I0657326

Grand Lodge A.F. & A.M. of Ontario, Canada

Proceedings - Grand Lodge, A.F. & A.M. of Canada - 1874

Grand Lodge A.F. & A.M. of Ontario, Canada

Proceedings - Grand Lodge, A.F. & A.M. of Canada - 1874

ISBN/EAN: 9783337222819

Printed in Europe, USA, Canada, Australia, Japan

Cover: Foto ©Andreas Hilbeck / pixelio.de

More available books at **www.hansebooks.com**

PROCEEDINGS

OF THE

GRAND LODGE

OF

Ancient Free and Accepted Masons

OF CANADA,

AT A

Special Communication, held at the Village of Trenton,
on the 24th day of Sept,, A. D. 1873, A. L. 5873.

ALSO AT ITS

Nineteenth Annual Communication,

HELD AT TORONTO, ONT,

ON THE

8th & 9th days of July, A. D. 1874, A. L. 5874.

Ordered to be read in all Lodges and preserved.

WILLIAM MERCER WILSON, SIMCOE, ONT.,

GRAND MASTER.

THOMAS BIRD HARRIS, HAMILTON, ONT.,

GRAND SECRETARY.

Hamilton: Spectator Steam Printing House, James & Main Sts.

1874.

Grand Lodge of Canada.

PROCEEDINGS.

At a Special Communication of the Grand Lodge of Ancient Free and Accepted Masons of Canada, held at the Village of Trenton, on Wednesday, the 24th day of September, A. D. 1873, A. L. 5873.

PRESENT.

R. W. Bro. H. W. Day, P. D. D. G. M., as Grand Master.
" " " H. W. Delany, P.D.D.G.M.,as Dep. Grand Master.
" J. B. Christie, as   Grand Senior Warden.
" Jos. Black, as   "   Junior Warden.
" Rev.W. Bleasdell M.A. as " Chaplain.
" R. W. Williams, as   "   Treasurer.
V. W. Bro. Geo. S. Graham, as   "   Registrar.
" " Jas. Young, as   "   Secretary.
" Lewis Cruickshank, as   "   Senior Deacon.
" Adam Young, as   "   Junior Deacon.
" David Lynn, as   "   Supt. of Works.
W. " W. T. Barker, as   "   Dir. of Cer.
" Samuel Gooding, as   "   Sword Bearer.
W. " J. N. Lee, as   "   Organist.
" " Chas. Francis, as   "   Pursuivant.
" Wm. German, as   "   Tyler.
" G. H. Miller, as
" Wm. Little, as
" H. Morton, as   "   Stewards.
" J. H. Munn, as

Together with Masters, Past Masters, and brethren hailing from the following Lodges:

Trent, No. 38, United, No. 29, Frank, No. 127, Sterling, No. 69, Consecon, No. 50, Moira, No. 11, Colborne, No. 91, Hastings, No. 150, Golden Rule, No. 126.

The Grand Lodge having been opened in 𝔉𝔬𝔯𝔪 at Two o'clock P. M.

R. W. Bro. H. W. Day, stated that he had been empowered by the M. W. Grand Master, to perform the ceremonies of laying the foundation stone of the Union High and Public School Building, in the village of Trenton.

A procession was then formed in accordance with the regulations as laid down in the book of Constitution, and under the direction of the Acting Grand Director of Ceremonies, marched to the site of the new School Building, preceded by the band of the 49th Battalion.

The assembly was then addressed by the Acting Grand Master, and the Acting Grand Chaplain, after which Bro. the Rev. William. Bleasdell, invoked the blessing of the G. A. O. T. U. on the undertaking.

R. W. Bro. H. W. Delany, read the following scroll, to be deposited in the cavity of the stone:

By favor of the

Almighty God,

ON THE 24TH DAY OF SEPTEMBER, A. D., MDCCCLXXIII,

Of the era of Masonry, 5873,

And in the Thirty-seventh year of the reign of our beloved Sovereign

Victoria,

Whom may God preserve.

The Right Honorable Sir Frederick Temple, EARL OF DUFFERIN,
K. P. K. C. B., &c., &c.,

Being Governor General of the Dominion of Canada, &c., &c.,

The Honorable WILLIAM P. HOWLAND, C. B.,

Being Lieutenant-Governor of the Province of Ontario.

WILLIAM MERCER WILSON, Esq., Most Worshipful Grand Master.

The Corner Stone of this building to be used as the Union School House

Was laid by

Right Worshipful Brother HENRY WRIGHT DAY, M. D.,

Assisted by

Right Worshipful Brother F. RICHARDSON, District Deputy Grand Master

for the District,

And an especial Grand Lodge of Freemasons of Canada,

Attended by various Brethren,

And in the presence of a large concourse of people.

SCHOOL BOARD.—R. W. Williams, M.D., *Chairman;* James Richardson, *Secretary;* W. H. Austin, H. W. Delany, H. W. Day, M. D., Henry Gill, William Jeff, James Marsh, James Young, Shuter S. Bouter, Alexander Miller, William Guinn.

MUNICIPAL OFFICERS.—Chas. Francis. Esq., *Reeve :* Alex. Miller, Geo. A. Smith, R. W. Williams, M. D., Terence McCabe, *Councillors :* David Roblin, *Treasurer ;* Jeremiah Simmons, *Clerk.*

CLERGY.—Rev. W. Bleasdell, M. A., Episcopal; Rev. John R. Watt, Presbyterian; Rev. H. Brettargh, Roman Catholic; Rev. Isaac Welden, Wesleyan Methodist; Rev. R. W. Marsh, Episcopal Methodist.

OFFICERS TRENT LODGE, A. F. & A. M., No. 38.—R. W. Bro, H. W. Day, Master ; Rev. Bro. W. Bleasdell, Chaplain; Bro. J. B. Christie, S. W. ; Bro. Jas. Black, J. W. ; Bro. Jas. Young, Secretary; Bro. R. W. Williams, Treasurer ; Bro. Wm. German, Tyler; Bro. W. T. Barker, P. M.

Architect of the Building—John D, Evans, P. L. S.   *Builder*—David Lynn.   *Carpenters*—William W. Northcott and Walter Alford.   Engrossed by Bro. William Gulna.

The metallic case was then put in the stone containing the leading and local newspapers, the parchment inscription, together with the various silver and copper coins of the Dominion.

The Acting Grand Master was then presented with a massive silver trowel, manufactured for the occasion, which after receiving he made a few appropriate remarks, with thanks for the gift, and proceeded to spread the mortar on which to lay the stone, after which the stone was lowered to its place—the band playing appropriate music.

The proper implements having been applied to the stone by the G. J. Warden, the G. S. Warden and the D. G. Master, it was ascertained that the craftsmen had done their duty, the Acting Grand Master then said

"Having full confidence in your skill in our royal art, it remains for me as Grand Master, to finish the work." Three knocks were given upon the stone with the gavel and he said : " *Well made, truly laid, well proved, true and trusty.*"

As they were handed to him, he poured out the customary libations saying: "I strew corn upon the stone as the emblem of Plenty, I pour wine upon it as the emblem of Cheerfulness, and I anoint it with oil as the emblem of Comfort and Consolation. May corn, wine, and oil, and all the necessities of life, abound among men and may the G. A. O. T. U. who has so kindly blessed us in the proceedings of this day enable those engaged in the erection of this work to complete it. May he protect the workmen from accident, and long preserve the structure from decay and ruin, that it may serve for generations yet to come, the great purpose for which it is intended.

Response: So mote it be.

The plans of the intended structure designed by Bro. J. D. Evans, were then inspected by the Acting Grand Master, and being approved were returned to the Architect, with words to the following effect: "The foundation stone of this building being laid, I present you with the working instruments and also the plans, in full confidence that as a skilful workman you will use them so that the building will rise in harmony and beauty, and being perfected in strength, will answer the purpose for which it was intended, to your credit and to the satisfaction of all who have selected you for the work."

The proceedings being ended the procession was re-formed and returned to the Town Hall, escorting thither the Grand Lodge.

ATTEST.

Grand Secretary.

Grand Lodge of Canada.

PROCEEDINGS.

At the Nineteenth Annual Communication of the Grand
Lodge of Ancient Free and Accepted Masons of Canada,
held in the Music Hall, in the city of Toronto, commencing
on Wednesday the 8th day of July, A. D. 1874, A. L. 5874.

PRESENT.

M. W. Bro. William M. Wilson, Grand Master.

On the Throne.

R.	"	"	Thomas White jr.,	Deputy Grand Master.	
"	"	"	B. E. Charlton,	Grand Senior Warden.	
"	"	"	F. Mudge,	"	Junior "
"	"	"	Jas. Bain, as	"	Chaplain.
"	"	"	David McLellan, as	"	Treasurer.
"	"	"	John Nettleton,	"	Registrar.
"	"	"	Thos. B. Harris,	"	Secretary.
V.	"	"	R. Brierley, as	"	Senior Deacon.
"	"	"	A. D. Stevens,	"	Junior Deacon.
"	"	"	W. F. Biggar, as	"	Supt. of Works.
"	"	"	N. Gordon Bigelow,	"	Dir. of Cer.
"	"	"	Hugh Murray, Asst.	"	Secretary.
"	"	"	John Midgley, Asst.	"	Dir. of Cer
"	"	"	B. Saunders, as	"	Sword Bearer.
"	"	"	C. A. Sippi, Asst.	"	Organist.
"	"	"	A. G. Muir,	"	Pursuivant.
		"	John L. Dixon,	"	Tyler.

V. W. Bro. Chas. R. D. Booth, ⎫
"   "   "   D. McG. Malloch, |
"   "   "   S. H. McKitrick, |
"   "   "   G. B. Reeve, |
"   "   "   W. D. Hepburn, |
"   "   "   Ed. Allworth,   ⎬ Grand Stewards.
"   "   "   John McLean, |
"   "   "   C. R. Boswell, |
"   "   "   John C. Hoshal, |
"   "   Joshua G. Burns, as ⎭

DISTRICT DEPUTY GRAND MASTERS.

R. W. Bro. Thos. C. Macnabb,   St. Clair   District.
"   " • "   D. B. Burch,   London   "
"   "   "   John E. Harding,   Huron   "
"   "   "   W. S. Burnett,   Wellington   "
"   "   "   Robt. Kemp   Niagara   "
"   "   "   Hy. Robertson,   Toronto   "
"   "   "   J. B. Trayes,   Ontario   "
"   "   "   F. Richardson,   Prince Edward   "
"   "   "   James Reynolds,   St. Lawrence   "
"   "   "   Wm. Mostyn,   Ottawa   "
"   "   "   Wm. Nivin,   Montreal   "

GRAND REPRESENTATIVES.

M. W. Bro. William M. Wilson, Representative of the Grand Lodges of Kentucky,and Illinois,and the Grand Orients of St. Domingo,and Central America.

R. W. Bro. Thomas B. Harris, Representative of the Grand Lodges of Kansas, Tennessee, Missouri, and Oregon, and the Grand Orient of Lusitana, Portugal.

M. W. Bro. Thos. Douglas Harington, Representative of the Grand Lodges of Quebec, Vermont, Nova Scotia, and Pennsylvania.

M. W. Bro. A. A. Stevenson, Representative of the Grand Orient of Brazil, and the Grand Lodges of Connecticut, and Minnesota.

R. W. Bro. Henry Macpherson, Representative of the Grand
   Orient of Uruguay.
R. W. Bro. J. K. Kerr, Representative of the Grand Lodge
   of Texas.
R. W. Bro. Thomas White, jr, Representative of the Grand
   Lodge of Nevada, and the Grand Orient of
   France.
M. W. Bro. James Seymour, Representative of the Grand
   Lodge of Mississippi.
R. W. Bro. Kivas Tully, Representative of the Grand Lodge
   of Ireland.
R. W. Bro. David McLellan, Representative of the Grand
   Lodge of Georgia.
R. W. Bro. Jas. A Henderson, Representative of the Grand
   Lodge of New York.
R. W. Bro. W. H. Frazer, Representative of the Grand Lodge
   of Wisconsin.

PAST GRAND OFFICERS.

M. W. Bro. T. D. Harington, P. G. M.
 "   "   "   A. A. Stevenson,   "
 "   "   "   Jas Seymour,   "
R. W. Bro. J. Urquhart, jr. P. D. D. G. M.
 "   "   "   Jas. A. Henderson,   "
 "   "   "   A. S. Kirkpatrick,   "
 "   "   "   C. D. Macdonnell,   "
 "   "   "   Thos. Wilkinson,   "
 "   "   "   L. H. Henderson,   "
 "   "   "   S. B. Harman,   "
 "   "   "   Thos. Ridout,   "
 "   "   "   W. G. Storm,   "
 "   "   "   W. H. Weller,   "
 "   "   "   J. K. Kerr,   "
 "   "   "   John Parry,   "
 "   "   "   P. J. Brown,   "
 "   "   "   F. Westlake,   "
 "   "   "   John E. Brooke,   "

R. W. Bro. E. C. Barber, P. D. D. G. M.
"   "   "   Geo. Billington, "
"   "   "   Kivas Tully, "
"   "   "   R. Kincaid, "
"   "   "   Isaac F. Toms. "
"   "   "   Wm. McCabe, "
"   "   "   Thos. Matheson, "
"   "   "   Jas. H. Rowan, "
"   "   "   F. Richardson, "
"   "   "   Chas. Hendry, "
"   "   "   Otto Klotz, "
"   "   "   John W. Murton,   P. G. S. W.
"   "   "   James Bain, "
"   "   "   Allan McLean, "
"   "   "   Henry Macpherson, "
"   "   "   R. C. Hamilton.   P. G. J. W.
"   "   "   R. P. Stephens, "
"   "   "   M. Crombie, "
"   "   "   David McLellan,   P. G. R.
"   "   "   Daniel Spry, "
"   "   "   Chauncy Bennett, "
V.   "   "   John F. Lash,   P. G. S. D.
"   "   "   John Boyd, "
"   "   "   W. F. Biggar,   P. G. S. of W.
"   "   "   A. T. Houel, "
"   "   "   James Gibson,   P. G. D. of C.
"   "   "   R. Brierley,   P. Asst. G. Sec.
"   "   "   W. R. Harris, "
"   "   "   John Wilson,   P. Ass't. G. D. of C.
"   "   "   B. Saunders,   P. G. S. B.
"   "   "   Jas. M. Rogerson,   P. Ass't. G. O.
"   "   "   N. L. Steiner, "
"   "   "   F. H. L. Staunton,   P. G. P.
"   "   "   John Paterson,   P. G. Steward.
"   "   "   Geo. Hodgetts, "
"   "   "   W. Carey, "
"   "   "   Wm. H. Archer. "
"   "   "   D. McMurchy, "

V. W. Bro. D. A. Creasor,   P. G. Steward.
"   "   "   W. R. White,   "
"   "   "   J. G. Cormack,   "
"   "   "   W. C. Morrison,   "
"   "   "   Thos. Sargant,   "
"   "   "   Geo. E. Bull.   "

PAST MASTERS.

R. W. Bro. J. Urquhart, jr.   W. Bro. J. W. Platt.
V. "   "   A. D. Stevens.   M. "   "   A. A. Stevenson.
    "   "   J. M. Clement.   R. "   "   Thos. White, jr.
M. "   "   Jas. Seymour.   "   "   Rev. E. M. Myers.
R. "   "   J. A. Henderson.   "   "   W. D. Davidson.
    "   "   A. S. Kirkpatrick. R. "   "   David McLellan.
    "   "   James Watson.   " "   "   Daniel Spry.
R. "   "   C. D. Macdonnell. V. "   "   A. T. Houel.
    "   "   E. R. Smith.   "   "   Jas. Morris.
R. "   "   Thos. Wilkinson.   "   "   A. L. Skeele.
    "   "   Gavin Stewart.   "   "   D. A. Fergusson.
R. "   "   T. C. Macnabb.   R. "   "   R. P. Stephens.
V. "   "   R. Brierley   "   "   "   M. Crombie.
R. "   "   B. E. Charlton.   "   "   "   J. K. Kerr.
    "   "   J. W. Murton.   V. "   "   A. R. Boswell.
    "   "   Wm. Forbes.   "   "   "   John F. Lash.
V. "   "   W. F. Biggar.   "   "   "   W. R. Harris.
    "   "   A. G. Muir.   "   "   W. T. O'Reilly.
    "   "   H. L. Geddes.   "   "   E. Peplow, jr.
    "   "   G. A. Wright.   R. "   "   J. B. Trayes.
    "   "   S. S. Lazier.   V. "   "   Jas. M. Rogerson.
R. "   "   L. H. Henderson.   "   "   Walter Kerr.
    "   "   Wm. Doctor.   "   "   Peter Begg.
    "   "   J. S. Mendell.   "   "   G. H. Dartnell.
    "   "   J. F. Kennedy.   "   "   C. A. Jones.
R. "   "   Jas. Bain.   R. "   "   F. Mudge.
    "   "   S. B. Harman.   "   "   Wm. Braund.
    "   "   Thos. Ridout.   "   "   T. L. M. Tipton.
    "   "   R. C. Hamilton.   R. "   "   John Parry.
    "   "   W. G. Storm.   "   "   John R. Park, jr.

V. W. Bro. John Paterson.
" " " Geo. Hodgetts.
" " F. H. Medcalf.
" " R. J. Winch.
R. " " W. H. Weller.
" " E. Allworth.
R. " " F. Westlake.
" " Jas. S. Scarff.
V. " " John Midgley.
" " Geo. W. Morgan.
R. " " John E. Brooke.
V. " " Jas. Gibson.
" " J. S. Loomis.
" " A. Rockwell.
" " Joseph Figg.
" " C. Burrell.
" " Thos. Ellison.
R. " " E. C. Barber.
V. " " Hugh Murray.
" " John W. Pickup.
" " John R. Peel.
V. " " W. Carey.
" " H. A. Baxter.
" " R. Lewis.
" " J. B. Nixon.
" " Hugh Kerr,
R. " " Allan McLean.
" " Albert Chard.
V. " " Geo. E. Bull.
R. " " W. S. Burnett.
" " " J. E. Harding.
" " " Jas. Reynolds.
V. " " N. L. Steiner.
" " " B. Saunders.
" " J. Erskine.
" " F. J. Menet.
" " W. T. Parsons.
" " Jno W. H. Wilson.

V. W. Bro. John A. Hoshal.
" " E. C. Thomas.
R. " " P. J. Brown.
" " C. H. Sorley.
R. " " Thos. B. Harris.
" " W. D. McGloghlon
R. " " Geo. Billington.
" " W. G. VanStaden.
V. " " D. McG. Malloch.
" " David Mansell.
R. " " Kivas Tully.
V. " " W. H. Archer.
" " Chas. Hunter.
" " Robt. Vardon.
" " Jas. Spaight.
V. " " D. McMurchy.
R. " " Hy. Macpherson.
V. " " D. A. Creasor.
" " John Creasor.
" " H. R. Corson.
R. " " John Nettleton.
" " " Hy. Robertson.
" " H. M. Cleland.
" " J. J. Campbell.
" " Robt. Nancollas.
" " C. R. Baker.
" " Robt. King.
" " Hy. Mosier.
" " G. Watson.
" " Jas. Sykes.
V. " " F. H. L. Staunton.
R. " " R. Kincaid.
" " Walter Beal.
" " P. McCarty.
R. " " Fred. Mudge.
" " J. M. Banghart.
R. " " D. B. Burch.
" " Jas. O'Connor.

W.	Bro.	W. H. Walkem.		W.	Bro.	S. D. Brown.
"	"	Geo. Mansfield.		"	"	John Satchell.
"	"	G. E. Earl.	R.	"	"	Wm. Nivin.
"	"	D. H. Bedford.	"	"	"	Chauncy Bennett
R.	"	Isaac F. Toms.		"	"	Geo. Risk.
"	"	A. McMichael.	V.	"	"	W. D. Hepburn.
R.	"	Robt. Kemp.		"	"	G. W. Pontine.
"	"	W. R. Jamieson.		"	"	John S: Tennant.
"	"	Thos. Aishton.		"	"	John Sinclair.
"	"	Jas. Dinwoodie.	V.	"	"	W. Carey.
V.	"	W. R. White.		"	"	T. Beattie.
"	"	J. G. Cormack.		"	"	John McLean.
"	"	S. E. Mitchell.		"	"	Thos. Swan.
"	"	Andrew Forbes.		"	"	John Ormiston.
"	"	F. W. Strange.		"	"	Francis Dalby.
"	"	Wm. Carrack.		"	"	J.W.MacEdward
"	"	Robt. Matheson.		"	"	Wm. Matheson.
"	"	G. R. Vanzant.	V.	"	"	S. H. McKitrick.
"	"	L. Jones.		"	"	J. C. Ross.
"	"	M. Gilbranson.		"	"	J. G. Burns.
V.	"	John Boyd.	V.	"	"	W. C. Morrison.
R.	"	Wm. McCabe.		"	"	M. H. Starr.
V.	"	John Midgley.		"	"	Jas. Lawson·
R.	"	Thos. Matheson.		"	"	N. Greening.
"	"	A. G. Macdonell.		"	"	Robt. Brown.
"	"	Chas. Paeckert.	V.	"	"	John McLean.
"	"	John Gibson.		"	"	W. Morton.
"	"	Peter Johnston.	V.	"	"	Geo. B. Reeve.
"	"	J. H. Thrall.		"	"	Alex. Mitchell.
R.	"	Wm. Mostyn.		"	"	E. E. Kitchen.
M.	"	T. D. Harington.		"	"	Ben. Bell.
R.	"	Jas. H. Rowan.		"	"	J. C. Thurston.
"	"	Silas Hoover.		"	"	T. F. Blackwood.
"	"	Jas. Sutton,	R.	"	"	John Parry.
"	"	Wm. Cameron.		"	"	C. F. H. Forbes.
"	"	R. H. Preston.		"	"	Robt. Scott.
"	"	J. B. Neff,		"	"	E. W. Town.
"	"	Jas. H. Benson.		"	"	R. B. Hannah.

W. Bro. D. W. Ferrier.	W. Bro. Philip Taylor.
" " John A. Ash.	" " H. B. O'Connor.
" " E. B. Fralick.	R. " " F. Richardson.
" " Wm. Hayden.	V. " " Thos. Sargant.
" " W. J. R. Holmes.	" " Wm. Young.
" " Wm. Knight.	R. " " Chas. Hendry.
" " J. A. Somerville.	" " " Otto Klotz.
" " Lauchlin Leitch.	

A constitutional number of Lodges being represented, the Grand Chaplain implored a blessing from the G. A. O. T. U. upon all the proceedings.

The Grand Lodge of Ancient Free and Accepted Masons of Canada was opened in 𝔄𝔪𝔭𝔩𝔢 𝔉𝔬𝔯𝔪 at 3 o'clock, P. M.

The Board of General Purposes, as required by the Constitution, appointed R. W. Bros. J. B. Trayes and Allan McLean and W. Bros. J. B. Nixon and Hugh Kerr, a Committee on the Credentials of Representatives and Proxies from Lodges, who reported the following as being present, viz:

Antiquity Lodge, Montreal, Que.
W. Bro. L. Cohen, W. M.; R. W. Bro. John Urquhart, Jr., P.M.

No. 1.   *Prevost Lodge, Dunham, Que.*
V. W. Bro. A. D. Stevens, P. M.

No. 2.   *Niagara Lodge, Niagara Ont.*
W. Bro. Robert Shearer, W. M.; W. Bro. John M. Clement, P. M.; M. W. Bro. James Seymour, P. M.

No. 3.   *St. John's Lodge, Kingston, Ont.*
R. W. Bro. James Henderson, W. M.; Bro. J. Geo. King, S. W.; Bro. Chas. H. Corbett, J. W.; R. W. Bro. A. S. Kirkpatrick, P. M.; W. Bro. James Wilson, P. M.; R. W. Bro. C. D. Macdonnell, P. M.

No. 4.   *Dorchester Lodge, St. John's Que.*
W. Bro. E. R. Smith, W. M.

No. 5.   *Sussex Lodge, Brockville, Ont.*
R. W. Bro. Thos. Wilkinson, W. M.

No. 6.   *Barton Lodge, Hamilton, Ont.*
W. Bro. Chas. Davidson, W. M.; Bro. Wm. Gibson, S. W.; Bro. Jas. Ferguson McClure, J. W.; W. Bro. Gavin Stewart, P. M.; R. W. Bro. Thos. C. Macnabb, P. M.; R. W. Bro. B. E. Charlton, P. M.; R. W. Bro. John W. Murton, P. M.; V. W. Bro. Richard Brierley, P. M.

No. 7.   Union Lodge, Grimsby, Ont.
W. Bro. Joseph Chambers, W. M.; W. Bro. Wm. Forbes, P. M.
V. W. Bro. W. F. Biggar, P. M.; V. W. Bro. A. G. Muir, P. M.

No. 9.   Union Lodge, Napanee, Ont.
W. Bro. H. L. Geddes, W. M.; W. Bro. G. A: Wright, P. M.

No. 10.   Norfolk Lodge, Simcoe, Ont.
W. Bro. Robt. Rochester, W. M.; Bro. James Hayes, S. W.;
V. W. Bro. John Wilson, P. M.; M. W. Bro. Wm. M. Wilson,
P. M.

No. 11.   Moira Lodge, Belleville, Ont.
W. Bro. S. S. Lazier, W. M.; Bro. A. A. Farley, S. W.; R. W.
Bro. L. H. Henderson, P. M.; W. Bro. Wm. Doctor, P. M.;
W. Bro. J. S. Mendell, P. M.

No. 14.   True Britons Lodge, Perth, Ont.
W. Bro. J. F. Kennedy, W. M.

No. 15.   St. George's Lodge, St. Catharines, Ont.
Bro. Wm. Dougan, S. W.

No 16.   St. Andrew's Lodge, Toronto, Ont.
V. W. Bro. N. Gordon Bigelow, W. M ; Bro. Andrew Smith,
S. W ; Bro. W. C. Wilkinson, J. W.; R W. Bro. James Bain,
P. M.; R W. Bro. Sam. B. Harman, P. M ; R. W. Bro. Thos.
Ridout, P. M.; R. W. Bro. R. C. Hamilton, P. M.; R. W. Bro.
W. G. Storm, P. M.; V. W. Bro. John Paterson, P. M.; V. W.
Bro. George Hodgetts, P. M.; W. Bro. F. H. Medcalf, P. M.

No. 17.   St. John's Lodge, Cobourg, Ont.
W. Bro. R. J. Winch, W. M.; R W. Bro. W. H. Weller, P. M.

No. 18.   Prince Edward's Lodge, Picton, Ont.
W. Bro. J. M. Platt, W. M.

No. 19.   St. George's Lodge, Montreal, Que.
W. Bro. M. Lesser, W. M.; Bro. A. A. Boudreau, J. W.; M.
W. Bro. A. A. Stevenson, P. M.; R. W. Bro. Thos. White, Jr,
P. M.; W. Bro. Rev. E. M. Myers, P. M. .

No. 20.   St. John's Lodge, London, Ont.
W. Bro. R. Luxton, W. M.: W. Bro. M. D. Dawson, P M.

No. 22.   King Solomon's Lodge, Toronto, Ont.
W. Bro. Thos. Langton, W. M.; Bro W. J. Hambly, S. W.
Bro. S. R. Richardson, J. W.; R. W. Bro. David McLellan,
P. M.; R. W. Bro. Daniel Spry, P. M.; V. W. Bro. A. T. Houel,
P. M.; W. Bro. James Morris, P. M.

No. 23.   Richmond Lodge, Richmond Hill, Ont.
W. Bro. James McConnell, W. M.; Bro. Jas. M. Lawrence,
S. W.; Bro. R. E. Shaw, J. W.; W. Bro. A. L. Skeele, P. M.

No. 24.   St. Francis Lodge, Smith's Falls, Ont.
W. Bro. D. A. Fergusson, W. M.

No. 25.   *Ionic Lodge, Toronto, Ont.*

W. Bro W. D. Otter, W. M.; R. W. Bro. R. P. Stephens, P. M.; R. W. Bro. M. Crombie, P. M.; R. W. Bro. J. K. Kerr, P. M.; V. W. Bro. A. R. Boswell, P. M.; V. W. Bro. John F. Lash, P. M.; V. W. Bro. W. R. Harris, P. M.; W. Bro. W. T. O'Reilly, P. M.

No. 26.   *Ontario Lodge, Port Hope, Ont.*

W. Bro. E. Peplow, Jr., W M ; Bro. Chas. Doebler, J. W.; R. W. Bro. J. B. Trayes, P. M.

No. 27.   *Strict Observance Lodge, Hamilton, Ont.*

W. Bro F. R. Despard, W. M.; Bro. Robt. A. Hutchison, S.W.; Bro. John Henery, J. W.; R. W. Bro. David McLellan, P. M.; V. W. Bro. James M. Rogerson, P. M.

No. 28.   *Mount Zion Lodge, Kemptville, Ont.*

W. Bro. Walter Kerr, P. M.

No. 29.   *United Lodge, Brighton, Ont.*

W. Bro. Peter Begg, P. M.

No. 30.   *Composite Lodge, Whitby, Ont.*

W. Bro. Geo. Hopkins, W. M.; W. Bro. G. H. Dartnell. P.M.; W. Bro. C. A. Jones, P. M.; R. W. Bro. Fred Mudge, P. M.

No. 31.   *Jerusalem Lodge, Bowmanville.*

V. W. Bro. Chas. R. D. Booth, S. W.

No. 32.   *Amity Lodge, Dunnville, Ont.*

W. Bro. Wm. Braund, W.M.; W. Bro. Thomas L. M. Tipton, P. M ; R. W. Bro. John Parry, P. M.

No. 33.   *Goderich Lodge, Goderich, Ont.*

W. Bro. J. R. Miller, W. M.; Bro. O. G. Anderson, S. W.

No. 34.   *Thistle Lodge, Amherstburgh, Ont.*

W. Bro. C. W. Thomas, W. M.; W. Bro. John R. Park, jr. P.M.

No. 35.   *St. John's Lodge, Cayuga, Ont.*

V. W. Bro. John A. Hoshal, P. M., Proxy.

No. 36.   *Welland Lodge, Fonthill, Ont.*

W. Bro. E. C. Thomas, P M., Proxy.

No. 37.   *King Hiram Lodge, Ingersoll, Ont.*

W. Bro. C. H. Slawson, W. M.; R. W. Bro. P. J. Brown, P. M.; W. Bro. C. H. Sorley, P. M.

No. 38.   *Trent Lodge, Trenton, Ont.*

W. Bro. Peter Begg, P. M.

No. 39.   *Mount Zion Lodge, Brooklin, Ont.*

Bro. W. J. Murray, S. W.; Bro. W. A. Kester, J. W.

No. 40.   *St. John's Lodge, Hamilton, Ont.*

W. Bro. Donald McPhie, W. M.; Bros. D. Aitchison, S. W.. John Malloy, J. W.; R. W. Bro. Thos. B. Harris, P. M.

No. 41.   *St. George's Lodge, Kingsville, Ont.*
W. Bro. Ed. Allworth, W. M.

No. 42.   *St George's Lodge, London, Ont.*
W. Bro. Wm. Thornton, W. M ; Bro. Wm. Fleming, J. W.;
R. W. Bro. F. Westlake, P. M.

No. 43.   *King Solomon's Lodge, Woodstock, Ont.*
W. Bro. R. M. Revell, W. M.; W. Bro. Jas. S. Scarff, P. M.

No. 44.   *St. Thomas Lodge, St. Thomas, Ont.*
V. W. Bro. John Midgley, W. M.; Bro. Robt. McCully, J. W.
W. Bro. Geo. W. Morgan, P. M.

No. 45.   *Brant Lodge, Brantford, Ont.*
W. Bro. John Bishop, W. M.; R. W. Bro. Fred Mudge, P. M.

No. 46.   *Wellington Lodge, Chatham, Ont.*
W. Bro. Wm. Young, W. M.; R. W. Bro. John E. Brooke, P. M.

No. 47.   *Great Western Lodge, Windsor, Ont.*
W. Bro. A. Whittaker, W. M.; Bro. Robt. McNaught, J. W.;
V. W. Bro. James Gibson, P. M.

No. 48.   *Madoc Lodge, Madoc, Ont.*
W. Bro. J. S. Loomis, W. M.; Bro. F. E. Dean, S. W.

No. 50.   *Consecon Lodge, Consecon, Ont.*
W. Bro. A. Rockwell, Proxy.

No. 51.   *Corinthian Lodge, Grahamsville, Ont.*
W. Bro. Joseph Figg, W. M.; Bro. Wm Fale, S. W.; W. Bro.
C. Burrell, P. M.

No. 52.   *Dalhousie Lodge, Ottawa, Ont.*
W. Bro. Jas. Egleson, W. M.

No 54.   *Vaughan Lodge, Maple, Ont.*
W. Bro. Thos. S. Raith, P. M., Proxy.

No. 55.   *Merrickville Lodge, Merrickville, Ont.*
W. Bro. Wm. Weir, W. M.

No. 56.   *Victoria Lodge, Sarnia, Ont.*
W. Bro. Thomas Ellison, P. M.

No. 58.   *Doric Lodge, Ottawa, Ont.*
W. Bro. Charles Esplin, W. M.; Bro. Wm. Kerr, S. W.; Bro. J. J.
Smyth, J. W.

No. 59.   *Corinthian Lodge, Ottawa, Ont.*
Bro. Frederick H. Hunton, S. W.; R. W. Bro. E. C. Barber,
P. M., Proxy.

No. 61.   *Acacia Lodge, Hamilton, Ont.*
Bro. Jas. Acheson, J. W.; V. W. Bro. Hugh Murray, P. M.
R. W. Bro. Thomas B. Harris, P. M.

2

No. 62.   *St. Andrew's Lodge, Caledonia, Ont.*
W. Bro. A. J. Nelles, W. M.

No. 63.   *St. John's Lodge, Carleton Place, Ont.*
W. Bro. John W. Pickup, P. M. Proxy.

No. 64.   *Kilwinning Lodge, London, Ont.*
Bros. C. A. Sippi, S. W.; Angus Grant, sr., J. W.; W. Bro·
John R. Peel, P. M.; V. W. Bro. W. Carey, P. M.; W. Bro·
H. A. Baxter, P. M.; W. Bro. R. Lewis, P. M.

No. 65.   *Rehoboam Lodge, Toronto, Ont.*
W. Bro. James E. Day, W. M.; Bro. George Patterson, S. W.;
Bro. Wm. Brydon, J. W.; W. Bro. Jas. B. Nixon, P. M.; R. W.
Daniel Spry, P. M.; R. W. Bro. W. H. Fraser.

No. 68.   *St. John's Lodge, Ingersoll, Ont.*
W. Bro. Hugh Kerr, W. M.; Bros. John Kerr, S. W.; James
Badden, J. W.; R. W. Bro. Allan McLean, P. M.

No. 69.   *Stirling Lodge, Stirling, Ont.*
W. Bro. Albert Chard, W. M.; V.W. Bro. Geo. E. Dull, P. M.

No. 72.   *Alma Lodge, Galt Ont.*
R. W. Bro. W. S. Burnett, P. M., Proxy.

No. 73.   *St. Jame's Lodge, St. Mary's Ont.*
Bro. W. Tytler, S. W.; R. W. Bro. John E. Harding, P. M.

No. 74.   *St. James' Lodge, Maitland, Ont.*
R. W. Bro. James Reynolds, Proxy.

No. 75.   *St. John's Lodge, Toronto, Ont.*
W. Bro. Seymour Porter, W. M.; Bro. R. J. Hovenden, S. W.;
Bro. H. W. Blain, J. W.; V. W. Bro. N. L. Steiner, P. M.;
V. W. Bro. B. Saunders, P. M.; W. Bro. J. Erskine, P. M.;
W. Bro. F. J. Menet, P. M.; W. Bro. W. T. Parsons, P. M.

No. 76.   *Oxford Lodge, Woodstock, Ont.*
W. Bro. C. L. Beard, W. M.

No. 77.   *Faithful Brethren Lodge, Lindsay, Ont.*
R. W. Bro. C. D. Macdonnell, Proxy.

No. 79.   *Simcoe Lodge, Brantford, Ont.*
W. Bro Wm. H. Porter, W. M.; W. Bro. John W. H.
Wilson, P. M.; W. Bro. W. Bro. Wm. Hy. Walkem, P. M.

No. 80.   *Albion Lodge, Newbury, Ont.*
W. Bros. Geo. Mansfield, W. M.; W. D. McGloghlon, P. M.

No. 81.   *St. John's Lodge, Mount Brydges, Ont.*
R. W. Bro. George Billington, W. M.

No. 82.   *St. John's Lodge Paris, Ont.*
Bro. J. C. Forsyth, S. W.; Bro. Geo. Angus, J. W.

No. 83.   *Bearer Lodge, Strathroy, Ont.*
R. W. Bro. George Billington, Proxy; W. Bro. W. G.
VanStaden, P. M.

No. 84.   *Clinton Lodge, Clinton, Ont.*
V. W. Bro. D. M. Malloch, W. M.; Bro. R. A. Barton, S. W.;
Bro. George. Glasgow, J. W.

No. 85.   *Rising Sun Lodge, Farmersville, Ont.*
W. Bro. David Mansell, P. M., Proxy.

No. 86.   *Wilson Lodge, Toronto, Ont.*
W. Bro. George C. Moore, W. M.; Bro. Alexander Patterson,
S. W.; Bro R. T. Coady, J. W.; R. W. Bro. Kivas Tully, P. M.;
V. W. Bro. Wm. H. Archer, P M.; W. Bro. Chas. Hunter, P. M.

No. 87.   *Markham Union Lodge, Markham, Ont.*
W. Bro. George Godfrey, W. M.; Bro. John R. Hall, S. W.;
Bro. David Johnston, J. W.; W. Bro. Robert Vardon, P. M.;
W. Bro. James Spaight, P. M.; V. W. Bro. D. McMurchy, P.M.

No. 88.   *St. George's Lodge, Owen Sound, Ont.*
W. Bro. Thomas Scott, W. M.; Bro. James McLaughlin, J. W.;
W. Bro D. R. Dobie, P. M.; R. W. Bro. H. Macpherson, P.M.;
V. W. Bro. D. A. Creasor, P. M.; W. Bro. John Creasor, P. M.;
W. Bro. H. R. Corson, P. M.

No. 90.   *Manito Lodge, Collingwood, Ont.*
R. W. Bro. John Nettleton, W. M.; Bro. John Ferguson, S. W.;
R. W. Bro. Henry Robertson, P. M.; W. Bro. Cleland, P. M.

No. 91.   *Colborne Lodge, Colborne, Ont.*
W. Bro. J. J. Campbell, W. M.; W. Bro. J. D. Henderson, P. M.

No. 92.   *Cataraqui Lodge, Kingston, Ont.*
Bro. Thomas Gordon, J. W.; W. Bro. Robert Nancollas, P. M.

No. 93   *Northern Light Lodge, Kincardine, Ont.*
W. Bro. Jas. A. Macpherson, W. M.; W Bro. C. R. Barker, P.M.

No. 94   *St. Mark's Lodge, Port Stanley, Ont.*
W. Bro. Thomas Robinson, W. M.

No. 95.   *Ridout Lodge, Otterville, Ont.*
R. W. Bro. P. J. Brown, Proxy.

No. 96.   *Corinthian Lodge, Barrie, Ont.*
W. Bro. R. King, W. M ; Bro. A. B. McPhie, S. W.

No. 97.   *Sharon Lodge, Sharon, Ont.*
W. Bro. James Kavanagh, W. M.; W. Bro. Henry Mosier, P.M.

No. 98.   *True Blue Lodge, Albion, Ont.*
W. Bro. G. Watson, P. M. and Proxy.

No. 99.   *Tuscan Lodge, Newmarke', Ont.*
W. Bro. A. M. Hood, W. M.; Bro. J. H. Widdifield, S. W.;
W. Bro. James Sykes, P. M.

No. 100.   *Valley Lodge, Dundas, Ont.*
W. Bro. Duncan McMillan, W. M.; Bro. W. A. Foley, J. W.;
V. W. Bro. F. H. L. Staunton, P. M.

No. 101.   *Corinthian Lodge, Peterboro', Ont.*
W. Bro. John J. Lundy, W. M.; R. W. Bro. R. Kincaid, P. M.;
W. Bro. Walter Beal, P. M.

No. 103.   *Maple Leaf Lodge, St. Catharines, Ont.*
W. Bro. P. McCarty, P. M.

No. 106.   *Burford Lodge, Burford, Ont.*
R. W. Bro. Fred Mudge, P. M.

No. 107   *St. Pauls Lodge, Lambeth, Ont.*
W. Bro. J. M. Banghart, W. M.; R. W. Bro. D. B. Burch, P. M.;
W. Bro. James O'Connor, P. M.

No. 108.   *Blenheim Lodge, Drumbo, Ont.*
W. Bro. S. D. Brown, W. M.

No. 109.   *Albion Lodge, Harrowsmith, Ont.*
R. W. Bro. James A. Henderson, Proxy.

No. 110.   *Central Lodge, Prescott, Ont.*
W. Bro. John Satchell, W. M.; R. W. Bro. James Reynolds,
P. M.; W. Bro. Geo. En. Earl, P. M.

No. 111.   *Morpeth Lodge, Ridgetown, Ont.*
W. Bro. D. H. Bedford, P. M. and Proxy.

No. 112,   *Maitland Lodge, Goderich, Ont.*
Bro. Charles E. Robertson, S. W.; Bro. James Garrow, J. W.;
R. W. Bro. Isaac F. Toms, P. M.

No. 113.   *Wilson Lodge, Waterford, Ont.*
W. Bro. B. L. Chipman, W. M.; Bro. J. S. Upper, S. W.; Bro.
Thomas Hayne, J. W.; W. Bro. A. McMichael, P. M.

No. 114.   *Hope Lodge, Port Hope, Ont.*
W. Bro. A. Purslow, W. M.

No. 115.   *Ivy Lodge, Beamsville, Ont.*
R. W. Bro. Robert Kemp, P. M.

No. 116.   *Cassia Lodge, Widder, Ont.*
W. Bro. H. L. Morphy, W. M.

No 118   *Union Lodge, Schomberg, Ont.*
W. Bro. A. Armstrong, Jr. W. M ; W. Bro. W. R. Jamieson,
P. M.

No. 119.   *Maple Leaf Lodge, Bath, Ont.*
W. Bro. Thomas Aishton, W. M.

No. 120.   *Warren Lodge, Fingal, Ont.*
R. W. Bro. D. B. Burch, Proxy.

No. 121.   *Doric Lodge, Brantford, Ont.*
W. Bro. W. H. Masterson, S. W.

No 123   *The Belleville Lodge, Belleville, Ont.*
W, Bro. Geo. D. Dickson, W. M.; Bro. George H. Pepe, J. W.

No. 125.   *Cornwall Lodge, Cornwall, Ont*
W. Bro. John McIntyre, W. M.

No. 126.   *Golden Rule Lodge, Campbellford, Ont.*
W. Bro. Jas. Dinwoodie, P. M., Proxy.

No. 127   *Franck Lodge, Frankford, Ont.*
W. Bro. A. Rockwell, P. M., Proxy.

No. 128   *Pembroke Lodge, Pembroke, Ont.*
W. Bro. Andrew Irving, jr., W. M.; Bro. Asher Ansell, S. W.;
V. W. Bros. W. R. White, P. M.; J. G. Cormack, P. M.; W.
Bros. S. E. Mitchell, P. M.; Andrew Forbes, P. M.

No. 129.   *The Rising Sun Lodge, Aurora, Ont.*
W. Bro. Fred. W. Strange, W. M.; Bro. D. B. Warren, J. W.

No. 133.   *Lebanon Forest Lodge, Exeter, Ont.*
W. Bro. Wm. Carrack, P. M., Proxy.

No. 135.   *St. Clair Lodge Milton, Ont.*
W. Bro. J. D. Matheson, W. M.; Bro. Wm. Panton, S. W.;
W. Bro. Robert Matheson, P. M.

No. 136.   *Richardson Lodge, Stouffville, Ont.*
W. Bro. G. R. Vanzant, W. M.; W. Bro. L. Jones, P. M.

No. 137.   *Pythagoras Lodge, Meaford, Ont.*
Bro. Robert McIntosh, J. W.

No. 139.   *Lebanon Lodge, Oshawa, Ont.*
W. Bro. M. Gilbranson, W. M.; V. W. Bro. John Boyd, P. M.;
R. W. Bro. William McCabe, P. M.

No. 140.   *Malahide Lodge, Aylmer, Ont.*
V. W. Bro. John Midgley, Proxy.

No. 141.   *Tudor Lodge, Mitchell, Ont.*
R. W. Bro. Thomas Matheson, W. M.; Bro. Wm. Walkinshaw,
J. W.

No. 142.   *Excelsior Lodge, Morrisburg Ont*
W. Bro. A. G. Macdonell, W. M.

No. 143.   *Friendly Brothers' Lodge, Iroquois, Ont.*
W. Bro. David Fink, W. M.

No. 144.   *Tecumseh Lodge, Stratford, Ont.*
Bro. George J. Waugh, S. W.; W. Bro. Chas. Paeckert, P. M.;
W. Bro. John Gibson, P. M.

No. 145.   *J. B. Hall Lodge, Millbrook, Ont.*
R. W. Bro. C. D. Macdonnell, Proxy.

No. 146.   *Prince of Wales Lodge, Newburg, Ont.*
W. Bro. A. K. Ailsworth, W. M.; W. Bro. Peter Johnston, P. M

No. 147.   *Mississippi Lodge, Almonte, Ont.*
W. Bro. J. H. Thrall, W. M.; R. W. Bro. Wm. Mostyn, P. M.

No. 148.   *Civil Service Lodge, Ottawa, Ont.*
M. W. Bro. T. D. Harington, P. M.; R. W. Bro. James H. Rowan, P. M.

No. 149.   *Erie Lodge, Port Dover, Ont.*
W. Bro. Silas Hoover, P. M.

No. 151.   *The Grand River Lodge, Berlin Ont.*
W. Bro. W. Hendry, W. M.; Bro. C. O. Sizer, S. W.

No. 154.   *Irving Lodge, Lucan, Ont.*
W. Bro. James Sutton, W. M.; Bro. Robert Fox, S. W.

No. 155.   *Peterboro' Lodge, Peterboro, Ont.*
W. Bro. James Millar, W. M.; Bro. Samuel White, S. W.; W. Bro. Wm. Cameron, P M.

No. 156.   *York Lodge, Eglinton, Ont.*
W. Bro. John F. Ellis, W. M; Bro. T. Armstrong, S. W.; M. E. Snider, J. W.

No. 157.   *Simpson Lodge, Newboro', Ont.*
W. Bro. R. H. Preston, M. M.

No. 165.   *Burlington Lodge, Wellington Square, Ont.*
W. Bro. Robt. Halson, W. M.; Bro. Walter S. Bastedo, J. W.

No. 168.   *Merritt Lodge, Welland, Ont.*
W. Bro. J. H. Burgar, W. M.

No. 169.   *Macnab Lodge, Port Colborne, Ont.*
W. Bro. J. B. Neff, P. M., Proxy.

No. 170.   *Britannia Lodge, Seaforth, Ont.*
W. Bro. H. L. Vercoe, W. M.; Bro. A. J. McIntosh, J. W.; W. Bro. J. H. Benson, P. M.

No. 172.   *Ayr Lodge, Ayr, Ont.*
W. Bro. A. H. Kay, W. M.

No. 173.   *Victoria Lodge, Montreal, Que.*
R. W. Bro. Wm. Nivin, P. M., Proxy.

No. 174.   *Walsingham Lodge, Port Rowan: Ont.*
R. W. Bro. Chauncy Bennet, P. M., Proxy.

No. 176.   *Sparta Lodge, Sparta, Ont.*
R. W. Bro. D. B. Burch, Pooxy.

No. 177.   *The Builders Lodge, Ottawa, Ont.*
W. Bro. E. B. Butterworth, W. M.

No. 178.   *Plattsville Lodge, Plattsville Ont.*
W. Bro. George Risk, W. M.

No. 179.   *Bothwell Lodge, Bothwell, Ont.*
W. Bro. N. H. Avery, W. M.

No. 180.   *Speed Lodge, Guelph, Ont.*
W. Bro. P. Bish, W. M.; V. W. Bro. W. D. Hepburn, P. M.

No. 181.   *Oriental Lodge, Port Burwell, Ont.*
              Bro. Wm. H. Cosseboom, S. W.; W. Bro. G. W. Pontine, P.M.

No. 184.   *Old Light Lodge, Lucknow, Ont.*
              W. Bro. John S. Tennant, P. M., Proxy.

No. 185.   *Enniskillen Lodge, York, Ont.*
              W. Bro. R. A. Weir, W. M.; Bros. William Clark, S. W.;
              G. B. Stephenson, J. W.

No. 186.   *Plantagenet Lodge, Plantagenet, Ont.*
              R. W. Bro. E. C. Barber, Proxy.

No. 189.   *Filiæ Viduæ Lodge, Adolphustown, Ont.*
              W. Bro. P. D. Davis, W. M.

No. 190.   *Belmont Lodge, Belmont, Ont.*
              W. Bro. James O'Connor, Proxy.

No. 192.   *Orillia Lodge, Orillia, Ont.*
              Bro. E. B. Alport, S. W.

No. 193.   *Scotland Lodge, Scotland, Ont.*
              R. W. Bro. Fred Mudge, P. M.

No. 194.   *Petrolia Lodge, Petrolia, Ont.*
              W. Bro. John Sinclair, P. M., Proxy.

No. 195.   *The Tuscan Lodge, London, Ont.*
              V. W. Bro. W. Carey, P. M., Proxy.; W. Bro. T. Beattie, P. M.

No. 196.   *Madawaska Lodge, Arnprior, Ont.*
              W. Bro. John W. Pickup, Proxy.

No. 200.   *St. Alban's Lodge, Mount Forest, Ont.*
              W. Bro. John McLaren, W. M.; W. Bro. Thos. Swan, P. M.

No. 201.   *Leeds Lodge, Gananoque, Ont.*
              W. Bro. John Ormiston, W. M.

No. 203.   *Irvine Lodge, Elora, Ont.*
              W. Bro. John McDonald, W. M.; Bro. J. H. Kenning, S. W.;
              W. Bro. Francis Dalby, P. M.

No. 205.   *New Dominion Lodge, New Hamburg, Ont.*
              Bro. Philip Erback, J. W.

No. 207.   *Lancaster Lodge, Lancaster, Ont.*
              W. Bro. A. Falkner, W. M.; R. W. Bro. John Urquhart, jr.
              P. M ; W. Bro. J. W. MacEdward, P. M.

No. 209a.   *St. John's Lodge, London, Ont.*
              W. Bro. D. McPhail, W. M.

No. 209.   *Evergreen Lodge, Lanark, Ont.*
              R. W. Bro. Wm. Mostyn, Proxy.

No. 210.   *Hawkesbury Lodge, Hawkesbury, Ont.*
              R. W. Bro. E. C. Barber, Proxy.

No. 212.   *Elysian Lodge, Garden Island.*
W. Bro. Bobt. Nancollas, P. M.

No. 213.   *Dominion Lodge, Ridgeway, Ont.*
W. Bro. J. B. Neff, Proxy.

No. 214.   *Craig Lodge, Ailsa Craig, Ont.*
W. Bro. Richard Sands, W. M.; Bro. D. J. Watson, S. W.;
W. Bro. Wm. Matheson, P. M.

No. 216.   *Harris Lodge, Orangeville, Ont.*
W. Bro. Thomas Y. Greet, W. M.; Bro. A. MacGowan, J. W.;
V. W. Bro. S. H. McKitrick, P. M.

No. 217.   *Frederick Lodge, Delhi, Ont.*
Bro. Robert Wood, S. W.; W. Bro. J. C. Ross, P. M.

No. 218.   *Stevenson Lodge, Toronto, Ont.*
W. Bro. Geo. Chanter, W. M.; Bro. James Robertson, S. W.;
Bro. J. W. Minor, J. W.; W. Bro. Joshua G. Burns, P. M.;
V. W. Bro. W. C. Morrison, P. M.

No. 219.   *Credit Lodge, Georgetown, Ont.*
W. Bro. John R. Barber, W. M.; Bro. Daniel McKenzie, S. W.;
Bro. W. McLeod, J. W.; W. Bro. M. H. Starr, P. M.

No. 220.   *Zeredatha Lodge, Uxbridge, Ont.*
W. Bro. Geo. H. Dartnell P. M.

No. 221.   *Mountain Lodge, Thorold, Ont.*
W. Bro. Jas. Lawson, P. M., Proxy.

No. 222.   *Marmora Lodge, Marmora, Ont.*
W. Bro. Thos. Warren, W. M.; V. W. Bro. Geo. E. Bull, P.M.

No. 223.   *Norwood Lodge, Norwood, Ont.*
Bro. S. H. Dewart, J. W.

No. 224.   *Zurich Lodge, Zurich, Ont.*
Bro. Michael Zeller, J. W.; W. Bro. Robt. Brown, P. M.

No. 226.   *Mount Moriah Lodge, Montreal, Que.*
V. W. Bro. John McLean, P. M., Proxy; R. W. Bro. John
Urquhart, jr. P. M.

No. 228.   *Prince Arthur Lodge, Odessa, Ont.*
W. Bro. A. P. Booth, W. M.; Bro. Thos. K. Ross, J. W.

No. 230.   *Kerr Lodge, Bell Ewart, Ont.*
W. Bro. J. W. H. Wilson, P. M.

No. 231.   *Lodge of Fidelity, Ottawa, Ont.*
W. Bro. Wm. Rea, W. M

No. 232.   *Cameron Lodge, Wallacetown, Ont.*
W. Bro. J. W. Luton, W. M.

No. 233.   *Doric Lodge, Park Hill, Ont.*
V. W. Bro. Geo. B. Reeve, P. M., Proxy.

No. 234.	*Beaver Lodge, Clarksburg, Ont.*
W. Dro. Alex. Mitchell, P. M., Proxy.

No. 236.	*Manitoba Lodge, Bondhead, Ont.*
W. Dro. W. C. Law, W. M.; Bro. Donald Gunn, S. W.; Dro. W. R. Fenton, J. W.

No. 240.	*Prince Rupert's Lodge, Winnipeg, Man.*
R. W. Dro. R. Kincaid, Proxy.

No. 241.	*Quinte Lodge, Shannonville, Ont.*
W. Bro. H. P. Redour, W. M.

No. 242.	*Macoy Lodge, Escott, Ont.*
Dro. R. B. Aylsworth, S. W.

No 243.	*St. George's Lodge, St. George, Ont.*
W. Dros. E. E. Kitchen. W. M.; Benjamin Bell, P. M.

No. 244.	*Lisgar Lodge, Mapleton, Man.*
R. W. Dro. R. Kincaid, Proxy.

No. 245.	*Tecumseh Lodge, Thamesville, Ont.*
W. Dro. B. L. Chipman, W. M.

No. 246.	*Union of Strict Observance Lodge, Montreal, Que.*
W. Dro. J. C. Thurston, W. M.

No. 247.	*Ashlar Lodge, Yorkville, Ont.*
W. Bro. W. C. Pridham, W. M.; Bro. Geo. Coles, S. W.; Bro. Joseph Dain, J. W.; W. Dro. Thos. F. Blackwood, P. M.

No. 248.	*Eureka Lodge, Pakenham. Ont.*
W. Dro. John W. Pickup, P. M., Proxy.

No. 249.	*Caledonia Lodge, Angus, Ont.*
W. Bro. John McKimmie, W. M.

No. 250.	*Thistle Lodge, Embro, Ont.*
Dro. Henry Adams, S. W.

No. 253.	*Minden Lodge, Kingston, Ont.*
Bros. J. M. Pollock, S. W.; James Redden, J. W.

No. 254.	*Clifton Lodge, Clifton, Ont.*
R. W. Dro. John Parry, P. M.

No. 255.	*Sydenham Lodge, Dresden, Ont.*
Bro. J. W. Sharpe, J. W.; R. W. Dro. Thos. C. Macnabb, P.M.

No. 256.	*Farran's Point Lodge, Farran's Point, Ont.*
W. Dro. Chas. F. H. Forbes, P. M., Proxy.

No. 257.	*Gall Lodge, Galt, Ont.*
Bro. Alfred Taylor, S. W.

No. 259.	*Springfield Lodge, Springfield, Ont.*
Dro. D. McKenzie, S. W.; W. Bro. Robt. Scott, P. M.

No. 260.   *Washington Lodge, Petrolia, Ont.*
W. Bro. Wm. Stevenson, W. M.

No. 261.   *Oak Branch Lodge, Innerkip, Ont.*
W. Bro. E W. Town, W. M.

No. 262.   *Harriston Lodge, Harriston, Ont.*
W. Bro. Alex. Irvine, W. M.

No. 263.   *Forest Lodge, Forest, Ont.*
W. Bro. H. J. Nash, W. M.

No. 264.   *Chaudiere Lodge, Ottawa, Ont.*
W. Bro. W. H. Timbers, W. M.

No. 265.   *Patterson Lodge, Concord, Ont.*
W. Bro. W. C. Patterson, W. M.; Bro. John Lane, J. W.

No. 266.   *Northern Light Lodge, Stayner, Ont.*
W. Bros. Thos. H. George, W. M.; R. B. Hannah, P. M.

No. 267.   *Parthenon Lodge, Chatham, Ont.*
W. Bro. H. J. Eberts, W. M.

No. 268.   *Verulam Lodge, Bobcaygeon, Ont.*
R. W. Bro. C. D. Macdonnell, Proxy.

No. 269.   *Brougham Union Lodge, Brougham, Ont.*
W. Bro. D. W. Ferrier, W. M.; Bro. Geo. Godfrey, J. W.

No. 270.   *Cedar Lodge, Oshawa, Ont.*
W. Bro. Philip Taylor, W. M.; Bro. Francis Rae, S. W.; Bro. Daniel McKay, J. W.

No. 271.   *Wellington Lodge, Erin, Ont.*
Bro. R. D. Boomer, S. W.

No. 274.   *Kent Lodge, Blenheim, Ont.*
W. Bro. Lewis Kinne, W. M.; W. Bro. John A. Ash, P. M.

No. 275.   *Pontiac Lodge, Onslow, Ont.*
R. W. Bro. Wm. Mostyn, Proxy.

No. 276.   *Teeswater Lodge, Teeswater, Ont.*
W. Bro. H. B. O'Connor, W. M.

No. 277.   *Seymour Lodge, Port Dalhousie, Ont.*
Bro. Wm. Scott, J. W.; M. W. Bro. James Seymour, P. M.

No. 278.   *Mystic Lodge, Roslin Ont.*
W. Bro. E. B. Fralick, P. M., Proxy.

No. 280.   *Mount Sinai Lodge, Napanee, Ont.*
R. W. Bro. F. Richardson, W. M.; Bro. J. F. Ferguson, S. W.; Bro. J. R. Pruyn, J. W.

No. 281.   *Thorne Lodge, Holland Landing, Ont*
W. Bro. A. Williams, W. M.; Bro. W. H. Thorne, S. W.

No. 282.   *Lorne Lodge, Glencoe, Ont.*
                W. Bro. Wm. Hayden, W. M.
No. 283.   *Eureka Lodge, Belleville, Ont.*
                R. W. Bro. L. H. Henderson, W. M.; Bro. W. C. Hamilton,
                J. W.
No. 284.   *St. John's Lodge, Brussels, Ont.*
                W. Bro. W. J. R. Holmes, W. M.
No. 285.   *Seven Star Lodge, Allitton, Ont.*
                V. W. Bro. Thomas Sargant, P. M.; W. Bro. Wm. Knight, P.M.
No. 286.   *Wingham Lodge, Wingham, Ont.*
                W. Bro. J. E. Tamlyn, W. M.
No. 287.   *Shuniah Lodge, Prince Arthur's Landing.*
                R. W. Bro. P. J. Brown, Proxy.
No. 288.   *Ancient Landmark Lodge, Winnipeg, Man.*
                R. W. Bro. Thos. B. Harris, Proxy.
No. 289.   *Doric Lodge, Lobo, Ont.*
                W. Bro. W. D. McGloghlon, Proxy.
No. 290.   *Leamington Lodge, Leamington, On'.*
                W. Bro. Wm. Young, Proxy.
No. 291.   *Dufferin Lodge, West Flamboro, Ont.*
                V. W. Bro. F. H. Lynch Staunton, Proxy.
No. 292.   *Robertson Lodge, Nobleton, Ont.*
                W. Bros. James Bowman, W. M.
No. 294.   *Moore Lodge, Mooretown, On'.*
                W. Bro. J. A. Sommerville, W. M.
No. 295.   *Conestogo Lodge, Drayton, Ont.*
                R. W. Bro. Chas. Hendry, W. M.
No. 296.   *Temple Lodge, St. Catharines, Ont.*
                W. Bro. Lauchlin Leitch, W. M.
No. 297.   *Preston Lodge, Preston, Ont.*
                Bro. Nelson Mulloy, S. W.; R. W. Bro. Otto Klotz, P. M.
No. 298.   *Eddy Lodge, Hull, Que.*
                W. Bro. E. B. Butterworth, Proxy.
No. 299.   *Victoria Lodge, Centreville, Ont.*
                W. Bro. John S. Miller, W. M.
No. 300.   *Mount Olivet Lodge, Thorndale, On'.*
                W. Bro. M. Forster, W. M.
No. 301.   *Hanover Lodge, Hanover, Ont.*
                R. W. Bro. John E. Harding, Proxy.
U. D.   *St. Davids Lodge, St. Thomas, Ont.*
                W. Bro. Josiah Corlis. W. M.

U. D.   *Blyth Lodge, Blyth, Ont.*
            W. Bro. Wm. Wilson, W. M.

U. D.   *Minerva Lodge, Victoria, Ont.*
            W. Bro. Robt. King, W. M.; Bro. Thomas Brunskill, S. W.,
            Bro. A. M. Morden, J. W.

U. D.   *Humber Lodge, Weston, Ont.*
            W. Bro. F. W. Forbes. W. M.; Bro. Wm. Brown, S. W.

U. D.   *Durham Ledge, Durham, Ont.*
            W. Bro. Jas. H. Hunter, W. M.

U. D.   *Morning Star Lodge, Smiths Hill, Ont.*
            W. Bro. John Varcoe, W. M.

U. D.   *Enterprise Lodge, Beachburg, Ont.*
            W. Bro. Andrew Irving, Proxy.

U. D.   *Blackwood Lodge, Woodbridge, Ont.*
            W. Bro. Thos. F. Blackwood, W. M.

U. D.   *Pnyx Lodge, Wallaceburg, Ont.*
            Bro. John Scott, J. W.

U. D.   *Clementi Lodge, Lakefield, Ont.*
            R. W. Bro R. Kincaid, W. M.

U. D.   *Blair Lodge, Palmerston, Ont.*
            R W. Bro. Thos. B. Harris, Proxy.

U. D.   *Clifford Lodje, Clifford, Ont.*
            W. Bro. K. M. Walton, W. M.

U. D.   *Doric Lodge, Toronto, Ont.*
            R. W. Bro. R. P. Stephens, W. M.; W. Bro. Jas. B. Nixon, P.M

U. D.   *The Hiram Lodge, Dundas, Ont.*
            W. Bro. N. Greening, W. M.

U. D.   *Wilmot Lodge, Baden, Ont.*
            W. Bro. Wm. Merton, P. M.

On motion, the report of the Committee on Credentials was received and adopted.

The M. W. Grand Master, granted permission for the admission of all Master Masons in good standing, as visitors.

The Grand Secretary read the rules and regulations for the government of Grand Lodge during time of business.

The Grand Secretary commenced reading the minutes of proceedings at the last annual Communication, when

It was moved by R. W. Bro. Thos. White jr., seconded by M. W. Bro. T. D. Harington, and

RESOLVED,—That the minutes of the proceedings of Grand Lodge at its Eighteenth Annual Communication, held at the city of Montreal, on the 9th and 10th days of July, A. D. 1873, having been printed, and copies thereof forwarded to the Subordinate Lodges, the same be considered as read and now confirmed.

The M. W. Grand Master delivered the following address to the brethren assembled in Grand Communication.

ADDRESS.

Brethren of Grand Lodge:

I avail myself of the earliest moment to announce to you officially, that the long pending difficulties between ourselves and the Masons of Quebec have now been happily arranged.

Under authority of the resolution adopted by this Grand Lodge in July, 1871, and after certain preliminary arrangements had been made, by which all concerned were bound to accept, abide by, and carry out, all the conditions and terms which might be agreed upon by a joint committee, taken from both bodies in the Province of Quebec, a Masonic Conference of the members of committees appointed respectively by the Grand Lodge of Quebec, and by myself on your behalf, met at Montreal on the 17th of February last, and after much careful consideration, agreed upon terms of union between our Lodges in Quebec and the Lodges already affiliated with and composing the Grand Lodge of Quebec.

Copies of the official protocols of this Conference were, by my directions, promptly forwarded to all our Lodges, so that you were at once placed in possession of the important intelligence, that a satisfactory settlement of these unhappy difficulties had at length been arrived at.

In order, therefore, to give full effect to the arrangements thus entered into, all that now remains to be done on your part, is to pass a resolution to formally withdraw from the territory, and recognize fraternally the Grand Lodge of Quebec as the supreme Masonic Authority in that Province, extending to her the right hand of fellowship, with our best wishes for her future prosperity and usefulness.

In concluding my remarks upon this very important

matter, I avail myself of the present opportunity to express my warmest acknowledgements to our R. W. Bro , the Deputy Grand Master, for his valuable co-operation. His advice and assistance largely contributed to bring about a peaceful solution of these unhappy troubles, and I would be pleased to see his valuable services upon this and other occasions suitably acknowledged by Grand Lodge. The truly Masonic spirit and feeling which existed and was evinced on both sides, enabled our brethren to overcome all obstacles, and eventually led to a union, which I hope will prove perpetual. We shall part from our brethren of Quebec with unfeigned regret; we will miss their "familiar faces" and pleasant voices at our annual meetings, but they carry with them our best wishes and heartfelt prayers for their happiness and prosperity. The link that bound us in the chain of brotherly love remains unbroken, and we shall still continue working together for the promotion of the great cause which lies near all our hearts. The change about to take place is, after all, only a change of jurisdiction, and can make but a very slight change in our fraternal relations.

The intelligence that the Quebec difficulties were on the eve of arrangement was promptly followed by edicts from the Grand Lodges of Vermont and Illinois, revoking their former edicts of non-intercourse with this Grand Lodge. These were met in a fraternal spirit by me as your representative, and all bars to the resumption of fraternal relations have thus been removed. I have again assumed the office of Grand Representative of the Grand Lodge of Illinois, and had much pleasure in appointing R. W. Bro. Wiley M. Egan, of Chicago, as our representative near that Grand Body.

LOUISIANA.

An earnest appeal properly attested by the Grand Master of Louisiana, praying for a contribution in aid of a fund then being raised for the relief of many brethren who were suffering from an inundation in the State of Louisiana, was forwarded to me by our Grand Secretary on the 27th of May last. Feeling that "he gives twice who gives quickly" I was desirous that a contribution should at once be forwarded, but it was considered prudent to await the meeting of Grand Lodge before taking any action in the matter. I am unable to say whether the opportunity of assisting our distressed brethren is still open to us or not; but, if, upon inquiry, we find that we are still in time to alleviate distress and suffering by a contribution, I am quite sure that an appeal to your sympathy and benevolence will not be made in vain.

In connection with the Grand Lodge of Louisiana, and the interruption of our friendly relations with that Grand Body, arising, I believe, from a misapprehension on their part as to our action in regard to the Orient of France, I may here state that by my directions a letter was addressed to the Grand Representative of the Grand Orient on the 25th of November last, requesting him to communicate to the Grand Orient our views on the point at issue, and to express the hope that the Grand Orient would reconsider her action, and withdraw the recognition which she had accorded to an antagonistic body within the jurisdiction of the Grand Lodge of Louisiana. No reply to this communication has yet been received, but I sincerely hope that the G. O. will on mature consideration, withdraw her recognition and recede from the unfriendly position she has assumed towards the Grand Lodge of Louisiana.

CORRESPONDENCE

My Masonic correspondence during the past year has been unusually large, and while I am happy to believe that all letters addressed to me have been promptly replied to, I feel it a duty, in the interests of future Grand Masters, to suggest that, except in special cases, much time would be saved by a close adherence to the requirements of that section of the constitution which enacts that—"The Grand Master shall not be applied to officially on any business

concerning masons or masonry, but through the Grand
Secretary, the Deputy G. M., the District Deputy G. M.'s
or the Board of General Purposes." The reason for this
clause is sufficiently obvious. Many of the matters written
about are connected with affairs that have extended over long
periods; the documents connected with which are on file in
the archives of the office of the Grand Secretary, therefore
when the application is made through the proper official,
all the information is submitted at the same time, and the
Grand Master is thus enabled to give an intelligent decision
upon the question submitted, without having to refer to the
Grand Secretary for further information.

FUNERALS.

The question as to the propriety of permitting other
Societies to take part in Masonic funerals, has been prominently brought under my notice during the past year. My
views on the subject (which are strongly opposed to the
practice) were expressed in a letter addressed by me to the
Secretary of a lodge in reply to one from him, requesting
information on the subject. This letter was subsequently
published in the *Craftsman*, and I now introduce the matter
to you, in the hope that a formal decision of Grand Lodge
will be given on the subject; I have always felt in the same
way as to the impropriety of our lodge-rooms being used
jointly with other societies, or indeed, used for any purpose
outside of Masonry, and would recommend that an expression
of the views of Grand Lodge be also given upon this point.

ON SUSPENSION.

In the course of the discharge of my official duties during
the past year, an appeal was made to me by a Brother Mason
against an order of his lodge made some months previously,
suspending him indefinitely for a Masonic offence of which
he had been found guilty. After much careful consideration
of the whole matter, I concurred in the judgment pronounced
by the lodge, but as I considered that the brother referred to
had already been sufficiently punished, I declared the sus-

pension removed, and ordered that the brother be restored to his former standing in his lodge. The point to which I at present desire to direct your especial attention is as to the propriety of Grand Lodge, (I raise no question as to her authority) ordering that a brother who had been indefinitely suspended shall be restored to his former standing in his lodge.

In ordering as I did, that the brother referred to should be restored to full fellowship with his lodge, I acted in direct opposition to my own former rulings, and also to my present convictions on the point; but I felt bound to carry out the decision of the Grand Lodge, as expressed in a report of the Board of General Purposes, which report was received and adopted at the annual Communication in 1870—(see printed proceedings, page 461 *et seq*). I would be much pleased to have this question carefully re-considered, as it involves a point of the greatest importance.

'Suspension may be for a definite or for an indefinite period. If for a definite period, the party suspended, at the expiration of the time mentioned, at once assumes his former position and standing in his lodge and with the craft generally, and no action of the lodge is either requisite or necessary; but, if the suspension is for an indefinite period then the procedure is entirely different. A sentence of indefinite suspension conveys to my mind the idea that, although the Grand Lodge may remove the suspension in so far as the relationship of the party to the general craft is concerned, it would neither be wise nor prudent for the Grand Lodge to compel a lodge to receive back as a member one whom a majority of the lodge declined to receive. There are not many lodges that would not receive back a member after Grand Lodge had removed the suspension; but I am strongly of the opinion that no lodge should be compelled to receive back a brother who had been indefinitely suspended, unless by ballot, a majority of the members declared their assent to his return. I leave the matter, however in your hands, and again request for it your careful consideration.

3

NEW JERSEY.

I received a communication from the Grand Master of the Grand Lodge of New Jersey, informing me that a person of doubtful character had applied to one of their subordinate Lodges for initiation, and had been rejected, and that he had recently returned to that State a Master Mason and member of one of our Canadian Lodges. Upon inquiry, I ascertained that the party alluded to had resided for one year within the jurisdiction of the Lodge which had received him, and that they had not considered it necessary to make inquiries as to character at his former place of residence in New Jersey. I may mention that the subsequent conduct of this brother has led to charges being made against him. From this, and other incidents of a similar nature which have come to my knowledge, I would earnestly exhort the Masters and officers of Lodges to be more prudent and careful in their inquiries as to the character of those who seek admission to our Order, and it has occurred to me that perhaps it would be prudent to add a clause to the usual petition, to the effect that the applicant had not been rejected by any other Lodge within the last twelve months—the object of this addition would be, that if it was afterwards ascertained that the statement was untrue, the offender might be expelled.

NEW LODGES.

During the past year I have granted dispensations for the formation of nineteen new Lodges, a list of which I here append for your information. I declined granting one for a new Lodge at Fort Erie, as I did not consider that a Lodge was required in that particular locality, and for a similar reason I also refused a dispensation for an additional Lodge at Sarnia—the petitioners may apply to Grand Lodge for warrants, and I have no doubt that the applications will receive consideration.

LIST OF LODGES GRANTED DISPENSATIONS SINCE MEETING
OF GRAND LODGE IN JULY, 1873.

Dispensation date.	Name of Lodge.	Where Held.	Worshipful Master Elect.
1873.			
July 21...........	St. David's......	St. Thomas.........	Josiah Corlis.
October 16.....	Blyth	Blyth...............	William Wilson.
November 22...	Minerva.........	Victoria	Robert King.
December 26..	Humber........	Weston	Frank W. Forbes.
December 26...	Durham.......	Durham	James H. Hunter.
1874.			
January 13.....	Arkona.........	Arkona	John Dallas.
January 15....	Grafton	Grafton	Francis Drake.
January 31.....	Morning Star ..	Smith's Hill........	John Varcoe.
February 14....	Enterprise	Beachburg	George Forbes.
February 16...	Blackwood.....	Woodbridge.......	Thomas F. Blackwood.
February 17....	Onyx	Wallaceburg.......	Harvey Morris.
February 27....	Clementi.......	Lakefield.........	Robert Kincaid.
February 28....	Hiram	Cheapside.........	Jesse V. Hoover.
March 9.......	Blair...........	Palmerston........	Hugh Hyndman.
April 10........	Clifford.........	Clifford	Kenneth McL. Walton.
April 11	Doric	Toronto...........	Richard P. Stephens.
April 22........	The Hiram	Dundas	Nathaniel Greening.
June 4	Chesterville....	Chesterville.......	William Wilson French.
June 17........	Wilmot........	Baden.............	John Moran.

INSURANCE.

I regret to announce that the rooms, warrants, jewels and furniture of Craig Lodge, No. 214, at Ailsa Craig, Bernard Lodge, No. 225, at Listowel, and Aylmer Lodge, No. 138, at Aylmer, were respectively destroyed by fire in the month of March last; duplicate warrants were at once prepared and forwarded to them free of charge. I believe that neither of these Lodges had effected insurance upon their Lodge property, and I would now earnestly advise all our Lodges to avail themselves of the protection afforded by a policy in a good insurance company.

FINANCES.

On examining the accounts submitted by R. W. Bro. Groff, our most efficient and trustworthy Grand Treasurer, I am much pleased to be able to report that our finances are in a most satisfactory condition. In advance of the report of the Auditors, I submit the following extracts of grand totals:—

```
Investments—Stocks.................................... 28 800 00
    "        Bank of Toronto....................... 1 681 66
    "        Bank of Commerce..................... 15 683 58

        Total......................................... $56 135 24
Carried to credit of General Fund...................................... 32 969 98
    "        "      Asylum Fund... ........................ 6 451 66
    "        "      Investment Benevolence...................... 15 079 20
    "        "      Benevolence Account......................... 1 604 40

                                                    $56 135 24
```

FORMS, ETC

During the present session I hope o be able to submit, first for the consideration of the Board of General Purposes, and afterwards for your approval, with a view to secure greater uniformity :—Forms of procedure to be used in Masonic trials, and the ceremonies and forms to be used at installation of officers of a Lodge, and at the dedications of Masonic Halls. These have been prepared since our last annual communication, and when approved, will, I hope, be ordered to be made known to those having to act on the same in a due Masonic manner. I have here to acknowledge the valuable services of my learned and R. W. Bro. J. K. Kerr, in preparing the first of these, and for the latter I am much indebted to the labours of that most zealous, intelligent, and hard-working brother, R. W. Bro. Klotz.

CORNER STONE DEDICATIONS, 1873.

July 28th. At Port Hope, assisted by the brethren of that beautiful and thriving town, and by large numbers from Peterboro', Cobourg, and elsewhere, I laid the corner stone of a chapel and dining-hall, in connection with Trinity College School. The interest in the proceedings was much enhanced by the attendance of a large number of the clergy, and by the presence of the boys attending the College. A banquet, given by the Masons of Port Hope, formed a pleasing termination to my very pleasant visit.

Aug. 20th. I laid with Masonic ceremonies on this day the corner stone of an Episcopal Church at Parkhill, on which occasion I was assisted by the D. G. M., and a large attendance of our western brethren. R. W. Bro. Innes, the present Grand Chaplain, also took part in the proceedings.

Our reverend brother is now slowly recovering from a dangerous illness, which, I regret to say, will prevent his attendance at this meeting.

Aug. 21st. I visited Doric Lodge, No. 289, Lobo, and dedicated their new hall. Past D. D. G. M. Westlake, and a number of brethren from London were present and assisted me in the ceremonies.

Sept. 5th. The corner stone of a Methodist Episcopal Church was laid at Teeswater, on which occasion I was ably represented by R. W. Bro. Harding, D. D. G. M., of Huron District.

Sept. 20th. A similar ceremony took place at New Boyne. The work was most efficiently performed by R. W. Bro. Reynolds, D. D. G. M. of St. Lawrence District, who kindly acted for me on that occasion.

Sept. 24th. The foundation stone of a public school was laid with Masonic ceremonies at Trenton, when R. W. Bro. Dr. H. W. Day, P. D. D. G. M. of Prince Edward District, officiated in my absence.

Oct. 2nd. Having received an invitation from the Governor of the State of Michigan, to be present at the laying of the foundation stone of a new capitol about to erected at Lansing. I gladly availed myself of the opportunity of witnessing a ceremony which I felt assured would be most correctly and ably performed. As a full account of the proceedings on this very interesting occasion was published in the *Craftsman*, I will only say that the kind reception accorded, and the honors paid me as your representative, were most gratifying.

Jan. 3rd, 1874. The corner stone of a Methodist Episcopal Church was laid with appropriate ceremonies at Brockville, by R. W. Bro. Reynolds, D. D. G. M. as my representative. From the published accounts this must have been a most interesting gathering.

Jan. 6th. On this day I visited the brethren of St. Mary's

and dedicated their new Hall to Masonry, under the auspices of our indefatigable and R. W. Bro. Harding, the D. D. G. M. of that District. The craft within his jurisdiction are in a most flourishing condition.

Feb. 6th. I visited Waterford and installed the officers of Wilson Lodge, No. 113.

June 24th. I spent St. John's Day with the brethren of Port Hope, as their guest; the Masons of Cobourg, with their wives and children, were also sharers in their liberal hospitality.

The gathering took the form of a pic-nic, and a most beautiful spot had been selected for the place of meeting; the day was most pleasantly spent, and the arrangements made by R. W. Bros. Trayes and Wright, and the other brethren on the Committee of Management were most admirable. I had the pleasure of passing the evening at the club-rooms, where I met many of my Masonic brethren.

July 1st. On Dominion Day I laid the corner-stone of a Methodist Episcopal Church at St. Thomas, assisted by R. W. Bro. Burch, D. D. G. M. of London District. The attendance was large and most respectable. I cannot refrain from mentioning, in connection with this visit, the agreeable surprise I felt to find that St. David's Lodge, to form which I had only granted a dispensation a year since, already numbered over sixty members—a class of men, too, who would be an ornament to any Lodge. By their united exertions, and under the able guidance of W. Bro. Corlis, their zealous and most efficient Master, they have erected a large and handsome edifice, the upper storey of which is to be used as their lodge room, and when completed and furnished (and it is now very nearly so), St. David's Lodge will occupy one of the handsomest and most convenient halls in this jurisdiction. All power to such workers.

During the past year I was enabled to visit my brethren in various parts of our jurisdiction. When in Montreal in September last, I received much kind attention from our warm-hearted brethren of that city, and I have only to mention that I met M. W. Bros. Stevenson and Bernard, to convince you that I had no reason to complain of any absence of kindness or hospitality when in their vicinity. I paid a very pleasant visit to Peterboro', also during the month of February, and in June last I was the recipient of a banquet given in my honor, by the brethren of London. On these and all other Masonic occasions the kind attentions paid me will ever be remembered.

As suggested at our last annual Communication, I have made enquiries with reference to the establishment of the Grand Lodge of Utah, and I have now much pleasure in recommending that she be recognized as a Sister Grand Lodge, and the right hand of fellowship extended towards her.

FRATERNAL DEAD.

I noticed with regret that Grand Master Keith, of Nova Scota, died on the 14th of December last, at the age of 78 years. Our Most Worshipful Brother was beloved and respected by all who knew him. By his earnest efforts to promote Masonic interests, formerly as Provincial Grand Master, and latterly as Grand Master of the Grand Lodge of Nova Scotia, he had endeared himself to the fraternity, and we tender our sympathy and condolence to the Grand Lodge of Nova Scotia on the loss of her distinguished Grand Master.

I may also refer to the death of Earl Dalhousie, P. G. M. of the Grand Lodge of Scotland, which was announced by cable yesterday.

In our own jurisdiction we have to lament the untimely death of R. W. Bro. James V. Noel, P. D. D. G. M., and R. W. Bro. B. C. Davy, P. G. J., Warden of this Grand Lodge; both of them were distinguished for their zeal and their love of Masonry. Though dead, their memories will long live in the hearts of their brethren. Other brethren have been called from labor to rest; but as their names will appear in the reports of the D. D. G. M.'s, I consider it unnecessary to refer to them more directly in this address.

MASONIC ASYLUM FUND.

The further consideration of this very interesting subject, which was so ably discussed at our last annual Communication, was then laid over to the present meeting, and will again be brought up before you by the trustees of the Masonic Asylum Trust in their annual report. My views on the subject were so fully expressed in my last annual address that I consider it unnecessary now to repeat them. The report for the last year has been printed and will be distributed among the members of the Grand Lodge, from the perusal of which you will observe that the Trustees still rely with confidence upon receiving your sanction to enable them to carry out, in a modified form, the truly philanthropic object which they have so much at heart. The practical suggestions made by the distinguished brethren who form the Board of Trustees, will, I have no doubt, receive your most favorable consideration.

I commenced my present address by announcing the termination of our Quebec difficulties, and I had hoped to be able to conclude it by informing you that another difficulty, which I regard as only second in importance to that of Quebec, had also been removed. The matter is one to which during the past year I have given much anxious thought and attention, but as (contrary to my sanguine expectations) it is not yet finally and absolutely closed, I do not consider it prudent to mention it in more direct terms at present. I may say, however, that I entertain no doubt of such a conclusion as will prove gratifying to the members of the Grand Lodge.

I now leave you, brethren, to consider the various matters I have suggested, with such other business as may be brought before you. The past history of this Grand Lodge proves that each passing year has but added to her prosperity, her influence, and her respectability; 'tis true, we have also

had our share of trouble and anxiety, but the good has far
outbalanced annoyance of every kind—and as to the future,
if we only act up to the true principles of Freemasonry, if
we direct our most earnest efforts to the great object of
making men wiser, better, and happier, we must succeed in
securing for Masonry the respect and admiration of all good
men.

WILLIAM M. WILSON,
Grand Master.

It was moved by R. W. Bro. Thos. White jr., seconded by
M. W. Bro. T. D. Harington, and

RESOLVED,—That the address of the M. W. Grand Master be referred
to the Board of General Purposes to report thereon.

Telegrams were received and read from M. W. Bro. W. B.
Simpson, and R. W. Bro. Rev. G. M. Innes, Grand Chaplain,
regretting their inability to be present at this Communication
of Grand Lodge.

It was moved by M. W. Bro. T. D. Harington, seconded
by R. W. Bro. J. E. Harding, and.

RESOLVED,—That the following reports from the various District
Deputy Grand Masters be received and considered as read, viz:

ST. CLAIR DISTRICT.

To the Most Worshipful the Grand Master, Officers and Members of the Grand
Lodge of A. F. &. A. M. of Canada.

MOST WORSHIPFUL SIR AND BRETHREN,—In accordance
with the requirements of the Constitution of Grand Lodge
and the discharge of the duty devolving upon me, I have the
honor to submit, this my first annual report of the condition
of Freemasonry in this District.

I have, during my term of office, visited all the Lodges in
the District, and have pleasure in reporting to Grand Lodge
that Freemasonry is still continuing in a flourishing and
satisfactory condition throughout the District.

During the year, upon petitions duly recommended, I
applied to the M. W. the Grand Master for Dispensations to
open two new Lodges at the following places, viz:—one at

Arkona, called Arkona Lodge, W. Bro J. Dallas, W. M., and the other at Wallaceburg, called Pnyx Lodge, W. Bro. II. Morris, W. M.; to both of which, the M. W. the Grand Master was pleased to issue dispensations. On subsequent visits to said Lodges, I found them working satisfactorily.

All the Lodges in the District, I am happy to say, are working in accordance with the adopted ritual of Grand Lodge.

The usual dispensations for wearing Masonic Regalia have been granted to the brethren on proper occasions, and in this connection I am pleased to report that many of them were for the purpose of attending Masonic Lectures and Divine services.

Several of the brethren during the year who have been removed from our midst by death, were duly reported to the Grand Secretary, as required by the Constitution, and they received Masonic burial.

I cannot close this my report without expressing my gratitude and sincere thanks to the officers and brethren of all the Lodges, for the universal kindness, attention and fraternal welcome with which I was received when paying my official visits, and will look back with unfeigned pleasure to the time when I had the honor to hold the high position of D. D. G. M. of St. Clair District.

All of which is respectfully submitted.

THOMAS C. MACNABB,

Chatham, 1st July, 1871.   D. D. G. M., St. Clair District.

LONDON DISTRICT.

To the Most Worshipful the Grand Master and the Grand Lodge of Canada.

MOST WORSHIPFUL SIR AND BRETHREN,—In compliance with the Constitution, I beg to submit my report upon the condition of Masonry in this District.

Owing to the extent of the District, I was not able to visit all of the twenty-five Lodges comprising it—but such as I did visit, I found well skilled and the Lodges properly furnished—and from enquiries made, learned that .the remainder, unvisited, were in an equally prosperous condition, as their returns to Grand Lodge will fully show.

On the 10th of August, 1873, I granted a dispensation to St. John's Lodge, No. 20, to appear in regalia to meet their brethren from Cleveland Ohio, at a promenade concert and supper in London, on which occasion, I was ably assisted by R. W. Bro. F. Westlake, P. D. D. G. M., R. W. Bro. Rev. G. M. Innes, Grand Chaplain, Bro. Medicraft, Tuscan Lodge, 195, and other distinguished brethren. A very enjoyable evening was spent, and great credit is due to the Masons of London, for the liberal and spirited manner in which the entertainment was carried out.

A dispensation was also granted to the brethren at London, for holding their annual Festival.

I attended the M. W. Grand Master, at three Special Communications of Grand Lodge in my District.

The first on the 20th August, 1873, at Park Hill, for the purpose of laying the foundation stone of an English Church in that village.

The second on the 21st August, 1873, at Lobo, for the purpose of dedicating a new Masonic Hall.

The third on the 1st July,at St. Thomas,for the purpose of laying the corner stone of a new Episcopal Methodist Church in that thriving town.

At all of the above Special Communications, large numbers of the craft turned out to assist the M. W. the Grand Master and Grand Officers in the performance of their duties. After the ceremony at each place, the brethren suitably entertained the Grand Master and visiting brethren assembled.

In reporting the formation of a new lodge at the Town of St. Thomas, under the name of "St. David's Lodge," for which a dispensation was issued by the M. W. the Grand

Master, I take pleasure in stating that the lodge is in a most flourishing condition, the brethren having displayed a great amount of enterprise in erecting one of the finest edifices in Western Ontario, which is not only an ornament to the Town of St. Thomas, but reflects great credit on the brethren of St. David's Lodge.

The minute book and records have been admirably kept, and it is with great pleasure I recommend that a warrant be granted.

The few complaints which have arisen during the year have, I believe, been adjusted to the satisfaction of all concerned.

I have to report the total loss by fire, of two Lodge-rooms and their contents, viz: Malahide Lodge, No. 104, and Springfield Lodge, No. 258, and would recommend to the consideration of Grand Lodge, the remitting of their dues for the year.

The following Bros. have been reported to me as having gone to their rest, viz: Bro. R. Ferguson of St. John's Lodge, No. 20, W. Bro. Wm. Hemphill of St. Mark's Lodge, No. 94, and Bro. Donald Seaton of St. John's Lodge, No. 81.

I find many enquiries being made by the brethren of the district, as to the advisability of Grand Lodge reducing the annual fees from 50 to 25 cents per year.

In conclusion allow me to return to the Grand Master and Grand Secretary my sincere thanks for the promptness and courtesy extended to me, and to the brethren of the London District for their courtesy and kindness evinced at all times to me officially or otherwise.

All of which is most respectfully and fraternally submitted.

D. B. BURCH,

London, July 4th, 1871.   D. D. G. M. London District.

WILSON DISTRICT.

To the Most Worshipful the Grand Master and Grand Lodge of Canada.

MOST WORSHIPFUL SIR AND BRETHREN, I have the honor to report that during the year just closed I visited ten of the lodges in my District, with one exception I found them in a most prosperous condition, while peace and harmony prevailed throughout. It had been my full intention and earnest desire to visit every lodge under my charge, but a most desirable position being offered me in Detroit, Michigan, I accepted it in January last, since which time it has been simply impossible for me to visit the Wilson District. I have, however, been in correspondence with all the lodges in my charge, and am pleased to say that no matter of so serious a nature has been brought under my notice, that special mention need be made of it in this report. During the year a number of lodges made application to me for permission to appear in public in Masonic clothing, I gave the desired permission in all but one instance, in which the brethren wished to attend a ball, this application I referred to the M. W. the Grand Master, who was pleased to grant a dispensation.,

In closing this brief report, I would respectfully advise my successor to hold a District Lodge of Instruction at the earliest possible moment, as it was most apparent to me, there is not that thorough uniformity in the Ritual work that is desirable. In some lodges little innovations had been allowed to creep in, that I believe a General Lodge of Instruction would more effectually eradicate than half a dozen visits to each lodge. Had I remained in the District I had intended to have held such a lodge as I recommend, before my term of office expired. I would thank the brethren of the District for the uniform kindness and courtesy that I have met with at their hands.

All of which is respectfully submitted.

W. S. MARTIN,

Paris, July 3rd, A. D. 1874.   D. D. G. M.

HURON DISTRICT.

To the Most Worshipful the Grand Master and the Grand Lodge of Canada.

MOST WORSHIPFUL SIR AND BRETHREN,—I have the honor to submit my report on the condition of Masonry in Huron District, for the year A. L. 5873-4.

There are twenty-one lodges working under warrants and two under dispensations. All lodges in the District are working in harmony, and are in a prosperous and flourishing condition. I regret that I have been unable to visit any great number of lodges in the District owing to circumstances over which I had no control.

I have held two general Lodges of Instruction during the year, the first at Walkerton, in the month of October last. This lodge was a failure owing to the Battalion of the County of Bruce being out for drill, and most of the brethren being volunteers. The second was held at Seaforth, on the 17th, 18th and 19th of June last, and was most successful and satisfactory. The work was exemplified in accordance with the Ritual of this Grand Lodge and a large amount of information obtained as to the working of a lodge in this jurisdiction. There were the representatives of ten lodges in attendance, who appeared highly satisfied with the result of the meeting.

In September last I laid the foundation stone of a new stone Church at Teeswater, under a dispensation empowering me to do so.

The Most Worshipful the Grand Master granted a dispensation for holding a lodge at Blyth, in the County of Huron, and also for holding a lodge at Smith's Hill, in the County of Huron. I recommend that warrants be granted to both lodges.

The difficulties existing in Tudor Lodge, No. 141, at the date of my last report, are happily dissipated, and the lodge is now in a prosperous condition under the able mastership of R. W. Bro. Matheson.

I installed the officers of St. James' Lodge, No. 73, St. Mary's, and assisted at the dedication of their lodge by the Grand Master.

Two deaths have been reported to me during the year, viz., of W. Bro. Rainee of Clinton Lodge. No. 84, and of Bro. Smith of Tecumseh, No. 144, both were buried with Masonic honors. I have been notified of the suspension of Bro. Tait Scott for unmasonic conduct, by Forest Lodge, No. 162, Wroxeter,and of Bro.R. J. Sloan, for non-payment of dues, by the same lodge. I have also been notified by the Secretary of the lodge,of the suspension of Bro. Thomas Kirk Anderson, by Britannia Lodge, No. 170. I have also been notified of the restoration of Bro. Charles Zoller, by Tecumseh Lodge, No. 144. Bro. Scott has appealed to the Board of General Purposes against the ruling of the lodge and the Board referred the appeal to me. I have endeavored to have the matter disposed of, but Bro. Scott alleges that he cannot find an important witness, and the matter will have to be disposed of by my successor in office.

I beg leave to append a letter that I received from W. Bro. Nicol, W. M. of Bernard Lodge, No. 225, Listowel, asking for assistance from Grand Lodge, their lodge room and furniture having been destroyed by fire. and I recommend it to your favorable consideration.

I beg leave to return my thanks to the brethren of Huron District, for their great kindness and courtesy to me at all times.

Respectfully submitted,

JOHN E. HARDING. .

St. Mary's, July 2nd, A. D. 1874.   D. D. G. M. Huron District.

WELLINGTON DISTRICT.

To the Most Worshipful the Grand Master and the Grand Lodge of A. F. and A. M. Canada.

MOST WORSHIPFUL SIR AND BRETHREN,—I beg to submit the following report on the progress and condition of Freemasonry in the Wellington District, for the year just ended.

There are fifteen lodges working under warrants from Grand Lodge and three under dispensations. I have visited officially nearly all of these during the year, and I take pleasure in acknowledging the general correctness and the large measure of uniformity displayed in the working of the lodges, as well as the general harmony and good will that evidently prevail throughout the district. Two lodges I had not the pleasure of visiting, viz., "Preston" and "Conestogo" but I am sure I need only to mention the fact that these are presided over by R. W. Bro. Otto Klotz and Charles Hendry, respectively, to satisfy you of their efficient working. Only one case of difficulty has come under my notice, viz., the suspension of Bro. John A. Mackie by the "Grand River" Lodge, and his appeal against the decision of the lodge. This difficulty, which unfortunately is of more than one year's standing, will, I trust, be very shortly adjusted. As an evidence of the progress Masonry is making in Western Ontario, I may mention the fact that Wellington District was constituted five years ago with seven lodges. Let us hope that with increased numbers and apparent, at least, efficiency of working of the lodges, there are being disseminated those great principles of the order which should lead to greater intelligence, and a higher sense of honor and morality throughout the Craft and the country generally.

Several deaths, but considering the extent of the District, comparatively few, have occurred in the Craft during the year. The last offices of respect were becomingly paid by the Craft to the remains of most of those who have left us. I shall mention the names of only three, who were well known in the craft, Bros. John Scott, Galt, Robert Chance, Guelph, and William Walden, Berlin.

Several dispensations were granted by me to the brethren to appear in regalia in public, for social purposes. These meetings, I am happy to say, were entirely successful.

In conclusion, I beg to recommend to your favorable consideration the prayer for warrants of the lodges now working under dispensations. Without being invidious, I think it only my duty, in this connection, to mention the very business-like and thorough manner in which the Palmerston brethren have begun operations. They cannot fail to make a very successful lodge so long as they retain their present zeal and energy.

Respectfully submitted.

W. S. BURNETT,

Galt, June 27th, A. D. 1874.   D. D. G. M. Wellington District.

HAMILTON DISTRICT.

To the Most Worshipful Grand Master and the Grand Lodge of Canada.

MOST WORSHIPFUL SIR AND BRETHREN,—I have the honor to submit herewith the Annual Report of the condition of Masonry in the Hamilton District.

I have visited all the lodges in the District, but one, during the past year, and have pleasure in reporting that prosperity generally has attended them, and that they are governed by able and zealous brethren.

There are now thirteen warranted lodges in the district and one under dispensation, having a present total membership of 1029.

On the 23rd October last I had the pleasure of dedicating and consecrating Dufferin Lodge, No. 291, West Flamboro', and I am glad to learn that a large number of good men and true Masons have been added to its membership since its institution.

A number of brethren in Dundas, believing that it would be of advantage to the best interests of the craft to institute a new lodge in that Town, forwarded me a petition asking for a dispensation to open a new lodge to be called "The Hiram Lodge," which petition I recommended and forwarded to the M. W. the Grand Master; a dispensation was issued on the 22nd April last, and I am informed that

4

several meetings have already been held under the dispensation.

During the year, amongst others, two eminent brethren
have been called from their labors—V. W. Bro. Thomas
Duggan, M. D., who died 4th March, A. D. 1874, and W.
Bro. George King Chisholm, who died 14th April, 1874.

Bro. Duggan was born in Toronto, in 1812, removed to
Hamilton in 1840 ; and in 1841 was made a Mason in Barton
Lodge, of which he continued to be a member till his death.
Ho early reached the East, and soon afterwards became a
member of the Hiram Chapter of Royal Arch Masons, in
which for many years he occupied the position of presiding
officer as High Priest, now recognized as First Principal Z.

At the formation of the Grand Lodge of Canada in 1855,
he was appointed Grand Superintendent of Works. In 1857,
on the institution of the Grand Chapter, R. E. Comp. Duggan was elected Grand Third Principal J.; the following
year Grand Second Principal H.; and during the year 1860-
61 was chosen Grand Superintendent of Royal Arch Masonry
for the Hamilton District. In consideration of the valuable
and faithful services rendered to the Royal Arch Masons of
the Hiram Chapter by R. E. Comp. Duggan, in his capacity
of Most Excellent High Priest, they, in 1856, presented him
with a very handsome piece of plate and a laudatory address.

Bro. Chisholm was an old resident of Oakville, and some
twenty years ago he represented the County of Halton in
the Parliament of the Province of Canada, which has since
outgrown its Provincial character and developed into a
Dominion, embracing many provinces and not inaptly designated the "Greater Britain." He was about sixty years of
age.

Col. Chisholm connected himself with the Masonic fraternity some sixteen years ago, being initiated into St. Andrew's
Lodge, No. 16, Toronto, on the 11th May, 1858. He was
subsequently made a Royal Arch Mason in St. Andrew's

Chapter, Toronto. He was a charter member of Royal Oak Lodge, No. 198, Oakville, and its first master. He also held the position of master in the same lodge at the time of his death. He was buried with Masonic honors on the 17th April, 1874.

Having been selected as one of the marksmen to represent Canada at the annual meeting of the National Rifle Association of England, I regret that I will be unable to attend in my place at the approaching communication of Grand Lodge, and I trust that the circumstances which will cause my absence, will be considered of sufficient importance to warrant Grand Lodge in readily excusing it.

Respectfully submitted.

J. J. MASON,

Hamilton, 18th June, 1874.   D. D. G. M. Hamilton District.

NIAGARA DISTRICT.

To the Most Worshipful Grand Master and Grand Lodge of A. F. & A. Masons of Canada.

Most Worshipful Sir and Brethren,—In accordance with the requirements of the Constitution of Grand Lodge, I now submit this my second annual report, on the working condition and prosperity of the various Masonic Lodges in the old Niagara District for the past Masonic year, and in so doing I will be as brief as possible, not wishing to occupy the valuable time of this Grand Lodge with a lengthy report.

Permit me here to state from the amount of public duties devolving upon me, and the large District to travel over, I have been unable to visit all the eighteen Lodges in this District, yet I have visited those Lodges which from past experience I knew needed further assistance, and I have very much pleasure to be able to state, there is at the end of my term of office a marked improvement in the working and management of such Lodges, yet at the same time I must earnestly urge the necessity of the W. Masters of some

Lodges carrying out the suggestions advanced when officially visiting them.

After having been re-elected for the Niagara District, I deemed it advisable to hold a Lodge of instruction in St. Catharines, (as recommended in my last years report) but having given the subject my most careful attention, supplemented by the opinions of several eminent Masters in reference to the same, I came to the conclusion to abandon the idea, yet I am not unmindful of the necessity of a more general uniformity in the working of the country Lodges in the District, and I am confident that the delegates present from said District will admit I have used all the means within my power in order to accomplish more uniformity of the work as required by this Grand Lodge, and I trust that the work thus commenced will be carried to completion by my successor.

The communications officially received during the past Masonic year although extensive, have been more of a pleasing than of a serious nature, as only a few cases needed my official attention for their adjustment, and only in one instance have I been obliged to appeal to the M. W. Grand Master for his decision, which I trust will be taken by this Grand Lodge as a satisfactory proof of the flourishing condition of Masonry in the old Niagara District.

During the past year I have received three petitions for granting dispensations to open Lodges in this District, viz: one at Fort Erie, to be named Morning Star Lodge, W. Bro. Hume, to be first W. Master, the second at Cheapside, Selkirk, to be named "Hiram Lodge," W. Bro. Jessie V. Hoover, to be first W. Master, the third petition came from Port Robinson, accompanied by a resolution passed by Welland Lodge, No. 31, held at Font Hill, but only just having received said petition, I deem it advisable to hand it over to my successor for such action as he in his wisdom may deem advisable.

I would state in reference to opening a Lodge under

dispensation, I appointed W.Bro.S. Smith, of Drummondville, a well skilled Mason, to examine the W. Master and get any other necessary information, which having forwarded to the M. W. Grand Master, he very justly refused to grant the dispensation.

In reference to the petition from Cheapside, Selkirk, everything proving favourable, the M. W. Grand Master granted the dispensation, which I trust under the guidance of W. Bro. Hoover, will prove a benefit to the craft.

I granted a dispensation to Mountain Lodge, No. 221, Thorold, permitting that Lodge to wear Masonic clothing on the celebration of the Festival of St. John the Evangelist, in December last.

I also granted a dispensation to the brethren of Dominion Lodge, No. 213, Ridgeway, to wear Masonic Regalia at a Pic-Nic, held on the Festival of St. John the Baptist, at which there were over a thousand persons present, a cordial invitation having been sent to the surrounding Lodges.

By special invitation I had the honor of being present, and was made the recipient of a present from a committee of ladies, which having feebly acknowledged, P. D. D. G. M., I. P. Willson, of Welland, took the platform and addressed the assemblage in a truly Masonic spirit, as also did the Rev. Bro. Cammel, Chaplain of the Lodge, and I have every reason to believe that much good in the cause of Masonry was accomplished, every thing passing off with the utmost quietude, nothing but the true spirit of Masonry prevailing.

The balance of the business in connexion with the past year is not of much importance to Grand Lodge, being confined to the alteration of the By-laws of some Lodges which have received the sanction of the M. W. Grand Master in due course.

I will now call your attention to the fact, that although the Great Architect of the Universe has permitted us to assemble together at this the nineteenth annual Communication of Grand Lodge, many brethren have been removed from our midst. In my district five deaths from various causes have been reported, and although not having held many high positions amongst the craft, as Masons their names will long be cherished, from their strict adherence to the true principles of Masonry; each brother was interred with Masonic ceremonies.

I cannot close this report without making special mention of some lodges in my district for their correct work and carefully recorded minutes, viz., Niagara, No. 2, Niagara; Union, No. 7, Grimsby; St. John's, No. 35, Cayuga; St. Andrew's, No. 62, Caledonia; Maple Leaf, No. 103, St. Catharines; Merritt, No. 168, Welland; McNab, No. 169, Port Colborne; Enniskillen, No. 185, York; and Clifton, No. 254, Clifton. I must also state that the balance of the lodges are using every exertion in order to carry out .my directions.

I have now only to repeat the closing remarks of last year's report, by returning my thanks to the lodges in the district, for the kindness I have received from them upon every occasion, as also for the confidence reposed in me for the second year as their D. D. G. Master, and may peace, harmony, and prosperity prevail amongst them.

As usual, the replies of the Grand Secretary have been prompt and instructive, for which I now tender him my thanks, and may he long continue to hold the position he has so ably filled up to the present time.

All of which is respectfully submitted.

ROBERT KEMP,
July 1st, 1574.   D. D. G. M. Niagara District.

TORONTO DISTRICT.

To the M. W. the Grand Master and the Grand Lodge of A. F. and A. M. of Canada.

MOST WORSHIPFUL SIR AND BRETHREN,—In accordance with the constitution, I beg to submit the following report on the Toronto District:

Five new lodges have been opened in this District during the past year, located as follows, namely: Minerva Lodge at Victoria; Humber Lodge at Weston; Durham Lodge at Durham; Blackwood Lodge at Woodbridge; Doric Lodge at Toronto.

Their record, since opening, will be submitted to Grand Lodge, and I am satisfied that they are in good hands, and that their prospects for successful operation are very favorable. I recommend that they receive warrants.

On the 26th February last I authorized the removal of York Lodge, No. 156, from Davisville to Eglinton.

I have been asked, several times, as to the eligibility of candidates for initiation, who were physically deformed. In replying, I proceeded upon the rule, which seems to be now well established, that candidates must be physically capable of complying with all the requirements of the degrees.

One complaint against a lodge, involving an important question, came before me, in which I decided that it was incorrect and highly improper to ballot for a candidate at any meeting without his name and other particulars appearing on the summons for that meeting. In this case, however, there did not appear to be any wilful or intentional violation of the constitution: I therefore, admonished the lodge and its officers, for their improper action, and cautioned them to be more careful in the future.

In this district there are now forty lodges, and I have much pleasure in stating that nearly all are in a prosperous condition, and efficiently worked.

In retiring from this honorable position, I beg to assure the brethren of the Toronto District of my continued regard for the welfare of our beloved institution among them, and also of my gratitude for their many acts of kindness and courtesy towards myself.

All of which is fraternally submitted.

HENRY ROBERTSON,
Collingwood, July 3rd, A. D. 1874.   D. D. G. M. Toronto District.

ONTARIO DISTRICT.

To the M. W. the Grand Master and Grand Lodge of A. F. & A. M. of Canada

MOST WORSHIPFUL SIR AND BRETHREN,—In accordance with the requirements of the constitution, I have the honor to submit my report of the state of Masonry in Ontario District during the past year, and shall do so as briefly as possible.

I am happy to report that, of the twenty-five Lodges in this District, all, with the exception of two, are in a most prosperous condition, financially and otherwise; and I have on all occasions found the work performed in a highly creditable manner.

In the course of the year I have held General Lodges of Instruction at Brighton, Colborne, Oshawa and Whitby, all of which were well attended, nearly every Lodge in the district being represented, and I believe they resulted in permanent benefit to the officers and brethren who were at all anxious to acquire the work. On these occasions I was ably assisted in demonstrating the work by W. Bro. James Miller, of Peterboro'; W. Bro. R. J. Winch, of Cobourg; W. Bros. Wellington and Thayer, of Brighton; W. Bro, Campbell, of Colborne; W. Bro. Lockhart, of Orono; V. W. Bro. John Boyd, W. Bros. Taylor and Gilbranson, of Oshawa; W. Bro. Hopkins, of Whitby, and others.

I regret that, owing to the demands of my private business upon my time, I have been unable to visit all the Lodges in Ontario District. All accessible by rail I have had the pleasure of visiting with one exception. I trust those Lodges which I have not had an opportunity of visiting officially during the year, will not attribute my absence to a lack of interest in their welfare and progress, as it is for their especial benefit I have held Lodges of Instruction. The Lodges I have not visited lie in country Districts, connected with the railways by stage, and I have never been able to persuade myself that anything like an adequately good result would follow from my travelling 20 to 80 miles by rail and from 30 to 40 by stage, in order to spend three or four hours in one of those Lodges, as I have always held the opinion that very little instruction, to be of any permanent use, could be communicated in one evening, while paying a Lodge an official visit. A Lodge of Instruction, held in a central locality, is easily accessible to a number of Lodges, and two or three days spent at a time in this way, in all cases yield very good results, substantial benefits being derived by the officers and members who attend, which cannot fail to effect permanent good to the Lodges participating therein, and the Craft generally.

The M. W. the Grand Master has been pleased to issue, on my recommendation, dispensations for two new Lodges in this District, one, the "Grafton Lodge," in the village of Grafton, County of Northumberland, presided over by Bro. Francis Drake, a zealous Mason and a good worker; the other, the "Clementi Lodge," (named after our distinguished R. W. P. G. C.,) in the village of Lakefield, County of Peterboro', R. W. Bro. Dr. Kincaid, P. D. D. G. M., of Ontario District, being appointed the first W. M. So distinguished a brother requires no recommendation at my hands, as it is universally admitted that he is one of the best workers connected with the Craft under the jurisdiction of this Grand Lodge. I was present at the opening of both the above Lodges, and take pleasure in stating the spirit and zeal of the officers and members inspired the hope that the lapse of a very few months would only be necessary to develop excellent Lodges, as they have both good material and bright masons connected with them. A recent visit to each confirmed this good opinion, and it affords me extreme pleasure to recommend that warrants be granted to both Lodges.

I have issued during the year seven dispensations to Lodges to appear in public in regalia ; of these five were for the purpose of enabling Lodges to attend Divine service, and I would strongly recommend the Lodges in this District to more generally in future set aside one day in each year on which to worship the Most High, clothed as Masons. Piety

virtue and morality being the necessary qualifications of
every candidate for Freemasonry, I think the public recognition of the G. A. O. T. U. occasionally, in this way, would
perhaps lessen the prejudices entertained towards our beloved
Order by over-zealous, pious, but misinformed people, who
represent a large class in every community. These people
would learn to respect our institution, and, as it is our desire
to increase our numbers from the wise and good, doubtless
other advantages would accrue, besides the benefit to the
members of our Lodges, who are taught by the beautiful and
solemn ceremonies of our Order to act according to the
commands of the Divine Creator.

While the Lodges throughout the District are well-officered
I desire to take this opportunity of cautioning Installing
Masters to exercise more care in future with regard to the
installation of brethren incapable of discharging the onerous
duties devolving upon them. In every case I warmly urge
them to closely examine the Worshipful Masters elect, so
that the high standing of our Lodges may be maintained.
Two Lodges in this District, owing to the negligence of the
Installing Masters, while they might rank with the highest,
have been barely in existence for the past two years.

It is gratifying to be in a position to state that harmony
prevails throughout this large District. A few complaints
have been brought before me, but in nearly all I have had
the gratification of being able to arrange the difficulties
satisfactorily to the parties concerned. One complaint was
placed in my hands by the M. W. the Grand Master, at whose
command I collected the evidence bearing thereon, and forwarded it to him for final disposition. Another, which I
laid before the M. W. the Grand Master, a case of one Lodge
encroaching upon the jurisdiction of another, was promptly
disposed of by him.

I would respectfully call the attention of our Lodges to
the fact that, by an alteration of the Constitution, made at
a recent session of Grand Lodge, the M. W. the Grand
Master alone possesses the power to grant permission for

the initiation of a candidate who resides in the jurisdiction of another Lodge, and that a dispensation is required from the M. W. the Grand Master before such candidate can be initiated. I find this amendment is not generally understood, as I have observed, on examining the books of Lodges, several instances wherein the consent of Lodges had been asked and given for the initiation of such candidates.

I desire again to recommend the division of the Ontario District, or a re-arrangement of it and adjoining Districts, as I deem the District, as at present constituted, altogether too large to be properly and efficiently looked after by one D. D. G. M.

I cannot close my report without expressing my warmest thanks to W. Bro. E. Peplow, W. M. of Ontario Lodge, No. 26, Port Hope, for the able manner in which he has discharged the duties of District Secretary during the past two years, and for having accompanied me upon many of my official visits; also to Bro. J. C. Doebler, J. W. of Ontario Lodge, Port Hope, for his able assistance and company on nearly every visit made by me during the past year; to R. W. Bro. Harris, Grand Secretary, for his valuable counsel so cheerfully and courteously given on very many occasions; and, finally, to the officers and members of Ontario District, for their uniform, courteous and kindly treatment of me upon all occasions. In surrendering the charge of the District back into their hands, I feel that my labors for the advancement of the Order in this District have not been altogether in vain. During the time I have held the office of D. D. G. M., I think I have made few enemies, and rejoice that I have had the opportunity of making so many good, true, and trusty friends.

All of which is respectfully submitted.

J. B. TRAYES,

Port Hope, July 1st, A. D. 1874.   D. D. G. M. Ontario District.

PRINCE EDWARD DISTRICT.

To the Most Worshipful the Grand Master and Grand Lodge A. F. and A. M. of Canada.

MOST WORSHIPFUL SIR AND BRETHREN,—In compliance with the requirements of the constitution, I have the honor to submit the following report:

Owing to a protracted absence in the United States, I have not been able to visit all the lodges in the district, but have much pleasure in stating that, as far as I know, peace and harmony prevail.

I have constituted one lodge, Victoria, No. 299, of Centreville, which received its charter at the last annual Communication of Grand Lodge. I had the pleasure of installing its officers, and must say that under the mastership of W. Bro. Miller it is doing good work and is in a very healthy condition. I also had the pleasure of installing the officers of Mount Sinai Lodge, No. 280, and Union Lodge, No. 9, Napanee.

The only deaths reported to me are Brothers George C. Stinson and Joseph Cummings, both members of Star in the East Lodge, No. 164, Wellington. They were buried with the usual Masonic ceremonies.

On the 17th of June I received a communication from W. Bro. E. B. Fralick, stating that at the last communication of Mystic Lodge the brethren had elected to the office of W. Master a brother who had not served as Warden, and stating the reason for the breach of the Constitution ; also stating that he had communicated with the M. W. the Grand Master on the subject, and asking for dispensation for confirmation, informing me at the same time that the M. W. the Grand Master had referred the matter to me, and to install the brother should I find the circumstances warranted doing so.

On the same day I received a communication from the M. W. the Grand Master, through the Grand Secretary, giving me authority to act in accordance with the above facts; also to examine the brother as to his ability to confer the three degrees.

I accordingly met the brethren at their last communication and found that the departure from the constitution was a necessity, and finding the brother well skilled, I installed him and the other officers elect in the usual manner.

Fraternally submitted.

FRED. RICHARDSON,
Napanee, 21st June, 1874.   D. D. G. M. Prince Edward District.

ST. LAWRENCE DISTRICT.

To the Most Worshipful the Grand Master and Grand Lodge A. F. and A. M. of Canada.

Most Worshipful Sir and Brethren,—As District Deputy Grand Master for the St. Lawrence District, I have the honor to submit the following report:

On the 10th September last, at the request of and acting for the M. W. the Grand Master, and attended by the Worshipful Master, Wardens and brethren of Simpson Lodge, No. 157, and a large number of influential brethren from the neighboring Lodges, I proceeded to New Boyne, in the Township of Bastard, in the County of Leeds, and there laid the foundation stone of St. Peter's (Episcopal) Church.

The church will be a very imposing structure, and there was a concourse of over 3000 assembled to witness the ceremonies, which were performed in accordance with the ancient usages of the Order.

On the 3rd of June last, also acting on behalf and at the request of the M. W. the Grand Master, and attended by the brethren of Sussex Lodge, No. 5, and a large number of brethren from other Lodges, I proceeded to Brockville and there laid with proper Masonic ceremonies the foundation stone of a new (Methodist Episcopal) Church.

The absence of the Grand Master was very much regretted by all, on both occasions, but with the aid and hearty co-operation of several well skilled brethren, the rites were made as imposing as possible, and created a very favorable impression upon all who witnessed them. On the latter occasion I was presented with a silver trowel by the congregation of the Brockville Church to mark the event.

During the year I installed the officers of six different Lodges, viz., Central, No. 110; Friendly Brothers, No. 143; Cornwall, No. 125; Lancaster, No. 207; Simpson, No. 159; and Rising Sun, No. 85; and visited the majority of the Lodges in my District.

I believe Masonry in the St. Lawrence District to be in a most flourishing and prosperous condition.

Having received an application from several brethren residing at and near Chesterville in the County of Dundas, for the establishment of a new Lodge there, I visited the locality, and having satisfied myself that it would be in the interests of Masonry that a Lodge should be opened there, recommended the application.

The number of deaths reported to me in my District has not been large, but amongst them has been that of Brother Adiel Sherwood, who for the better part of half a century filled with credit to himself and satisfaction to the community, the office of High Sheriff of the united Counties of Leeds and Grenville. He died at the age of 95 years, and had been an active member of the Order for over 70 years. He was an exemplary man and a good Mason.

All of which is respectfully submitted.

JAMES REYNOLDS,

Prescott, 3rd July, A.D. 1874.　　　D. D. G. M. St. Lawrence District.

OTTAWA DISTRICT.

To the Most Worshipful the Grand Master and Grand Lodge of A. F. and A. M. of Canada.

MOST WORSHIPFUL SIR AND BRETHREN,—In accordance with the requirements of the Grand Lodge Constitution, I beg leave to make a brief report of Masonry in the Ottawa District. To give a lengthy report of matters regarding the statistics of Masonry in this District would be only a waste of time of Grand Lodge, as these are already in the hands of the Grand Secretary.

I have visited a large number of Lodges in this District, but having been laid up by sickness for a space of nearly five months, I have been unable to visit them all. Those Lodges which I have been unable to visit officially are known to have as Masters, brethren well skilled in the noble art, I have, therefore, every reason to suppose they are in a flourishing state.

I have had the pleasure of installing the W. M. and officers of the following Lodges during the past year, viz., Pembroke, No. 128; Renfrew, No. 122 : Eureka, (Pakenham), No. 248; Mississippi, No. 147; and on all those occasions the meeting of the brethren together was very pleasing and profitable.

I granted several dispensations to Lodges to appear in regalia on proper occasions, the reason, for so appearing having been set forth in the applications. The principal one of these was granted to two of the Ottawa Lodges, viz., the Eddy, No. 298, and Fidelity, No. 231, to entertain the brethren from Ogdensburgh, who paid a visit to the Capital. I am very sorry that I was unable to attend the entertainment, but have been informed that a most pleasant evening was spent and the brethren from the United States were delighted with their reception. I take this opportunity of thanking R. W. Bro. Featherston, P. D. D. G. M., for having taken my place at the banquet and most creditably filling the same.

The required number of brethren having petitioned for a Dispensation to hold a Lodge at Beachburg, in the County of Renfrew, I had no hesitation in recommending it, as I had examined Bro. Forbes, the W. M. elect, and found him fully informed in the work laid down by the Grand Lodge; and as it was a section of country without any Lodge. The Grand

Master was pleased to grant a dispensation to the Lodge, under the name of "Enterprise." I trust a warrant will in due time be granted to this Lodge. A petition was also presented by a large number of brethren to open a new Lodge at Ottawa City. This one I could not recommend as I thought the number of Lodges in Ottawa City and its immediate vicinity are at present too great, and that, as a rule, if there were fewer Lodges we would have better ones, for I believe the multiplying of Lodges hurts Masonry, as improper material may then be taken in for the purpose of keeping the Lodge up; however, it remains for the Grand Master and Grand Lodge to grant the petition or not.

At the request of the Most Worshipful the Grand Master I proceeded to Ottawa to investigate a charge made by Bro. Smith against Dalhousie Lodge of that city; but the offence, if any, having taken place previous to the joining of that Lodge with this Grand Lodge, I could not recommend the Grand Master to take any action in the matter as I thought the matter should be referred to the Grand Lodge of England under which Dalhousie formerly held its charter. The Grand Secretary having all the papers in this case will, I have no doubt, lay them before the Board of General Purposes, by whom I hope the matter will be finally settled, as it has been the cause of a great deal of scandal to Masonry in Ottawa City. By instructions, I also held an enquiry in St. Francis Lodge of Smithsfalls, with regard to a charge made against the W. M. and the acting Wardens, of having declared a ballot clear when the same contained two black balls against the candidate. Previous to the time the candidate was initiated I wrote to the W. M. telling him of the charge and advising him to cause another ballot to be taken but he paid no attention to my letter and proceeded with the initiation, passing and raising of the candidate. At the investigation the two brethren who placed the black balls testified to their having done so, and also gave their reason for so doing, and were positive that they had made no mistake. Under these circumstances I saw no other way than

to suspend the W. M. until the G. M. had given his decision
in the matter. The Grand Master shortly afterwards re-in-
stated the W. M., not wishing to establish a precedent that
the ballot might be disputed after being declared clear by
the Master and Wardens. There has been a charge preferred
by a member of Pontiac Lodge against the W. M. for certain
irregularities, but I have not taken any action in it, only
recommended the brother to wait until after the Grand Lodge
met when the new order of things in contemplation would
be finally settled on, and his Lodge being in the Province of
Quebec he could then lay his charges before his own Grand
Lodge.

I am happy to be able to report that the only Lodge in
Ontario hailing from a foreign Grand Lodge is about to come
in to this Grand Lodge ; and that the long standing differences which have existed between the Lodge at L'Orignal
under the Grand Lodge of Ireland, and Hawkesbury and Plantagenet Lodges under this Grand Lodge, are about to be
settled amicably for all the parties concerned. Having, at
the request of the G. M., visited these Lodges, I managed to
obtain the following mutual agreement: "The Lodges at
Hawkesbury and L'Orignal to surrender their warrants
to their respective Grand Lodges; then this Grand Lodge
to grant a warrant to the United Lodge ; the place of holding the Lodge to be decided by a committee of equal numbers
chosen from each Lodge or by Grand Lodge." I am sure
that this will be received with that satisfaction it deserves,
and that the Grand Lodge will have no hesitation in complying with the terms of the agreement, which I would strongly
recommend to be done.

A number of other Masonic questions have been referred
to me which I have decided to the best of my ability, in
accordance with the Constitution and Masonic jurisprudence,
and am happy to say that in no case has my advice or
decision been found fault with by the brethren, but, on the
contrary, have been heartily carried out.

During the last year, I had the pleasure of dedicating to

5

Masonry two new halls, one at Renfrew, on the 31st December, and the other at Arnprior, on the 24th June; at both of these large numbers of the brethren attended. Both halls are creditable to the Lodges which furnished them, but more particularly the one at Arnprior, which would be a credit to a much larger town.

There have been very few Masonic burials reported to me, True Briton's Lodge, Perth, however, has lost two brethren that it will be very hard to replace ; Bro. Campbell, who had filled the office of Secretary for a number of years with credit to himself and honor to the Craft; the other is Bro. Walker, one of the editors and proprietors of the *Perth Courier*, who from the time of his admission into Masonry took a lively interest in everything appertaining to the welfare of the Lodge and its members; the only other funeral was that of Bro. Hudson, of Renfrew Lodge, a Roman Catholic, the clergy of whose church refused to give him Christian burial on account of his being a Mason. He was buried with full Masonic honors by one of the largest gatherings of Masons ever held in this part of the country.

I cannot conclude this report without expressing my thanks to the officers and brethren of the Lodges in my District, for the courtesy and kindness shown me on all occasions in the discharge of my duties, particularly Pembroke, Arnprior, Renfrew, and Hawkesbury.

All of which is respectfully submitted.

WILLIAM MOSTYN

D. D. G. M. Ottawa District.

Almonte, July 4th, 1874.

MONTREAL DISTRICT.

To the M. W. Grand Master and G. L, of A. F. and A. M. Canada.

Most Worshipful Sir and Brethren,—I have the honor to report that during my term of office I have made repeated visits to the various Lodges in this District and am happy to state that I have found them working most creditably according to the ritual of Grand Lodge.

With the exception of one instance of Masonic complaint (that preferred against V. W. Bro. Alex. Chisholm of Lodge of Antiquity) I have to report that the harmony which should at all times characterize Masons has happily been undisturbed and that the utmost cordiality and fraternal good feeling prevail.

On St. John's Day I had the honor of installing the officers of six Lodges, and in January I performed the same duty to the officers elect of Mount Moriah Lodge, in all of which I was most ably assisted by R. W. Bro. J. Urquhart, jr.

I granted a dispensation to Mount Royal Lodge, No. 202, permitting the members to wear regalia on the occasion of their Annual Ball, as also to the members of Antiquity, St. George's, Zetland, and Mount Moriah Lodges for a Dinner, (in celebration of St. John's Day,) held at the Ottawa Hotel.

I convened one Lodge of Instruction for the benefit of the craft in this District, but as some of the brethren were disposed to make it the arena for religious discussion, I did not at that time consider it expedient to offer further instruction.

The result of the labors of the Committee appointed to settle the differences which existed between ourselves and the Quebec brethren, has, on the whole, given very great satisfaction, and with my permission, and pending the receipt of the Edict of the M. W. the Grand Master in reference to the matter, many fraternal visits were exchanged among the brethren hailing from the Lodges under the hitherto two Grand Lodges, and it is to be hoped that while your Grand Lodge is in session you will ratify and confirm the proceedings of your committee, which, together with the brethren from the Sister Grand Lodge of Quebec, have brought about so satisfactory a result.

I have made enquiry of the various Lodges to report any deaths that have occurred, but the replies so far received do not announce the decease of any brother.

In retiring from office, I tender my sincere thanks to the

brethren for the courtesy and kindness which have always been extended to me in the discharge of my duty.

All of which is respectfully submitted.

WILLIAM NIVIN,

Montreal, 22nd June, 1874.   D. D. G. M. Montreal District,

BEDFORD DISTRICT.

To the Most Worshipful the Grand Master and Grand Lodge of A. F. & A. M. of Canada.

MOST WORSHIPFUL SIR AND BRETHREN,—I sincerely regret my inability to make a more satisfactory report of my official duties for the past year, during which I have had the honor of presiding over the Bedford District. The doubts expressed at the time of my election, as to my ability to devote the necessary time for the faithful discharge of the duties appertaining to the office, have been too fully realized, and the number of my official visits has consequently been limited. I have however, had the pleasure of visiting some of the Lodges and installing their officers. I have also been in communication with several of the most prominent and active members in the district, and as far as can be thus ascertained, I am confident the Lodges generally are in a healthy state, the majority of them being very prosperous. It is also pleasing to report that during my term of office not a complaint has been made. Owing to my official position rather than any other qualifications, I had the honor of being one of the committee appointed on the Quebec difficulty, and I trust our humble efforts may have laid the foundation for an amicable settlement of the unfortunate matter, and the restoration of peace and harmony among the craft in this province. While however, a large number in this district would still prefer to remain allied with the Grand Lodge of Canada, and feel proud of their allegiance to such a body, I think they are generally prepared to accept the new regime, if by so-doing the interests of the craft in general are to be subserved.

In conclusion I would thank those Lodges which I had the pleasure of visiting, for the kind manner in which I was received, and also the several Lodges in the district for the honor conferred in electing me to the high and responsible office, and I trust their choice of a successor may result in the election of one who will be able to devote more time and fill the office more satisfactorily than it has been in my power to do.

Fraternally, &c.,

GEO. H. WILKINSON,

St. John's Q. 20th June, 1874.   D. D. G. M., Bedford District

MANITOBA.

To the Most Worshipful the Grand Master and the Grand Lodge of Canada, A. F. & A. M.

MOST WORSHIPFUL SIR AND BRETHREN,—I have the honor to submit the following annual report, for the province of Manitoba.

I am pleased to be able to report all the Lodges in this District, in a prosperous condition, and working harmoniously. No complaints of any importance have been brought under my notice.

Death has visited us, our late Bro. Murray, an old and highly respected member of Lisgar Lodge, has been called away.

I granted a dispensation to wear Masonic clothing at the funeral, which was attended by a very large number of Masons.

Two others, members of Prince Rupert Lodge, have also been summoned to the Grand Lodge above. Although at the time of their decease they were not residing in this Province, they were still members of that Lodge. I allude to R. W. Bros. J. V. Noel, and B. C. Davey, both leading members of the Order, the former having been our former D. D. G. M. We remember their services with gratitude, and would add our tribute of respect to their memories.

Their families have our sincerest sympathy in their bereavement.

On the festival of St. John the Evangelist, I had the pleasure, with the assistance of W.Bros. Black and Henderson, of installing and investing the officers of Lisgar Lodge ; and on the same day, with the assistance of the same brethren, I installed the officers of Prince Rupert Lodge and Ancient Landmark Lodge ; W. Bro. Champion, having been elected W. M. of the former, and W. Bro. J. H. Bell, of the latter; both worthy brethren, under whose direction these Lodges are prospering and will prosper.

On the same evening I was presented with an address, and a beautiful D. D. G. M's. Jewel, for which I again return the brethren my warmest thanks.

The spirit of charity has not died out among the Lodges here. In addition to many instances of private benevolence in this somewhat wide field for its exercise, the Lodges in the city, with the assistance of our leading amateur musicans, connected with the Order and otherwise, gave a Grand Concert, in aid of the funds of the City General Hospital. I granted a dispensation for the members to appear in regalia at it. The proceeds amounted to about $300. Too much praise cannot be given to the members of the committee, particularly to Bro. G. McMicken, the chairman, for their praiseworthy and successful exertions in this matter.

I have officially and otherwise visited the different Lodges in the District, several times during the year, although I regret that private duties prevented me from visiting Lisgar Lodge as often as I would have wished, but I always heard with pleasure the last accounts from it, and I know that with such worthy and skilled brethren as W. Bros. Black and Burns at its head, it must prosper.

I held a General Lodge of Instruction in the city of Winnipeg, occupying three days, which was well attended by the brethren in the city. In consequence of bad roads, very few attended from a distance. With the valuable assistance of W. Bros. Henderson, Clark, Champion, Bell, and other skilled brethren, the work in the three degrees was exemplified, and the usual instructions given as far as time permitted.

We are very much pleased to observe that owing to the large immigration, numbers of visitors are attending our meetings, and many of them are joining our Lodges. We give them all a hearty welcome.

All of which is respectfully submitted.

WM. N. KENNEDY,

Winnipeg, June 24th, A. D. 1874.   D. D. G. M., Manitoba District.

The foregoing Reports were referred to the Board of General Purposes, to report thereon to this Grand Lodge.

R. W. Bro. Thomas White, Jr., President of the Board of General Purposes, submitted the following

ANNUAL REPORT.

The Board of General Purposes beg to present this their annual report.

The annual meeting was held in the Town of Belleville, on Tuesday, the 10th day of February last. The Books of the Grand Secretary and the Grand Treasurer, together with the accounts, statements, and vouchers, for the financial year ending 31st December, 1873, were submitted and properly audited, and the Board have pleasure in stating that they were found to be correct.

The Receipts and Expenditure were as follows:

RECEIPTS.

Certificates	3,502 00
Dues	6,490 01
Fees	2,176 50
Dispensations	526 00
Warrants	220 00
Constitutions	605 23
Proceedings	12 75
	$13,532 49

EXPENDITURE.

General Expenses Account..............6,490 40
Expenses, Board of General Purposes. 1,542 40
Testimonials 400 00
Reprinting Proceedings 175 50
Chicago Grant Repaid.................. 387 21 8,995 51

Balance............................ 4,536 98

Of which sum there has been carried to
credit of the Benevolent Fund........... 4,257 14

Leaving a balance over Expenditure of $279 84

The funds belonging to Grand Lodge are invested as follows:—

Dominion Stock bearing 6 per cent..   28,800 00
  "   "   "   5 per cent..   10.000 00
Debentures, County of Middlesex,
  6 per cent............................   1,600 00
Bank of Toronto, bal. 30th Nov.... 1,393 66
  "   "   Interest Account
  Dominion Stock..................... 144 00 1,537 66
Canadian Bank Commerce...........   10,601 81

$52,539 47

Which represents the following amounts at credit of the
various accounts, viz:

General Fund 30,267 90
Asylum " 6,337 66
Benevolence Fund, Investment acct.   13,725 95
  "   "   Current acct 2,207 96

$52,539 47

The Grand Treasurer having transferred $87.29 to the
Benevolent Investment Fund in excess of ten per cent on the
receipts for the year 1872, the Board recommend that the
amount be allowed to remain in preference to making all
the corrections that would be otherwise necessary.

The Board recommend that the President be authorized
to draw orders upon the Grand Treasurer for the following
amounts, remitted by Grand Lodge.

King Hiram Lodge, No. 37 ....,   34 50
Great Western Lodge, No. 47...............   43 50
St. John's Lodge, No. 68.....................   38 50
Prince Albert Lodge, No. 183 ....   25 00
Sutton Lodge, No. 227......................   12 50
                                            ————
                                            $154 00

The Board having examined the following accounts and found them to be correct, have ordered their payment.

Lawson, McCulloch & Co.,Constitutions,&c   696 55
Buntin, Gillies & Co., Stationery...........   22 48
Richard Haigh, binding 22 50
G. Ennis, jr., printing 4 00
Copp, Clark & Co., certificates..............   249 29
Grand Secretary, Incidentals................   83 92
  "   "   Travelling Expenses....   59 00
Grand Treasurer, Postages and Stationery   4 00
Otto Klotz, for box and covering...........   11 50
James Bain...............................   3 00
                                            ————
                                            $1,156 24

BENEVOLENCE.

R. W. Bro. Klotz, the worthy and painstaking Chairman of the Committee on Benevolence, prepared and submitted to the Board the following interesting report, accompanied by tabulated statements, which have been entered upon the books of the Board. The general report is herewith sub-mitted for the information of Grand Lodge.

The number of individual grants made to private parties during the years 1872 and 1873 appears to be 138.

The number of City Boards of Relief to which grants have been made during the same period is 6.

And the grants made to Lodges during the same period 9 in number, 7 of which being for special grants of particular cases of emergency, while two of the 9 grants were made to the Lodges at Winnipeg, in a similar way as the grants to the several city Boards of Relief.

Among the above 138 individual grants to private parties

there are 38 to needy brethren, 91 to widows of deceased brethren, 2 to widows and orphans of deceased brethren, 4 to orphans of deceased brethren, 1 to a son of a deceased brother, and 2 to daughters of deceased brethren.

During the same period there have died out of above 138, 4 brethren, leaving 34 on our books, and of these 9 received grants only in 1872, and none in 1873, while 25 received grants in 1872, as also in 1873.

Of the 91 widows 14 received no grants in 1873, and 77 received grants in 1872, and in 1873 one of the 14 was refused an application for aid, not being found needy, and one of the 14 got married and was reported as being well off.

The joint grants to 2 widows and orphans were made in 1873. Of the 4 grants to orphans 2 were in 1872 only, and 2 in 1872 and 1873. The 1 son to whom a grant was made is now off our list. Of the 2 daughters 1 received a grant in 1872 only, and 1 in 1872 and 1873.

During the twelve months considerable information has been procured through correspondence, in relation to the particulars of parties who have received aid, and such information has been duly recorded in the Grand Lodge Book on Benevolence, so that at present information is only wanting concerning one brother out of above 138.

The Board have had under consideration the several applications for relief, and after due consideration made the following appropriations to be paid from the funds of Benevolence:

No.	Applicant.	Sum allowed.	Payable through.
1	Toronto Board of Relief..........	$150	Bro. J. S. Spooner.
2	Hamilton Board of Relief.......	75	R. W. Bro. J. J. Mason.
3	London Board of Relief..........	75	" " F. Westlake.
5	Kingston Board of Relief.	40	" " G. N. Wilkinson.

No.	Applicant.	Sum allowed.	Payable through.
6	Montreal Board of Relief.	75	R. W. Bro. Wm. Nivin.
7	Bro. F.............	25	W. " Thos. Aishton.
8	Bro. O'............	20	R. W. " L. H. Henderson.
10	Bro. T...............	20	W. M. Colborne Lodge, No. 91.
12	Bro. C.....	25	R. W. Bro. Otto Klotz.
13	Bro. S.......	20	W. M. Union Lodge, No. 9.
14	Bro. I.......	40	" New Dom.Lodge, " 205.
15	Bro. T.............	20	R. W. Bro. C. D. Macdonnell.
16	Bro. N......	15	W. M. Corinthian Lodge,No. 101.
17	Bro. M.............	25	R. W. Bro. J. B. Trayes.
18	Bro. C.............	20	" " "
19	Mrs. B.....	10	" " "
10	Mrs. M.............	20	W.M.Madawaska Lodge,No. 196.
21	Mrs. M...	20	R. W. Bro. L. H. Henderson.
22	Mrs. T.............	20	R. W. Bro. John Milne.
23	Mrs. S.............	15	W.M.Mount Zion Lodge, No. 39.
24	Mrs. B......... ...	20	R. W. Bro. W. H. Weller,
25	Mrs. M.............	20	W. M. Thistle Lodge, No. 225.
26	Mrs. V.............	10	R. W. Bro. J. J. Mason.
27	Mrs. Q..	15	" " "
28	Mrs. B......, ...	20	" " "
29	Mrs. S......	20	" " "
20	Mrs. B.............	20	" " "
31	Mrs. P.............	25	" " "
32	Mrs. H.............	25	W. M. St. John's Lodge,No. 68.
33	Mrs. McD.........	25	R. W. Bro. A. S. Kirkpatrick.
34	Mrs. K......... ...	20	W. M. Irving Lodge, No. 154.
35	Mrs. M.............	20	" Corinthian Lodge, " 59.
36	Mrs. G.............	25	" Lebanon Lodge, " 139.
37	Mrs. S............	20	R. W. Bro. C. D. Macdonnell.
38	Mrs. S.............	25	" " Robt. Kincaid.
39	Mrs. B.......	20	W.M.Plattsville Lodge, No. 178.
30	Mrs. G.............	20	R. W. Bro. A. S. Kirkpatrick.
41	Mrs. G.............	20	W. M. Composite Lodge,No. 30.
42	Mrs. W.	15	" " " " 30.
43	Mrs. W............	20	" Oxford Lodge, " 76.

No.	Applicant.	Sum allowed.	Payable through.
44	Mrs. H............ ...	25	R. W. Bro. Daniel Spry.
45	Mrs. K.............	15	Bro. J. S. Spooner.
46	Mrs. P.......	15	" " "
47	Mrs. G.............	25	" " "
48	Mrs. D......	20	" " "
49	Mrs. H.............	15	" " "
40	Mrs. O.........	20	" " "
51	Mrs. K.............	20	" " "
52	Mrs. G.....	15	" " "
53	Bro. M.............	20	" " "
54	Bro. C.............	40	" " "
55	Bro. H.............	35	" " "
56	Miss P.............	20	R. W. Bro. A. S. Kirkpatrick.
57	Mrs. J.............	30	" " " "
58	Mrs. G............ ...	25	" " F. Westlake.
59	Mrs. W	20	" " "
50	Mrs. T......	15	" " "
61	Mrs. C.............	20	" " "
62	Mrs. McI...... ...	20	" " "
63	Mrs. McD........	15	" " "
64	Bro. M.............	25	R. W. Bro. Allan McLean.
65	Bro. C.............	25	" " " "
66	Mrs. W............	40	W. M. Hope Lodge, No. 114.
67	Mrs. D.............	20	R. W. Bro. J. J. Mason.
68	Mrs. E......,......	15	" " F. Richardson.
69	Wid'w & orphans		
	Bro. D.........	50	" " A. S. Kirkpatrick.
70	Misses N...........	40	" " " "

$1,785

The Board rejected the application of Mrs. Whitney, of Whitby, the papers submitted not containing necessary information.

The application of Bro. Anthony Lucy was rejected, the applicant desiring to invest the grant asked for in real estate and merchandise. The application on behalf of Bro. Francis Poole was referred to the local Relief Board at Kingston.

It appearing that the cheque issued in July, 1872, in favor of Bro. Jos. Cornick, sr., for $20, was not cashed, owing to the death of that brother, and application now being made by Bro. Samuel Cornick for this grant, it is recommended that the cheque referred to be issued to the latter brother on account of the family of the brother deceased.

The Board are of opinion that under her present circumstances, Mrs. Dale is not entitled to make any claim upon the funds of Grand Lodge.

The Board regret to notice that in some instances no relief has been afforded by local Boards and private Lodges to applicants who have received and are receiving grants from the Benevolent Fund of Grand Lodge. The Board is glad to state that the information supplied at this meeting respecting the applications submitted, is much fuller than usual, but, in a number of instances, is far from being complete. It is found that strict justice is not always meted out to the various applicants, and this is almost entirely owing to the fact that, comparatively speaking, scanty information is furnished to the Board. It is recommended that all applications should be made on the printed form as advised, and which, is carefully filled up, will be of valuable assistance to the Board in fairly and impartially considering the numerous applications for relief that are presented.

GRIEVANCES AND APPEALS.

The Board had before them certain cases of Grievances and Appeals, and came to the following conclusions which they submit to Grand Lodge.

In the matter of the complaint of Bro. A. H. Taylor, against Bro. George Logan and R. W. Bro. E. C. Barber, the Board found that all the parties had been duly summoned to appear. The complainant did not appear, nor did he give any sufficient reason for his non-appearance. R. W. Bro. Barber appeared for himself and Bro. Logan, and denied the charge, stating his readiness to submit evidence in rebuttal of it. In view of these facts, the Board recommend the dismissal of the charges for want of prosecution; and in doing so must avail themselves of the opportunity of remarking upon the great impropriety of brethren making charges without following them up in the evidence, thus putting the accused to great inconvenience and expense in obeying summonses calling upon them for their defence.

In the matter of the appeal of Bro. John A. Mackie, the Grand River Lodge, No. 151, not having appeared to sustain its decision, and the Board having heard the appellant and the remarks of the W. Master of the Lodge, do recommend that the appeal of Bro. Mackie be allowed and the suspension removed.

In the matter of Bro. C. C. Baird, suspended by Acacia Lodge, No. 61, for unmasonic conduct, and recommended by said Lodge for expulsion, which was referred to the D. D. G. M. of the Hamilton District, to report thereon. The D. D. G. M. having confirmed the opinion of the Lodge, it was ordered that Bro. C. C. Baird, be summoned to appear at this meeting of Grand Lodge, to show cause why he should not be expelled for unmasonic conduct.

MISCELLANEOUS.

The Board recommend that the sum of £50 be given as an addition to the salary of Bro. Muir, the assistant in the office of the Grand Secretary, thus making the salary $700 per annum.

The Board cannot close this, their annual report, without expressing their acknowledgements to the brethren of Belleville for the cordial hospitality extended to them during their meeting in that town.

All of which is respectfully submitted.

THOMAS WHITE, Jr.
President B. of G. P.

It was moved by R. W. Bro. Thos. White, Junr., seconded by R. W. Bro. Hy. Macpherson, and

RESOLVED,—That the annual report of the Board be received.

R. W. Bro. T. White, Jr., on behalf of the Board submitted and read the following semi-annual report on

AUDIT AND FINANCE.

The Board of General Purposes beg to report as follows :

That the receipts for the half year ending 30th June 1874, amounted to $7,368.57, all of which has been paid over by the Grand Secretary, into the hands of the Grand Treasurer.

The Statement of the Grand Treasurer as on the 30th June, 1874, is as follows:

ASSETS.

```
Dominion Stock, at 6 per cent.,    28,800
    "          "    at 5 per cent.,   10,000
                                    ————————  38,800 00
Bank of Toronto, 31st Dec. '73. 1537,66
Interest, deposited since..........  144 00
                                    ————————   1,681 66
Cash in Bank of Commerce.....       15,653 58
                                               —————————
                                               $56,135 24
```

Representing the following balances at the credit of the various accounts in the books of the Grand Lodge.

```
General Fund.............................$32,969 98
Benevolence Fund, investment account .  13,725 95
Ten per cent of receipts for 1873..........  1,353 25
Benevolence Fund, current account......  1,604 40
Asylum Fund as at 31st Dec., 1873........  6,337 66
Interest on Stock..........................    144 00
                                            —————————
                                            $56,135 24
```

In view of the fact of the very large amount of cash in hand at the present time, the Board recommend that the sum of five thousand dollars be invested in Government securities.

The Board recommend the payment of the following accounts, viz.:

Lawson, McCulloch & Co., for printing ...   224 45
Copp, Clark & Co., for certificates..........   154 82
Buntin, Gillies & Co., for stationery.........   13 00
Richard Haigh, for binding..................   26 00
British America Assurance Company, for
  premiums of Insurance on Regalia, &c.   21 00
Grand Secretary, attending An'l. Meeting
  of Board at Belleville......................   19 90
Lash & Co., Testimonials to M. W. Bro.
  Stevenson, and to R. W. Bro. Otto
Klotz, as per resolution of Grand Lodge   600 00

The Board recommend that Lawson, McCulloch & Co.'s tender for printing Constitutions, viz: for first 1,000 $150. Each additional 1,000 $100, be accepted.

The brethren of Hamilton having erected a Hall with vaults suitable for the requirements of the craft in that city, and for the accomodation of the offices of the Grand Lodge, the Board recommend that the local members of the Board be a committee empowered to make the necessary arrangements for transferring the offices of Grand Lodge to the said Hall, the lease whereof not to exceed the term of five years absolute, with right of renewal for five years more.

All of which is respectfully submitted.

THOMAS WHITE,
President B. of G. P.

It was moved by R. W. Bro. T. White, jr., seconded by M. W. Bro. T. Douglas Harington, and

RESOLVED,—That the semi-annual report of the Board on Finance be received.

R. W. Bro. Otto Klotz, chairman of the sub-committee on Benevolence, gave notice that on to-morrow he will apply to Grand Lodge for the sum of $3000, to be taken from the General Funds, and transferred to the fund of Benevolence.

M. W. Bro. T. D. Harington, gave notice, that on to-morrow he would move that the next annual Communication of Grand Lodge, be held at Ottawa.

R. W. Bro. F. Westlake, gave notice, that on to-morrow, he would move that the next annual Communication of Grand Lodge be held at London.

W. Bro. Hayden, gave notice, that on to-morrow, he would move that the next annual Communication of Grand Lodge be held at St. Catharines.

In accordance with notice given,

It was moved by R. W. Bro. Thomas White, jr., seconded by R. W. Bro. Otto Klotz:

That Article 1, "Of Deputy Grand Master," Book of Constitution, which requires that the Deputy Grand Master shall not be elected from that portion of the Province in which the Grand Master resides, be amended by striking out the words: "and in order that both sections of the Province may enjoy a proper representation, he shall not be elected from that portion of the Province in which the Grand Master resides."

In amendment,

It was moved by W. Bro. Lesser, seconded by W. Bro. Cohen,

That this question be laid on the table until the position of the Lodges of Lower Canada is finally settled.

A vote of Grand Lodge having been taken on the amendment, it was declared in the negative.

The original resolution was then adopted.

In accordance with notice given,

It was moved by W. Bro. J. M. Banghart, seconded by W. Bro. Hayden,

That the last clause in the Article "Of Fees" in the Book of Constitution be amended, by striking out the word "fifty" and inserting therefor the word "twenty five."

In amendment,

It was moved by W. Bro. H. L. Vercoe, seconded by W. Bro. Gibson,

That the motion be laid on the table till the full settlement of the financial matters with the Grand Lodge of the Province of Quebec, shall have been effected.

C

A vote of Grand Lodge having been taken on the amendment, it was declared *lost*.

The original motion on a vote being taken, was also declared *lost*.

R. W. Bro. T. White, jr., President of the Board of General Purposes, submitted the following report on

MASONIC ASYLUM TRUST.

The Trustees of the Masonic Asylum Trust beg leave to submit their Annual Report as follows :

Commencing as usual with a financial reference, the balance reported last year consisted of; Investments in Dominion Stocks, $4,800 ; Bank Deposits, $1,393.66 ; Total, $6,193.66.

Crediting a year's interest, $352.95, and debiting premium and brokerage $94.22 on $1,400 additional stock purchased, the Funds of the Trust now stand as follows :

```
Dominion Stock............................ ............$6,200  00
Cash in Bank................................... ......   252  39
                                                       _____
    Total................................... ......$6,452  39
```

Having, last year, given an analysis showing the yearly growth of the *Fund* from the inception of the Trust in 1860, your Trustees on this occasion, so far trespass on the time of Grand Lodge, by referring to the leading *Reports* which have from time to time been presented in advocacy of the main object sought to be attained, and which are to be found in the annual proceedings of Grand Lodge as follows :

1861—Original Report by R. W. Bro. Harman as Chairman—setting out features and particulars of project in full detail—pp. 191 to 200.

1862—Report of progress by R. W. Bro. Emilius Irving, Chairman *pro tem*—pp. 305 to 307.

1867—Report of progress by R. W. Bro. Spence as Chairman—pp. 344 to 349—Feb., 1867.

Report of same in fuller detail, and with valuable suggestions, by R. W. Bro. Spence—pp. 367 to 370, July, 1867.

1868—Report of progress and recording the lamented decease of R. W. Bro. Spence—pp. 596 to 599, by R. W. Bros. Tully, Harman, DeGrassi, and Bain.

1869—Report of progress—pp. 102 to 104, by R. W. Bros. Tully, Harman, DeGrassi, and Bain.

1870—Report of progress—pp. 451 to 452, by R. W. Bros. Tully, Bain, and DeGrassi.

1871—Report of progress—p. 840, by R. W. Bros. Tully, Bain, and Harman.

1873—Report with full recapitulation of funds received and invested, and of proposed action and naming the lamented death of R. W. Bro. DeGrassi—pp. 398 to 400, by R. W. Bro. Tully as Chairman.

Sensible of the liability to oblivion to which the best efforts are subject, unless promptly acted upon, your Trustees express the hope that the arguments and considerations urged in these reports, may be reviewed and fully considered by Grand Lodge in coming to a deliberate and final decision.

Reverting to the action of Grand Lodge at its *last* Session, your Trustees turn, (1) to their Report, at page 398, proceedings, 1873; (2) to the reference to the same in the address of the M. W. The Grand Master, at page 347; (3) to the Report of the Board of General Purposes on the same, at page 501, and (4), to the action of the Grand Lodge, at page 504.

In the first, their Report, they made use of these expressions:

" In the matter of the great object indicated in the original report of 1869, when the proposal of an Asylum was first enunciated, regret at apparent delay is counterbalanced by the knowledge that among the most valued evidences of benevolence are to be found instances which, cautiously enter-

tained at their first inception, have in time forced their utility
to be conceded; in this view the trustees confidently await
the time when the genius of Masonry will irresistibly assert
itself, in requiring evidences to be afforded to the outer
world that the great masonic landmark "brotherly love"
needs a warmer illustration than the distribution of casual
benevolence, and that while many a private home has been
gladdened thereby, it may be both more visibly and more
fraternally illustrated in the creation of an institution
where,to quote the words of the original report ' the indigent
and decayed Mason, his bereaved widow and his helpless
orphan may enter, NOT as into an institution where the feeling
of dependence, almost aggravates distress, *but* as in a HOME
provided by Masons, who by the goodness of the Great
Architect of the Universe, have been blessed with a
continuance of means, for those who, from unforeseen and
unavoidable causes, are plunged into the depths of poverty
and want, but who are nevertheless brethren, and brethren
whose claims to the appellation are in the true spirit of
Masonry enhanced by misfortune."—p. 398.

And again,

" To return to the matter of funds, a comparative reference
to the financial position of Grand Lodge in 1860, when the
scheme of an asylum was first mooted, and that presented by
last years accounts, proves that Grand Lodge had good
grounds for faith in her resources, when in 1860 on the
motion of the revered Grand Master who again presides over
us, *she pledged herself to a liberal support* of a project which
commended itself *with an unprecedented enthusiasm* to Masonic
recognition, as evidenced by the series of commendatory
resolutions unanimously adopted on the motions of the
leaders of the craft from every section of Canada, and the
trustees feel convinced that the voice of Masonry will
pronounce that the scheme should be now matured, the very
circumstance of protracted delay, in carrying out a benevolent project, the necessity for which has been so long
announced, almost inviting reflections injurious to the craft."
—page 400.

And again,

"By reference to previous reports, it will be seen that several liberal propositions from Lodges who were desirous of seeing the asylum located in their neighborhood, lapsed from want of action, one in particular from the town of Niagara, of several acres of land, a substantial building, and $3,000 in money, it is to be regretted was not accepted by Grand Lodge, though strongly recommended by the Trust, but while the lands and building thus originally offered have been since appropriated and were gladly availed of for the useful and benevolent objects of "Miss Rye's Female Emigration Home" your trustees have pleasure in adding that they have ascertained that the monetary offer of $3,000 is still held to be binding on the Masons of Niagara, should that unrivalled site for salubrity and centrality, as your trustees are bound after a recent visit of inspection to regard it, be selected, and there is every reason to believe that on due and timely application there might be secured on advantageous terms a most beautifully located plot of ordnance land with a substantial building (formerly a military hospital) admirably adapted, with comparatively slight modifications, to be immediately utilized as the nucleus of the proposed institution, which once opened, will lack neither interest, encouragement nor support to become the cherished monument of the spirit of Masonry."—p. 400.

In the second, The M. W. The Grand Master in his annual address gives his views thereon as follows :

"A report from the trustees of the Masonic Asylum Trust, will be submitted for your consideration. This important subject was first officially brought forward in 1859, but up to this period no decided action has been taken in the matter. I venture to express a hope that during the present session the subject will receive your careful consideration, and that you will decide either at once to give instructions for the carrying out of the suggestions made by the trustees, as to the purchase of lands and the erection of a suitable building, or to abandon the scheme altogether, for it does

appear to me that (as expressed in the report) the protracted
delay in carrying out a benevolent project, almost invites
reflections injurious to the craft. When the scheme was first
submitted, it was received with universal approbation, and
a liberal support was promised; but it was subsequently
argued by many of our leading Masons, that the class of
persons in this country requiring this kind of benevolence,
were very different from those for whom the great charities
of England were established, and that but very few of them
would be found willing to accept a HOME which would
separate them from their children and relatives. From my
own personal knowledge I may say, that there are many
whose hearts are now gladdened by your bounty, that would
rather relinquish it altogether than accept it upon the terms
suggested. There are a few, however, who do not thus
regard it, and as our country increases in population, so will
these cases increase also. From our ample resources a commencement on a limited scale might now be inaugurated,
the land required for this purpose may be obtained at a
comparatively low price at present, and I am inclined to
believe that the fund now at the disposal of the trustees,
would be found amply sufficient to purchase the land and
to secure a HOME which, for some years to come at all
events, would be large enough to meet the necessities of our
present position. I leave the whole matter in your hands,
firmly believing that you will take such action as will seem
to you to be most wise and prudent. Appeals from *poverty*
and *distress* have never been disregarded by this Grand
Lodge. The open hand, prompted by the generous heart,
has ever been cheerfully extended to relieve the wants of
our poor brethren, their widows or orphans; and the delay
which has occurred in the matter of the Masonic Asylum,
has really arisen from the anxious desire of the members of
this Grand Lodge to ascertain the best way of directing the
stream of their benevolence so as to secure the greatest good
to the greatest number. And I am proud to say that the
Grand Lodge of Canada not only appreciates but practices
that beautiful sentiment of Galt, "that whenever we do

"an act of justice or kindness to another, it is the "benevolence of Heaven directing us to achieve some good "for ourselves."—p. 348.

In the third, The Board of General Purposes report on the above paragraph of the Grand Master's address as follows:

"With reference to the Masonic Asylum, the Board agree that there is much in the condition of Canada and Canadian Masons to render advisable a different mode of applying and distributing their benevolence from that adopted by their brethren in England, and that among us "few would be found "willing to accept a *home* which would separate them from "their children and relatives." The successful establishment of such an asylum, and the erection of stately buildings in connection therewith, in which aged Masons and their wives and widows might find the comforts of a home, would no doubt be gratifying to Masonic pride, and might be pointed out to the "profane" as conclusive evidence of Masonic benevolence and zeal; but to produce an effect on the uninitiated is not the Mason's mission, and it may well be questioned whether such a gratification would not be bought too dear. The sole question for Grand Lodge is how best to dispose of its funds available for purposes of benevolence, and there can be no doubt that the establishment of such an institution would be a severe tax for all time on the resources of Grand Lodge, that its benefits would not, in the present condition of Canada, be availed of to any very large extent, and that little would be left, after paying the yearly expenses of maintenance, to be distributed amongst equally deserving out-door applicants for relief. "*The greatest good to the greatest number*" should be the object aimed at in the distribution of our benevolence, and there can be little doubt that the present mode of affording relief is at the same time the most economical for the donors and the most acceptable as well as beneficial for the large majority of the recipients. The Board adopt the suggestion of the M. W. Grand Master that some definite action should be taken at the present session of Grand Lodge, and would therefore recommend

that for the present the scheme be abandoned, and the money with its accumulated interest be returned to the donors."
—pp. 501 to 502.

In the fourth, The Grand Lodge resolved as follows :

RESOLVED.—That the consideration of so much of the report of the Board of General Purposes upon the address of the M. W. Grand Master, referring to the Masonic Asylum, be postponed to the next annual communication.—p. 504.

The whole matter would, therefore, appear to stand over for consideration at the present Grand Lodge, on the Grand Master's reference to the Report of the Trust for 1873, and the Report of the Board of General Purposes thereon. And, in furtherance of such consideration, your Trustees, as the committee to whom the project has been so long and specially referred to by Grand Lodge, and who have necessarily given it their gravest attention, beg leave to offer the following remarks:

1st. In the matter of The M. W. Grand Master's address. They submit that the M. W. The Grand Master conveyed his remarks on the Report of the Trustees, with great fairness and under a two-fold aspect.

I. From the stand-point, held by some, of the requirements of Masonic benevolence in Canada, so far differing from those in England, that the majority of those availing themselves of the same, would prefer an external or out-door dispensation as at present carried out, to an internal or indoor system of relief, such as an Asylum would furnish; but

II. That, as there are those who do not consider this an exposition of the entire Masonic mind, "from our ample resources, a commencement (of the proposed institution) on a limited scale, might now be inaugurated, the land required for the purpose being obtainable at a comparatively low price, while he was inclined to believe the fund now at the disposal of the Trustees, would be found sufficient to acquire the land and to secure a HOME which, for some years, to come, at all events, would be large enough to meet the necessities of our present position."

2nd. While your Trustees regret that the Board of General Purposes of last year, were not prepared to do so, they trust the present Board may, on consideration, see their way to a recommendation of this latter *most moderate* course of action, which would thus, by adopting the M. W. Grand Master's view of commencing on a limited scale, afford an opportunity for testing the utility of a scheme which even, if not unanimously entertained, is still, *from a large and influential advocacy*, open to respect and consideration ; and they must repudiate, though always in a becoming Masonic spirit, the entirely false argument, as however reluctantly, they are compelled to term it, that, "the carrying out of this scheme, would be a mere gratifying of Masonic pride to be pointed out to the profane as conclusive evidence of Masonic benevolence and zeal ; that "it might well be questioned whether such a gratification would not be bought too dear." And, "that there could be no doubt that the expense of such an institution would be a severe tax for all time on the revenues of Grand Lodge." From such reasoning, your Trustees entirely differ as both an unfair and an unjust reflection *on the large portion of the craft in Canada who conscientiously advocate the movement*; nay more, on Masonry in general, wherever such expositions of its principles are to be found in every portion of the masonic world ; and as well might it apply to any other efforts of the benevolent outside of the craft, to rear enduring monuments of piety, charity and benevolence, and the founders of hospitals, orphanages, and even schools and seminaries for the succour of the afflicted, and the improvement of our race, might be thus erroneously charged with false views in their inception. As to the argument of expense and its being a severe tax for all time on the revenues of Grand Lodge, it will be presently shown that such a result is entirely imaginary.

To deal, however, practically with the main question of Masonry in Canada having an institution of a permanent character to supplement in extreme cases, the present system of Masonic aid, (*and with which it has never been for a*

moment contemplated to interfere,) your Trustees would now
ask of Grand Lodge to permit them to assume the responsibility of instituting a commencement on a limited scale,
as recommended by the M. W. the Grand Master, and
towards such commencement, all they would require is the
sanction to make an appeal to the Lodges for support, *quite
apart from other contributions to Grand Lodge funds*, and to act
on the response, which under the blessing of T. G. A. O. T. U.,
they have a full confidence, will be such as will tend to
promote as well His glory, as the benefit of their fellow
creatures, by liberal and hearty contributions. They speak
advisedly in saying that to "return the funds already
received with the accumulated interest" as proposed by the
Board of General Purposes, would be not only most distasteful
to the subscribing Lodges, but to numbers of other Lodges
and Masons who are anxiously awaiting a call on them to
follow in the course of those who subscribed in 1861, and
who are known to regret the delay. And the appeal can be
the more confidently made when it can be pointed out to
the Lodges that the Trust has carefully husbanded the funds
committed to their charge, the accumulated and reinvested
interest alone amounting to nearly $2,700 or more than a
third of the present fund of the Trust. The opportunity for
founding the institution at Niagara, as set forth in the report
of last year, is, they believe, still open, and, from the pecuniary
inducements so liberally offered in that old town, the birth-
place of Freemasonry in Western Canada, and the world-
known name of which seems peculiarly attractive, could be
at once made available, with little, if any, application of the
principal of the fund. On the head of revenue for the annual
maintenance of the institution, there will be no difficulty
in raising funds for the same. An income of from $1,000 to
$1,500, they have reason to anticipate, would be readily
obtained from an enrolment in that behalf of numbers of
unaffiliated Masons, who, while not having the disposition or
time for the active exercise of a Masonic life, would be glad
to avail themselves of an opportunity thus afforded them of
contributing to that which they were early taught to regard

as the great bond of the order, "Brotherly Love and Relief.'
An annual payment of *ten cents a head* from *affiliated* Masons
would produce a like sum and more, and these resources,
with the interest on the present investment, would
amply suffice for the maintenance of a "limited" institution,
wholly apart from any tax, much less "a severe one," on the
revenues of Grand Lodge, already so largely and worthily
directed in the fulfilment of the great objects of our time
honoured institution.

KIVAS TULLY, *Chairman.*
SAMUEL B. HARMAN,
JAMES BAIN,
VINCENT CLEMENTI,
JAMES K. KERR,

It was moved by R. W. Bro. T. White, jr., seconded by
R. W. Bro. J. K. Kerr, and

RESOLVED, That the report be received and distributed.

R. W. Bro. P. J. Brown gave notice that on to-morrow he
would move that the rank of Past Grand Master of this
Grand Lodge be conferred upon R. W. Bro. Thos. White, jr.

W. Bro. John Ormiston gave notice that at the session of
Grand Lodge to-morrow morning he would move, That it is
not expedient to interpret Sec. 3 of proposing members, page
55, Book of Constitution, as giving to the M. W. the
Grand Master power to grant a dispensation without first
referring to the Lodge in whose jurisdiction the candidate
may reside.

The M. W. Grand Master announced that the election of
officers would take place to-morrow at the session immediately
following the morning session.

The Grand Lodge was called from labor to refreshment to
meet on to-morrow (Thursday) morning at ten o'clock.

THURSDAY, July 9th, A. D. 1874.

The Grand Lodge resumed its sittings at 10.30 o'clock, a. m.

PRESENT.

M. W. Bro. W. M. Wilson, Grand Master,

On the Throne.

Grand Officers, Members, and Representatives.

In accordance with notice given,

It was moved by R. W. Bro. Otto Klotz, seconded by R. W. Bro. J. E. Brooke, and

RESOLVED,—That the sum of $3000, be taken from the general funds of Grand Lodge and transferred to the funds of benevolence.

R. W. Bro. Otto Klotz, on behalf of the Board of General Purposes, submitted the following report on

BENEVOLENCE.

The Board have had, under consideration a very large number of applications for assistance, and after due consideration made the following appropriations, to be paid from the funds of Benevolence at the disposal of the Board, viz.:

No.	To whom granted.	Amount.	Through whom payable.
1	Toronto Board of Relief	$200	Bro. James S. Spooner,
2	Hamilton "	" 100	R. W Bro. J. J. Mason,
3	London "	" 100	W. Bro. H. A. Baxter,
4	Ottawa "	" 50	V. W. Bro. D. S. Eastwood,
5	Kingston "	" 50	Bro. L. Clements,
6	Mrs. S...............	40	R. W. Bro. Robt. Kincaid,
7	Mrs. G...............	50	W. M. Albion Lodge, 80
8	Mrs. McC	40	R.W. Bro. Robert Kemp,
9	Mrs. H	30	R. W. Bro. Allan McLean,
10	Bro. C...............	25	" " "
11	Mrs. B...............	20	W. M. Plattsville Lodge, 178
12	Mrs. G	30	R. W. Bro. H. D. Pickel,
13	Bro. E...............	20	" " "
14	Mrs. O...............	25	Bro. James S. Spooner,
15	Bro. P...............	50	" " "

16 Mrs. H........	25	Bro. James S. Spooner,			
17 Mrs. K.........……......	30	"	"	"	
18 Mrs. G......	30	"	"	"	
19 Mrs. H.....	20	"	- "	"	
20 Mrs. K....	20	"	"	"	
21 Bro. M....................	20	"	"	"	
22 Mrs. P..............	20	"	"	"	
24 Mrs. D.....	20	"	"	"	
24 Mrs. G..........	25	"	"	"	
25 Bro. H....................	35	"	"	"	
26 Mrs. G.....................	25	Bro. L. Clements,			
27 Misses N..................	40	"	"		
28 Mrs. H........	20	"	"		
29 Mrs. L......	25	"	"		
30 Mrs. J.....................	40	"	"		
31 Miss P..............	25	"	"		
32 Mrs. D.....................	50	"	"		
33 Mrs. A............	30	W. M. Wilson	Lodge, 113		
34 Orphans of Bro. P.....	30	"	"	"	"
35 Bro. D....................	40	"	Prince Art'r "	228	
36 Mrs. B...	30	"	Albion	"	80
37 Orphan child of Bro. T.	20	"	"	"	"
38 Bro. L.....................	15	"	St. Andrews "	62	
39 Bro. F.....................	25	"	Maple Leaf "	119	
40 Bro. O'C..................	20	R. W. Bro. L. H. Henderson,			
41 Mrs. M................	20	"	"	"	"
42 Mrs. W....................	40	R W. Bro. J. B. Trayes,			
43 Mrs. C.	25	W. M. Rising Sun Lodge,129			
44 Bro. D......'...........	30	W. Bro. J. A. Macpherson,			
45 Mrs. W.........	40	R. W. Bro. J. J. Mason,			
46 Mrs. P.....................	30	"	"	"	
47 Mrs. Q.........	25	"	"	"	
48 Mrs. B.....................	30	"	"	"	
49 Mrs. D.........	20	"	"	"	
50 Mrs. B.............	25	"	"	"	
51 Mrs. P.....	25	"	"	"	
52 Mrs. S...........	25	"	"	"	
53 Mrs. B............	20	R. W. Bro. W. H. Weller,			

54 Orphans of Bro. F......	30	W. M. Colborne	Lodge,	90
55 Bro. C........................	40	"	United	"	29
56 Bro. M.......................	40	"	"	"	.:
57 Bro. R.......................	30	"	Tuscan	"	99
58 Bro. LcC............	40	"	St. John's	"	209a
59 Mrs. McD............	25	"	"	"	"
60 Mrs. McD................	25	"	"	"	"
61 Mrs. McI.........	25	"	Kilwinning	"	64
62 Bro. S............	20	"	Union	"	9
63 Mrs. T................	20	Bro. R. Armour,
64 Mrs. K.....................	25	W.M. Great West'n. "	47
65 Orphans of Bro C	30	"	St. John's	"	20
66 Mrs. G....................	25	"	St. Francis	"	24
67 Mrs. C....................	50	"	Niagara	"	2
68 Mrs. T....................	25	"	"	"	2
69 Mrs. M....................	30	"	Richardson	"	136
70 Mrs. A.........	30	"	"	"	"
71 Mrs. C....................	25	R. W. Bro. Otto Klotz,
72 Mrs. K......	40	W. M. Irving	Lodge, 154
73 Mrs. H	30	"	Sharon	"	97
74 Bro. T....................	30	R. W. Bro. C. D. Macdonnell,
75 Mrs. G............	25	W. M. J. B. Hall Lodge, 145
76 Mrs. G............	30	"	True Britons "	14
77 Mrs. S..............	25	"	Mountain	"	221
78 Bro. I....................	40	"	New Domi'n. "	205
79 Mrs. M....................	40	"	Eureka	"	248
80 " A......	30	"	Union	"	118
81 " M...................	20	"	Thistle	"	250
82 Bro. M......	25	"	King Solom. "	43
83 Mrs. T.........	25	"	Wilson	"	113
84 " S....................	30	"	Mount Zion	"	39
85 " G...................	25	"	Lebanon	"	139
86 Bro. B....................	30	"	"	"	"
87 Mrs. C..	25	"	Composite	"	30
88 " G....................	40	R. W. Bro. J. B. Trayes,
89 " W....................	20	W. M. Composite Lodge, 30
90 " C................	25	"	"	"	"
91 " W.........	30	R. W. Bro. F. Westlake,

92	"	T............	30	R. W. Bro. F. Westlake,		
93	"	G......	30	"	"	"
94	Bro. N.........		20	R. W. Bro. R. Kincaid,		
95	Winnipeg Lodges......		100	R. W. Bro. W. N. Kennedy,		
96	Miss S....................		40	W. M. P. of W. Lodge, 146		
97	Mrs. B..................		40	"	Grand River	" 131
98	"	K.............	50	"	Alexandra	" 158
99	"	H.........	30	R. W. Bro. Otto Klotz,		
100	"	K...................	40	W. M. Welland Lodge, 36		
101	"	D......	30	R. W. Bro. Thos. White, jr.,		
102	"	McC............. ...	30	W. M. St. James' Lodge, 74		
103	Mrs. E....................		25	R. W. Bro. F. Richardson,		
104	Bro. K....................		20	W. Bro. G. W. Morgan,		
105	Mrs. M....................		20	"	"	"
106	Irvine Lodge No. 203..		30	W. M. Irvine Lodge, 203		
107	Bro. J.......		20	V. W. Bro. James Gibson,		
108	Mrs. H.........		30	W. M. King Solom. Lodge,22		
109	"	McG....	30	W. M. Ionic	" 63	
110	Bro. T...............		40	"	Brant	" 45
111	"	A....	50	"	Orillia	" 192
112	Mrs. C.........		25	"	Clinton	" 84
113	"	B....................	30	"	"	" "
114	"	R.......	50	"	St. John's	" 82
115	"	C............	30	"	Macoy	" 242
116	"	McC................	25	"	Amity	" 32

$3,840

The Board rejected the application made by Rising Sun Lodge, No. 129 Aurora, for the sum of ninety three dollars twenty-five cents, the funds of Benevolence of Grand Lodge not being intended to make good the pecuniary losses sustained by private Lodges through their own negligence, or the carelessness and mistakes of individual members of such Lodges.

The Board submit a condensed statement made by several of the City Boards of Relief as required by Grand Lodge resolution of July 1873, the city of Ottawa failing to comply.

TORONTO BOARD OF RELIEF.

Balance on hand from last return...........$	578	15
Direct grant from Grand Lodge............	150	00
Special grants from Grand Lodge to individual applicants.......................	265	00
Total receipts from private Lodges.........	489	00
	$1482	15
Total paid for Relief......	1163	05
Balance on hand................................$	319	10

HAMILTON BOARD OF RELIEF.

Balance on hand from last return...........$	53	35
Direct grant from Grand Lodge............	75	00
Special grants from Grand Lodge to individual applicants.......................	95	00
Collections St. Paul's Church, 27th Dec..	76	07
Total receipts from private Lodges.........	116	68
Balance due Treasurer.......................	25	67
	$ 441	77
Total paid for Relief and Funerals..........$	441	77

LONDON BOARD OF RELIEF.

Balance on hand from last return...... ....$	9	50
Received from Grand Lodge......	75	00
" " Private Lodges...............	150	00
	$ 189	50
Total paid for Relief and Funerals.........	178	50
Balance on hand.............................$	11	00

KINGSTON BOARD OF RELIEF.

Balance on hand from last return...........$	26	43
Received from Grand Lodge.................	40	00
" " St John's Lodge............	54	88
	$ 121	31
Total paid for Relief and Funerals..........	84	52
Balance on hand.............................$	36	79

Upon comparing the modo of rendering these several accounts, it is found that while London and Kingston only show the amount granted by Grand Lodge directly to the Local Board of Relief, without bringing in the sums granted by Grand Lodge to individual brethren in their locality; Toronto and Hamilton show both the direct grant to the Local Board and the individual grants. Again Hamilton, London, and Kingston include in their benevolent accounts the funeral expenses, Toronto does not. It also appears that in Kingston only one Lodge contributes to the local fund of Benevolence.

The Board desire to express their surprise that while there are two parties in Kingston, who for several years have made large claims upon the funds of Grand Lodge, and collectively received the large sum of four hundred and twenty dollars, the Kingston Board of Relief does not appear to have given any aid except twice, a small sum in all, $40, to one of those parties, notwithstanding their returns invariably show a considerable balance on hand.

The Board strongly recommend that parties soliciting aid from the funds of Benevolence, if they reside in a place where there is a Local Board of Relief formed by the Lodges in that locality, that the applications for such aid be made through such Local Board, and that in all cases, applications for relief be made either through such Local Board, or through a private Lodge, and not in any case through individual brethren.

The Board also recommend that wherever there is more that one Lodge in any City, Town or Village, that such Lodges form among themselves a Local Board of Relief.

It was moved by R. W. Bro. Otto Klotz, seconded by M. W. Bro. A. A. Stevenson, and

RESOLVED,—That the report of the Board on Benevolence be received.

It was moved by R. W. Bro. T. White, jr., seconded by R. W. Bro. R. P. Stephens, and

RESOLVED,—That the annual report of the Board of General Purposes be adopted.

7

It was moved by R. W. Bro. T. White, jr., seconded by W. Bro. Taylor, and

RESOLVED,—That the semi-annual report of the Board of General Purposes on Audit and Finance be adopted.

R. W. Bro. T. White, jr., on behalf of the Board submitted the following report on

WARRANTS.

The Board of General Purposes beg to report that they have made a thorough examination of the books, papers etc., forwarded by the various Lodges under dispensation named below, and recommend that warrants be granted.

Blackwood Lodge,		..................Blackwood, Ont.
Doric	"	..................Toronto, "
Enterprise,	"	..................Beachburg, "
Humber	"	..................Weston, "
Morning Star	"	..................Smith's Hill, "
St. David's	"	..................St. Thomas, "
Arkona	"	..................Arkona, "
Pnyx	"	..................Wallaceburg, "
Durham	"	..................Durham, "
Blyth	"	..................Blyth, "
Minerva	"	..................Victoria, "
Grafton	"	..................Grafton, "
Wilmot	"	..................Baden, "
Blair	"	..................Palmerston, "
Clifford	"	..................Clifford, "

The petiton from brethren at Acton for a dispensation for a Lodge at that place to be called the " Walker" Lodge, the Board recommend be held over for the action of the Grand Master, no dispensation having yet been issued.

In regard to the application for a Lodge at Dundas, to be called The Hiram Lodge, dispensation for which has been issued by the M. W. Grand Master, and a petition having been filed from several members of the Valley Lodge, Dundas, praying that the warrant be not granted : the Board regret to find that an unpleasant and unhappy state of affairs exists between Valley Lodge and the petitioners for The Hiram Lodge, the Board therefore recommend that a warrant be issued to The Hiram Lodge so soon as the difficulties between the parties be amicably settled to the satisfaction of the M. W. the Grand Master, and that until the warrant be granted, the Grand Master be requested to continue his dispensation.

Respectfully submitted.

THOS. WHITE, Jr.,
President B. of G. P.

It was moved by R. W. Bro. Thos. White, jr., seconded by R. W. Bro. Otto Klotz, and

RESOLVED,—That the report of the Board on Warrants be received and adopted.

W. Bro. Ormiston, brought up the following motion, of which notice had been given yesterday, viz:—That it is not expedient to interpret Section 3 of proposing members, page 55, of the Book of Constitution, as giving to the M. W. the Grand Master, power to grant dispensations without first referring to the Lodge in whose jurisdiction the candidate may reside.

The M. W. Grand Master ruled the motion out of order.

R. W. Bro. R. P. Stephens, on behalf of the Board, submitted the following report on the

GRAND MASTER'S ADDRESS.

In reply to the Address of the M. W. the Grand Master, the Board of General Purposes beg to submit the following report:

1. The Board cannot but express the great gratification which every member feels that the settlement of the difficulties between our brethren in the Province of Quebec, referred to in the opening paragraph of the Grand Master's Address, should have been effected during the administration of one who took such an able and active part in the formation of this Grand Lodge, who conducted it so wisely and so well through its earlier and weaker years, and who has since administered

its affairs with so much skill and ability through the successive terms of his re-election to the high office of Grand Master.

The Board feel that to the many great qualities of mind and heart, of the Grand Master, we are in a great measure indebted for that restoration of peace and harmony now so happily effected.

To brethren now leaving us the Board would say, we part from them with regret, we shall miss their friendly greeting at our annual assemblies, and their wise and able counsel in our deliberations, but under existing circumstances that parting, either now, or in the not distant future, was inevitable. We wish them a hearty God-speed.

However, we, as a Grand Lodge, may have differed on some points from our brethren in Quebec who left us, we have always felt that a restoration of harmony was necessary for the good of Masonry, and that any concession short of an abandonment of vital principles should be made to accomplish that end. The Board join their congratulations to those of the Grand Master at the amicable settlement of questions of great difficulty and join him in wishing the Grand Lodge of Quebec a career of great usefulness and prosperity.

The Board would bear testimony to the great zeal and ability, as well as tact and temper, with which the negotiations were conducted by the Deputy Grand Master, R. W. Bro. Thomas White, jr., and which so materially contributed to their success, and they cheerfully concur in the recommendation of the Grand Master, that these and his many other valuable services to the Craft should be suitably acknowledged by Grand Lodge.

2. The Board learn with pleasure that the settlement of our difficulties in Quebec has led to the resumption of friendly intercourse with the Grand Lodges of Vermont and Illinois.

3. The Board have heard with great pain of the sufferings of our Brethren in Louisiana, and would recommend that a

sum of $200 be voted by Grand Lodge towards their relief, if on enquiry assistance should still be found necessary.

4. The action of the Grand Master in communicating the views of this Grand Lodge to the Grand Orient of France on the points at issue between it and the Grand Lodge of Louisiana, meets with the cordial approbation of the Board, and they concur with the Grand Master in the expression of the hope that it may help to restore friendly relations between those two bodies.

5. For the reasons given by the Grand Master and others, which he might feel a delicacy in urging, the Board approve of his suggestion, that Brethren should not, except on very special occasions, communicate directly with him, and would urge on the Brethren the propriety of transmitting all official communications to the Grand Secretary, or, in proper cases, to the Deputy Grand Master or District Deputy Grand Masters, as directed in the Book of Constitution.

6. The Board cordially endorse the views of the Grand Master as to the impropriety of allowing other societies to take part in the conduct of Masonic funerals, and also as to Lodge rooms to be used jointly with other societies, or for other than Masonic purposes.

7. The Board agree with the Grand Master on the great importance of re-considering the question of standing in the Lodges, of brethren whose suspensions have been removed by Grand Lodge, and would suggest that the proper steps be taken to have the matter discussed and their position and rights defined by Grand Lodge.

8. The Board cannot too strongly approve of the recommendation of the Grand Master that Lodges should in all cases, especially when applicants for initiation have not been long residents in their midst, make the closest and most searching enquiry as to their character and standing, and they also approve his suggestion that a clause should be added to the ordinary form of petition, stating that the applicant had not been rejected by any other Lodge within twelve months.

9. In view of the fact that Lodges frequently.suffer on account of the destruction of their property by fire, and that Grand Lodge is sometimes asked to make good losses arising entirely from their own neglect, the Board would urge upon Lodges the propriety of attending to the recommendation of the Grand Master, that they should in all cases effect an insurance on their property in some Company of good standing.

10. The Board desire to express their pleasure at the con tinued prosperity of the order as evinced by the number of dispensations granted during the year, the large amount of material brought into the masonic building in the older Lodges, and the increasing desire of the public to secure the attendance and services of the order at the ceremony of laying the foundation stones of churches and buildings of importance.

The Board would also bear testimony to the zeal and assiduity of the Grand Master, (at a great sacrifice of time and expense) on those occasions of ceremony, and in the dedication of Masonic Lodges,in the installation of officers, and in paying fraternal and official visits in different sections of the country.

11. The Board express great gratification that to the many eminent services of those highly esteemed and able brethren, R. W. Bro. J. K Kerr, and R. W. Bro. Klotz; they have added the important one of respectively providing for the craft forms of procedure in Masonic Trials, and forms of the Dedication and Installation ceremonies, which will tend to secure uniformity in procedure and work. Those brethren deserve the thanks of Grand Lodge, and the Board recom- mend that the proper means be taken to cause those forms of procedure to be communicated to the Lodges and the forms of ritual required by the officers whose duty it is to exemplify them.

12. Enquiry as to the establishment and position of the Grand Lodge of Utah, having been found satisfactory, the Board cordially recommend recognition and the establish- ment of fraternal relations with that Grand Lodge.

13. With reference to the Masonic Asylum Trust, the report of this Board made at the last Annual Communication is still before Grand Lodge for consideration. The Board, therefore, do not at present deem it expedient to offer any further suggestion on the subject.

14. In conclusion, the Board desire to express their thankfulness at the removal during the year of the one great obstacle to the establishment of Masonic peace and harmony in the Dominion, and the near prospect of the removal of another, less in degree, and the last of general importance, and the hope that these difficulties being removed, an extended career of usefulness and increased prosperity may await us in the future.

Respectfully submitted,

R. P. STEPHENS,
Chairman Special Com.

It was moved by R. W. Bro. R. P. Stephens, seconded by R. W. Bro. Hy. Macpherson, and

RESOLVED, that the report of the Board on the Grand Master's address be received.

R. W. Bro. T. White jr., on behalf of the Board submitted the following report on the

CONDITION OF MASONRY.

The Board of General Purposes beg leave to present the following report on the Condition of Masonry.

The Board have examined the reports of the D. D. G. Masters for all the Districts, and are gratified to be again assured of the satisfactory condition of the subordinate Lodges in their several districts, unaccompanied by any difficulties to disturb the general harmony.

The D. D. G. Masters have, during the past year, visited the most of the Lodges under their jurisdiction, and there can be but little doubt that the present flourishing condition of Masonry, is in great part due to their faithful discharge of this duty.

Several Lodges of Instruction have been held during the past year with great success. The D. D. G. M. of the Ontario District having held no less than four, at all of which there was a large attendance, and much care was taken in the instruction of the brethren present.

Attention has been called to the want of due caution in the installation of Masters of Lodges, without a thorough examination as to their qualification for so high and important an office. It is impossible to over-estimate the importance of requiring from those called upon to preside over our Lodges perfect familiarity with the duties of the Master as well as an accurate acquaintance with the ritual prescribed by Grand Lodge. This should invariably be insisted upon *before* the Master is installed into office, for if there be any indifference on this subject before the installation on the part of the Master elect, it is greatly to be feared that less effort will be made to acquire "the work" perfectly after the gavel has been placed in his hand Neglect in this particular form for a single year, has in some instances, worked almost irreparable injury to many Lodges.

One D. D. G. M. exceeded his authority by granting a dispensation permitting brethren to appear in Masonic regalia at a ball. This power is vested in the M. W. the Grand Master alone.

The Board regret to find that in one Lodge there has been an enquiry as to the manner in which the ballot has been used by members. The enquiry arose upon a charge that the W. M. and Wardens of a Lodge had declared the ballot clear when two black balls had been cast against a candidate for initiation. The matter having been brought before the M. W. the Grand Master, he has adjudicated upon the question. It therefore only remains for the Board to' add that the sacred character of the ballot should be borne in mind by officers as well as members of all Lodges, and any disclosure of the secrecy of the ballot is not to be countenanced under any circumstances.

The attempts of an impostor in our midst, who had with considerable success ingratiated himself with many of our order, and it is said, has gained admission into some lodges in the United States, induce the Board to remind the brethren that they cannot be too cautious in extending the hand of fellowship to those who are not provided with the credentials furnished to members, and to exhort the Masters and officers of Lodges to rigidly examine all applicants for admission as visitors before they permit the portals of the Lodge to be passed by any applicant. The impostor now especially referred to, is named [Alexander Craig, and the letter rejecting him from the sanctuary of Hall Kanawha Lodge, No. 20, Charleston, West Virginia, will be laid before Grand Lodge for the information of the brethren.

We desire to join in congratulating the M. W. the Grand Master on the happy settlement of the difficulties existing for some years past in the Province of Quebec, to which reference has been made in the reports already presented to Grand Lodge.

We would desire to record the unfeigned regret with which we have learned that so many of our beloved brethren have passed from their sphere of usefulness amongst us. Though absent from our councils, alas forever, their memory will live in our hearts. We would recommend that suitable memorial pages in the printed proceedings of Grand Lodge, be set apart to record the name, rank, and date of death of our late departed brethren, viz.: R. W. Bro. John V. Nool, R. W. Bro. B. C. Davy, and V. W. Bro. Thomas Duggan, all of whom were Past Grand Officers of this Grand Lodge.

All of which is respectfully submitted,

THOMAS WHITE, Jr.,
President B. of G. P.

It was moved by R. W. Bro. T. White, jr., seconded by R. W. Bro. J. K. Kerr, and

RESOLVED,—That the report of the Board on Condition of Masonry be received and adopted.

R. W. Bro. J. K. Kerr read a letter from a Brother of St. John's Lodge, No. 82, Paris, as likewise a circular from Hall Kanawha Lodge, No. 20, Charleston, West Virginia, warning the brethren against one Alexander Craig, who claims falsely to hail from the latter Lodge, and who under various *aliases* has been travelling through the country by means of money fraudulently and unlawfully obtained from different Lodges and also from individual brethren.

The consideration of the report on the Asylum Trust was resumed, when

It was moved by R. W. Bro. S. B. Harman, seconded by R. W. Bro. James Bain:

That the report of the Trustees of the Masonic Asylum Trust be received and adopted.

That the M. W. the Grand Master be requested to act with the Chairman of the Board of General Purposes, the Grand Secretary, and the Trustees, hereby constituted as a standing committee, to take such steps as may be required to give effect to the report just adopted, and if necessary to conclude arrangements by which the truly liberal offer of Niagara Lodge may be availed of and the institution at once organized. And further, in the event of such last named action being taken, to advise all Lodges and the authorities of Royal Arch, Templar, and all other Masonic bodies, thereof, with a view to obtaining additional aid, and enlisting the fullest sympathy in the happy inauguration of this great work.

In amendment it was moved by R. W. Bro. B. E. Charlton, seconded by R. W. Bro. P. J. Brown,

That all after the words "Masonic Asylum Trust" be struck out, and the following be substituted in lieu thereof, "that that portion of the report of the Board of General Purposes for 1873, which was laid over for the consideration of Grand Lodge at this Communication, be now adopted."

On a vote of Grand Lodge being taken on the foregoing amendment it was declared *lost*.

Subsequently it was moved in amendment by W. Bro. Wm. Forbes, seconded by R. W. Bro. B. E. Charlton.

That the matter of the final settlement of the Masonic Asylum Trust Fund, be laid over until the next annual Communication of Grand Lodge, and that in the interim the subordinate Lodges be appealed to, enquiring what annual aid they will give towards its support, either by way of bonus or yearly grant, with a further statistical report of the numbers and nature of the requirements of such as may have claims on our Benevolence, within the jurisdiction, as well as the number of non-affiliated Masons likely to assist the project.

The foregoing amendment having been put to the Grand Lodge, it was declared adopted.

R. W. Bro. T. White, jr., on behalf of the Board, submitted the following report on

GRIEVANCES AND APPEALS.

The Board of General Purposes beg leave to report on the following cases which have been brought before them, namely :

1. *In re* St. John's Lodge, No. 3, Kingston. A candidate was proposed in this Lodge on St. John's Day, 27th Dec. last, which day is by the by-laws of that Lodge, made a regular meeting. The Constitution provided that the ballot shall take place at the next regular meeting following the proposal. In this case the next regular meeting occurred within seven days after the 27th, when the candidate was balloted for by order of the W. M. Notice of the ballot having been given, but not seven days notice as required by the by-laws. The Grand Master has ordered that this question should be submitted to the Board.

To avoid any question as to the regularity of such proceedings in the future, the Board recommend that the Constitution be amended, so as to provide that four weeks shall elapse in all cases between the proposal of a candidate and the ballot on the same.

2. In the matter of Grand River Lodge, No. 151, against Bro. John A. Mackie, which has been already reported upon, (the Board at the meeting in February last, having recommended the removal of suspension on the ground of want of prosecution on the part of the Lodge,) the Grand Master has ordered fresh evidence to be taken, which has now been considered.

The charge preferred is one of violation of his O. B. as a M. M. The Board find that the charge as laid, is not sustained by the evidence, although in their opinion a Masonic offence has been committed. They recommend that as the accused has now been suspended for over a year, the Grand Master be requested to remove the suspension as soon as he thinks proper to do so.

3. In the matter of the complaint of Bro. George Smith, against Dalhousie Lodge, No. 52. The Board find that the whole matter has already been disposed of by them. They recommend that the Grand Secretary be instructed to forward to Bro. Smith, a copy of their previous decision, and to express to him their strong dis-approval of the offensive tone employed by him in his letter on this subject.

4. In the matter of Corinthian Lodge, No. 101, against Bro. Maurice Dunsford, the charges are incendiarism and misappropriation of his employers' moneys. The Board recommend that the case be referred back to the Lodge for the proper trial of the accused in the usual way.

5. In the appeal of Bro. W. R. Yuill, against the action of Clinton Lodge, No. 84, in recommending him to Grand Lodge for expulsion, the Board find that the charge is one which if committed by the accused, was so committed before his initiation, and in view of that fact, is not in the opinion of the Board of sufficient gravity to warrant so severe a penalty. They therefore recommend that the appeal be allowed.

6. *In re* Gosslee, *vs.* J. J. Campbell, the W. M. of Colborne Lodge, No. 91, the complaint is for refusing to initiate a candidate who has been regularly balloted for and accepted.

Having heard both parties, the Board is of opinion that the action of the Master should be sustained.

7. Acacia Lodge, No. 61, *vs.* Bro. Chas. C. Baird.—After proper trial before the D. D. G. M. of the Hamilton District, the accused has been recommended to appear at this meeting and show cause why he should not be expelled.

He appeared and showed such cause as he could. After

consideration of the circumstances of the case, it was recommended that the Brother be not now expelled, but that his suspension be confirmed in the hope that his conduct in the future will be such as to justify his restoration to full Masonic privileges.

All of which is respectfully submitted.

THOS. WHITE, Jr.,

President B. of G. P.

It was moved by R. W. Bro. T. White, jr., seconded by R. W. Bro. Otto Klotz, and

RESOLVED,—That the report of the Board on Grievances and Appeals be received.

The Grand Lodge was called from labor to refreshment. to meet at 2.30 o'clock, p. m.

———

The Grand Lodge resumed its sittings at 4.45 o'clock. p. m.

PRESENT.

M. W. Bro. W. M. Wilson, Grand Master,

On the Throne,

Grand Officers, Members and Representatives.

The M. W. Grand Master appointed the following Brethren Scrutineers of the Ballot for Grand Officers and elective members of the Board of General Purposes, viz: R. W. Bros. Wm. Nivin and R. P. Stephens, and W. Bro. F. J. Menet.

It was moved by R. W. Bro. Otto Klotz, seconded by W. Bro. Somerville, and

RESOLVED,—That in order to avoid unnecessary delay in the distribution of the ballots at future Communications of Grand Lodge, the ballot papers be handed to delegates when they report themselves to the Committee on credentials, and enter their names in the attendance book, and that delegates be only admitted on presentation of ballot papers.

It was moved by R. W. Bro. Otto Klotz, seconded by R. W. Bro. J. E. Brooke, and

RESOLVED,—That the report of the Board on Benevolence be adopted.

It was moved by W. Bro. Wm. Forbes, seconded by R. W. Bro. John Parry, and

Resolved,—That at future Communications of Grand Lodge, each District have a distinct position assigned it in Grand Lodge, to be designated by the name of the District, prominently exhibited, and each Lodge its respective position in said District.

It was moved by R. W. Bro. T. White, jr., seconded by R. W. Bro. James Seymour, and

Resolved,—That the report of the Board on Grievances and Appeals be adopted.

The M. W. Grand Master availed himself of the opportunity at this stage of the proceedings to present R. W. Bro. Otto Klotz, the Chairman of the Sub-committee of the Board on Benevolence, with a very suitable Testimonial, consisting of an elaborate Bronze Mantle Time Piece, with silver mountings, and silver plate on which was engraved the "good Samaritan," as a slight acknowledgement of the arduous duties he has performed for twenty years past.

The Grand Lodge was called from labor to refreshment, to meet at 8 o'clock, p. m.

The Grand Lodge resumed its sittings at 8.45 o'clock, p.m.

PRESENT.

M. W. Bro. W. M. Wilson, Grand Master,

On the Throne,

Grand Officers, Members and Representatives.

The M. W. the Grand Master took occasion to present M. W. Bro. A. A. Stevenson, P. G. M., on behalf of Grand Lodge, with a Testimonial which had been procured in accordance with a resolution of Grand Lodge, as a slight recognition of his services rendered to Masonry, and particularly to this Grand Lodge during his occupancy of the Grand East for three years in succession.

The presentation consisted of a full suit of Regalia, chain, collar, apron and gauntlets of a P. G. M. A solid silver pitcher, two silver goblets and a silver salver, with a suitable inscription thereon.

It was moved by R. W. Bro. S. B. Harman, seconded by R. W. Bro. J. Reynolds,—That all difficulties among our Brethren in the Province of Quebec, being now finally and happily terminated, by mutual agreement, this Grand Lodge formally cedes to the Grand Lodge of Quebec, all her rights and privileges hitherto claimed in that territory, and cordially welcomes the Grand Lodge of Quebec, as a Sister Grand Lodge, trusting that the most cordial bond of union may ever exist between them and this Grand Lodge, and wishing them a long and uninterrupted career of true Masonic success and prosperity.

In amendment,

It was moved by W. Bro. Cohen, seconded by R. W. Bro. J. Urquhart, jr.,—That if this Grand Lodge sees that it is essentially necessary to cede their territory in the Province of Quebec, that this be done with distinct proviso, that any Lodge in that Province desiring to retain their allegiance to this Grand Lodge may do so, and can never be alienated except for offence against the Constitution as laid down, or by their own free will.

The amendment having been put to Grand Lodge, it was declared *lost.*

The original resolution was then put to Grand Lodge, and declared *carried.*

It was moved by R. W. Bro. B. E. Charlton, seconded by R. W. Bro. R. P. Stephens, and

RESOLVED,—That the M. W. Grand Master be requested to appoint a special committee for the purpose of carrying out the recommendation made to this Grand Lodge in regard to procuring a suitable Testimonial, for presentation to R. W. Bro. Thomas White, jr., in recognition of his many valuable services rendered to the Craft, and as a mark of high esteem and regard entertained towards him personally by this Grand Lodge.

The M. W. the Grand Master appointed the following Brethren as the Committee, viz.: M. W. Bros. A. A. Stevenson and W. B. Simpson, and R. W. Bro. J. K. Kerr.

It was moved by M. W. Bro. James Seymour, seconded by R. W. Bro. P. J. Brown, and unanimously

RESOLVED,—That in consideration of the lasting benefit which Masonry in general has received from the labors of R. W. Bro. Thos White, jr., in conducting the several conferences, which have so happily resulted in bringing about a settlement of the differences and difficulties relating to Masonry in the Province of Quebec, that the rank and dignity of a Past Grand Master be accorded to him by this Grand Lodge.

M. W. Bro. T. White, jr., on behalf of the Board submitted the following supplementary report on

WARRANTS.

The Board of General Purposes beg to report that they have had under consideration, applications from the following Lodges applying for Warrants, viz: "Clementi" Lodge, Lakefield, "Chesterville" Lodge, Chesterville, "Hiram" Lodge, Cheapside, and recommend that a Warrant be issued to "Clementi" Lodge.

In the matter of Chesterville Lodge, the Board learn from R. W. Bro. Reynolds D. D. G. M., St. Lawrence District, that they have held but one or two meetings, (the dispensation being granted by the G. M. only on 3rd of May) that he has inspected their hall and Lodge furniture and found them suitable for the requirements of a Masonic Lodge. That the minute book of the Lodge while under dispensation has not been submitted for inspection, the Board therefore recommend that a warrant be not granted, but that the G. M. be requested to continue his dispensation.

In the matter of "Hiram Lodge," Cheapside, dispensation for which was issued on the 28th of February, 1874. No evidence having been laid before the Board to show that the petitioners have availed themselves of the dispensation, the Board recommend that a warrant be not granted.

The business of the Board has been very seriously delayed by the neglect of petitioners for new Lodges to forward the minute books for examination until after the assembling of Grand Lodge, and it is therefore recommended that in future all Lodges under dispensation be required to forward their books to the Grand Secretary in time to be laid before the Board at its first meeting.

All of which is respectfully submitted,

THOS. WHITE, Jr.,

President B. of G. P.

It was moved by M. W. Bro. T. White, jr., seconded by V. W. Bro. N. G. Bigelow, and

RESOLVED,—That the supplementary report of the Board on Warrants be received and adopted.

R. W. Bro. P. J. Brown, on behalf of the Board, submitted the following report on

PART OF THE ADDRESS OF THE GRAND MASTER.

The Board of General Purposes beg to report.

In reference to that part of the address of the M. W. the Grand Master referring to Financial arrangements arising out of the settlement of the Masonic differences in the Province of Quebec, the Board recommend the adoption of the following resolution.

That on the occasion of our brethren from Quebec retiring from among us, to unite with the brethren of the Grand Lodge of Quebec, we present them with $4,000, for purposes of benevolence, with our heartiest good wishes for their future prosperity, and that the said funds be placed in the hands of M. W. Bro. White, in trust for the retiring Lodges, until a meeting of their representatives, who shall by a majority determine the disposition thereof.

They also recommend that the blank in the report in the Grand Master's address be filled up with the sum of $200.

All of which is respectfully submitted.

THOS. WHITE, Jr.,

Presiden: B. of G. P.

It was moved by R. W. Bro. P. J. Brown, seconded by W. Bro. Robinson, and

RESOLVED,—That the report of the Board just read be received and adopted.

M. W. Bro. Harington, P. G. M., presented his credentials as the accredited representative of the Grand Lodges of

S

Vermont and Quebec, respectively, which were accepted and the representative was saluted with the usual honors.

In accordance with notices given, the following places were proposed for holding the next Annual Communication, viz.:

R. W. Bro. F. Westlake, City of London.
M. W. Bro. T. D. Harington, City of Ottawa.
M. W. Bro. James Seymour, Town of St. Catharines.

A vote of Grand Lodge having been severally taken on the various places put in nomination, the majority of the votes were in favor of the City of London, and London was declared to be the place for the holding of the next annual Communication.

It was moved by M. W. Bro. Thomas White, jr., seconded by R. W. Bro. P. J Brown, and unanimously

RESOLVED,—That the thanks of Grand Lodge be tendered to the Grand Lodges of Iowa, Massachusetts, Rhode Island, Texas, Maine and Nevada, for their donations of bound volumes of their Proceedings, Constitutions, &c., for the use of Grand Lodge Library, and also to Bro. Leon Hyneman of Philadelphia, for a copy of his History of Initiation, and that the Grand Secretary be instructed to reciprocate the kindness.

The Scrutineers having reported, the following brethren were declared duly elected Office Bearers for the ensuing term, viz.:

GRAND OFFICERS.

M. W. Bro. W. M. Wilson, Simcoe,   Grand Master.
R. " " J. K. Kerr, Toronto,   Deputy " "
" " " W. R. White, Pembroke,   " Senior Warden.
V. " " Hugh Murray, Hamilton,   " Junior "
R. " " Rev. G. MInnes, London, re-elected " Chaplain.
" " " Henry Groff, Simcoe,   " " Treasurer.
V. " " D. McG Malloch, Clinton,   " Registrar.
R. " " T. B Harris, Hamilton,   " " Secretary.
    By an open vote of Grand Lodge,
" James Heron, London,   " Tyler.

DISTRICT DEPUTY GRAND MASTERS.

The following brethren were nominated by the representatives of Lodges, as District Deputy Grand Masters for their respective Districts, and approved by the M. W. Grand Master, viz:

R. W. Bro. Thos. C. Macnabb,	Chatham,	St. Clair	District.
" " " W. D. McGloghlon,	London,	London	"
" " " Chauncy Bennett,	Port Rowan,	Wilson	"
" " " J. H. Benson,	Seaforth,	Huron	"
" " " W. F. Savage,	Elora,	Wellington	"
" " " J. J. Mason,	Hamilton,	Hamilton,	"
" " " D. E. Broderick,	Caledonia,	Niagara	',
" " " R. P. Stephens,	Toronto,	Toronto	"
" " " J. B. Trayes,	Port Hope,	Ontario	"
" " " S. S. Lazier,	Belleville,	Prince Edward	"
" " " A. S. Kirkpatrick,	Kingston,	St. Lawrence	"
" " " John W. Pickup,	Pakenham,	Ottawa	"
" " " Geo. Black,	Mapleton,	Province of Manitoba

The M. W. Grand Master proceeded with the installation and investiture of the newly elected officers, who were proclaimed and saluted with the customary Masonic honors.

At a subsequent date the M. W. Grand Master was pleased to notify the Grand Secretary of the following appointments to office for the ensuing Masonic year, viz:

V. W. Bro. Fred J. Menet, Toronto,	Grand	Senior Deacon.	
" " " Geo. S. Birrell, London,	"	Junior "	
" " " James H. Rowan, Ottawa,	"	Superintendent of Works.	
" " " And. Irving, jr. Pembroke,	"	Director of Ceremonies.	
" " " F. R. Despard, Hamilton, Asst.	"	Secretary.	
" " " James Miller, Peterboro, "	"	Director of Ceremonies.	
" " " John M. Clement, Niagara,	"	Sword Bearer.	
" " " C. A. Sippi, London,	"	Organist.	
" " " Thos Aishton, Bath, Asst.	"	"	
" " " Hugh Kerr, Ingersoll,	"	Pursuivant.	

V. W. Bro. James Sutton, Lucan,
" " " A. Whittaker, Windsor,
" " " Isaac Waterman. London,
" " " J. R. Leggett, L'Orignal,
" " " R. Rochester, Simcoe,
" " " Josiah Corlis, St. Thomas, } " Stewards.
" " " E. Peplow, Jr., Port Hope,
" " " H. T. Champion, Winnipeg
" " " T. F. Blackwood, Yorkville
" " " John Gibson, Stratford,
" " " D. A. Fergusson, Smith'sF'ls
" " " A. Hudspeth, Lindsay,

It was moved by R. W. Bro. R. P. Stephens, seconded by M. W. Bro. T. White, jr., and

RESOLVED,—That the report of the Board on the address of the **Grand Master** be adopted.

It was moved by M. W. Bro. Thos. White, jr., seconded by R. W. Bro. J. E. Brooke, and

RESOLVED,—That the cordial thanks of this Grand Lodge are due, and are hereby heartily tendered to the committee of management of the Toronto Lodges, for the ample and satisfactory arrangements made for the holding of the present Annual Communication.

It was moved by R. W. Bro. Chauncy Bennett, seconded by R. W. Bro P. J. Brown, and

RESOLVED,—That the thanks of this Grand Lodge be tendered to the various Railway and Steamboat Companies, for their liberality in reducing the fares to delegates attending this Annual Communication.

It was moved by R. W. Bro. P. J. Brown, seconded by M. W. Bro T· White, jr., and

RESOLVED,—That a cordial vote of thanks be tendered to the committee on Credentials of representatives, for the satisfactory manner in which they have discharged the duties devolving upon them.

It was moved by R. W. Bro. James Reynolds, seconded by R. W. Bro. J. E. Brooke, and

RESOLVED,—That the thanks of Grand Lodge be tendered to the Scrutineers of the ballot for the satisfactory manner in which they have discharged their arduous duties.

It was moved by R. W. Bro. Harding, seconded by R. W. Bro. Benson,

That the dues of Bernard Lodge, No. 225 Listowel, for the past year, be remitted, the said Lodge having lost all its furniture and property by fire

The M. W. Grand Master ruled the motion out of order.

NOTICES OF MOTION.

W. Bro. John Ormiston, gave notice, that at the next Annual Communication he will move to amend the Constitution by striking out the words "unless by Dispensation of the Grand Master," in section 3, "Of proposing members," and inserting in lieu thereof the words "without having first obtained the consent of the last named lodge."

V. W. Bro. F. H. Lynch Staunton, gave notice, that at the next Annual Communication he will move that the following clause be added to that part of the Constitution relating to private Lodges.

"That no Brother shall be an ordinary member of more

than one Lodge in the same City, Town, or incorporated Village."

The President of the Board of General Purposes, gave notice, that at the next Annual Communication he will move that the article "Of proposing members," clause 2, be amended by adding thereto, the words following:

"And in all cases at least four weeks must elapse between the proposal of the candidate and the ballot for the same."

Also—to add to the declaration of candidates previous to initiation, the words "and that I have not been rejected by this or any other Lodge within twelve months from the date of my present application,"

W. Bro. James B. Nixon, gave notice, that at the next Annual Communication he will move that the Toronto District be divided into two Districts, the counties of York and Peel to constitute the Toronto District, and the counties of Simcoe and Grey to constitute a new District, to be named the Georgian District.

M. W. Bro. Seymour gave notice, that he would, at the next Annual Communication, move to amend the Constitution, so as to provide against Dual Membership in all cities, towns, and villages.

R. W. Bro. J. K. Kerr gave notice, that at the next Annual Communication, he will move to make all amendments in the Constitution, necessary or expedient, in consequence of, or occasioned by, the change in Territorial Jurisdiction of Grand Lodge, by this session withdrawing from that part of our territory known as the Province of Quebec.

R. W. Bro. Benson gave notice, that at the next Annual Communication he will move an amendment to the Constitution,—That no Money Grant shall be made on the last day of Grand Lodge, providing the proceedings extend over two days.

W. Bro. J. A. Sommerville gave notice that he would move

at the next Annual Communication, to amend the Constitution, "of proposing members" section 7, by striking out all the words after "ballot" and inserting the words "one black ball appear against him" in lieu thereof.

The Scrutineers of the ballot reported that the following named brethren had received the largest number of votes for members of the Board of General Purposes for the ensuing term, and were declared duly elected, viz.:

R. W. Bro. Otto Klotz,   Preston   Lodge, No. 207, Preston.
"   "   "   D. Spry,   St. Andrew's "   "   16, Toronto.
"   "   "   P. J. Brown,   King Hiram   "   "   37, Ingersoll.
"   "   "   Allan McLean,   St. John's   "   "   68,   "
"   "   "   Hy. Macpherson, St. George's "   "   88, Owen Sound

The M. W. Grand Master was pleased to announce the following appointments as members of the Board of General Purposes for the ensuing term, viz.:

R. W. Bro. Hy. Robertson,   Manito.   Lodge, No. 90, Collingwood.
"   "   "   Rev. V. Clementi, Clementi   "   " 313, Lakefield.
"   "   "   David McLellan, Strict Ob'c. "   "   27, Hamilton.
"   "   "   E. C. Barber,   Corinthian   "   "   57, Ottawa.
"   "   "   C. D. Macdonnell, St. John's   "   "   3, Kingston.

And for one year to fill vacancies, viz.:

R. W. Bro. J. A. Henderson, St. John's Lodge, No. 3, Kingston.
"   "   "   J. E. Harding,   St. James   "   "   73, St. Mary's.
"   "   "   L. H. Henderson, The Belle'e. "   " 123, Belleville.

The business of Grand Lodge being ended, it was closed, in Ample Form.

ATTEST.

THOS. B. HARRIS,
Grand Secretary.

NOTE.

Owing to the illness, resulting in the death, of our late R. W. BRO. THOMAS BIRD HARRIS, Grand Secretary, the duty of preparing the present Proceedings of Grand Lodge, for publication, has devolved upon the undersigned, who on the 21st August last, was appointed by the M. W. the Grand Master, Grand Secretary, *pro tem.*

Nothwithstanding the fact, that every care has been exercised in the preparation of the Proceedings, it is possible that inasmuch as the undersigned has had to rely nearly altogether upon the rough minutes, and papers and memoranda found in the office, a few errors may have crept in unawares.

The indulgence of Grand Lodge may under these circumstances be fairly and confidently claimed.

The Report on Foreign Correspondence was printed and paged before the meeting of Grand Lodge.

Too little allowance had been made for the general Proceedings, and the paging of the the former is consequently incorrect.

The Foreign Correspondence should commence with page *72* and end with page *840* instead of the present numbers 629 and 742 respectively.

J. J. MASON,

GRAND SECRETARY'S OFFICE, }   Grand Secretary, *pro tem.*
HAMILTON, 30th Sept., 1874. }

GRAND SECRETARY'S ANNUAL REPORT.

R. W. BRO. THOMAS B. HARRIS, Grand Secretary, in account current with the Grand Lodge of Canada. Moneys received from the 1st January to the 31st December, 1873.

NAMES OF LODGES.		NAMES OF LODGES.	
— Antiquity Lodge	$ 25 50	68 St. John's	71 25
1 Prevost	59 25	69 Stirling	31 00
2 Niagara	46 25	72 Alma	79 75
3 St. John's	83 25	73 St. James'	56 75
4 Dorchester	19 44	74 St. James'	59 00
5 Sussex	57 75	75 St. John's	61 75
6 Barton	128 25	76 Oxford	62 00
7 Union	65 75	77 Faithful Brethren	28 00
8 Nelson	7 50	78 King Hiram	67 50
9 Union	14 04	79 Simcoe	15 75
10 Norfolk	81 50	80 Albion	27 50
11 Moira	41 50	81 St. John's	38 25
13 Western Light	3 00	82 St. John's	85 50
14 True Briton's	53 00	83 Beaver	55 00
15 St. George's	80 00	84 Clinton	39 00
16 St. Andrew's	118 50	85 Rising Sun	25 75
17 St. John's	110 75	86 Wilson	10 00
18 Prince Edward	73 00	87 Markham Union	68 75
19 St. George's	68 00	88 St. George's	18 75
20 St. John's	59 00	90 Manito	105 25
21 Zetland	49 45	91 Colborne	90 38
22 King Solomon's	132 50	92 Cataraqui	87 00
23 Richmond	29 25	93 Northern Light	56 25
24 St. Francis	49 25	94 St. Mark's	23 25
25 Ionic	85 50	95 Ridout	45 25
26 Ontario	43 00	96 Corinthian	61 00
27 Strict Observance	123 00	97 Sharon	36 25
28 Mount Zion	43 50	98 True Blue	27 75
29 United	35 25	99 Tuscan	53 43
30 Composite	45 25	100 Valley	48 12
31 Jerusalem	62 75	101 Corinthian	56 75
32 Amity	83 00	103 Maple Leaf	122 75
33 Goderich	64 00	104 St. John's	25 75
34 Thistle	65 00	105 St. Mark's	39 75
35 St. John's	45 75	106 Burford	110 00
36 Welland	26 25	107 St. Paul's	43 47
37 King Hiram	53 50	108 Blenheim	39 00
38 Trent	67 25	109 Albion	50 74
39 Mount Zion	17 50	110 Central	25 50
40 St. John's	77 50	111 Morpeth	66 75
41 St. George's	56 50	112 Maitland	61 50
42 St. George's	99 25	113 Wilson	46 48
43 King Solomon's	63 50	114 Hope	38 50
44 St. Thomas	82 50	115 Ivy	30 25
45 Brant	66 00	116 Cassia	23 00
46 Wellington	71 75	118 Union	11 00
48 Madoc	25 00	119 Maple Leaf	28 00
50 Consecon	29 25	120 Warren	34 75
51 Corinthian	16 50	121 Doric	46 50
53 Shefford	92 50	122 Renfrew	51 75
54 Vaughan	86 50	123 The Belleville	73 25
55 Merrickville	57 50	126 Golden Rule	95 25
56 Victoria	62 00	128 Pembroke	85 00
58 Doric	37 00	129 The Rising Sun	53 25
59 Corinthian	66 75	130 Yamaska	7 50
61 Acacia	181 75	131 St. Lawrence	44 75
62 St. Andrew's	23 00	133 Lebanon Forest	56 75
63 St. John's	63 80	135 St. Clair	21 23
64 Kilwinning	53 75	137 Pythagoras	41 79
65 Rehoboam	78 00	139 Lebanon	112 50
66 Durham	37 23	140 Malahide	63 50

GRAND SECRETARY'S ACCOUNT.—[*Continued.*]

NAMES OF LODGES.		NAMES OF LODGES.	
141 Tudor	18 00	223 Norwood	20 25
143 Friendly Brothers	6 00	224 Zurich	21 25
144 Tecumseh	95 50	225 Bernard	20 25
145 J. B. Hall	23 75	226 Mt. Moriah	43 00
146 Prince of Wales	44 75	227 Sutton	14 50
147 Mississippi	73 25	228 Prince Arthur	20 25
148 Civil Service	30 00	229 Ionic	49 75
149 Erie	88 00	230 Kerr	58 50
150 Hastings	23 00	231 Lodge of Fidelity	51 25
151 The Grand River	112 00	232 Cameron	74 25
153 Burns	42 00	233 Doric	51 50
154 Irving	47 25	234 Beaver	32 75
155 Peterborough	49 00	235 Aldworth	87 50
156 York	17 00	236 Manitoba	19 25
157 Simpson	36 25	237 Vienna	49 25
158 Alexandra	59 75	238 Havelock	6 00
159 Goodwood	14 50	239 Tweed	30 00
161 Percy	69 75	240 Prince Rupert's	85 75
162 Forest	59 25	241 Quinte	58 00
163 Browne	19 00	242 Macoy	51 00
164 Star in the East	32 00	243 St. George	15 75
165 Burlington	42 00	244 Lisgar	37 70
166 Wentworth	71 00	245 Tecumseh	64 50
168 Merritt	47 75	246 U. of S. Observance	27 25
169 Macnab	85 25	247 Ashlar	57 25
170 Britannia	30 75	248 Eureka	56 00
172 Ayr	16 00	249 Caledonian	33 50
173 Victoria	23 75	250 Thistle	25 00
174 Walsingham	93 23	253 Minden	74 50
176 Spartan	42 25	254 Clifton	46 50
177 The Builders'	65 44	255 Sydenham	56 25
178 Plattsville	44 90	256 Farran's Point	72 00
179 Bothwell	53 75	257 Galt	76 75
180 Speed	100 00	258 Guelph	29 50
181 Oriental	44 50	259 Springfield	67 00
183 Prince Albert	47 00	260 Washington	84 75
184 Old Light	28 50	261 Oak Branch	54 00
185 Enniskillen	39 50	262 Harriston	28 75
186 Plantagenet	6 00	263 Forest	28 50
187 Royal Canadian	50 75	264 Chaudiere	76 75
189 Filius Viduæ	37 00	265 Patterson	24 25
190 Belmont	61 00	266 Northern	21 50
192 Orillia	79 75	267 Parthenon	130 50
193 Scotland	40 75	268 Verulam	49 13
194 Petrolia	64 00	269 Brougham Union	15 50
195 The Tuscan	26 50	270 Cedar	19 25
196 Madawaska	52 50	271 Wellington	10 00
197 Saugeen	54 75	272 Seymour	58 50
198 White Oak	46 26	274 Kent	47 50
200 St. Alban's	43 73	275 Pontiac	41 00
201 Leeds	120 25	276 Teeswater	26 00
202 Mount Royal	1 00	277 Seymour	34 25
203 Irvine	95 75	278 Mystic	17 25
205 New Dominion	14 50	279 New Hope	21 25
209 Evergreen	50 44	280 Mt. Sinai	33 25
210 Hawkesbury	25 50	281 Thorne	26 50
211 Brome Lake	13 25	282 Lorne	63 00
212 Elysian	41 00	283 Eureka	28 75
213 Dominion	63 00	284 St. John's	28 91
214 Craig	36 25	285 Seven Star	62 50
215 Lake	29 25	286 Wingham	59 25
216 Harris	49 25	287 Shuniah	14 00
217 Frederick	13 50	288 Ancient Landmark	20 00
218 Stevenson	222 21	289 Doric	30 50
219 Credit	60 44	290 Leamington	69 75
220 Zeredatha	46 50	291 Dufferin	47 50
221 Mountain	42 50	292 Robertson	39 50
222 Marmora	23 50	294 Moore	56 25

GRAND SECRETARY'S ACCOUNT.—[*Continued.*]

NAMES OF LODGES.		NAMES OF LODGES.	
295 Conestogo.....................	30 25	U. D. Humber...................	20 00
296 Temple.....................	73 00	" Durham....................	20 00
297 Preston	85 50	" Arkona...	20 00
298 Eddy.......................	37 50	Cash.........................	5 81
299 Victoria....................	30 00	D. D. G. M. Ontario District....	1 00
300 Mt. Olivet...................	28 50	" " Toronto "	9 00
301 Hanover.....................	20 00	" " Niagara "	1 00
U. D. St David's...............	20 00		
" Blyth.....................	20 00	Total................\$13,532 49	
" Minerva..................	20 00		

CASH STATEMENT.

Moneys received by the Grand Secretary and paid over to the Grand Treasurer, from the 1st January to the 31st December, 1873.

CR.   DR.

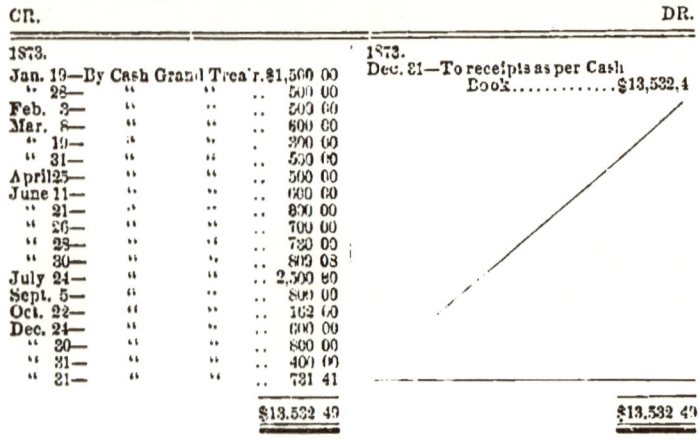

1873.					1873.	
Jan. 19—By Cash Grand Trea'r.				\$1,500 00	Dec. 31—To receipts as per Cash	
" 28—	"	"	..	500 00	Book...........\$13,532,4	
Feb. 3—	"	"	..	500 00		
Mar. 8—	"	"	..	600 00		
" 19—	"	"	.	300 00		
" 31—	"	"	..	550 00		
April25—	"	"	..	500 00		
June 11—	"	"	..	600 00		
" 21—	"	"	..	800 00		
" 26—	"	"	..	700 00		
" 28—	"	"	..	730 00		
" 30—	"	"	..	809 08		
July 24—	"	"	..	2,500 00		
Sept. 5—	"	"	..	800 00		
Oct. 22—	"	"	..	162 00		
Dec. 24—	"	"	..	600 00		
" 30—	"	"	..	800 00		
" 31—	"	"	..	400 00		
" 31—	"	"	..	731 41		
				\$13,532 49		\$13,532 49

RECAPITULATION.

Certificates...	\$ 3,502 00
Dues..	6,490 00
Fees	2,176 59
Dispensations	526 00
Warrants..	220 00
Constitutions..	605 29
Proceedings, &c..	12 75
	\$13,532 49

BALANCE SHEET.

The Grand Lodge of Ancient Free and Accepted Masons of Canada. R. W. Bro. HENRY GROFF, Grand Treasurer.

DR.

1873.	$	cts.	$	cts.
Dec. 31—Stocks, Dominion, 6 per cent.$28,800 00				
" 5 " . 10,000 0)			38,800	00
—Debentures, Co. of Middlesex......			1,600	00
—Bank of Toronto, balance as reported on 30th June....	1,393	66		
—Bank of Toronto, Deposit in October......	144	00	1,537	66
Canadian Bank of Commerce, Simcoe..			10,601	81
			$52,539	47

CR.

1873.	$	cts.	$	cts.
Dec. 31—General Account........				
—Asylum Fund, balance as reported by Asylum Trust 30th June..............			30,267	90
Six month's Interest on Do. Stock, 1st Oct..........	6,193	66		
	144	00		
—Benevolent Fund (investment acc't), viz., balance 31st December, 1872......			6,337	66
Add 10 per cent. of receipts for 1872......	12,468	81		
	1,257	14	13,725	95
—Benevolent Fund (current account)......			2,207	96
			$52,539	47

SIMCOE, 2nd January, 1874.

E. E.   HENRY GROFF, GRAND TREASURER.

The Middlesex Debentures have been paid, and amount deposited in Bank since the amount was made up.—H. G.

The foregoing statements have been audited and found correct.

ALLAN McLEAN, CHAIRMAN COM.

GENERAL FUND.

The Grand Lodge of Ancient Free and Accepted Masons of Canada in account with HENRY GROFF, Grand Treasurer.

DR. 1873.		$	cts.	CR. 1873.		$	cts.
	To paid the President's orders as follows, viz.:			Jan. 3—By Balance per account........		29,988	06
Jan. 9—	To Grand Secretary, for office rent.....	60	00	20— " received from Grand Secretary.....		1,500	00
"	" for quarter's salary.	400	00	28— " " "		500	00
Feb. 8—	" For expenses of B. of G. P..........	376	40	Feb. 3— " " "		600	00
"	" " "	22	30	Mar. 8— " " "		300	00
26—	" T. & R. White, for wood cuts........	10	50	19— " " "		500	00
"	" Grand Treasurer, for contingencies..	3	73	31— " " "		500	00
Mar. 3—	" Master, "	21	00	Apr. 25— " " "		600	00
—	" Copp, Clark & Co, for certificates...	301	64	June 11— " " "		300	00
—	" Duncan, Stuart & Co., for blank book.	2	05	21— " " "		700	00
—	" Lawson, McCulloch & Co., printing..	382	88	27— " " "		730	06
—	" " "	277	00	28— " " "		800	08
—	" W. Bruce, for engrossing.........	43	19	30— " " "		2,300	00
—	" R. Haigh, for a registry book........	37	00	July 24— " " "		800	00
—	" W. W. Summers, for repairs........	5	25	Sept. 4— " " "		162	00
—	" Grand Secretary, for assistance......	325	60	Oct. 22— " " "		600	00
—	" M. Howles, for a tin case...........	5	25	Dec. 26— " " "		800	00
—	" Grand Secretary, for continguncies ..	200	00	31— " " "		400	00
—	" " for balance of contingencies ..	17	77	1874.			
13—	" Buntin, Gillies & Co., for stationery.	28	91	Jan. 2— " " "		731	41
—	" transferred to Benevolence Investment account, 10 per cent. of gross receipts for 1872..............	1,257	14				
Apr.17—	" Grand Secretary, for quarter's salary.	400	00				
—	" " for regalia......	21	00	By amount carried forward......$43,520			55

GENERAL FUND.—(CONTINUED)

1873.		$ cts. 1873.	By amount brought forward..... 43,520 55 $ cts.
Apr.19—	To Copp, Clark & Co., for certificates...	124 18	
23—	" Lash & Co., for testimonial to M. W. Bro. Seymour....	400 00	
June23—	" Buntin, Gilles & Co., for paper......	175 50	
28—	" Grand Secretary, for quarter's salary.	400 00	
July 8—	" Lawson, McCulloch & Co., for rent..	60 00	
16—	" For expenses B. of G. P.	1,013 20	
—	" "	130 50	
—	" transferred to Benevolence current ac't	3,000 00	
Aug. 5—	" Deputy Grand Master, for incidentals	10 00	
—	" T. & R. White, for printing.........	17 50	
—	" the Grand Master, for travelling ex's.	500 00	
—	" " " incidentals...	9 50	
—	" the Grand Secretary, for incidentals..	100 00	
—	" " "	109 31	
—	" " " for assistance in his office	325 00	
—	" the Grand Secretary, for expenses attending Board.......	30 66	
8—	" Copp, Clark & Co., for certificates...	165 75	
—	" Lawson, McCulloch & Co., printing.	400 00	
—	" Buntin, Gillies & Co, for stationery.	131 00	
—	" Bro. A. L. Petrie, proportion Chicago fund................	19 33	
—	" Bro. A.K. Boswell, preportion Chicago fund............	182 73	
11—	" "	169 61	

GENERAL FUND.—(CONTINUED.)

1873.		$	cts.
Aug 13—	" P. J. Brown, proportion Chicago fund.	34	84
15—	" Lash & Co. for repairing regalia ..	50	00
23—	" Bro. Robertson, F. Correspondence..	50	00
Oct. 6—	" Grand Master, half-yearly allowance.	250	00
8—	" " Secretary, for quarter's salary.	400	00
24—	" " " assistance in his office..	162	00
874.			
Jan. 2—	" " " " ..	161	00
—	" " " quarter's salary......	400	00
—	" " " office rent.........	60	00
—	" Wm. Bruce, for engrossing warrants.	12	00
—	" To balance down............	30,267	90
	Total............	$43,520	55

1873.		$	cts.
	By amount brought forward......	43,520	55
	Total................	$43,520	55
	By Balance due G. Lodge on this acc't.	$30,267	90

E. F.

SIMCOE, 2nd January, 1874.

HENRY GROFF, GRAND TREASURER.

DR.   The Grand Lodge of A. F. & A. M. Masons of Canada in account with the Canadian Bank of Commerce, Simcoe.   CR.

1873.		$	cts.
June 28—	To Cash Payments as per Cheques....	$25,265	55
	Balance......................	11,725	24

1873.		$	cts.
Jan. 3—	By Balance per account............	$8,214	31
21—	" deposit per H. Groff, G. Treasurer...	1,500	00
29—	" " "	500	00
Feb. 4—	" " "	500	00
Mar. 10—	" " "	600	00
21—	" " "	300	00
Apr. 2—	" " "	500	00

				CR.
May	3—	"		720 00
	26—	"		500 00
June	3—	"		250 50
	12—	"		600 00
	23—	"		300 00
	28—	"		700 00
	30—	" Interest calculated on daily balances, at 5 per cent.....		219 50
July	2—	" deposit per H. Groff, G. Treasurer...		1,539 08
	——	"		48 00
				$16,990 79

1873.
July 2.—By Balance to new account........$11,725 21

J. COWAN,
Ledger Keeper.

$16,990 79

E. E.

CANADIAN BANK OF COMMERCE,
SIMCOE, 2nd July, 1873.

DR.   The Grand Lodge of A. F. & A. M. Masons of Canada in account with the Canadian Bank of Commerce, Simcoe.   CR.

			$	cts.				$	cts.
1874.					1873.				
Jan.	3—To Cash Payments, as per Cheques..		8,369	96	July	3—By Balance per account.......		11,725	24
	Balance......		10,601	81		— " deposit per H. Groff, G. Treasurer...		2,500	00
					Sept.	6— "		800	00
					Oct.	13— "		720	00
						24— "		162	00
					Nov.	8— "		250	00
					Dec.	26— "		600	00
	To amount carried forward $18,971 77					By amount carried forward......$16,757 24			

ACCOUNT WITH BANK OF COMMERCE.—CONTINUED.

		$	cts.				$	cts.
1874.					**1873.**			
To amount brought forward.....		18,971	77		By amount brought forward....		16,757	24
					30— " deposit per H. Groff, G. Treasurer...		49	00
					31— " " "		800	00
					— " Interest calculated on daily balances at 5 per cent.		235	12
					1874.			
					Jan. 2— " deposit per H. Groff, G. Treasurer...		400	00
					3— " " "		731	41
					Total..............		$18,971	77
					Deduct Cheques as above...........		8,369	96
		$18,971	77		By Balance due G. Lodge......		$10,601	81

CANADIAN BANK OF COMMERCE, }
SIMCOE, 3rd Jan., 1874.

E. E.

FUND OF BENEVOLENCE.—CURRENT ACCOUNT.

The Grand Lodge of Ancient Free and Accepted Masons of Canada in account with HENRY GROFF, Grand Treasurer.

DR.		$	cts.				$	cts.	CR.
1873.					**1873.**				
To paid the President's orders, viz.:					Jan. 2— " By Balance as per account audited..		1,357	34	
Feb. 17— " Mrs. C............		20	00		April 3— " 6 months' Interest on $24,000 Do.				
28— " Montreal Board of Relief....		50	00		" 6 per cent. Stock.......		720	00	
Mar. 1— " Bro. M............		25	00		May 3— " 6 months' Interest on $10,000 Do.				
3— " " R............		30	00		" 5 per cent. Stock.......		250	00	

Date	Description	Amount
3—	" Mrs. C.	20 00
3—	" London Board of Relief	40 00
3—	" Mrs. K.	20 00
3—	" Bro. S.	20 00
5—	" " T.	25 00
5—	" Mrs. A.	25 00
5—	" Toronto Board of Relief	50 00
5—	" Mrs. H.	20 00
5—	" " D.	20 00
5—	" Bro. M.	20 00
5—	" " B.	25 00
5—	" Mrs. T.	25 00
5—	" " G.	20 00
7—	" " B.	60 00
8—	" Bro. T.	40 00
8—	" Hamilton Board of Relief	40 00
8—	" Bro. S.	40 00
8—	" " I.	40 00
8—	" " W.	35 00
13—	" Mrs. G.	50 00
15—	" Kingston Board of Relief	25 00
15—	" Mrs. C.	20 00
15—	" " T.	20 00
19—	" " J.	30 00
	" " S.	25 00
	" " M.	25 00
20—	" Toronto Board of Relief	
	" "	
22—	" Mrs. I.	
—	" " II.	
24—	" Bro. C.	
31—	" Mrs. McD.	

Date	Description	Amount
June 30—	" 6 months' Interest on Middlesex Debentures, $1,000	48 00
30—	" Interest on Bank account	219 50
July 24—	" General Fund	3,000 00
Oct. 13—	" 6 months' Interest on $24,000 Do. Stock	720 00
Nov. 7—	" 6 months' Interest on $10,000 Do Stock...	250 00
Dec. 31—	" 6 months' Interest on Middlesex Debentures, $1,600	48 00
31—	" Interest on Bank account	235 12

9

FUND OF BENEVOLENCE.—(Continued.)

1873.		$	cts.
Mar.31—	" Miss P............		25 00
April 1—	" Mrs. F............		25 00
7—	" " B............		20 00
15—	" Ottawa Board of Relief....		40 00
17—	" Mrs. B............		25 00
—	" " C............		20 00
—	" Orphans of Bro. B......		20 00
—	" Mrs. W............		30 00
June 9—	" " S............		30 00
—	" " F............		25 00
Aug. 6—	" Bro. M............		25 00
8—	" " K............		25 00
—	" Mrs. W............		30 00
—	" " H............		40 00
—	" Harris Lodge, No. 216....		100 00
9—	" Montreal Board of Relief....		40 00
—	" Bro. T............		35 00
—	" Mrs. G............		20 00
—	" Bro. E............		30 00
—	" Mrs. G............		25 00
—	" " S............		25 00
—	" " G............		25 00
—	" " S............		30 00
—	" " B............		40 00
11—	" Bro. C............		50 00
—	" Mrs. F............		50 00
—	" Great Western Lodge, No. 47....		30 00
—	" Bro. S............		

Date	Name	Amount
	" Mrs. N	20 00
	" Bro. K	40 00
13	" Hamilton Board of Relief	100 00
	" Mrs. Q	20 00
	" " G	25 00
	" " T	20 00
	" " W	40 00
	" " B	40 00
	" " DeG	100 00
13	" Bro. T	25 00
	" Mrs. S	50 00
	" " C	25 00
14	" Bro. M	20 00
	" Kingston Board of Relief	50 00
	" Bro. G	50 00
	" Orphans of Bro. T	25 00
	" Mrs. B	20 00
	" Bro. S	25 00
15	" Mrs. C	20 00
	" " G	30 00
	" " W	40 00
	" " OC	20 00
	" " McC	20 00
	" London Board of Relief	100 00
18	" Mrs. B	20 00
21	" " D	20 00
	" " S	20 00
Aug11	" Bro. M	25 00
22	" Toronto Board of Relief	200 00
	" Mrs. McI	25 00

FUND OF BENEVOLENCE.—(CONTINUED.)

1873.			$	cts.
Aug. 22	"	K..........	30	00
"	"	P..........	20	00
"	"	G..........	30	00
"	"	Bro. M..........	20	00
"	"	B..........	20	00
"	"	Mrs. D..........	20	00
"	"	H..........	20	00
"	"	O..........	20	00
"	"	K..........	25	00
"	"	G..........	25	00
"	"	S..........	40	00
26	"	Bro. I..........	20	00
27	"	Mrs. Q..........	30	00
28	"	B..........	50	00
30	"	G..........	30	00
"	"	McD..........	20	00
"	"	C..........	25	00
"	"	C..........	30	00
"	"	B..........	25	00
"	"	Bro. R..........	25	00
Sept. 1	"	DcG..........	25	00
"	"	Mrs. L..........	30	00
4	"	W..........	25	00
4	"	J..........	25	00
5	"	B..........	25	00
9	"	J..........	25	00
"	"	M..........	20	00

Date	Recipient	Amount	
Sept 12—	" T..............	20 00	
16—	" R..............	50 00	
15—	" Bro. C...........	50 00	
—	" M..............	40 00	
—	" Mrs. G...........	30 00	
—	" C..............	25 00	
—	" S..............	30 00	
—	" C..............	20 00	
—	" C..............	25 00	
—	" McD..............	40 00	
—	" Miss P...........	25 00	
—	" Mrs. H...........	20 00	
—	" A..............	20 00	
—	" Orphans of late Bro. I'.....	30 00	
—	" Mrs. W...........	20 00	
30—	" Shuniah Lodge.......	50 00	
Oct. 8—	" Winnipeg Board of Relief....	50 00	
—	" Mrs. J...........	50 00	
13—	" E..............	25 00	
24—	" Bro. H...........	30 00	
Nov 11—	" Mrs. B...........	40 00	
—	" Bro. G...........	20 00	
—	" Mrs. H...........	30 00	
Dec.23—	" S..............	20 00	
	Balance..............	2,207 96	
		$6,847 96	

1874.
Jan. 2.—By Balance due G. Lodge on this account. $2,207 96

HENRY GROFF, GRAND TREASURER.

$6,847 96

E. E.

SIMCOE, 2nd January, 1874.

RETURNS OF SUBORDINATE LODGES, RENDERED 24TH JUNE, 1874.

Lodges marked (*) hold their Installation of Officers on the Festival of St. John the Evangelist: all others on that of St. John the Baptist.

NO.	LODGE.	WHERE HELD.	NIGHT OF MEETING.		W. MASTER.	SECRETARY.
2	Niagara	Niagara	Wed'day on or before full moon every mth.		Robt. Shearer	Hy. Woodington
3	The Anc't St. John's	Kingston	First Thursday	"	Jas. A. Henderson	I. J. Christie
5	*Sussex	Brockville	Wednesday on or before full moon.	"	Thos. Wilkinson	Alex. Stewart
6	Barton	Hamilton	Second Wednesday	"	Chas. Davidson	John Mowat
7	Union	Grimsby	Thursday on or before full month.	"	Jos. Chambers	John A. Nelles
9	*Union	Napanee	Friday on or before full moon.	"	H. I. Geddes	J. H. W. Bedford
10	*Norfolk	Simcoe	Tuesday on or before full moon.	"	Robt. Rochester	A. J. Donly
11	*Moira	Belleville	Wednesday on or before full moon	"	S. S. Lazier	R. R. Lloyd
14	*True Briton's	Perth	First Monday.	"	J. F. Kennedy	Robt. Miller
15	St. George's	St. Catharines	Tuesday on or before full moon.	"	Robert Kane	Sam. A. Dougan
16	*St. Andrew's	Toronto	Second Tuesday.	"	N. G. Bigelow	Jas. S. Lovell
17	St. John's	Cobourg	Monday on or before full moon.	"	George Pringle	Robt. C. Bruce
18	*Prince Edward	Picton	Thursday on or before full moon.	"	John M. Platt	Bela Johnson
20	*St. John's	London	Second Tuesday	"	R. Luxton	M. D. Dawson
22	*King Solomon's	Toronto	Second Thursday	"	Thos. Langton	John Campbell
23	Richmond	Richm'nd Hill	Monday on or before full moon	"	Jas. McConnell	Thos. Newton
24	St Francis	Smith's Falls	Friday on or before full moon	"	D. A. Ferguson	Stewart Mong.
25	*Ionic	Toronto	First Tuesday.	"	W. D. Otter	J. G. Robinson
26	*Ontario	Port Hope	Third Thursday.	"	E. Peplow, Jr.	Geo. W. Lambert
27	*Strict Observance	Hamilton	Third Tuesday.	"	F. R. Despard	R. L. Gunn
28	*Mount Zion	Kemptville	Wednesday before full moon.	"	Rich. Chambers	A. McPherson
29	*United	Brighton	Thursday on or before full moon.	"	Ira B. Thayer	W. A. Mabew
30	*Composite	Whitby	First Thursday	"	Geo. Hopkins	Robt. Willis
31	*Jerusalem	Bowmanville	Wednesday on or before full moon.	"	Thomas Bassett	Wm. McKay
32	*Amity	Dunnville	Wednesday on or after full moon.	"	Wm. Brand	Wm. Fry

No.	Lodge	Place	Meeting		Officer	Officer
33	•Goderich	Goderich	First Wednesday	"	John R. Millar	Wm. Dickson
24	•Thistle	Amherstb'rgh	Tuesday before full moon	"	Chas. W. Thomas	G. Middleditch
35	St. John's	Cayuga	Thursday on or after full moon	"	Duncan Cameron	Thos. Bridger
36	Welland	Fenthill	Thursday on or before full moon	"	David W. Horton	S. C. Howey
37	•King Hiram	Ingersoll	Tuesday on or before full moon	"	Chas. H. Slawson	L. Y. Chadwick
38	•Trent	Trenton	Tuesday before full moon	"	Henry W. Day	Wm. Little
39	•Mount Zion	Brooklin	Tuesday on or before full noon	"	Chas. H Sweetapple	P. B. Browne
40	•St. John's	Hamilton	Third Thursday	"	Donald McPhie	Joseph Kneeshaw
41	•St. George's	Kingsville	Thursday on or before full moon	"	E. Allworth	Lewis Mulott
42	•St. George's	London	First Wednesday	"	Wm. Thornton	Fred. J. Hood
43	King Solomon's	Woodstock	Tuesday on or before full moon	"	R. M. Revell	Samuel Stephens
44	•St. Thomas	St. Thomas	First Thursday	"	John Midgley	J. J. Bourne
45	•Brant	Brantford	Tuesday on or before full moon	"	John Bishop	George Lindlay
46	•Wellington	Chatham	First Monday	"	Wm. Young	G. F. Horsford
47	•Great Western	Windsor	Thursday on or before full moon	"	A. Whittaker	Jas. C. Guillot
48	•Madoc	Madoc	Tuesday on or before full moon	"	J. S. Loomis	James O'Hara, Jr
50	•Consecon	Consecon	Friday on or before full moon	"	A. G. Whittier	James E. Glenn
51	•Corinthian	Grahamville	Tuesday on or before full moon	"	Joseph Figg	Alex. F. Campbell
52	Dalhousie	Ottawa	First Tuesday	"	James Egleson	W. C. MacAgy
54	•Vaughan	Maple	Tuesday on or before full moon	"	George A. Enony	H. W. Bolitho
55	•Merrickville	Merrickville	Tuesday after full moon	"	William Weir	Alf. W. Bottom
56	Victoria	Sarnia	Tuesday on or before full moon	"	James Gowans	Charles Fisher
57	•Harmony	Binbrook	Monday after full moon	"	Jas. Russell	John Brown, jr
58	•Doric	Ottawa	First Wednesday	"	Chas. Esplin	D. P. Williams
59	•Corinthian	Ottawa	Third Thursday	"	Robert Watson	Joseph Potts
61	•Acacia	Hamilton	Fourth Friday	"	John H. Tilden	James Widger
62	•St. Andrew's	Caledonia	Wednesday on or before full moon	"	Alex. J. Nelles	H. Park
63	•St. John's	CarletonPlace	Wednesday on or before full moon	"	David McNab	Wm. Carley
64	•Kilwinning	London	Third Thursday	"	John Ferguson	H. A. Baxter
65	•Rehoboam	Toronto	First Thursday	"	James E, Day	Thos. J. McClelland
66	•Durham	Newcastle	Tuesday on or before full moon	"	W. F. Lockhart	J. P. Lovekin, jr
68	•St. John's,	Ingersoll	Thursday on or before full moon	"	Hugh Kerr	Wm. Ewart

RETURNS OF SUBORDINATE LODGES.—[CONTINUED.]

NO.	LODGE	WHERE HELD.	NIGHT OF MEETING.	W. MASTER.	SECRETARY.
69	Stirling	Stirling	Thursday after the full moon..each month	Albert Chard	John S. Black
72	Alma	Galt	Thursday on or before full moon. "	John Cavers	Jas. Hetherington
73	*St. James'	St. Mary's	Fist monday "	D. S. Rupert	A. Carman
74	*St. James'	Maitland	Monday nearest full moon "	John Chapman	Thomas Fleming
75	St. John's	Toronto	First Monday "	Seymour Porter	John Eastwood, jr.
76	*Oxford	Woodstock	Second Wednesday "	C. L. Beard	Joseph Rippon
77	*Faithful Brethren	Lindsay	First Thursday "	S. C. Wood	H. Gladman
78	*King Hiram	Tilsonburg	Wednesday on or before full moon "	A. H. Brown	John Secord
79	*Simcoe	Bradford	Thursday after the full moon "	Wm. H. Porter	J. K. Stevenson
80	Albion	Newbury	First Tuesday "	Geo. Mansfield	Joseph Mills
81	*St. John's	Mt. Brydges	Tuesday on or before full moon. "	Geo. Billington	E. Handy
82	*St. John's	Paris	Tuesday on or before full moon. "	P. Buckley	Jas. Inckland
83	*Beaver	Strathroy	Friday on or after full moon "	Wr. W. Hoare	Chales Mole
84	*Clinton	Clinton	Friday on or after full moon "	D. McG Malloch	John Bansford
85	Rising Sun	Farmersville	Thursday nearest the full moon "	J. B. Saunders	Jas. H. Blackburn
86	*Wilson	Toronto	Third Tuesday "	George C. Moore	Chas. Callighen
87	Markham Union	Markham	Friday on or before full moon "	George Godfrey	Jas. S. Wilson
88	St. George's	Owen Sound	Wednesday on or before full moon "	Thomas Scott	W. Boyd Stephens
90	*Manito	Collingwood	Wednesday on or after full moon. "	John Nettleton	Henry Nolan
91	*Colborne	Colborne	Friday on or before full moon "	J. J. Campbell	George Keyes
92	*Cataraqui	Kingston	Second Wednesday "	Henry S. Minnes	F. Rowland
93	*Northern Light	Kincardine	First Thursday "	Jas. A. Macpherson	Jas. Le Gear
94	*St. Mark's	Port Stanley	Second Tuesday "	Thomas Robinson	W. H. Edgcombe
95	*Ridout	Otterville	Thursday on or before full moon. "	W. F. Kay	J. E. Clark
96	*Corinthian	Barrie	Thursday on or before full moon. "	Robert King	Wm. Mansoll

No.	Lodge	Location	Meeting		Officer	Officer
57	•Sharon	Sharon	Tuesday on or before full moon	"	Jamse Kavanagh	William Dodds
98	True Blue	Albion	Friday on or before full moon	"	George Watson	James Neeley
99	•Tuscan	Newmarket	Second Wednesday	"	A. M. Hood	David W. Mayes
100	Valley	Dundas	Friday on or before full moon	"	Duncan McMillan	John A. Fisher
101	•Corinthian	Peterboro'	Wednesday after full moon	"	John J. Lundy	Robt. W. Smylie
103	•Maple Leaf	St. Catharines	Thursday on or after full moon	"	J. B. Somerset	Edward Gardiner
104	St. John's	Norwichville	Wednesday after the full moon	"	Egbert C. McLees	William Topham
105	St. Mark's	Drum'ndville	Tuesday on or before full moon	"	John Wills	M. B. Morris
106	•Burford	Burford	Wednesday on or before full moon	"	W. G. Nelles	W. B. Underhill
107	St. Paul's	Lambeth	Second Wednesday	"	J. M. Banghart	A. E. Griffith
108	Blenheim	Drumbo	Wednesday on or before full moon	"	Robert Kelly	J. G. Terryberry
109	•Albion	Harrowsmith	Friday on or before full moon	"	Joseph Purdy	James Cooke
110	•Central	Prescott	First Tuesday	"	John Satchell	J. J. French
111	•Morpeth	Ridgetown	Second Thursday	"	Ed. H. Tiffany	D. H. Bedford
112	Maitland	Goderich	Second Tuesday	"	Ed. Campaigne	P. F. Walker
113	•Wilson	Waterford	Wednesday on or before full moon	"	B. L. Chipman	David Wilson
114	•Hope	Port Hope	First Thursday	"	Adam Purslow	Wm. Gothwaite
115	•Ivy	Beamsville	Tuesday on or after full moon	"	George Walker	James Allan
116	•Cassia	Widder	Monday on or before full moon	"	H. L. Morphy	Robert F. Manly
118	Union	Schomberg	Monday on before full moon	"	A. Armstrong, jr	James S. Hughes
119	•Maple Leaf	Bath	Monday before full moon	"	Thos. Aishton	John Belfour
120	Warren	Fingal	Second Thursday	"	James Miller	George A. Gray
121	•Doric	Brantford	Friday on or before full moon	"	Jas. W. Digby	Fred. T. Wilkes
122	•Renfrew	Renfrew	First Friday	"	John C. Wright	James Watt
123	•The Belleville	Belleville	First Thursday	"	George D. Dickson	E. L. Aunger
125	•Cornwall	Cornwall	First Tuesday	"	John McIntyre	Charles Poole
126	•Golden Rule	Campbells f'd	Tuesday on or after full moon	"	Hugh O'Neil	Robert Linwoodie
127	Franck	Frankfort	Monday before full moon	"	Samuel Gunter	Tobias Alley
128	•Pembroke	Pembroke	First Tuesday	"	Andrew Irving, jr	Robert G. Scott
129	The Rising Sun	Aurora	Friday on or after full moon	"	F. W. Strange	J. Anderson
131	St. Lawrence	Southampton	Second Tuesday	"	Andrew Lindsay	John Eastwood
133	•Lebanon Forest	Exeter	Monday on or before full moon	"	George Eacrett	M. Eacrett

RETURNS OF SUBORDINATE LODGES.—[CONTINUED.]

NO.	LODGE.	WHERE HELD.	NIGHT OF MEETING.	W. MASTER.	SECRETARY.
135	*St. Clair	Milton	Thursday on or before full moon each mth.	John D. Matheson	Wm. Robson.
136	Richardson	Stouffville	Wednesday on or before full moon	G. R. Vanzant	Hiram Johnson.
137	*Pythagoras	Meaford	Friday on or after full moon	R. R. Fulton	S. D. McCallum.
139	Lebanon	Oshawa	Second Tuesday	Martin Gilbranson	John Boyd.
140	*Malahide	Aylmer	Wednesday on or after full moon	S. S. Clutton	John Weisbhrod.
141	*Tudor	Mitchell	Tuesday or or before full moon	Thomas Matheson	Thomas Babb.
142	*Excelsior	Morrisburgh	Thursday on or before full moon	A. G. Macdonell	Wm. Carlyle.
143	*Friendly Brother's	Iroquois	Wednesday before full moon	David Fink	John N. Tuttle.
144	*Tecumseh	Stratford	First Thursday	C. T. Campbell	Isaac S. Griswold.
145	J. B. Hall	Millbrook	Second Thursday	J. W. Wallace	George Knowlson.
146	*Prince of Wales	Newburgh	Wednesday before full moon	A. K. Aylsworth	Wm. Maitland.
147	Mississippi	Almonte	Friday on or before the full moon	Jason H. Thrall	Thomas Coulter.
148	*Civil Service	Ottawa	Second Tuesday	N. W. McLean	Colin Campbell.
149	*Erie	Port Dover	Monday on be-fore full moon	H. H. Sovereign	A. F. Turnbull.
150	*Hastings	Hastings	Thursday on or before full moon	Wm. M. Orr	H. Morton.
151	The Grand River	Berlin	Tuesday on or before full moon	Wm. Hendry	Alexander Roy.
153	*Burns	Wyoming	Thursday on or before full moon	W. B. Collins	H. G. Taylor.
154	*Irving	Lucan	Thursday on or before full moon	James Sutton	William Porte.
155	*Peterborough	Peterboro'	First Friday	James Millar	D. D. Galletly.
156	*York	Eglinton	Friday on or before full moon	J. F. Ellis	John McCarter.
157	Simpson	Newboro'	Tuesday on or after full moon	Robert H. Preston	Levi S. Lewis.
158	*Alexandra	Oil Springs	Thursday on or after full moon	John McCann	John Q. Braund.
159	*Goodwood	Richmond	First Tuesday	John McLaren	James R. Hill.
161	*Percy	Warkworth	Wednesday before full moon	I. Humphries	George H. Boyce.
162	Forest	Wroxeter	Monday on or before full moon	S. B. Spaile	George Gibson.

No.	Lodge	Town	Meeting		
164	*Star in the East	Wellington	Tuesday on or before full moon	Joseph R. Ruttan	Joseph Stephenson
165	*Burlington	Wel'n Square	Wednesday on or before full moon	Robert Halson	Freder.ck Bray
166	*Wentworth	Stoney Creek	Monday on or before full moon	George Slingerland	Alva G Jones
168	*Merritt	Welland	Monday on or before full moon	J. H. Burgar	W. E. Burgar
169	*Macnab	Pt. Colborne	Tuesday on or before full moon	Thomas J. O'Neil	James A. Griffith
170	*Britannia	Seaforth	Monday on or before full moon	H. L. Vercoe	Wm. Ballantyne
171	*Prince of Wales	Iona	Friday on or before full moon	A. A. Boston	John Edgecombe
172	*Ayr	Ayr	Tuesday on or before full moon	Alex H. Kay	Wm. Pringle
174	*Walsingham	Port Rowan	First Thursday	John Hudson	Wm. Ross
176	Spartan	Sparta	Second Friday	Wm. B. Cole	John Callard
177	The Builders'	Ottawa	Friday on or before full moon	E. B. Butterworth	Wm Rea
178	*Plattsville	Plattsville	Wednesday on or before full moon	George Risk	Robt. J. Bourchier
179	*Bothwell	Bothwell	First Tuesday	N. H. Avery	P. L. Graham
180	*Speed	Guelph	Tuesday on or before full moon	Philip Bish	Joseph Minnuack
181	*Oriental	Port Burwell	Friday on or before full moon	James E. Deacon	M. G Barwell
183	*Prince Albert	Port Perry	Thursday on or before full moon	Abner Hurd	H. S. Campbell
184	*Old Light	Lucknow	Monday on or before full moon	Robert L. Weir	Robert L. Hunter
185	*Enniskillen	York	Wednesday on or before full moon	James VanBridger	George W. Murton
186	*Plantagenet	Plantagenet	Monday on or before full moon	Peter D. Davis	W. A. Chamberlain
199	*Filius Vidue	Adolphust'wn	Wednesday on or before full moon	J. B. Campbell	E. L. Sil's
190	Belmonte	Belmonte	Friday on or before full moon	Thomas S. Atkinson	F. W. Raikes
192	*Orillia	Orillia	First Monday	H. F. Teeter	John Perry
193	*Scotland	Scotland	Monday on or before full moon	John Highner	W. A. McLin
194	*Petrolia	Petrolia	Second Wednesday	Edw. de La Hooke	W. E. Paine
195	The Tuscan	London	First Monday	James G. Cranston	Donald Currie
196	*Madawaska	Arnprior	Thursday on or before full moon	James G. Cooper	A. Garrioch
197	*Saugeen	Walkerton	Second Tuesday		H. Davidson
198	*White Oak	Oakville	Tuesday on or before full moon	John McLaren	John McCorkindale
200	St. Alban's	Mount Forest	Friday on or before full moon	John Ormiston	Thomas G. Smith
201	*Leeds	Gananoque	Tuesday on or before full moon	John McDonald	Francis M. Baker
203	Irvine	Elora	Friday before full moon	Otto Pressprich	C. E. Perry
205	New Dominion	New Hamb'g	Monday on or after full moon		Wm. Millar

RETURN OF SUBORDINATE LODGES.—[CONTINUED.]

NO.	LODGE	WHERE HELD	NIGHT OF MEETING	W. MASTER	SECRETARY
206	*North Gower..	North Gower.	First Monday...........each month	Thomas Conley.	James Lindsay...
207	*Lancaster	Lancaster....	Second Wednesday.... "	Alex. Falkner....	D. McIntyre....
209a	*St. John's......	London......	Third Thursday.... "	Duncan McPhail...	John Burnett....
209	Evergreen	Lanark......	First Tuesday.... "	David Munro	Robt. Pollock....
210	*Hawkesbury	Hawkesbury.	First Wednesday.... "	John R. Legget	Geo. Manson....
212	*Elysian......	Garden Isl'nd	First Monday.... "	Geo. F. Charles..	Robt. Naucollas..
213	*Dominion......	Ridgeway...	Wednesday on or before full moon... "	John N. Fulmer...	A. R. Hardison...
214	*Craig......	Ailsa Craig.	Monday on or after full moon.... "	Richard Sands....	Wm. Hooper......
215	Lake.........	Ameliasburg.	Monday on or before full moon.. "	Edward Roblin....	W. A. Bertson...
216	*Harris........	Orangeville..	Tuesday on or before full moon.. "	Thos. G. Greet...	Thos J. Decatur..
217	*Frederick	Delhi.........	Monday on or before full moon.. "	Luke Cook......	Wm. Tilley......
218	*Stevenson	Toronto......	Second Monday...... "	Geo. Ghanter....	D. Roche......
219	*Credit......	Georgetown	Friday on or before full moon... "	John R. Barber..	Wm. Freeman
220	*Zeredatha......	Uxbridge	Monday on or before full moon. "	John Summerville.	Jas. J. Hillary..
221	*Mountain.....	Thorold......	Wednesday on or before full moon "	Wm. Orr Cowan..	Wm. T. Fish..
222	*Marmora......	Marmora.....	Tuesday before full moon...... "	Thos. Warren....	David Fitchett..
223	*Norwood......	Norwood	Tuesday on or before full moon. "	John A. Butterfield.	S. P. Ford ....
224	*Zurich......	Zurich.....	Friday on or before full moon... "	Wm Buchanan	Robt. Brown....
225	*Bernard......	Listowel	Wednesday on or before full moon "	John Nichol	James Trail....
228	*Prince Arthur....	Odessa.....	Monday after full moon....... "	A. P. Booth......	John D. D. Amey'
229	*Ionic......	Brampton...	Wednesday on or before full moon "	R. Cochrane.....	Jas. Fletcher....
220	*Kerr.....	Bell Ewart.	Tuesday on or before full moon. "	G. M. Simpson.	H. Belfry......
231	Lodge of Fidelity..	Ottawa......	Second Wednesday...... "	Wm. Rea......	A. G. McCormick..
232	*Cameron	Wallacetown	Wednesday on or before full moon "	J. W. Luton.....	Geo. Duncan....
233	*Doric......	Park Hill....	Tuesday on or before full moon. "	Wm. Caw........	Daniel Eccles....

No.	Name	Location	Meeting		Officers	
234	*Beaver	Clarksburg	Tuesday on or before full moon.	"	Robert H. Hunt	Joseph Rorke
235	Aldworth	Paisley	Friday on or before full moon	"	P. McLaren	James C. Gibson
236	*Manitoba	Bondhead	Tuesday on or after full mo.n	"	W. C. Law	Ira Doan
237	Vienna	Vienna	Friday on or before full moon	"	John Teal	John Dean
238	Havelock	Watford	Tuesday before full moon	"	George Shirley	Daniel McLachlan
239	Tweed	Tweed	Friday on or before full moon	"	George Easterbrooke	William Wray
240	*Prince Rupert's	Winnipeg, M.	Third Tuesday	"	H. T. Champion	John Macdonnell
241	*Quinte	Shannonville	Tuesday after full moon	"	H. P. Rether	R. A. Fullerton
242	*Macoy	Escott Front	Monday on or before full moon	"	Reuben Fields	Michael Conley
243	*St. George	St George	Thursday on or before full moon	"	E. E. Kitchen	R. G. Lawrason
244	*Lisgar	Mapleton, M	First Monday	"	Thomas Bunn	David Young
245	Tecumseh	Thamesville	Second Tuesday	"	B. L. Chipman	Wm. L. Judson
247	*Ashlar	Yorkville	Fourth Tuesday	"	W. E. Pridham	Wm. S. Robinson
248	Eureka	Pakenham	Wednesday on or after ful 1 moon	"	John Riddell	John Cowan
249	*Caledonian	Angus	Thursday on or after full moon	"	John McKimmie	Robert Wade
250	Thistle	Embro	Second Tuesday	"	John Ross	James Munro
252	*The International	N Pembina, M	Second Tuesday	"	Fred. T. Bradley	
253	*Minden	Kingston	First Monday	"	Stntel Woods	G. W. Andrews
254	Clifton	Clifton	Thursday on or before full moon	"	Robert Robinson	G. V. Le Vaux
255	Sydenham	Dresden	Wednesday on or after full moon	"	Harvey Morris	Sibree Clarke
256	*Farran's Point	Farran sPoint	First Wednesday	"	C. A. Summers	A. Archibald
257	Galt	Galt	Tuesday on or before full moon	"	James Patterson	John Shupe
258	Guelph	Guelph	Third Wednesday	"	A. C. Chadwick	W. J. Paterson
259	*Springfield	Springfield	Monday on or before full moon	"	J. B. Mills	E. Burnham
260	*Washington	Petrolia	First Tuesday	"	Wm. Stevenson	Thomas Callan
261	*Oak Branch	Innerkip	Thursday on or before full moon	"	E. W. Town	George Bates
262	*Harriston	Harriston	Monday on or after full moon	"	Alexander Irvine	T. Jones
263	*Forest	Forest	Wednesday on or before full moon	"	H. J. Nash	Wm. A. Jamieson
264	*Chaudiere	Ottawa	Thursday on or after full moon	"	W. H. Timbers	John C. Woods
265	Patterson	Thornhill	Thursday on or before full moon	"	W. C. Patterson	C. E. Jakeway
266	*Northern Light	Stayner	Tuesday before full moon	"	Thomas H. George	Charles Dunlop
267	*Parthenon	Chatham	First Wednesday	"	H. J. Erls	

RETURNS OF SUBORDINATE LODGES.- [CONTINUED]

NO.	LODGE.	WHERE HELD.	NIGHT OF MEETING.	W. MASTER.	SECRETARY.
268	*Verulam........	Bobcaygeon..	First Monday........... each month	John Kennedy.....	J. G. Edwards.....
269	Broughan Union .	Brougham....	Wednesday after full moon..... "	D. W. Ferrier......	Peter McIntyre....
270	*Cedar...........	Oshawa.....	Fourth Tuesday......... "	Philip Taylor.....	C. W. Smith......
271	Wellington	Erin.........	Wednesday on or before full moon "	James Brodly. ..	Hy. McNaughton..
272	Seymour	Ancaster	Wednesday on or before full moon "	Hy. Richardson...	Wm. Algier.......
274	*Kent.......	Blenheim....	Third Monday...... "	Lewis Kinnie.....	Robert H. Hall....
276	Teeswater......	Teeswater...	Friday on or before full meon... "	H. B. O'Connor...	John Gillies......
277	Seymour.......	Pt. Dalhousie	Wednesday on or before full moon "	Humphrey Julian	John Green.......
278	*Mystic........	Roslin.......	Thursday before full moon..... "	Edison B. Fralick.	P. G. Duncan.....
279	New Hope.....	Hespeler.....	Wednesday on or before full moon "	Archie Brydon....	Edward Musgrove.
280	Mount Sinai...	Napanee.....	First Thursday......... "	Fred. Richardson..	W. Fullerton.....
281	Thorne........	Holland Ld'g	First Tuesday......... "	Alex. Williams ...	David S. Ross.....
282	Lorne.........	Glencoe....	Thursday on or before full moon "	William Hayden..	John W. Campbell
283	*Eureka......	Belleville...	First Wednesday after full moon. "	H. H. Henderson..	J. S. Hurst.......
284	*St. John's.....	Brussels	Tuesday on or before full moon. "	Wm. J. R. Holmes	John Stewart.....
285	Seven Star	Alliston.....	Wednesday on or before full moon "	John Stewart.....	D. J. Greig.......
286	*Wingham.....	Wingham....	Tuesday on or before full moon. "	John E. Tamlyn..	W. E. Bray.......
287	Shuniah.......	Pr. Arthur's L	Tuesday on or before full moon. "	C. C. Forneri	John P. Vigars....
288	*Ancient Landmark.	Winnipeg, M.	Second Monday .... "	John H. Bell	D. Young ....
289	*Doric........	Lobo.......	Thursday on or before full moon "	John D. McLeay..	Joshua Irvine ....
290	*Leamington...	Leamington .	Tuesday on or before full moon. "	E. R. Sheply.....	George A. Morse..
291	*Dufferin	W. Flamboro'	Thursday on or before full moon "	Alfred Jones	R. Miller........
292	*Robertson.....	Nobleton	Wednesday on or before full moon "	James Bowman....	W. Stokes.......
293	*The Roy'l Sol Mother	Jerusalem Pal	First Wednesday..... "	Robert Morris....	
294	*Moore........	Mooretown ..	Thursday on or before full moon "	Jas. A. Sommerville	John Linton .....

No.	Lodge	Place	Meeting		Secretary	Master
295	*Conestogo	Drayton	First Tuesday	"	Charles Hendry	Silas P. Dales
296	*Temple	St. Catharines	First Wednesday	"	L. Leitch	John Henderson
297	Preston	Preston	Friday on or before full moon	"	John Chapman	Carl E. Klotz
299	Victoria	Centreville	Thursday on or before full moon	"	John S. Miller	Robert Henry
300	*Mount Olivet	Thorndale	Tuesday on or before full moon	"	Moffatt Forster	Noble Dickie
301	*Hanover	Hanover	Monday on or before full moon	"	George Landerkin	Wm. H. Colles, jr.
302	St. David's	St. Thomas	Monday on or before full moon	"	Josiah Corlis	H. G. Hunt
303	*Blyth	Blyth	Second Wednesday	"	William Wilson	John Hutchison
304	*Minerva	Victoria	Wednesday on or after full moon	"	Robert King	Ab. Leonard
305	*Humber	Weston	Wednesday on or before full moon	"	Frank W. Forbes	Charles Macmunn
306	Durham	Durham	Tuesday on or before full moon	"	James H. Hunter	Charles I. Grant
307	Arkona	Arkona	Thursday on or before full moon	"	John Dallas	E. Wintemute
308	*Grafton	Grafton	Tuesday on or before full moon	"	Francis Drake	Edward Hayward
309	*Morning Star	Smith's Hill	Second Wednesday	"	John Varcoe	Robert B. Scott
310	Enterprise	Beachburg	First Tuesday	"	George Forbes	H. R. Wiglesworth
311	*Blackwood	Woodbridge	Friday on or before full moon	"	Thos. F. Blackwood	C. H. Dunning
312	*Pnyx	Wallaceburg	Second Wednesday	"	Harvey Morris	Francis J. Sawyer
313	*Clementi	Lakefield	Friday after full moon	"	Robt. Kincaid	
314	*Blair	Palmerston	Friday after full moon	"	Hugh Hyndman	A. Bruce Munson
315	*Clifford	Clifford	Third Monday	"	K. McI. Walton	Ab S. Allan
316	*Doric	Toronto	Second Wednesday	"	R. P. Stephens	Chas. Cullighen
317	*The Hiram	Dundas	Second Tuesday	"	Nathaniel Greening	J. S. Baillie
318	*Wilmot	Baden	Friday on or after full moon	"	John Moran	
U.D.	Hiram	Cneapside	Wednesday on or before full moon	"	Jesse V. Hoover	C Zoeger
U.D.	Chesterville	Chesterville	Monday on or before full moon	"	Wm. Wilson French	
U.D.	North Star	Owen Sound	Wednesday after full moon	"	John Creasor	
U.D.	Alvinston	Alvinston	Tuesday on or after full moon	"	M. Matheson	
U. D.	Temple	Hamilton	Fourth Monday	"	J. M. Gibson	

SUSPENSIONS.—Unmasonic Conduct

No. 72.   *Alma Lodge, Galt, Ont.*
               T. S. Fisher,

No. 97.   *Sharon Lodge, Sharon, Ont.*
               John Dean.

No. 122.   *Renfrew Lodge, Renfrew, Ont.*
               Richard K. Cole.

No. 153.   *Burns Lodge, Wyoming, Ont.*
               J. C. McLauchlin.

No. 184.   *Old Light Lodge, Lucknow, Ont.*
               Wm. F. Read.

No. 205.   *New Dominion Lodge, New Hamburgh, Ont.*
               John Jackson.

No. 237.   *Vienna Lodge, Vienna, Ont.*
               Charles Thornthwaite.

No. 258.   *Guelph Lodge, Guelph, Ont.*
               Herbert F. Tuck.

No. 259.   *Springfield Lodge, Springfield, Ont.*
               Arch. Clunas.

SUSPENSIONS.—Non-payment of Dues.

No. 2.   *Niagara Lodge, Niagara, Ont.*
P. B. Clement, Thomas N. Ball, D. Thorburn, Geo. D. Prest, L. Stockman.

No. 3.   *The Ancient St. John's Lodge, Kingston, Ont.*
Rev. W. B. Moffat, Wm. D. Antrobus, P. T. McCuaig, John J. Linton, Jas. Smith, Jno. Bredon, jr., Rufus Stephens, Rev. William Stephenson.

No. 6.   *Barton Lodge, Hamilton, Ont.*
R. C. Holbrook, Thomas Marsden, Thomas Jeffrey, Charles Cumber, Joseph Craig.

No. 9.   *Union Lodge, Napanee, Ont.*
Robert Boyce, W. S. Detlor, A. N. Carscallan, I. Kinmerley, C. B. Perry, Josh Bowers, Rev. F. Chisholm, John M. Bogart, D. W. Perry, John W. Sixsmith, Thomas Fleming, William Morrison.

No. 10.   *Norfolk Lodge, Simcoe, Ont.*
R. C. Lyons, W. P. Kelly, J. Hanna, W. H. Heally, John Duckman, W. H. Covernton, Charles C. Ritchie.

No. 14.   *True Briton's Lodge, Perth, Ont.*
Robert Moffatt, John Morris.

No. 20.   *St. John's Lodge, London, Ont.*
James Robertson, John Fleming.

No. 22.   *King Solomon's Lodge, Toronto, Ont.*
George B. Douglass, Robert Ware, Wm. H. D. Kennedy,
Gilbert Pearcy.

No. 24.   *St. Francis Lodge, Smith's Falls Ont.*
Arthur Wall.

No. 25.   *Ionic Lodge, Toronto, Ont.*
Walter M. Ross.

No. 29.   *United Lodge, Brighton, Ont.*
Robert Barker, William M. Platt, S. Bulkley, Jas. Stanley.

No. 31.   *Jerusalem Lodge, Bowmanville, Ont.*
Edward Silver.

No. 33.   *Goderich Lodge, Goderich, Ont.*
Alexander Kinnear.

No. 40.   *St. John's Lodge, Hamilton, Ont.*
M. W. Attwood, James F. Egan, James McKay.

No. 42.   *St. George's Lodge, London, Ont.*
Thomas Bennett, A. H. Bailey, T. Babington, J. W. Cryer,
W. H. Code, J. Copeland, J. Law, Wm. Marshall, N. McFee
T. W. Harrison, I. D. R. McLean, John Auld, G. Rossler.

No. 43.   *King Solomon's Lodge, Woodstock, Ont.*
W. H. Bradley, John Hay, John Mitchel, George Oswald,
David S. Ross.

No. 47.   *Great Western Lodge, Windsor, Ont.*
Chris. A. Vetter, Thomas D. Allen.

No. 55.   *Merrickville Lodge, Merrickville, Ont.*
Robert Gwynne, P. Y. Merrick, Adam Lamb.

No. 62.   *St. Andrew's Lodge, Caledonia, Ont.*
Josh Fisher, John McDonald, Wm. Ryan, R. Canfield, Wm
Munroe.

No. 64.   *Kilwinning Lodge, London, Ont.*
Robert Bullen, Charles Cater, W. B. Nichols, J. Elson, J. W.
Scott.

No. 68.   *St. John's Lodge, Ingersoll, Ont.*
J. Whaley, W. J. Piper, Jno. Hetherington, B. Galbraith,
James Tune, J. G. Chown, A. Boyce, S. W. Jacobs, J. B.
Choat, H. Hearn, Geo. Wiseman, Jno. Gayfer, J. B. Crawford,
Thomas C. McKenzie, Hy. Charles, A. McKenzie.

No. 69.   *Stirling Lodge, Stirling, Ont.*
Jas. Heagle, I. Wativer, C. Craige, Wm. Duffy, Jno. Ackers,
F. McManus, Jno. C. Brentnall, A. C. Hinds, A. Shearing,
A. McConaghy, O. Ferguson, C. A. Garrison, P. G. Cheese-
borough, F. Meyers, W. Scott.

10

No. 72.   *Alma Lodge, Galt, Ont.*
T S. Fisher,

No. 75.   *St. John's Lodge, Toronto, Ont.*
Wm. J. Bryan, Daniel Hick, John Simson, Robert G. Trotter,
T. Dill, E. Gledhill, H. G. Rutledge, Wm. J. Taylor.

No. 77.   *Faithful Brethren Lodge, Lindsay, Ont.*
Hy. Fowler, Thomas C. Bartholemew.

No. 81.   *St. John's Lodge, Mt. Brydges, Ont.*
D. A. Campbell, W. A. D. Fraser, L. L. Griffith, John
McLauchlin, E. Rockhey, Robert Tucker.

No. 82.   *St. John's Lodge, Paris, Ont.*
E. L. P. Osler, Wm. McRae, Wm. S. Wilkinson, Robert
Doller, John McLean. T. Millington, Geo. R. Pattrello.

No. 83.   *Beaver Lodge, Strathroy, Ont.*
James Sommerville, W. McLeod, John McBride, Jno. Black,
J. A. Campbell, A. Cameron, D. Ross, Jos. H. Scott.

No. 86.   *Wilson Lodge, Toronto, Ont.*
T. W. Medley, Hy. Burden, A. E. Fairfield, John Parr.

No. 87.   *Markham Union Lodge, Markham, Ont.*
N. Button, James Maclin, George Gilchrist, J. McArdell.

No. 90.   *Manito Lodge, Collingwood, Ont.*
F. Hewson, T. Musgrove, James Cross, Joseph Jardine, W. G.
Patterson.

No. 91.   *Colborne Lodge, Colborne, Ont.*
William Errington, James Black.

No. 95.   *Ridout Lodge, Otterville, Ont.*
William A. McLim, William Miller.

No. 96.   *Corinthian Lodge, Barrie, Ont.*
G. Caswell, E. Beazer, John Patterson, John Barclay, John
Finch, Alex Campbell, Hy. Gilpin.

No. 97.   *Sharon Lodge, Sharon Ont.*
James, S. Hunt, Gideon P. Knight.

No. 104.   *St. John's Lodge, Norwichville, Ont.*
William H. Coker.

No. 106.   *Burford Lodge, Burford, Ont.*
Henry Hipkins, W. H. Serpell.

No. 107.   *St Paul's Lodge, Lambeth, Ont.*
J. M. Crenklaw, C. Bryant, James Davis, J. Fitzallan, J. L.
Baker, T. Scott, C. N. Harris, G. Weir, W. Scott, W. E. Scott,
W. Sumner.

No. 109.   *Albion Lodge, Harrowsmith, Ont.*
George Benheim, John Milmine.

No. 118.   *Union Lodge, Schomberg, Ont.*
William Moore, William Nelson.

No. 119.   *Maple Leaf Lodge, Bath, Ont.*
James Wemp,

No. 121.   *Doric Lodge, Brantford, Ont.*
Robert John Westlake, Hy. Lemmon.

No. 129.   *The Rising Sun Lodge, Aurora, Ont*
Alf. Graham, Thomas G. Ransom, Samuel Harris, James
Fitzgerald, Thomas Armstrong.

No. 136.   *Richardson Lodge, Stouffville, Ont.*
W. Bertram, S. W. Freel, Frederick Chinn, George Pringle,
James Brunskill.

No. 137.   *Pythagoras Lodge, Meaford, Ont.*
S. C. Saunders, Thomas Fields.

No. 141.   *Tudor Lodge, Mitchell, Ont.*
R. J. Widdis.

No. 142.   *Excelsior Lodge, Morrisburg Ont.*
Gavin Moffat, John Allison.

No. 143.   *Friendly Brothers' Lodge, Iroquois, Ont.*
John Patten, Elijah Barber, James Roarke, Mat. McCarty.

No. 144.   *Tecumseh Lodge, Stratford, Ont.*
Peter M. Oronhyatekha, Benj. Schantz, A. R. Kerby.

No. 145.   *J. B. Hall Lodge, Millbrook, Ont.*
William Turner, J. H. Sootheran, Thomas Medd.

No. 150.   *Hastings Lodge, Hastings, Ont.*
John L. Slater.

No. 151.   *The Grand River Lodge, Berlin Ont.*
John Y. Savage.

No. 153.   *Burns Lodge, Wyoming, Ont.*
William Boyce, J. G. Bolt, J. Bright, Thomas C. Clement,
John Vansickle, A. S. Vanalstine, P. L Hawkins, T. Donnelly,
J. C. Stickle, E. Sherwood, Duncan A. McLauchlin.

No. 154.   *Irving Lodge, Lucan, Ont.*
Pat. Franklin, Thomas A. Stewart.

No. 155.   *Peterborough Lodge, Peterboro' Ont.*

James Aikens, Hy. Calcutt, Wm. Goodwin, William E. James,
Hy. Lawson, John Turner.

No. 164.   *Star in the East Lodge, Wellington, Ont.*
H. N. Todman, L. B. Stinson, Richard Murphy, Ira Clinton.

No. 165.   *Burlington Lodge, Wellington Square, Ont.*
James Wilson, John Osborne.

No. 168.   *Merritt Lodge, Welland, Ont.*
Robert Stevenson, Jacob Cushman, Thomas Brown.

No. 169.   *Macnab Lodge, Port Colborne, Ont.*
Edward P. Broughton.

No. 170.   *Britannia Lodge, Seaforth, Ont.*
John E. Price.

No. 174.   *Waltingham Lodge, Port Rowan, Ont.*
Richard English, Charles Raymond, Charles Bingham, A. C.
Shaplay,Geo.Lough,Jas.Drew,Isaiah Becker,Michael O'Brian.

No. 180.   *Speed Lodge, Guelph, Ont.*
Alexander Goodfellow.

No. 185.   *Enniskillen Lodge, York Ont.*
John McDonald, John Howard, Joshua Howard.

No. 180.   *Filius Viduæ Lodge, Adolphustown, Ont.*
John Wilmer.

No. 192.   *Orillia Lodge, Orillia, Ont.*
Thomas C. Noble, Samuel Bridgland, James A. Murray,
Thomas Myers, T. Larard, John C. Forsythe, John A. Frost,
Charles H. Kermott, James W. Anderson, Cecil Wright, Alex.
Munro, A. M. Empey. H. T. Henley, A. Kak, H. McK.
Sutherland.

No. 198.   *White Oak, Lodge, Oakville, Ont.*
       James Rioch, David Grig.

No. 203.   *Irvine Lodge, Elora, Ont.*
Louis Glick.

No. 218.   *Stevenson Lodge, Toronto Ont.*
David Smith, Frederick Walstron.

No. 219.   *Credit Lodge, Georgetown, Ont.*
David McMillan.

No. 230.   *Bell Lodge, Ewart, Ont.*
Charles H. Kermott.

No. 232.   *Cameron Lodge, Wallacetown, Ont.*
Thomas Cussock, E. Osborne, John Partridge, Oliver Cruise.

No. 236.   *Manitoba Lodge, Bondhead, Ont.*
Thomas C. Scholfield.

No. 238.   *Havelock Lodge, Watford, Ont.*
James McPherson.

No. 247.   *Ashlar Lodge, Yorkville, Ont.*
. John S. Henderson.

No. 272.   *Seymour Lodge, Ancaster, Ont.*
William J. Ratsey.

No. 277.   *Seymour Lodge, Pt. Dalhousie, Ont.*
W. A. McCollough.

RESTORATIONS.

No. 2.   *Niagara Lodge, Niagara, Ont.*
John Rousseau.

No. 6.   *Barton Lodge, Hamilton, Ont.*
John Harte. Ethelbert Servos.

No. 7.   *Union Lodge, Grimsby, Ont.*
W. W. Kitchen,

No. 15.·   *St. George's Lodge, St. Catharines, Ont.*
Thomas H. Towers.

No. 18.   *Prince Edward Lodge, Picton, Ont.*
David W. Allison.

No. 20.   *St. John's Lodge, London, Ont.*
William Hy. Niles.

No. 22.   *King Solomon's Lodge, Toronto, Ont.*
E. P. Osborne.

No. 23.   *Richmond Lodge, Richmond Hill Ont.*
George A. Bernard.

No. 25.   *Ionic Lodge, Toronto, Ont.*
Robert Ramsay.

No. 27.   *Strict Observance Lodge, Hamilton, Ont.*
Robert C. W. MacCuaig.

'No. 32.   *Amity Lodge, Dunnville, Ont.*
John Swartz.

No. 35.   *St. John's Lodge, Cayuga, Ont.*
Thomas Bridger.

No. 36.   *Welland Lodge, Fonthill, Ont.*
George Gamble.

No. 37.   *King Hiram Lodge, Ingersoll, Ont.*
W. S. King, Thomas Dawes.

No. 40.   *St. John's Lodge, Hamilton, Ont.*
Robert R. Waddel.

No. 42.   *St. George's Lodge, London, Ont.*
Joseph Copeland, Edward Woodbury, William Marshall.

No. 45.   *Brant Lodge, Brantford, Ont.*
Charles H. Waterous.

No. 46.   *Wellington Lodge, Chatham, Ont.*
Walter Patterson.

No. 50.   *Consecon Lodge, Consecon, Ont.*
S. B. Nethery.

No. 55.   *Merrickville Lodge, Merrickville, Ont.*
Adam Lamb.

No. 58.   *Doric Lodge, Ottawa, Ont.*
Robert Stanley.

No. 75.   *St. John's Lodge, Toronto, Ont.*
David E. Morton, William Moulds, William J. Bryan,
Royal Hill.

No. 76.   *Oxford Lodge, Woodstock, Ont.*
Thomas Callan, John M. Burns, D. K. Perry, Jas. Callan

No. 80.   *Albion Lodge, Newbury, Ont.*
Abraham Challis.

No. 81.   *St. John's Lodge, Mt. Brydges, Ont.*
Robert Pujolas, Julius D. Corneil.

No. 82.   *St. John's Lodge, Paris, Ont.*
John A. Gillespie, C. S. Eastman.

No. 83.   *Beaver Lodge, Strathroy, Ont.*
John W. McVicar.

No. 86.   *Wilson Lodge, Toronto, Ont.*
John Power.

No. 91.   *Colborne Lodge, Colborne, Ont.*
W. A. Sills.

No. 92.   *Cataraqui Lodge, Kingston, Ont.*
William McCadden.

No. 99.   *Tuscan Lodge, Newmarket, Ont.*
James J. Hunter.

No. 103.   *Maple Leaf Lodge, St. Catharines, Ont.*
William Read.

No. 104.   *St. John's Lodge, Norwichville, Ont.*
Abraham P. Miller, E. W. Burgess, Wm. F. Cocker.

No. 107.   *St. Pauls Lodge, Lambeth, Ont.*
William Sumner.

No. 108.   *Blenheim Lodge, Drumbo, Ont.*
Thomas Cowan, J. B. Capron.

No. 113.   *Wilson Lodge, Waterford, Ont.*
John McLaren.

No. 126.   *Golden Rule Lodge, Campbellford, Ont.*
J. M. Lindsay.

No. 129.   *The Rising Sun Lodge, Aurora, Ont.*
Frederick Long.

No. 130.   *Richardson Lodge, Stouffville, Ont*
W. Bertram, A. McMurray.

No. 137.   *Pythagoras Lodge, Meaford, Ont.*
Wm. H. Taylor, Thomas Andrews.

No. 139.   *Lebanon Lodge, Oshawa, Ont.*
George F. Munroe.

No. 140.   *Malahide Lodge, Aylmer, Ont.*
Robert H. Man.

No. 144.   *Tecumseh Lodge, Stratford, Ont*
Charles Zeollner.

No. 151.   *The Grand River Lodge, Berlin, Ont.*
John Y. Savage.

No. 158.   *Alexandra Lodge, Oil Springs, Ont.*
C. N. Brooks.

No. 162.   *Forest Lodge, Wroxeter, Ont.*
John Sanderson.

No. 164.   *Star in the East Lodge, Wellington, Ont.*
Joseph Cummings.

No. 170.   *Britannia Lodge, Seaforth, Ont*
Thomas Kirk Anderson.

No. 178.   *Plattsville Lodge, Plattsville, Ont.*
James W. Brundle, John Robinson.

No. 205.   *New Dominion Lodge, New Hamburg, Ont.*
Alex. L. Beach, Jacob Wagner.

No. 333.   *Doric Lodge, Park Hill, Ont.*
Thomas S. Murray.

No. 247.   *Ashlar Lodge, Yorkville, Ont.*
Walter Hurrell.

No. 280.   *Mount Sinai Lodge, Napanee, Ont.*
H. Betts.

AT REST.

NAMES.	NO. NODGE.	DATE.
John M. Horsey...	3 St. John's.........	June 25 1874
Adiel Sherwood.........	} 5 Sussex...........	March 25........ "
Pratt Ferm		April 15.......... "
Wm. Donn..		January 5....... "
David Knox...........	} 6 Barton	March 18........ "
John C. Fields........		May 13.......... "
Wm. Gibs n...........	} 10 Norfolk..	June 27.........1873
Edmund Jackson...		May 12.........1874
Arch. Campbell........	} 14 True Briton's.	September 14.....1873
Geo. L. Walker........		June 1.........1874
Neil McGregor.........	} 15 St. George's	May 12.......... "
Wm. Clendennan........		
Samuel M. Stephens......		February 15......1874
Joseph Rogers.........	16 St Andrews..	September 13....1873
James Austin..........	17 St. John's........	October 1.......... "
J. J. Dunlop..........	18 Prince Edward's..	March 20........ "
George A. Ferguson.....	20 St. John's........	April — 1874
Thomas Saulter.......	} 22 King Solomon's...	September 16.....1873
John Worthington........		December 25...... "
Wm. Cassidy...........		March 10.......1874
Robert Brodie.........	26 Ontario..	December 28 1873
Wm. W. Pringle........	} 27 Strict Observance.	August 24........ "
George W. Kirkendall...		November 1...... "
Thomas H. Brush.......	84 Thistle....	June 16.......... "
David Killins.........	86 Welland	
Edward Robinson........	37 King Hiram	December 28.....1873
Henry Wigle...........	} 41 St. George's......	April 12.........1874
Peter C. McDonald......		April 28.......... "
Wm. Carson...........	42 St. George's......	September 28.... 1873
James Singer.........	44 St. Thomas.......	October 5.......... "
Frederick Vanderlip.....	45 Brant.............	November 12...... "
R. H. Craik...........	} 47 Great Western....	November 27.....1872
P. Duncan.............		May 2 1873
John Newcombe........		May 4 1874
George Grant..........		January 11........ "
John Houston..........		January 1........ "
John G. McLaughlin. ...	} 52 Dalhousie	April 15........ "
John R. O'Connor		May 13.......... "
Henry Snelsor..	} 54 Vaughan	November 26.....1873
John M. Rupert..		April 20........ 1874
Adam Lamb............	} 55 Merickville.... ..	April 10........ "
Walter Wickwire........		August 25........ "
Andrew Kerr..........	58 Doric............	April 22.........1873
Michael J. May........	59 Corinthian.... ...	
John McKellar.........	} 64 Kilwinning..... ..	October — 1873
John Cousins...........		November — .... "
Abel Bristol....	68 St. John's	November 11.....1873
Benjamin Stedman.....	69 Stirling.....	January 16.......1874
Wm. A. Robinson.....	} 82 Alma............	January 18........ "
Wm. Walden... ......,		October—.......1873
John Scott............		April 29........1874
Donald Seaton.........	81 St. John's	June 17 .... "
Thos. A. Richards......	} 82 St. John's.... ...	July 4...........1873
Joshua Longhead........		September 30..... "
Samuel H. Rance	84 Clinton..........	January 8.......1874
John H. Bennett........	} 86 Wilson....	January 17.......1873
Josh Howson..........		July 21.......... "
Wm. R. Burnham	91 Colborne.........	May 9.. 1874
Wm. Boyce...........		
Daniel Chisholm........		January 12 187
James W. J. Andrew ...	} 92 Cataraqui........	January 13........ "
John V. Noel		January 15....... "
Henry S. Minnes........		January 20....... "
Wm. McCadden........		May 17.......... "
Wm. Hemphill.........	} 94 St. Marks........	February 27...... "
Duucan McLean		May 28........... "

AT REST.

NAMES.	No.	LODGE.	DATE.
Edward Hickman	98	True Blue	
George C. McManus	99	Tuscan	May 27............1874
Charles C. Averill			November 15......1873
A. D. Calder	100	Valley	December 28......1873
Donald Sutherland	101	Corinthian	September 2....... "
Wm. H. Ette	103	Maple Leaf	September 19..... "
Francis Kroft	105	St. Mark's	June 27............ "
Wm. Ormiston	110	Central	April 7............1874
Michael Traxler	111	Morpeth	March 27.......... "
Wm. Piper	112	Maitland	February — ...... "
A. S. Proctor	116	Cassia	August 3.......... "
Wm. Scholfield	118	Union	....
John Anderson			
Charles Champion	119	Maple Leaf	August 25.........1873
Benjamin Canning Davy			February 10......1874
Charles Hudson	122	Renfrew	June 4............ "
John Adair	126	Golden Rule	November 22......1873
John G. Mills	128	Pembroke	August 25......... "
Leonard Morden	136	Richardson	
Patrick J. Duffy	139	Lebanon	July 18...........1873
James Caister	144	Tecumseh	September 4....... "
Wm. Smiley			January 10.......1874
J. G. Northrup	147	Mississippi	November 22...... "
Reuben Keys	154	Irving	August 25.........1873
Thomas Whealy	157	Simpson	January 6.........1874
George C. Stinson	164	Star in the East	December 25. 1873
Jos. Cummings			January 9.........1874
Wm. Irving	165	Burlington	September 3.. 1873
S. N. Pattison	168	Merritt	April 15..........1874
James Lyons	172	Ayr	March 16.......... "
A. B. Hutchinson	174	Walsingham	December 11......1873
James R. Doan			March 5...........1874
John Harvey	177	The Builders'	September 1.......1873
Isaac Read			December 5...... "
M. M. O'Connor	178	Plattsville	August 31.........1874
Henry Godhill	184	Old Light	October 1........ 1873
Samuel Campbell	186	Plantagenet	....
John McLlin	193	Scotland	September 18......1873
George K. Chisholm	198	White Oak	April 14 1874
Samuel White			March 26.......... "
John Lauder	200	St. Albans	September 24.....1873
Jacob Wagner	205	New Dominion	December 6.......1873
James H. McCutchen			May — 1874
Joseph Faulkner	210	Hawkesbury	August 26... 1873
Hugh Caldwell	218	Stevenson	September 10..... "
George W. Smith	221	Mountain	September 17..... "
John Wesley Jones	222	Marmora	....
Casper Hill	224	Zurich	September 15...... "
George A. Carey	235	Aldworth	March 9 1874
James F. Wright	237	Vienna	November 21......1873
David Huston	238	Havelock	August 16........1872
John V. Noel	240	Prince Rupert's	January 16.......1874
Philip Kennedy	244	Lisgar	July — 1873
Daniel B. Shaw	245	Tecumseh	August 12........1874
Wm. H. Munro	248	Eureka	November 15......1873
Wm. Shaw			May 23.. 1874
Irving Nelson	249	Caledonian	December 8.......1873
Henry Ross	250	Thistle	March 31..........1874
George W. Mastin	254	Clifton	October 16........1873
Wm. H. Sparrow			May 1.............1874
Frederick Guggisberg	257	Galt	March 25.........1873
Robert Chance	258	Guelph	February 24.......1874
James Allan	262	Harriston	October 14........1873
R. P. Stanton	265	Patterson	September 13.....1874
Teodore Thompson	266	Temple	June 17........... "
....	....	....	....

In Memoriam.

RIGHT WORSHIPFUL BROTHER

JOHN V. NOEL,

PAST MASTER CATARAQUI LODGE, No. 92, AND
MINDEN LODGE, No. 253, KINGSTON ONT.,
AND PRINCE RUPERT'S LODGE, No.
240, WINNIPEG, MANITOBA.

Past District Deputy Grand Master,
Manitoba.

DIED 15th January, A. D. 1874.

AGED 66 YEARS.

AT REST.

En Memoriam.

RIGHT WORSHIPFUL BROTHER

BENJAMIN C. DAVY,

PAST MASTER UNION LODGE, No. 9, NAPANEE,
ONT., MAPLE LEAF LODGE, No. 119, BATH
ONT., AND PRINCE RUPERT'S LODGE,
No. 240, WINNIPEG, MANITOBA.

Past Grand Junior Warden

DIED 10th February, A. D. 1874.

AGED 51 YEARS.

AT REST.

En Memoriam.

VERY WORSHIPFUL BROTHER.

THOMAS DUGGAN, M.D.

PAST MASTER BARTON LODGE, NO. 6, AND ACACIA
LODGE, NO. 61, HAMILTON, ONTARIO.

Past Grand Superintendent of Works,

Past Grand Third Principal J.

Grand Chapter of Canada.

DIED 4th MARCH, A. D. 1874.

AGED 62 YEARS.

AT REST.

LIST OF GRAND OFFICERS FOR 1874-5.

M. W. Bro. W. M. Wilson, Simcoe, Grand Mast r.
R. " " James K. Kerr, Toronto, Deputy Grand Master.
" " " T. C. Macnabb Chatham, D. D. G. M., St. Clair   District
" " " W. D. McGloghlon, London,   "   London   "
" " " Chauncy Bennett, Port Rowan, "   Wilson   "
" " " J. H. Benson, Seaforth,   "   Huron   "
" " " W. F. Savage, Elora,   "   Wellington   "
" " " J. J. Mason, Hamilton,   "   Hamilton   "
" " " D. E Broderick, Caledonia,   "   Niagara   "
" " " R. P. Stephens, Toronto,   "   Toronto   "
" " " J. B. Trayes, Port Hope,   "   Ontario   "
" " " S. S. Lazier, Belleville,   "   Prince Edward   "
" " " A. S. Kirkpatrick,   "   Kingston   "
" " " John W. Pickup, Pakenham,   "   Ottawa   "
" " " George Back, Mapleton,   "   Manitoba   "
" " " W. R. White, Pembroke, Grand Senior Warden.
" " " Hugh Murray, Hamilton, Grand Juni r Warden.
" " " Rev. Can n Innes, London, Grand Chaplain.
" " " Henry Groff, Simcoe, Grand Treasurer.
" " " D. McG. Malloch, Clinton, Grand Registrar.
*" " " Thos. B. Harris, Hamilton, Grand Secretary.
V. " " F. J. Menet, Toronto, Grand Senior Deacon.
" " " Geo. S. Birrell, London, Grand Juni r Deacon.
" " " James H. Rowan Ottawa, Grand Superintendent of Works
" " " Andrew Irving, Jr , Pembroke, Grand Director of Ceremonies.
" " " F. R. Despard, Hamilton, Assistant Grand Secretary.
" " " James Miller, Peterboro Asst. Grand Director of Ceremonies.
" " " John M. Clement, Niagara, Grand Sword Bearer.
" " " C. A. Sippi, London, Grand Organist.
" " " Thomas Aishton, Bath, Asst. Grand Organist.
" " " Hugh Kerr, Ingersoll, Grand Pursuivant.
    " James Heron, London, Grand Tyler.
" " " James Sutton, Lucan,   ⎫
" " " A. Whittaker, Windsor,   ⎪
" " " Isaac Waterman, London,   ⎪
" " " J R. Leggett, L Original.   ⎪
" " " R Rochester, Simcoe.   ⎪
" " " Josiah Corlis, St. Thomas.   ⎬ Grand Stewards
" " " E Peplow, Jr., Port Hope   ⎪
" " " H. T. Champion, Winnipeg.   ⎪
" " " Thos. F. Blackwood, Yorkville ⎪
" " " John Gibson, Stratford.   ⎪
" " " D. A Ferguson, Smith's Falls, ⎪
" " " A. Hudspeth, Lindsay.   ⎭

*. Died 18th Aug, A. D. 1874. R. W. Bro. J. J. Mason, Hamilt n, appointed Grand Sec. *pro tem.*

BOARD OF GENERAL PURPOSES 1874-5.

PRESIDENT.

R. W. Bro. James K. Kerr, Deputy Grand Master, Toronto.

VICE-PRESIDENT :

R. W. Bro. Henry Macpherson, P. G. S. W., Owen Sound.

OFFICERS OF GRAND LODGE —[BY VIRTUE OF OFFICE.]

M W. Bro. W. M. Wilson,   Grand Master   Simcoe.
R. " " James K. Kerr, Deputy   "   "   Toronto.
 " " " W. R. White,   "   Senior Warden, Pembroke.
 ' " " Hugh Murray,   "   Junior   "   Hamilton.

PAST GRAND MASTERS.

M. W. Bro. T. Douglas Harington, P. G. M., Ottawa.
 "   "   " W. B. Simpson,   P. G. M., Montreal.
 "   "   " A. A. Stevenson, P. G. M.,   "
 "   "   " James Seymour,   P. G. M., St. Catharines.

DISTRICT DEPUTY GRAND MASTERS.

R. W. Bro. Thomas C Macnabb,   Chatham,   Ontario.
 "   "   " W. D. McGloghlon,   London,   "
 "   "   " Chauncy Bennett,   Port Rowan, "
 "   "   " J. H. Benson,   Seaforth,   "
 "   "   ' W. F. Savage,   Elora,   "
 '   "   " J. J. Mason,   Hamilton,   "
 "   "   " D. E. Broderick,   Caledonia,   "
 "   "   " R. P. Stephens,   Toronto,   "
 "   "   " J. B. Trayes,   Port Hope,   "
 "   "   " S. S. Lazier,   Belleville, "
 "   "   " A. S. Kirkpatrick,   Kingston,   "
 "   "   " John W. Pickup,   Pakenham,   "
 "   "   " Geo Black,   Mapleton,   Man.

ELECTED BY GRAND LODGE.

V. W. Bro. Fred. J. Menet, G. S. D.,   Toronto,   Ontario.
R. "   " W. H. Weller, P. D. D. G. M., Cobourg,   " '
 " "   " James Bain, P. G. S. W.,   Toronto,   "
 " "   " R. Kincaid, P. D. D. G. M.,   Peterborough, "
 " "   " S. B. Harman. P. D. D. G. M., Toronto,   "
 " "   " Otto K otz, P. D. D. G. M.,   Preston,   "
 " "   " Daniel Spry, P. G. R.,   Toronto,   "

BOARD OF GENERAL PURPOSES. — [CONTINUED.]

R. W. Bro P. J. Brown, P. D. D. G. M.,   Ingersoll,   "
" " " Allan McLean, P. G. S. W.,   Ingersoll.   "
" " " Henry Macpherson, P. G. S. W.,   Owen Sound,   "

APPOINTED BY THE GRAND MASTER.

R. W. Bro. John W. Murton, P. G. S. W.,   Hamilton,   Ontario.
" " " F. Westlake, P. D. D. G. M.,   London,   "
" " " J. A Henderson, P. D. D. G. M.,   Kingston,   "
" " " J. E. Harding, P. D. D. G M.,   St. Marys,   "
" " " L. H. Henderson, P. D. D. G. M.,   Belleville,   "
" " " Henry Robertson, P. D. D. G. M.,   Collingwood,   "
" " " Rev. Vincent Clementi, P. G. C.,   North Douro'   "
" " " David McLellan, P. G. R.,   Hamilton,   "
" " " E. C. Barber, P. D. D. G. M.,   Ottawa,   "
" " " C. D. Macdounell, P. D. D. G. M.,   Peterborough,   "

REPRESENTATIVES.

FROM THE GRAND LODGE OF CANADA.

R. W. Bro. The Right Hon. Lord De Tably,
      In the United Grand Lodge of England.
" " " James Vokes Mackey,   "   Ireland.
" " " Lindsay Mackersy,   "   Scotland.
" " " Henry W. Turner,   "   New York.
" " " Andrew Kerr Mackinley,   "   Nova Scotia.
" " " E. T. Carr,   "   Kansas.
Ill. " " Dr. Franc, DePaula Romas Grand Orient of Brazil.
" " " Jacinto DeCastro   "   St. Domingo.
" " " J. M. Samper Angiano,   "   New Grenada.
" " " Antonio M Mollejas,   "   Venezula.
" " " Joas Caetona D'Almeida,   "   Portugal.
" " " Luis Goapil, 33°,   "   Mexico.
" " " Francesco DeLuca,   "   Italy.
" " " A. M. Medina,   "   Chili.
" " " Laurentino Ximenez, 33°,   "   Uruguay.
" " " — Caubet,   "   France.
" " " Dr. L. Montafar,   "   Cent. America.
R. W. Bro. Geo. S. Blackie, 33°, M. D., Grand Lodge of Tennessee.
M. " " John V. Ellis,   "   New Brunswick
R. " " Samuel C. Perkins,   "   Pennsylvania.
" " " George Frank Gouley,   "   Missouri.
M. " " Henry R. Cannon,   "   New Jersey.

REPRESENTATIVES.—[CONTINUED.]

R.	"	"	R. C. Jordan, in the Grand Lodge of	Nebraska.
"	"	"	Wm. S. Fish,	"	Connecticut
"	"	"	Thomas W. Chubbuck,	"	Nevada.
"	"	"	Charles Kahn,	"	Wisconsin.
"	"	"	William H. Tuller,	"	Georgia.
"	"	"	W. M. Washburne,	"	Ohio.
M.	"	"	Harvey G. Hazelrigg,	"	Indiana.
R.	"	"	Wiley M. Egan,	"	Illinois.
"	"	"	Alex. Murray,	"	Quebec.
"	"	"	William Drummond Wilson	"	Utah.

REPRESENTATIVES

IN THE GRAND LODGE OF CANADA.

R. W. Bro. Sir John A. Macdonald, K C. B.,
From the Grand Lodge of England.

"	"	"	Kivas Tully,	"	"	Ireland
M.	"	"	Wm. Mercer Wilson,	"	Grand Orient of St. Domingo.
"	"	"	Wm. Mercer Wilson,	"	'	Cent. America
"	"	"	Wm. Mercer Wilson,	"	Grand Lodge of Kentucky.
"	"	"	Wm. Mercer Wilson,	"	"	Illinois.
"	"	"	T. D. Harington	"	"	Nova Scotia.
"	"	"	T. D. Harington,	"	"	Pennsylvania.
"	"	"	T. T. Harington,	"	"	Vermont.
"	"	"	T. D. Harington,	"	"	Quebec.
"	'	"	A. A. Stevenson,	"	Grand Orient of Brazil.
"	"	"	A. A. Stevenson,	"	Grand Lodge of Connecticut
"	"	"	A. A. Stevenson	"	'	Minnesota.
"	"	"	A. Bernard,	"	Grand Orient of New Grenada.
"	"	"	A. Bernard,	"	Grand Lodge of New Jersey.
"	"	"	A. Bernard,	"	"	New Brunswick
"	"	"	W. B. Simpson,	"	Grand Orient of Italy.
"	"	"	Thos. White, Jr,	"	"	France.
"	"	"	Thos. White, Jr,	"	Grand Lodge of Nevada.
"	"	"	James Seymour,	"	'	Mississippi
R.	"	"	James A. Henderson	"	"	New York.
"	"	"	Henry Macpherson,	"	Grand Orient of Uruguay.
"	"	"	Rev. V. Clementi,	"	"	Chili.
"	"	"	J. K. Kerr,	"	Grand Lodge of Texas.
"	"	"	R. Ramsay,	"	"	Nebraska.
"	"	"	R. Ramsay,	"	"	Ohio.
"	"	"	David McLellan,	"	"	Georgia.
"	"	Hugh A. Mackay,	"	"	Michigan.
"	"	"	W. A. Frazer,	"	Wisconsin.

Synopsis of the Returns of Lodges for tho year ending 24th June, 1874.—Continued.

LODGE.	WHERE HELD.	Initiations.	Passed.	Raised.	Joined.	Withdrawn.	Died.	Susp. N. P. D.	Susp. U. M. C.	Expelled.	Restored.	No. of Mem.
145 J. B. Hall........	Millbrook..........	4	2	3	..	1	..	3	..	..	..	35
146 Prince of Wales..	Newburg....	5	6	6	..	12	..	..	..	..	..	50
147 Mississippi	Almonte...	5	7	9	3	7	1	..	..	..	..	33
148 Civil Service.....	Ottawa...........	6	8	5	4	1	..	..	..	..	..	60
149 Erie...........	Port Dover	9	8	8	3	..	..	..	..	..	..	63
150 Hastings, ...	Hastings,.........	1	1	2	..	1	..	1	..	..	..	33
151 The Grand River.	Berlin.....	5	5	7	..	5	..	1	..	..	1	66
153 Burns...........	Wyoming	7	10	9	2	3	..	11	1	..	..	57
154 Irving.....	Lucan	10	10	9	..	1	1	2	..	..	..	46
155 Peterborough	Peterborough......	7	3	3	1	4	..	6	..	..	..	43
156 York............	Davisville......	7	8	10	2	3	..	..	..	..	..	47
157 Simpson........	Newboro	4	2	3	1	5	1	..	..	..	..	45
158 Alexandra......	Oil Springs......	5	6	8	1	2	..	..	..	..	1	51
159 Goodwood......	Richmond, ...	2	1	2	..	2	..	..	..	..	..	17
161 Percy...........	Warkworth	2	4	4	2	1	..	..	..	..	..	40
162 Forest	Wroxter...........	4	5	2	..	3	..	..	..	..	1	33
164 Star in the East .	Wellington......	3	1	1	1	1	2	4	..	..	1	43
165 Burlington	Wellington Square..	6	12	10	1	2	1	2	..	..	..	41
166†Wentworth	Stoney Creek......	..	..	..	..	..	..	..	..	..	..	30
168 Merritt	Welland...........	9	7	7	3	3	1	3	..	..	..	50
169 Macnab	Port Colborne.....	6	3	2	2	1	..	1	..	..	..	68
170 Britannia	Seaforth......	9	9	4	3	3	..	1	..	..	1	56
171†Prince of Wales..	Iona............	..	..	..	..	..	..	..	..	..	..	52
173 Ayr..... ...	Ayr...........	7	7	7	..	1	..	..	..	..	..	43
174 Walsingham.	Port Rowan	13	12	9	1	2	2	8	..	..	..	70
176 Spartan	Sparta............	12	9	10	1	..	..	..	..	..	..	48
177 The Builders'....	Ottawa........	13	11	11	1	2	2	..	..	..	..	53
178 Plattsville.......	Plattsville	4	3	4	1	2	1	..	..	..	2	28
179 Bothwell....	Bothwell	13	13	14	..	2	..	..	..	..	..	53
180 Speed	Guelph..........	11	12	13	2	10	..	1	..	..	..	97
181 Oriental	Port Burwell	5	3	2	..	1	..	..	..	..	..	60
183 Prince Albert....	Prince Albert.......	8	12	5	1	..	..	..	..	..	..	46
184 Old Light........	Lucknow........	4	3	2	..	..	1	..	1	..	..	42
185 Enniskillen	York	4	6	6	..	3	..	3	..	..	..	37
186 Plantagenet.....	Plantaganet......	6	6	4	..	1	1	..	..	..	..	26
189 Filius Viduæ...	Adolphustown......	..	..	..	..	8	..	1	..	..	..	18
190 Belmont........	Belmont.........	7	5	8	1	4	..	..	..	..	..	44
192 Orillia....-......	Orillia	8	8	7	..	7	..	15	..	..	..	61
193 Scotland..........	Scotland..... ...	6	4	5	..	1	1	..	..	..	..	40
194 Petrolia....	Petrolia..........	1	1	3	..	2	..	..	..	..	..	54
195 The Tuscan	London	5	5	3	1	4	..	..	..	..	..	47
196 Madawaska......	Arnprior....	1	..	..	..	1	..	..	..	..	..	44
197 Saugeen...	Walkerton.........	..	..	..	..	..	..	..	..	..	..	63
198 White Oak.......	Oakville........	5	3	3	1	3	2	2	..	..	..	63
200 St. Albans......	Mount Forest......	8	6	..	..	9	1	..	..	..	..	56
201 Leeds	Gananoque.........	5	4	8	..	1	..	..	..	..	..	77
203 Irvine	Elora	9	10	12	..	8	..	..	..	..	..	63
205 New Dominion...	New Hamburg......	6	6	5	1	4	2	..	1	..	2	45
206 †North Gower....	North Gower	..	..	..	..	..	..	..	..	..	..	16
207 Lancaster	Lancaster.........	7	4	4	1	3	..	..	..	..	..	43
209A St. John's......	London............	1	7	10	..	..	..	..	..	..	..	50
209 Evergreen......	Lanark..........	5	4	7	..	1	..	..	..	..	..	26
210 Hawkesbury	Hawkesbury......	9	9	8	..	2	1	..	..	..	..	26
212 Elysian	Garden Island......	6	5	3	..	..	..	..	..	..	..	51
213 Dominion......	Ridgeway.......	8	7	10	..	..	..	..	..	..	..	59
214 Craig'...........	Ailsa Craig.... ...	5	7	6	..	2	..	..	..	..	..	36
215 Leeds..........	Amcliasburg.......	1	6	8	..	1	..	..	..	..	..	20
216 Harris....	Orangeville......	7	7	7	2	1	..	..	..	..	..	65
217 Frederick.......	Delhi............	7	7	7	..	1	..	..	..	..	..	33
218 Stevenson......	Toronto	14	10	15	6	5	1	2	..	..	..	118
219 Credit	Georgetown	1	2	4	..	..	..	1	..	..	..	61
220†Zeredatha	Uxbridge........	..	..	..	..	..	..	..	..	..	..	48
221 Mountain........	Thorold...........	3	3	2	4	4	1	..	..	..	..	55
222 Marmora'........	Marmora	3	1	1	2	7	1	..	..	..	..	30

Synopsis of the Returns of Lodges for the year ending 24th June, 1874.—Continued.

LODGE	WHERE HELD.	Initiations.	Passed.	Raised.	Joined.	Withdrawn.	Died.	Susp. N. P. D.	Susp. U. M. C.	Expelled.	Restored.	No. of Mem.
223 Norwood	Norwood	3	4	3	..	..	..	..	..	..	..	26
224 Zurich	Zurich	..	..	..	..	2	1	..	..	..	..	20
225 Bernard	Listowel	9	8	8	1	..	..	..	..	..	..	26
223 Prince Arthur	Odessa	2	2	2	..	1	..	..	..	..	..	35
229 Ionic	Brampton	7	9	6	2	..	..	..	..	..	..	47
230 Kerr	Bell Ewart	5	8	6	..	3	..	1	..	..	..	25
231 Lodge of Fidelity	Ottawa	9	7	7	4	1	..	..	..	..	..	45
232 Cameron	Wallacetown	5	6	9	1	..	4	..	..	..	..	41
233 Doric	Park Hill	6	3	3	1	1	..	..	..	..	1	52
234 Beaver	Clarksburg	8	11	8	2	..	..	..	..	..	..	33
235 Aldworth	Paisley	3	3	3	2	..	1	..	.	..	..	31
296 Manitoba	Boudhead	1	..	6	..	1	..	1	..	..	..	28
297 Vienna	Vienna	3	4	5	..	..	1	..	1	1	..	39
298 Havelock	Watford	14	14	12	1	2	1	1	..	..	..	34
239 Tweed	Tweed	4	3	3	..	..	..	..	..	..	..	26
240 Prince Rupert's	Winnipeg, M	7	7	6	10	8	1	..	..	..	..	78
241 Quinte	Shannonville	7	7	4	2	5	..	..	..	..	..	47
242 Macoy	Escott Front	5	6	5	..	1	..	..	..	..	..	44
243 St. George	St. George	5	4	4	1	..	..	..	..	..	..	38
244 Lisgar	Mapleton	5	4	4	3	1	1	..	..	..	..	33
245 Tecumseh	Thamesville	5	5	5	..	4	1	..	..	..	..	35
247 Ashlar	Yorkville	4	7	5	3	4	..	1	..	..	1	44
248 Eureka	Pakenham	3	1	1	1	2	2	..	..	..	..	32
249 Caledonian	Angus	4	6	7	..	5	1	..	..	..	..	35
250 Thistle	Embro	7	9	9	..	..	1	..	..	..	..	31
252 †The International	North Pombina, M	..	..	..	..	..	..	..	..	..	..	..
253 Minden	Kingston	14	13	11	4	..	..	..	..	..	..	60
254 Clifton	Clifton	7	5	6	2	1	2	..	..	..	..	51
255 Sydenham	Dresden	9	10	7	8	..	..	..	..	..	..	41
256 Farran's Point	Farran's Point	4	12	13	..	1	..	..	..	..	..	30
257 Galt	Galt	9	10	10	1	4	1	..	..	..	..	55
253 Guelph	Guelph	..	..	..	..	..	1	..	1	..	..	53
259 Springfield	Springfield	8	8	8	..	..	1	..	1	..	..	47
260 Washington	Petrolia	2	2	..	..	2	..	..	..	..	..	30
261 Oak Branch	Innerkip	9	7	8	..	1	..	..	..	..	..	31
262 Harriston	Harriston	5	8	8	5	5	1	..	..	..	..	35
263 Forest	Forest	12	9	5	3	..	..	..	..	..	..	26
264 Chaudiere	Ottawa	13	10	14	1	10	..	..	..	..	..	64
265 Patterson	Concord	3	2	2	..	..	1	..	..	..	..	29
266 Northern Light	Stayner	6	5	5	..	..	..	..	..	..	..	32
267 Parthenon	Chatham	10	8	10	2	2	..	..	..	..	..	89
268 Verulam	Bobcaygeon	9	10	14	..	2	..	..	..	..	..	47
269 Bro'ham Union	Brougham	13	12	8	1	2	..	..	..	..	..	42
270 Cedar	Oshawa	8	5	5	1	2	..	..	..	..	..	51
271 Wellington	Erin	8	5	10	1	..	..	..	..	..	..	25
272 Seymour	Ancaster	8	7	5	1	2	..	1	..	..	..	27
274 Kent	Blenheim	18	19	24	2	2	..	..	..	..	..	50
276 Teeswater	Teeswater	2	1	5	..	..	..	..	..	..	..	22
277 Seymour	Port Dalhousie	13	12	8	1	1	..	1	..	..	..	47
278 Mystic	Roslin	3	4	..	..	..	..	..	..	..	..	22
279 New Hope	Hespeler	4	5	3	1	1	..	..	..	..	..	24
280 Mount Sinai	Napanee	4	4	5	1	1	..	..	..	..	1	43
281 Thorne	Holland Landing	..	..	..	..	1	..	..	..	..	..	16
282 Lorne	Glencoe	15	17	18	..	..	..	..	..	..	..	41
283 Eureka	Belleville	1	..	..	..	..	..	..	..	..	..	23
284 St. John's	Brussels	14	12	10	..	..	..	..	..	..	..	22
285 Seven Star	Alliston	3	4	3	..	..	..	..	..	..	..	18
286 Wingham	Wingham	6	6	6	1	1	..	..	..	..	..	27
287 Shuniah	Pr. Arthur's L'ndg	14	7	4	..	..	..	..	..	..	..	38
288 An't Landmark	Winnipeg, M	19	23	24	5	2	..	..	..	..	..	53
289 Doric	Lobo	4	5	6	2	1	..	..	..	..	..	27
290 Leamington	Leamington	10	9	11	..	..	..	..	..	..	..	33
291 Dufferin	West Flamboro	6	5	6	..	1	..	..	..	..	..	21
292 Robertson	Nobleton	7	7	3	4	3	..	..	..	..	..	19

Synopsis of the Returns of Lodges for the year ending 24th June, 1874.—Continued.

LODGE.	WHERE HELD.	Initiations.	Passed.	Raised.	Joined.	Withdrawn.	Died.	Susp. N.P.D.	Susp. U.M.C.	Expelled.	Restored.	No. of Mem.
293 Thelt.Sol.Moth.	Jerusalem, Pal....	..	..	..	..	..	..	..	..	..	..	20
214 Moore	Mooretown.	7	10	9	1	..	..	..	..	..	..	29
295 Conestogo	Drayton	9	7	7	1	4	..	..	..	..	..	25
296 Temple..	St. Catharines	11	7	6	6	..	1	..	..	..	..	36
297 Preston	Preston	17	17	17	1	..	..	..	..	..	..	56
299 Victoria	Centerville	..	..	..	..	..	..	..	..	..	..	9
300 Mount Olivet...	Thorndale	12	10	10	1	..	..	..	..	..	..	22
301 Hanover	Hanover	9	7	4	..	..	..	..	..	..	..	23
302 St. Davids	St. Thomas	30	25	17	..	..	..	..	..	..	..	53
303 Blyth	Blyth	8	7	5	..	..	..	..	..	..	..	15
304 Minerva	Victoria	11	8	7	1	1	..	..	..	..	.	21
305 Humber	Weston	12	9	9	..	1	..	..	..	..	..	26
306 Durham	Durham	11	3	..	..	..	..	..	..	..	..	19
307 Arkona	Arkona	2	2	1	.	..	..	..	..	..	..	13
308†Grafton	Grafton	..	..	..	..	..	..	..	..	..	..	10
309 Morning Star...	Smith's Hill	3	3	3	5	..	..	..	..	..	..	18
310 Enterprise	Beachburgh	1	1	..	2	..	..	..	..	..	..	12
311† Blackwood.	Woodbridge	5	4	2	1	2	..	..	..	..	..	19
312 Pnyx	Wallaceburgh	7	3	2	6	..	..	..	..	..	..	21
313†Clementi	Lakefield	..	..	..	..	..	..	..	..	..	..	9
314 Blair	Palmerston	8	3	3	..	..	..	..	..	..	..	24
315 Clifford	Clifford	..	..	..	..	..	..	..	..	..	..	11
316†Doric	Toronto	..	..	..	..	..	..	..	..	..	..	31
317 The Hiram	Dundas	1	..	..	..	..	..	..	..	..	..	16
318†Wilmot.	Baden	..	..	..	..	..	..	..	..	..	..	8
U. D. Hiram	Cheapside	..	..	..	..	..	..	..	..	..	..	12
U. D. Chesterville..	Chesterfield	..	..	..	..	..	..	..	..	..	..	11
U. D. Walker	Acton West	..	..	..	..	..	..	..	..	..	..	9
U. D. North Star...	Owen Sound	..	..	..	..	..	..	..	..	..	..	15
U. D. Alvinston	Alvinston	..	..	..	..	..	..	..	..	..	..	18
		1830	1710	1649	485	590	191	269	9		73	14530

RECAPITULATION.

OF THE RETURNS OF LODGES FOR THE YEAR ENDING 24TH JUNE, 1874,
AS FAR AS HEARD FROM.

Lodges organized and affiliated.............................. 320
   "   extinct.. 6
   "   Ceded to Grand Lodge of Quebec...... 38
   "   Number on Roll.. 276
   "   In arrear with Returns, 12 months and upwards........ 13
   "   Represented in Grand Lodge.... 252
Initiations reported... 1,830
Passings   "   1,649
Raisings   "   1,710
Joinings   "   435
Restorations.. 73
Resignations   "   590
Deaths... 131
Suspensions for non-payment of dues.................. 209
   "   unmasonic conduct.... 9
Members in good standing........................ 14,530

Receipts from Lodges for the Fiscal year ending 31st Dec.,
     1873, for fees, dues, &c..... ....$13,532 49
Masonic Asylum Fund, as reported 30th June, 1874..........6,452 39
Assets of Grand Lodge, as per Grand Treasurers statement
     30th June, 1874 ....56,135 24

FOREIGN CORRESPONDENCE.

To the Most Worshipful Grand Master and the Grand Lodge of A. F. & A. M. of Canada.

The Committee on Foreign Correspondence beg leave to present their annual report. The proceedings of thirty-seven Grand Lodges have been received and carefully examined, namely:—

1 Alabama	1873	20 Nevada	1873
2 Arkansas	1873	21 New Brunswick	1873
3 California	1873	22 New Hampshire	1873
4 Colorado	1873	23 New Jersey	1874
5 Delaware	1873	24 New York	1873
6 District of Columbia	1873	25 North Carolina	1873
7 Florida	1873	26 Nova Scotia	1873
8 Georgia	Emergent	27 Ohio	1873
9 Idaho	1873	28 Oregon	1873
10 Indiana	1873	29 Rhode Island	1873
11 Iowa	1873	30 South Carolina	1873
12 Kansas	1873	31 Texas	1873
13 Louisiana	1874	32 Utah	1873
14 Massachusetts	1873	33 Vermont	1873
15 Michigan	1874	34 Virginia	1873
16 Minnesota	1873	35 Washington	1873
17 Missouri	1873	36 West Virginia	1872
18 Montana	1873	37 Wisconsin	1873
19 Nebraska	1873		

It has been decided, this year, to make a change in the manner of publishing these Reports,—that is, to have them in print prior to the meeting of Grand Lodge. It is an experiment, which we think an improvement. It will, however, remain to be seen, whether it will work in practice, better than the old way.

This change necessitates the closing of our Report, at least a month earlier, than in previous years, and this will probably account for the non-reception of some of the Grand Lodge Proceedings, which do not appear in the present report.

9

The proceedings not noticed are those of the Grand Lodges of British Columbia, Connecticut, Georgia, Illinois, Kentucky, Maine, Maryland, Mississippi, Pennsylvania and Tennessee.

It is with feelings of the utmost gratification, that we are enabled to announce, the settlement of the difficulties, heretofore existing, among our brethren in the Province of Quebec, and the consequent recogniation, by the Grand Lodge of Canada, of the Grand Lodge of Quebec. The present session will, doubtless, see all formalities properly observed, and though we may part in sorrow, our Quebec brethren will have no more sincere and hearty well-wishes for their prosperity and success, than the brethren of the Grand Lodge of Canada.

We now proceed to the consideration of the proceedings, in the usual alphabetical order.

ALABAMA.

The fifty-third annual Communication was held at Montgomery, December 1st, 1873; M. W. Bro. Joseph H. Johnson, Grand Master, and R.W. Bro. Daniel Sayre, Grand Secretary.

From the Grand Masters address, we learn that

"Masonry, in Alabama, has not lost any of its interest, though, for reasons known to all of you, our numbers have not been augmented as in former years.

"Throughout the length and breadth of the jurisdiction, so far as we are informed, the brethren are working in harmony."

He decided the following matters, with a large number of others:—

"The Master of a Lodge has the right, and it is his duty, to require 'Blue Lodge clothing only' to be worn in all public processions. If Royal Arch Chapters are invited and are present "as Chapters," of course they wear their peculiar regalias.

"Refused to grant a dispensation to confer the Fellow Crafts and Master Masons degree in a shorter time than required by our laws. The Grand Master has no right to issue such a dispensation.

"A Lodge having by a vote of the Lodge, determined to celebrate publicly the festival of St. John the Baptist, the Worshipful Master of said Lodge *has the right* to revoke the action of the Lodge, by issuing his orders to the effect that no public celebration be had, such course, in his opinion, being for the good of the Order and the interest of the Lodge.

"A dimit is not sufficient evidence that a man is a mason. A petition for affiliation can be received, before the applicant is examined—the applicant must have a voucher, or be examined, before he can sit in the Lodge.

"I know of no authority for performing funeral ceremonies over the grave of a deceased mason several days after his burial."

The Grand Secretary reports that five of the fraternity fell victims to the yellow fever, during its prevalence there last fall.

Bro. Joel White was received as the representative of the Grand Orient of Hungary.

We deeply regret to learn of the death of Bro. Richard F. Knott, for some years the able chairman of correspondence. His loss will be sincerely regretted.

The conclusion of the report of the committee on appeals is well worthy of perusal:—

"In conclusion your committee beg to observe that Masonry, rightly considered, is not a mere toy to be assumed on communication days, or upon occasions when its appearance may give eclat, and then to be carefully put away, like a Sunday hat, until the next stated gathering of the brotherhood, but a principle, a rule of life which is to permeate all our intercourse with each other, and with the outside world. In communities like ours men need less to be *informed* than to be *reminded*. The brethren will, we trust, pardon the remark that there may, perhaps, be laid occasionally at our doors the charge of employing a time-serving policy. When there is a gross violation of Masonic Law, it matters not how respectable as the world goes, the offender may be, nor how much the 'material aid' which he can supply, may be appreciated by the Lodge, nor how wide his influence appears to be, nor yet how high may be his position in respect of social, religious, or civil affairs, the guilty party *must* be dealt with according to the laws and usages of our Order.

"As, in that material world, the higher a body rises the more stunning is its fall, so, in our moral atmosphere, the greater the eminence any one attains the more terrible, if he commit a grave offense and have his due, will be his precipitation from that high estate. Brethren, 'Let Justice prevail though the heavens fall.'

"If we fully discharge our duty all will be well. When we look back through the far distant and nearer past we see that our noble craft has steadily plowed her way down the sea of time, through the vicissitudes of twenty centuries; still she proceeds. The loud thunders of impotent rage may rattle above her; the fierce lightnings of malice may flash athwart her pathway, and the huge billows of envy yawn in front to swallow her up; yet, with all her timbers staunch and tight, with the Holy Bible for her chart, the Square and Compasses for her guide, she shall hold on her course to the port of everlasting peace."

The report on correspondence is presented in an unfinished condition, in consequence of the death of Bro. Knott, twenty-seven Grand Lodges are reviewed, including Canada for 1872.

M. W. Bro. Isaiah A. Wilson, was elected Grand Master, and R.W. Bro. Daniel Sayre, was re-elected Grand Secretary.

ARKANSAS.

Thirty-fifth annual Communication, held at Little Rock, October 13th, 1873, "in pursuance of the ordinance of the convention of the constituent lodges, held this day." M.W. Bro. E. R. DuVal, Grand Master, and R. W. Bro. L. E. Barber, Grand Secretary.

The Grand Master refers to the past year as one of uncommon trial and vexation. The reason was inauspicious, and the agricultural population were gloomy and despondent. Merchants, and others, unable to bear the prostration everywhere existing, were about to abandon the State. He suggests two legislative alterations: 1st an amendment to the form of the petition for initiation, stating whether the applicant had ever been rejected; and 2nd, an edict, requiring Lodges to keep a "Roll of Honor," containing the names of those who have been affiliated members for fifteen years, and who shall not be charged any dues after such enrolment.

He issued seventeen dispensations for new Lodges. From his decisions, we take the following:—

" An entry should never be made, either on the petition or Lodge books, of how a committee reported.

"The defamation of the origin, character and mission of the Son of God is unmasonic, and a Mason habitually guilty of such should be expelled.

" To traduce the good name and reputation of a deceased Brother Master Mason is unmasonic and grounds for charges.

"*Question*—A non affiliate applies for membership and is *rejected*. Shortly afterwards he dies; his family asks the Worshipful Master to bury him with masonic ceremonies; the Lodge refuses, upon the ground that the deceased Brother's character was notoriously bad. Did it do right?

"*Answer*—It did. The vicious should be buried in silence. 'Tis true, by the *literal* and *rigid* construction of the law, he was entitled to funeral honors, yet the Lodge, in according them to a bad character, would thereby be itself *debased*, and our beautiful and impressive ceremonies at the grave *sheer* mockery; hence I am of the opinion that in all such cases the Lodge *should* be permitted to exercise its *discretion*.

": The widow and orphans of a deceased Master Mason are entitled to protection, even if such necessitates *charges* against a Brother Mason for gross neglect and mismanagement of the interest of the estate.

" A Brother dying under suspension for non-payment of dues cannot be restored to membership in order that his widow may secure a certificate, as provided by Regulation eleven of this Grand Lodge. As the tree falls so it must lie.

"That a eunuch cannot lawfully be made a Mason.

"When the Lodge is at labor, the representatives of the lesser lights must be in due form and burning.

"All balloting for candidates, except upon proficiency, must take place at the altar.

"A Brother who establishes, to the satisfaction of the Lodge, that he is pecuniarily unable to pay dues, should not be suspended for their non-payment, but placed upon the 'Free List.' There is no offense in being too poor to pay. The effront to the law is in the ability to comply with its exactions and refusing.

"When a Brother has already been buried, the Lodge cannot appropriately perform any funeral rites around his grave. I have heard of Lodges in our jurisdiction, under such circumstances, going through the regular burial service, upon what authority, I know not.

"Before the ballot is spread, remarks upon the proficiency or moral fitness of the applicant for advancement are allowable; but when the result of the ballot is announced, it must be accepted as a finality without question or debate.

"The Grand Master also reports some curious work, done by West View Lodge, in this:—that in the absence of the Worshipful Master and Wardens, the Deacons assumed respectfully the East and West, filled the other stations by appointment, and proceeded to initiate, pass and raise candidates. I directed Dripping Springs Lodge No. 245, the the nearest chartered authority to the irregularly made Masons, to heal them by administering the obligation appropriate to each, respectively, explaining the informality practiced and reading the charge. The ceremony necessary to constitute the healing process was not clear to me; and I have made this report of the manner adopted in order that you may, if it be deemed necessary, give expression to your will by a edict as to the ceremony proper under such circumstances."

He closes an excellent address, with some particulars as to St. John's College, which is now in a fair way to succeed.

With one decision of the committee on appeals, we cannot agree. A Lodge collected dues from a member after he had withdrawn, and the committee say, the Lodge did right according to masonic law, because he held his dimit without application with any other Lodge. We say there is no masonic law, unless manufactured for the purpose, which will uphold so arbitrary a rule.

The Grand Orator delivered a good address.

A resolution of non-intercourse with Canada was passed, because of our "infringement" of the jurisdiction of Quebec. It all depends upon how you look at it. We rather think it was our jurisdiction that was "infringed," and can afford to smile at these futile resolutions. However, as our little difficulty is now peaceably settled, we presume the resolution is no longer in force.

The apron worn by the Master of the first Lodge in Arkansas, was presented to Grand Lodge by his son, and thanks voted therefor.

The amended Constitution, By-laws, and Rules for trials, are published with the proceedings.

The time of meeting of Grand Lodge was changed from the first Monday in November, to the second Monday in October.

The Masonic History of the State is continued, and biographical sketches of the Grand Masters are given.

No report on correspondence.

M. W. Bro. George A. Donnelly, was elected Grand Master, and R. W. Bro. L. E. Barber, re-elected Grand Secretary.

CALIFORNIA.

Twenty-fourth annual Communication, held at San Francisco, October 14th, 1873. M. W. Bro. L. E. Pratt, Grand Master, and R. W. Bro. A. G. Abell, Grand Secretary.

From the very able address of the Grand Master we extract the following:—

" While our own relations with foreign Grand Bodies have remained unchanged since your last annual Communication, I deem it prudent to call your attention to an apprehended danger, and to commend to your consideration the propriety of a prompt expression of the sentiment of this Grand Lodge upon the question of exclusive jurisdiction. The Grand Lodge of Hamburg and the Grand Orient of France not only persist in their unwarrantable invasion, or countenance of invasion of the jurisdiction of Grand Lodges on this continent, but seem to be growing more aggressive; and there are now indications that other foreign Grand Bodies are beginning to sympathise with them. I have no doubt that they are encouraged in this by the anomalous position which a majority of the American Grand Lodges have assumed towards the Grand Lodge of Quebec; and it would be difficult indeed, in my opinion, to draw any material distinction between what I deem the aggressions of the latter body, and those of the Grand Lodge of Hamburg and the Grand Orient of France. The Grand Bodies which deny the doctrine of exclusive jurisdiction, and without just ground, as I think, denounce this American doctrine, are still further encouraged by the recent, and, in my judgment, ill-advised and repre- hensible course of the Grand Lodges of Vermont and Illinois. These Bodies have now issued their edict prohibiting al intercourse with Masons holding allegiance to the Grand Lodge of Canada, until that Body shall have recognized the Grand Lodge of Quebec. I have never been able to reconcile my own judgment to the action of this Body in recognizing the Grand Lodge of Quebec. Much less can I reconcile myself to the extraordinary conduct of the Grand Lodges of Vermont and Illinois. If this Grand Lodge should to-day issue its edict of non-intercourse with Vermont and Illinois until they, in turn, should withdraw their edicts of non-inter- course with Canada, there would not be, upon principle, the shadow of a distinction between the two cases. Where, then, are these complications to end ?

So long as sundry of the American Grand Lodges contented themselves with the mere recognition of Quebec, the case presented only a question of differing judgments and opinions ; yet the sequel will show that, even in going thus far, they have placed a formidable weapon in the hands of the enemies of exclusive jurisdiction. But when the Grand Lodges of Vermont and Illinois pass beyond that, and, by hostile legislation, attempt to coerce and dragoon the venerable and respectable Grand Lodge of Canada into the recognition of what she honestly believes to be a case of absolute and un- mitigated insubordination and rebellion, a case is presented which, in my humble judgment, calls for something of resentment and indignation—something more decided and emphatic than the simple expression of a different opinion. It ceases to be a question of opinion or judgment, and becomes one of conscience, of independence, and of existence. As an individual Mason, at least, I can, and will, extend to the Grand Lodge of Canada the right hand of fellowship ; and while I regret and deplore her unhappy complications, I express to her the fervent hope that she will not yield her independence nor compromise her dignity, though all the

Grand Lodges in the universe hurl against her their edicts of non-intercourse. I do not see any possible justification for Vermont and Illinois, and I trust that, before you close your labors, you will express your fraternal disapprobation of the course they have pursued, in terms so round, ringing, and unmistakable, that henceforth there shall be no chance for a misconception of the attitude which we, of the Occident hold on the question of Grand Lodge jurisdiction, sovereignty, and independence.

"Several complaints have come to me as to the form of prayers used in some of the Lodges by the Chaplains, our brethren of the Hebrew faith objecting to seeking Jehovah through the intercession of Jesus Christ as our Lord and Redeemer. I have an indistinct recollection that a committee of the Grand Lodge of Massachusetts, some time since, after great labor and research, reached the conclusion that such prayers were proper, unexceptionable, and strictly Masonic. While I respectfully dissent from the conclusion of that committee, I do not think it necessary to dispose of the complaints upon the ground of strict right to use such prayers. Upon their religous faith men are usually sensitive and tender. Such feelings ought always to be respected; and fraternal courtesy and regard would seem to dictate the omission of non-essential form and expressions when known to be really offensive or objectionable to any brother.

"In two instances adjacent Lodges have expressed a desire to consolidate their property and membership. From the peculiar character of a portion of our jurisdiction, and from the excess of Lodges there and their proximity to one another, such a desire is likely to recur occasionally for many years. I understand that the committee on Revision will propose an amendment to our Constitution authorizing such consolidation in certain cases, and I most cordially recommend it to your favor.

"I have been twice asked if sitting in a Chapter of Royal Arch Masons with a given individual in this jurisdiction entitles the brother so sitting to vouch for such individual to a Lodge of Master Masons. I confess to have been at first a little staggered by the inquiry, for the rule is laid down with a great deal of exactness by the Masonic jurists whom we are accustomed to consult, and the case above stated would not come within the precise letter of that rule. He must have sat in the *Lodge*, says the rule, and a Chapter is

10

not a Lodge. But the question involved was probably not considered by those jurists. Had it been, I have little doubt that the rule would have been so stated as to include the case under consideration. I could not see any rational distinction between the two cases which should make the voucher good in the one case and not in the other, and my decision was pronounced accordingly.

"A misapprehension seems to have prevailed to a considerable extent as to the *status* of colored Masons and their right to visit. The question has been several times presented to me, and, as it is likely to occur more frequently hereafter until the matter is fully understood, I think it advisable once for all to have it settled in this jurisdiction. I have invariably answered that the color of the skin is a consideration to be entirely disregarded. It is surprising that, with the general intelligence of the Fraternity in this State, there should be any occasion to reiterate the fundamental doctrine that Masonry recognizes no such distinction. It is simply a question of regularity and standing, and whether the skin be black, red, or yellow, the applicant to visit is to be tried by those tests, and those only, which are applied to his white brethren. In one case the Master of a Lodge informed me that one of his subordinate officers, whom he highly esteemed, had declared that he could not sit in the Lodge with a black man, and that if the visitor was admitted he himself must retire. To this I replied that, although it was the duty of a master to preserve, if possible, the harmony of his own Lodge, yet he also owed a Masonic duty to members of other Lodges than his own; that they had some rights entitled to recognition, and that he did not owe to the members of his own Lodge any such special duty as called upon him to regard an absurd or unmasonic objection to a visitor; and that, if I were Master, and a member of my Lodge based his objection on the sole ground of the color of the visitor, I should disregard such objection and let the over-sensitive and offended member retire if he chose to do so. If, however, a member should object without assigning any reason, that would present another question, upon which I expressed my opinion one year ago, and they need not be here repeated. A colored Mason sat in this Grand Lodge from day to day at its last Communication, and I have yet to learn that any body's manhood has been seriously impaired thereby. I have but little patience with that Masonry which adopts any other tests than those of regularity, character, manhood, and intelligence, and it is time that there was an end of this child's babble about colored Masons.

"I cannot refrain from again expressing to you the pain and humiliation I have more than once experienced at the want of attendance on Masonic funerals. From this Temple I have seen the dead borne away to their last resting place with scarce enough of followers to lift the body from the hearse and lower it to the grave. This is not Masonic burial. The very term implies something more. The pauper from the almshouse and the felon from the scaffold are attended more respectfully that this. Let us remember that it is the last service which we shall ever be called upon or permitted to render to the departed, and let no trifling considerations of business or convenience interrupt the performance of this duty. If brethren cannot be awakened to a proper discharge of these rights by their own consciousness of right and wrong and the admonitions which have been given them already from this Body, it only remains for Masters to enforce their attendance by imperative summons—for our dead must be respectfully and decently entombed."

He issued eight dispensations for new Lodges, during the year, and twenty from special dispensations—twenty to re-ballot for rejected applicants within the time fixed by the Constitution, and four to elect officers at other than stated period. He does not believe in rotation in office, nor in naming Lodges after living men, and he thinks that Grand Lodges should always have a surplus of some thousands of dollars on hand.

The Grand Secretary presented a report, which is also very interesting. We quote as follows:—

"The usual, or perhaps rather more than the usual, number of letters from persons in the United States and Europe, inquiring for fathers, husbands, sons, or friends who have been lost in the great vortex of California, have been received; and it is gratifying to be enabled to say that this year, as heretofore, in most of the cases where such information was given as would afford an initial point for inquiry, the parties sought for have been traced and placed in communication with their relation or friends, either by a constant succession of letters to the place or places where they were last heard from, or by notes of enquiry appended to the bi-monthly lists of rejections &c., transmitted to the Lodges. Sometimes, however, it becomes rather difficult to obtain or give satisfactory information when, from Ireland,

France, Germany, or even portions of the United States, comes an inquiry regarding some person who was thought to have come to 'California' some twenty years ago, and who, being supposed to be a Mason, must probaby have joined 'the Lodge.' In such cases, unhappily, the trail is somewhat indistinct, inasmuch as the person may never have come to California—as California, covers sundry thousands of square miles—as the party may never have been a Mason at all—as he may never have joined 'the Lodge' here if he was—and as, if he did, there are nearly two hundred of 'the Lodges' in our State. And sometimes, too, comes a case where the solicitous inquirer has not been particularly anxious about the roving propensities, during life, of a wife or husband, either geographically or connubially, but when the death is heard of and a supposed amount of property is thought to have been left, the ties of kindred and the bonds of the fraternity are brought into service with an amount of tension which is very refreshing to let stretch. The following extract from a letter lately received, though done in rather worse English than some others, is a tolerably fair sample of some of the correspondence of that class:—

"I have the news of Sanfrancisco by a friend that my wife is ded and she is bury in the freemasons cemetery as I know that no person can not get in there without an order from the Gr∴ Lodge 1 beg to you the frat∴ of the order to se for get me a certificate of her burial, and to seek by the frat∴ Bros∴ of all Lodges to try to recover for me all she had, such as a policy of insurance and my life for $5000. two bank book where she was deposited money but allway and her old name Mrs.——, she had with her a large book the life of christ which my name is on the cover in gold letters, the certificat of mariage, and a big square Trunk which I buy in——for her and full of every thing for table use as table cloths fingers napp, cloths for herself any quantity as well quilts and blankets and cheets and pillow caises, the friend who wrot me this news say that she had give the lic that she was separated from me and had maried another man at——and not agree came in Sanfrancisco and die the parti told me she had maried a rich man and she had money to helself, so Dear bro∴ I hope that you will do all in your power by the frat∴ to find out all this things and the name of the Gentleman she had marrid for I will use the United States law for those get married with another man wife without Divorce, the Gentleman which I give you the name above is a witness of all for he have read the letter I have sent to her. hoping Dear Bro∴ that you will do all best for a poor unfortunate M∴ the Bank Books Was on New York banks I am goes to wrot a letter as well at——where she had married, I have the name of the W∴ M∴ of——Lodge for try to get the name and address of that gentleman have marriage, with her, and please give me the address of some Brother who are doing business in san francisco so I could get correspondence with them and that affair who is a great pity for me."

Bro. Abell takes peculiar pride in the library which he

says probably contains the largest collection of purely Masonic Books, to be found upon the continent. It numbers 711 volumes,and 349,788 pages,all handsomely and uniformly bound.

Number of existing Lodges 92.

From the report of the Grand Lecturer, the Lodges appear to be prosperous, and generally working well.

In the report of the committee on jurisprudence, which was adopted, we find the following:—"The political allegiance of the provinces of Alsace and Lorraine has been transferred from France to Germany, but that can in no way effect the *status* of the Masons of those provinces who yield allegiance and obedience to the Grand Orient of France."

A resolution was adopted, that no dispensation shall hereafter be granted to any Lodge, which shall have adopted the name of a living person.

We are glad to see that services of Bro. W. H. Hill, chair-man of correspondence, are appreciated by his brethren. The Finance Committee speak about the "rich fund of Masonic information" contained in his reports. Canada for 1872, receives a first class notice. We think our degree of prosperity almost unparalleled.

M. W. Bro. Isaac S. Titus, was elected Grand Master, and R. W. Bro. Alexander G. Abell, re-elected Grand Secretary.

COLORADO.

Thirteenth annual Communication; held at Denver, Sept. 30th, 1873. M. W. Bro. Henry M. Teller, Grand Master, and R. W. Bro. E. C. Parmelee, Grand Secetary.

The Grand Master delivered a brief address, in which he mentions having granted one dispensation for a new Lodge. He thinks the affiliation fee should be abolished, and the dues made as low as possible.

A memorial address was delivered on the Masonic character of Rt. Rev. and M. W. Bro. George M. Randall, P.G.M.

of Massachusetts, and Bishop of Colorado, Wyoming, and New Mexico, who died at Denver on Sept. 23rd, 1873.

M. W. Bro. Teller retired, after six years' service, and M. W. Bro. Webster D. Anthony was elected Grand Master, and the Grand Secretary was re-elected.

DELAWARE.

The sixty-seventh annual Communication was held at Wilmington, June 27th, 1873. M. W. Bro. Rev. J. C. McCabe, D. D., Grand Master, and R. W. Bro. J. P. Allmond, Grand Secretary.

The Grand Master delivered his address and valedictory, having filled the chair for three successive years, and being about to remove from the State. He records the death of P. G. M., Wm. T. Read.

The Grand Lodge is now in a good financial position, having new regalia and jewels, and a cash balance on hand.

In pursuance of a change made in the time of meeting of Grand Lodge, the 68th annual Communication was held at Wilmington, October 1st, 1873. R. W. Bro. C. J. Hall, D. G. M., presiding.

A resolution to repeal the resolution paying representatives, was adopted.

The state of their finances would not permit the publication of a report on correspondence. A suggestion was made that a full review every three years would be better than a meagre report every year. The receipt is acknowledged of our proceedings for 1872, amongst others.

M. W. Bro. John P. Allmond was transferred from the chair of Grand Secretary to that of Grand Master; and R. W. Bro. Wm. S. Hayes was elected Grand Secretary.

DISTRICT OF COLUMBIA.

The annual Communication was held at Washington, November 12th, 1873. M. W. Bro. C. F. Stansbury, Grand Master, and R. W. Bro. W. A. Yates, Grand Secretary.

On the question of " Mixed Funerals," the Grand Master has the following, which, we think, puts the matter on the proper ground :—

" I desired that, if the subject were to be re-opened, it should be on a full knowledge of the particular case which brought it up, and of the general sentiment of the Fraternity throughout the United States on the question. I have, therefore, taken care to investigate both, having addressed a letter to every Grand Master in the country, inquiring whether any agreement or regulation existed in his jurisdiction as to the relative positions or authority of our Fraternity and the Order of Odd-Fellows at funerals where the deceased had been a member of both societies ; and in case no agreement or regulation existed, what was the custom on such occasions. I have received replies from twenty-seven grand jurisdictions, and they are, almost without exception, uniform in declaring that there exists no regulation or agreement on the subject; that the Masonic fraternity always assumes exclusive control where it takes any part in the burial of a Brother, and performs its ceremony last where other associations participate at all in the funeral rites. The Masonic fraternity never attends a funeral except when the deceased, or his friends on his behalf, have expressed a desire for Masonic burial; and that wish is taken as the expression of a preference that the rites should be under their control. And that control cannot be divided with any other body, because no person not a Mason, can assist in the performance of Masonic work and it is only for the performance of Masonic work that the craft is ever permitted to appear in public. These are, in brief, the views of the Grand Masters who have responded to my inquiries.

" Anxious to show every courtesy to a great and useful society, I recommend that the whole of the papers in relation to this matter be referred to a special committee for examination and report. Leaving the matter wholly to the judgment of the Masters of the Lodges, does not seem to have fully met the requirements of the case, and often places a Master in an embarrassing position, in which he is liable to the accusation of discourtesy, if he carries out what he conscientiously believes to be his Masonic duty. The adoption of a strict and uniform rule appears to me to be the best method of avoiding painful and inappropriate discussions on these mournful occasions ; and I confess that I incline to a more rigid enforcement of the exclusiveness of our Fraternity.

"We shall do no injury and offer no discourtesy to other societies by this course. They are free to adopt a similar principle for the government of their own arrangements, and in so doing will never meet with opposition or jealousy from us. Seeking no publicity, avoiding parade and show as utterly opposed to the principles of our institution, we are never desirous of forcing our attentions or honors upon any. They must be sought before they will be bestowed, and no stranger hand should be permitted to assist in their bestowal."

He granted dispensations to several lodges to "call off," during the summer months.

The Grand Lodge Library has now 3219 volumes, and Bro. J. S. McCoy, the Librarian, receives a well merited compliment, for the energetic discharge of his duties.

They have a system of Grand Visitations to all the Lodges, which powerfully contributes to the harmony and efficiency of the Lodges. These Visitations are accompanied with lectures, addresses and readings, by eminent Brethren, and in most cases, they have the additional attraction of their celebrated Masonic choir; and they rarely fail in having interested and appreciative audiences. The consequence of this system is, that a very great deal of interest is taken in the Lodge meetings, and our Capitoline Brethren are able to boast, without exaggeration, of the elegance and perfection with which their Masonic work is now performed.

The following resolution was passed as a standing regulation:—

" *Resolved*, That in the burial of a deceased Brother by a Masonic Lodge, or in the performance of other Masonic labor in public, the control by the Lodge must be absolute, and that while the Lodge is exercising that control, no non-Masonic organization shall be permitted to participate."

The report on correspondence, by Bro. W. R. Singleton, covers 259 pages, and evinces the determination of the author, to spare no pains to keep his brethren well informed. Our proceedings for 1872 are fully noticed. We copy one of his comments:—

"This Grand Lodge keeps up the old Masonic Landmark, to transact its business in the Entered Apprentice Lodge, where legitimately only can be found the Treasurer and Secretary, which officers have no business in the F.·. C.·.'s or M.·. M.·.'s Lodge. In the United States all the Grand Lodges, since 1843, have changed from the old system, and now hold Lodges on the 1st, 2nd and 3rd *degrees* of Masonry. Originally they were called Lodges of E.·. A.·., F.·. C.·. and M.·. M.·., which is the true title, and we have never surrendered this point, nor consented to the *sin* and *iniquity* perpetrated by the Master Masons in snatching from the E.·. A.·. and F.·. C.·. all the rights to which they have been entitled from time immemorial."

The Grand Master and Grand Secretary were both re-elected.

FLORIDA.

The forty-third annual Communication was held at Jacksonville, February 11th, 1873. M. W. Bro. Samuel Pasco, Grand Master, and R. W. Bro. D. C. Dawkins, Grand Secretary.

The Grand Master reports a steady and constant improvement in their affairs. Nearly all the old Lodges have been restored. They now number sixty-five, with a membership of more than 2100. He thinks that notwithstanding the many discouragements that still attend them, the winter of their gloom is about to give way to a bright and glorious summer.

He issued dispensations for four new lodges, one at Key West, of which he speaks as follows:—

"The last named Lodge is composed of refugees from Cuba; their work is in the Spanish language, and the accounts of their progress that have reached me have been most encouraging. In my address, delivered here two years ago, I had occasion to refer to the enormities committed upon our Cuban brethren, and to express my abhorence of the outrages which it was alleged had been perpetrated upon them, and it has indeed been gratifying to have an opportunity to extend the hand of welcome to our infant Lodge of these unfortunate victims of tyranny, and to throw around

11

them the broad mantle of protection of this Grand Lodge.
Let us show these brethren that we know how to sympathize
with misfortune, and that we meet them around this altar as
brothers beloved, bound by a sacred tie that the outer world
does not comprehend."

We can hardly say too much in praise of the very excellent
report on correspondence, by Grand Secretary Dawkins.'
From his notice of our proceedings for 1872, we extract the
following :—

"Some Lodges established by this Grand Lodge in the
new Province of Manitoba, in what is known as the Dominion
of Canada, are in a flourishing condition. Question for
manufacturers of Masonic Jurisprudence in these fast times :
Is Manitoba unoccupied territory ?

"Two thousand dollars in gold was promptly contributed
to the Chicago sufferers.

"This Grand Lodge has made another effort without success
to quiet the Quebec dissenters.

"The pamphlet before us exhibits satisfactory and gratifying
evidence that the Grand Lodge of Canada is composed, and
its business in every department conducted by lively, true
and worthy craftsmen, in whose hands the reputation and
welfare of the fraternity there are eminently safe ; and that
they are not to be driven into humiliating disgrace, by
either any turbulence at home or outside pressure, however
formidable it may appear.

"Bro. E. Mitchell presented the report on Foreign Correspondence, reviewing in masterly style the proceedings of
thirty-three Grand Lodges, Florida for 1872 receiving
respectful notice. He likes the plan of our report better
than that of the year before, and acknowledges that we did
the 'right thing' in the Quebec case, and says that our
pamphlet was not in hand when he was gathering up the
'pros and cons' in his last report, &c. Well, let it go at
that, but we repel the insinuation that 'our labors in that
matter are all for Canada,' for we endeavor to consider it a
subject of general importance, in which all true Masons,
everywhere are interested. We do not, however, believe
that Bro. M. felt very serious in making such insinuation,
but look upon it as only a preparatory swell to giving vent
to the flow of fraternal emulation which followed in connection therewith.

"Bro. M. complains that one of our brethren has an unpronounceable name, which we will cordially 'invest him with' if he will pay us a visit and remain long enough in our genial clime to prepare his tongue to pronounce it. We assure him we have no difficulty anent it.

"We hope that when Bro. Drummond comes to consider Bro. Mitchell's defence of Canada in his review of Maine, he will see his erroneous position in the Quebec matter which has misled so many thousands to recognize contention and disorder in the Masonic Fraternity, and begin without further delay to repair the wrong done in the premises.

"All the Grand Lodges in the United States many years ago recognized the Grand Lodge of Canada as being regularly formed, and her jurisdiction as clearly defined as was that of Maine, or any other States of the Union, which jurisdiction embraced what is known as the Province of Quebec. And yet, within the last two years many of them, following in the lead of Bro. Drummond, have gone back upon that recognition, and assert in the face of stern and unyielding facts to the contrary that the Grand Lodge of Canada had not exclusive jurisdiction over that territory, simply because a few Lodges therein by consent continue to work under their mother Grand Lodges in Europe. This enormous departure from Masonic rectitude is startling and deplorable, and we are lost in wonder as to what will be the final result of the whole matter. It has been said that ' Truth crushed to earth will rise again,' and upon this basis we build our hope above expressed."

And also the following, from his review of Connecticut :—

" In his review of Nova Scotia, Bro. W. takes issue, and contends that seven constitute a quorum to transact business in a Master Mason's Lodge, and says : 'If only three are necessary, it seems to us that the same number should be all that is necessary to form a new Lodge, or to retain the Charter after being formed. Why require seven Master Masons to form a Lodge, or to retain the same, and allow three to undertake to do what they cannot, and do it properly?' We must bear in mind that a Lodge of the present day is not what it was in Ancient times, when three constituted a Lodge of Master Masons, and that the labors conducted may reasonably be supposed to be very different. We therefore believe that no Lodge should be opened for work or business unless there be seven present."

"We have ever been of opinion that seven constitutes a quorum in the First Degree, five in the Second, and three in

the Third, and now think that the transfer of business from
the First to the Third, by modern custom, does not affect
the quorum in the Third. The transaction of the business
has been taken from that department where there were at
least seven and transferred to that where three only are
requisite. We feel that that change should stand alone upon
its own foundation, whatever that may be, and we are un-
willing to concede that any material consequential changes
are thereby necessarily wrought in the original plan of
Masonry. If the number three is too small for the transaction of the Lodge business, it is an argument conclusive, in
our mind, that the change from the custom ' time immemorial' was a step in the wrong direction, and should therefore be retraced ; and if some of the older Grand jurisdictions will first fall back into the old line of doing the business in the First Degree, we will endeavor to follow in graceful
procession."

We have always insisted that all the ordinary business of
a lodge should be transacted in the first degree, and such is
our practice here. We never could understand why our
Brethren across the line should have departed from the
ancient custom in this particular. Will somebody please
enlighten us?

We had marked a number of extracts, anent Quebec, in
which the correct doctrine of Grand Lodge sovereignty,
with regard to our position, is ably upheld, but are compelled to refrain.

M. W. Bro. Albert J. Russell was elected Grand Master,
and R. W. Bro. D. C. Dawkins was re-elected Grand Secretary.

GEORGIA.

We have received the proceedings of an emergent Com-
munication of this Grand Lodge, in Macon, March 4, 1874.
M. W. Bro. Samuel D. Irvin, Grand Master, and R. W. Bro.
J. Emmett Blackshear, Grand Secretary.

The Grand Master says :—

"Brethren :—You have been called together in an Emergent meeting, to take such action as may be necessary to
correct a most grievous and unaccountable mistake committed

by the Grand Lodge at its Annual Communication in October last."

He then recapitulates the circumstances, from which it appears that the Junior Warden of a Lodge, (afterwards elected W. M.) was expelled by the Grand Lodge, without any charges having been preferred against him, and without apparently the slightest foundation, for any such action. We are not informed exactly how the mistake was made, but the occurrence is certainly an extraordinary one.

He was, of course, immediately restored by the unanimous adoption of the following report:—

"Your committee, to whom was referred the Address of the Most Worshipful Grand Master and accompanying documents, touching the case of brother Adolph Joseph, of Benevolent Lodge, No. 3, who was erroneously expelled by the Grand Lodge at its last regular session, in October, 1873, and against whom no charges had ever been preferred, respectfully report, that the Address of the Most Worshipful Grand Master, at the opening of this Emergent meeting of this Grand Lodge, gives the facts so fully and explicitly that no further elaboration is needed from your committee, except the declaration that the unfortunate mistake occurred by inadvertence in the committee on grievances, and that the fraternity had no worthier member than the brother thus unwittingly expelled. We accordingly recommend the adoption of the following resolution:

Resolved,—That brother Adolph Joseph be and is hereby declared restored to all the rights and privileges on Freemasonry.

IDAHO.

The sixth annual communication was held at Boise City, December 8th, 1873. M. W. Bro. John Kennaly, Grand Master ; and R. W. Bro. L. F. Cartee, Grand Secretary.

The Grand Master reports the past year as one of peace and prosperity. He decided that no lodge could grant a dimit to an entered apprentice, but does not say why, nor can we imagine any good reason for such a rule.

He recommends the repeal of a former resolution, making

saloon keeping a Masonic offence, and on this subject, the following report was adopted:—

"The undersigned, members of the select committee to whom was referred the subject of saloon keeping, temperance and kindred subjects, being unable to agree with the majority of the committee, beg leave to state that we consider such resolutions and edicts on those subjects as have heretofore been adopted by this Grand Lodge, as well as the one reported by the majority of this committee, an exercise of authority unwarranted by the ancient landmarks, that leads to confusion among the workmen, and is detrimental to the best interests of the Order. That the subordinate lodges possess already all the authority and power necessary for the proper discipline of members violating the moral law or their obligations as members of the Order, and such matters should be left entirely under their control. We therefore offer the following as a substitute for the resolutions reported by the majority of the committee:

"Whereas, At the last session of this Grand Lodge certain resolutions were adopted making the keeping of saloons by Masons in this jurisdiction, a Masonic offence, prohibiting Masons from engaging in said business, and notifying all Masons then engaged in the business to abandon the same prior to the 1st of October, 1873, under the penalty of being proceeded against, even to expulsion;

"And Whereas, The Master and Wardens of the several Lodges have, during the past year used their best efforts to carry the said resolution into effect, but have found it a moral impossibility to do so, therefore be it

"*Resolved,* That the resolutions adopted by the Grand Lodge at the annual Cummunication in December, A. L. 5872, prohibiting Masons from being engaged in the saloon business, and requiring them to close out their business on or before October 1st, 1873, and all resolutions and edicts of the Grand Lodge in any way affecting the legitimate business or pursuits of Masons in this jurisdiction, so far as the same are not forbidden and are not against the laws of the United States or Territory of Idaho, and the Ancient Landmarks of Masonry, be and the same are hereby repealed, and all proceedings had or done be declared null and void."

The Grand Master was re-elected. After the election of Bro. Chas. Himrod, as Grand Secretary, he was declared ineligible, being only a W. M., and not a P. M., and Bro.

Joseph Pinkham was thereupon appointed by the Grand Master to the vacant office.

INDIANA.

Fifty-sixth annual Communication held at Indianapolis, May 27th, 1873. M. W. Bro. Christian Fetta, Grand Master, and R. W. Bro. John M. Bramwell, Grand Secretary.

The Grand Master delivered his annual address, in which wo find that he issued dispensations for twenty-four new lodges. He appears to have performed his duties in no perfunctory manner, if we may judge from the following record of visits :—

" I have visited and examined the records of many lodges, from which I am enabled to present to you the following facts : —

" One third of these Lodges have good records accurately kept, an honor to the officers and creditable to the Fraternity.

"The minutes of one-third have not been signed by the W. M.

" The minutes of one-third of the Lodges do not show that candidates for advancement have shown suitable proficiency.

" One twenty-fifth of the Lodges ballot for candidates at called communications.

" One twenty-fifth of the Lodge records do not show that any of the officers or members were present at any of the communications.

" One-twelfth of the Lodges receive notes for the payment of dues. While this practice should be discourged and discontinued, it is, however, an improvement upon the custom of many Lodges who have no system of settlement whatever.

" One twenty-fifth of the Lodges do not ballot for candidates for the second or third degrees.

" One-twelfth of the Lodges follow a practice of calling off from one meeting to another, without ever closing.

" The records of one twenty-fifth of the Lodges do not show any reports from the committees on character.

"The records of one twenty-fifth of the Lodges do not show that any ballot has been had, and upon the report of the committee on character the candidate has been declared elected or rejected.

" One-twelfth of the Lodges declare cases of emergency to advance a candidate to the second or third degree.

" No argument is needed to show that these unlawful proceedings, if not checked, will undermine the very foundation of our organization. The existence of some of these Lodges would have been of short duration, had they not been able to show that some of these apparent irregularities were occasioned by omissions and mistakes in the records by the Secretary.

" In many of the Lodges the Secretaries are either ignorant or indifferent as to their duties. In some instances (from long continuance in office) the Secretary has become an Autocrat and rules the Lodge, his Master and Wardens. It is the duty of the Secretary to observe the W. Master's will and pleasure, and the Master is in duty bound to see that this officer does what is required of him. The Master should never permit any officer below him to usurp his authority. It is the Master's duty to supervise and direct all business, and to control and direct his subordinate officers.

" Lodge records should show who presided as Master and Wardens, and the names of all the officers, members and visitors present at each communication. It may be said that these are matters of mere form; but with equal truth it may be urged that the work of a Lodge is matter of form; the rites, the ceremonies, and the entire ritual of Masonry are matters of form; yet the preservation of these forms keeps alive the very substance of Masonry. The observance of prescribed forms is vital, not simply as a history of the Lodge, but to the existence and perpetuity of the fraternity."

He very properly suspended one Lodge for having buried an expelled member with Masonic Ceremonies. He decided that charges cannot be withdrawn without the unanimous consent of the Lodge.

We also extract the following : —

"The following question was submitted to me :

" ' Can a request from a Lodge in New York be received by a Lodge in our jurisdiction to confer the degree of M. M. upon a Bro. F. C. who had been elected to receive that

degree in the said New York Lodge, without a formal petition from the Bro. F. C., and a reference to a committee on
character?

"I held that the Lodge can receive the request, and if
there be no objection, and the Lodge is satisfied that the
person named in the request is a F. C. Mason, the Lodge
has a right to confer the degree as requested, without the
petition or reference.

"The following was submitted for decision. Grand Lodge
Regulations, paragraph 108:

"If a brother persists in the sale or use of intoxicating
liquors as a beverage, *after being admonished by the Lodge,* is
it the duty of the Lodge to suspend or expel him? Can a
brother be admonished by the Lodge without trial, and if
so, by what method should it be brought about?

"I answered: A Lodge may appoint some brother to wait
upon the offender, admonish him or notify him of the fact
that the sale or use of intoxicating liquors as a beverage
is a Masonic offence, and a violation of the rules and
regulations of our Grand Lodge. Or, the Master and
Wardens may counsel with him against the wrong practice,
admonish him to desist, or the law must be enforced.
After having been admonished, if he still continues, or does
not reform, prefer charges against him, and if found guilty
inflict the penalty according to Section 108 G. L. rules and
regulations.

"*Query.* Bro. D. D. N. was tried in our Lodge for unmasonic conduct, on five specifications. The fifth specification
was ruled out by the W. Master as being vague and indefinite. On the first and second he was acquited; on the
third and fourth he was found guilty and suspended for one
month, from which he took an appeal to the Grand Lodge.

"The Grand Lodge sustained the appeal, and remanded the
case back to the Lodge for a new trial. Now can the
Lodge try Bro. N. twice for the same offence? He has
already been tried on the first four specifications; on the
first and second he was acquitted, and on the third and
fourth he was found guilty, and has suffered the entire
penalty long before the Grand Lodge met. Can the Lodge
amend the fifth specification and try him on that alone?

"I held, you can not again put him on trial on the first
and second specifications.

"On the third and fourth specifications, it is your duty to
try him again.

12

" On the fifth specification, if it was matter not embraced in either of the other charges, that is, if it was a distinct transaction, a different offence, he can be proceeded against again, either in a new proceeding, or possibly together with the third and fourth specifications. But charges can not be amended, either in substance or form, after they have been read by the Secretary to the Lodge, except upon order of the W. Master, in open Lodge, upon cause shown.

" *Query.* Bro. ——— was expelled from our Lodge, from which he appealed. The Grand Lodge sustained the appeal, remanded the case to the Lodge for a new trial, with leave to amend specifications. Is it the duty of the Lodge to amend the specifications and go into trial if the aggrieved party does not wish the case tried again? Does the granting of a new trial reinstate him the same as he was before he was tried? Can the evidence taken at the last trial be received in the new trial in the absence of the witnesses?

" I hold,

" 1st. It is the *privilege* of the Lodge to amend.

" 2nd. It is the duty of the Lodge to proceed to trial unless the accuser, the accused and the Lodge unanimously assent to the withdrawal of the charges.

" 3rd. The defendant in the case referred to, stands (with reference to the Lodge) as he did after the charges were preferred, before trial.

" 4th. The depositions taken to be used at the last trial can be used in the second trial. Witnesses dead who testified at the former trial, can not of course be examined again. You may prove what they testified to on the former trial.

" *Question.* A Brother is elected a W. M. of a Lodge in 1871, elected again in 1872. Is a second installation required? Is the installation ceremonies adopted by our Grand Lodge the only ceremonial ritual to be observed at the installation of officers of subordinate Lodges?

" *Answer.* Every officer of a constituted Lodge must be installed before exercising any of the functions of his office. (See Sec. 30, R. and R. G. L.) A re-installation is necessary by the re-election. The ceremonial ritual for the installation of officers adopted by the Grand Lodge must be used and observed as a part and parcel of the rules and regulations of this Grand Lodge.

" *Question.* A man is superintendent of a brewery where they manufacture ale, has no interest in the concern; is he eligible for the degrees, or would the action of the Grand Lodge prevent him?

" Held, That his admission would be an infringement upon the spirit and meaning of the law. Every Lodge is pro- hibited from conferring any of the degrees of Masonry upon any one who makes it his business to manufacture.or sell intoxicating liquors to be used as a beverage. (See Sects. 108 and 109.) It needs no proof or argument to show that ale is intoxicating, or the brewery a place where liquor is manufactured, such as is contemplated by the law, and he who superintends is as guilty of the Masonic offence as the owner of the establishment."

In conclusion, he gives advice, well worthy of being care- fully studied ;—

"The total number of members reported in 1854 was 6,526, against 26,216 reported for 1872.

Since the year 1853 the Lodges in this jurisdiction have initiated 34,201. Of this number they have honorably discharged those who have dimitted and affiliated in the Grand Lodge above, 3,327, leaving a balance of 30,774, as charged against the Lodges. Of this number you have on hand, the difference between the number of members in 1854 and 1872, 19,790, or in other words you have retained but 19,790 out of 30,774 initiated. But the tables show that you have dimitted 17,528 against 9,741, who have affiliated, giving you the credit of all doubtful testimony, and pre- suming that the affiliations are those who have dimitted and removed from one part of the State to another.

"It is not begging the question when you take into con- sideration the increase of population in this State, to say that as many Masons have come into, and affiliated in this jurisdiction as have moved out of it. But admitting that you may have credit for those who have affiliated, you have trained and equipped an army of non-affiliates of 7,787.

"This vast army have turned their backs on you, and not one of them will be of any service to you in time of need and trouble. The question that first presents itself is, Why have so many dimitted? Why have 7,787, who were favorably impressed with the institution of Freemasonry, and received into the order as *men free born* and *well recommended*, who have assumed the duties and responsi- bilities of an organization based upon *Brotherly Love*, Relief and Truth, deserted you ?

"The answer is easily given. Sufficient care has not been taken in the selection of material, and in maintaining a healthy state of discipline and morals among officers and members.

"Those men who are captivated alone by the pomp and circumstances of public days, and have no realizing sense of the great principles of the Order, and no heart nor interest in the work and duties of Masonry, when the sick need help and the poor relief, when the cry of distress is heard, and small if not frequent sacrifices are to be made, and inconveniences incurred, to say nothing of going forth amid pestilence, contagion and death, soon fall by the way, and are seen and heard of no more among Masons. They are summer-day soldiers,

"In their natural constitution might have been discerned by inspection the deficiency which became apparent on trial.

"The true Mason must have high and noble aims and purposes in life. He must be a man of good morals, unselfish life, endeavoring to live so as to do the greatest good.

"A Lodge of such members will be an enduring institution.

"Again, the presence of unworthy members in the Lodge, if their public and private life is not a disgrace, their atmosphere can drive from the institution better and worthier men who, if prevailing in influence, would give the institution tone and character.

"In our experience how often have we found pure and upright men who fully accord with the principles of our institution, and having been induced ·to join our Order have sometimes found the officers of loose habits, and men among the members with whom it was not their choice to associate. After vainly trying to reform the members and establish the principles of the Order in the ascendency, nothing is more natural or more frequent than the attendance of the uncongenial members to become less frequent, and finally that a dimit should be prayed, and that the Mason who would otherwise have been an ornament to the Lodge, should go out into the world never again to affiliate.

"But your tables expose some worse and more damaging figures than all this—that of 6,883 suspensions and expulsions. While you may set up the plea that Masons have a right to dimit, and upon a slight provocation often sever their connection with the Order, no excuse can be urged for the latter. Let us change tactics. Let our motto be, Why should he be made a Mason? From this standpoint make your examinations, and if you find that an applicant is not positively honest, temperate, and with a positive object in life, reject him as unfit for your association."

The Grand Lodge differed from the Grand Master in his decision, quoted above, as to charges being withdrawn, holding that a majority vote is all that is necessary; and on the brewery question, the following was adopted:—

"A man is superintendent of a brewery where they manufacture ale, but has no interest in the concern; is he eligible for the degrees, or would the action of the Grand Lodge prevent him? The answer is in the affirmative; a decision that the committee would prefer not being called upon to defend, nor do they wish to attack it. How far the labourer who is engaged at his daily toils, or the husband-man who plants and raises hops, barley, corn, rye, etc., is a party to the crime of manufacturing intoxicating drinks, is rather too metaphysical and fine spun to be distinctly visible to the naked eye."

The question as to the liability of a Lodge to pay for the funeral, and other expenses, of one of their members who dies in a foreign jurisdiction, is being considerably dis. cussed. In our opinion the correct ground is taken in the subjoined report, which was adopted by the Grand Lodge of Indiana:—

"The Committee on Foreign Correspondence, to whom was referred so much of the Grand Master's Address as relates to the claim of Lincoln Lodge, No. 19, of Nebraska, against Noblesville Lodge, No. 57, have examined the papers in the case, and submit the following report:

"Bro. J. Greathouse, a member in good standing of Nobles-ville Lodge, No. 57, but residing within the jurisdiction of Lincoln Lodge, No. 19, of Nebraska, died, and was buried by the latter Lodge, which presented a bill to Noblesville Lodge for the expenses incurred in burying the deceased brother. Noblesville Lodge, No. 57, deemed the bill an extravagant one, and not being informed as to the reasons why the expense was incurred, the deceased being in good circumstances when he left their jurisdiction, declined to pay the amount, and the matter was referred to the Grand Lodge of Nebraska at its last annual Communication. On the report of the Committee on Jurisprudence it was held by that Grand Lodge that 'common usage' required the payment of the bill by Noblesville Lodge, No. 57, and the following resolution was adopted :

"*Resolved*, That the Grand Secretary of the Grand Lodge of Nebraska, be and is hereby instructed to ask through the Grand Secretary of the Grand Lodge of Indiana, that Noblesville Lodge, No. 57, pay Lincoln Lodge, No. 19. the amount expended by said Lincoln Lodge in the funeral expenses of deceased Bro. J. Greathouse.

"Your committee have not the time to investigate or discuss the question of what is 'common usage' in such cases, but so far as we are at present informed, are of the opinion that it is not in accordance with the position taken by the Grand Lodge of Nebraska. We find, however, that a pre-cedent has been established by this Grand Lodge in a similar case presented at the Annual Communication of 1869, when it was declared to be not in accordance with Masonic law or precedent to ask the Lodge with which he was affiliated to pay the expenses of burying a brother who had died under the jurisdiction of another Lodge.

"Your committee would further add, that a Master Mason in good standing is justly entitled to all the rights and benefits of Masonry, not only while under the jurisdiction of the Lodge which made him a Mason, or with which he may have subsequently affiliated, but he may claim them of any Lodge in the world under whose jurisdiction he may happen to be. His Lodge extends from east to west and from north to south, and may he always find Masonic Charity equally extensive."

Bro. M. H. Rice submitted the report on correspondence He was assisted by Bro. Daniel McDonald, and their joint production is very creditable. Canada for 1872 receives kindly mention.

The Grand Master and Grand Secretary were both re-elected.

IOWA.

Thirtieth annual Communication, held at Davenport, June 3rd, 1873. M. W. Bro. O. P. Waters, Grand Master, and R. W. Bro. T. S. Parvin, Grand Secretary. Representatives were present from 206 Lodges out of the 305 working Lodges in the jurisdiction.

The Grand Master had issued dispensations for 12 new Lodges during the year. He reversed the decision of a former Grand Master, which was to the effect that a Brother receiving the degrees in a Lodge, and failing to sign the by-laws, was not a member of that Lodge. The present Grand Master holds "that no Lodge has a right to make non-affiliates, and that a Brother raised to the sublime degree in a Lodge is, by that act, made a member of it, and that he has no more right to decline to sign its by-laws than he has to decline to perform any other Masonic duty; and that even if he does refuse to do so, he is, by the original petition, bound to abide by the laws of the order, one of the oldest of which is, that a Mason ought to belong to some Lodge."

He strongly urges the adoption of some plan to carry out their proposed Widows and Orphans' Home. He does not believe in special dispensations to ballot out of time, and thinks that if a fee were required to be sent with the application, the number of emergent cases would be rapidly lessened. He recommends the adoption of the practice, which prevails here, and in all European and some other jurisdictions—that of issuing Grand Lodge certificates.

The report of the Grand Secretary is just what we might expect from Brother Parvin, who is exceedingly thorough in his work. He enters largely into details, and gives much useful information.

The "Widows and Orphans' Home" was laid on the table.

Memorial pages are set apart to G. W. McCleary, P.G.M., Ansel Humphreys, P. G. M., J. B. Atherton, P. G. J. W., and W. F. Kidder, P. G. T.

Grand Secretary Parvin combines with these proceedings a number of interesting biographical sketches of the Past Grand Masters of Iowa.

The report on correspondence is by Bro. Thomas R. Ercanbrach. It covers 117 pages, and is exceedingly well written. Our proceedings of 1872 receive a good notice.

We copy the following from the address of the Grand Orator, Bro. John M. Crawford :—

"I close with the words of the great German poet, Goethe; words that find an echo in dark hours and in bright, in many a heart; words full of devoutness and piety. He calls it

"THE MASON LODGE.

"The Mason's ways are
A'type of existence:
And his persistence
Is, as the days are
Of men in this world.

"The Future hides in it
Gladness and sorrow;
We press still thorow,
Naught that abides in it
Daunting us—onward.

"And solemn before us
Veiled, the dark Portal,
Goal of all mortal;
Stars silent, rest o'er us,
Graves under us, silent.

"While earnest thou gazest,
Comes boding of terror,
Come phantasm and error,
Perplexes the bravest
With doubt and misgiving.

"But heard are the voices;—
Heard are the Sages,
The Worlds and the Ages;
'Choose well; your choice is
Brief and yet endless;

"'Here eyes do regard you,
In Eternity's stillness;
Here is all fulness,
Ye brave, to reward you:
Work, and despair not.'"

M. W. Bro. Joseph Chapman was elected Grand Master, and R. W. Bro. T. S. Parvin was re-elected Grand Secretary.

These proceedings are embellished with a fine steel engraved portrait of Bro. Chapman.

KANSAS.

Eighteenth annual Communication held at Lawrence, October 15th, 1873. M. W. Bro. John M. Price, Grand Master; and R. W. Bro. John H. Brown, Grand Secretary.

From the decisions of the Grand Master we take the following :—

"By a majority vote of the members present at a regular meeting, a Lodge can make a reasonable assessment on its own members for charitable purposes, or legitimate Lodge expenses, but not to assist in building a Masonic Hall. Funds for the latter purpose must be raised by voluntary contributions.

"A Lodge cannot grant a brother a new trial. If aggrieved,

his remedy is by appeal to the Grand Lodge, and that body can order a new trial.

"Lodges cannot compel non-affiliated Masons to pay dues.

"Lodges, while under Dispensation, cannot affiliate Masons—cannot dimit its members—cannot lay corner stones of public buildings—cannot dedicate Masonic Halls—cannot recommend a petition for dispensation to form a new Lodge—cannot give permission to another Lodge to advance a brother—cannot try one of its members for unmasonic conduct—in fact, can only *initiate, pass* and *raise* Masons, according to the express terms of their letters of Dispensation.

"When a brother received the first and second degrees in one Lodge, and by its request, the third degree was conferred in another, he becomes a member of the Lodge conferring the third degree, on signing the By-laws."

With several of these decisions we do not agree. It is our practice to require candidates to sign the By-laws on the night of their initiation, and as a part of that ceremony. He then becomes a member of that Lodge. If he receives the other degrees in another Lodge, at the request of the first, that does not alter his membership. The conferring of the degrees is simply an act of courtesy from one Lodge to another, and it stands as the work of the Lodge making the request.

During a recess the Grand Lodge dedicated a new Masonic Hall with imposing public ceremonies.

The following resolution was unanimously adopted. It is pretty strong, but not stronger, we suppose, than is required in Kansas:—

"*Resolved*, That whenever it shall come to the knowledge of the M. W. Grand Master, that any officer of this Grand Lodge, or of any subordinate Lodge in this jurisdiction, shall be engaged in keeping a saloon or dram shop, or in any other dishonorable or immoral occupation, he shall immediately suspend such person from the exercise of the duties of said office, until the next Annual Communication of this Grand Lodge, when such suspension shall be reported to this Grand Body for its action."

13

The Grand Officers were installed in public and the ceremony is thus reported :—

"The local interest which the session of the Grand Masonic Bodies created in Lawrence, was exemplified by the large and intelligent audience of ladies and gentlemen that was present in response to the very general invitation which had been given. Everything which could render such an occasion brilliant and attractive, united to satisfy the pride of Masons in their Order, and to convince them of its æsthetic and moral influence. The lights, the music, the richly appointed Lodge-room, the orderly and refined company, the glittering regalia, all testified to the fact that Freemasonry unites the useful and attractive to an admirable degree; and while convincing the mind, and appealing to the sterner moral sense, also satisfies the eye, and evokes what is best and purest in the sensuous and artistic nature of man. An Order that could attract about its altar such an assemblage as that brought together on this occasion, to witness the simple though impressive ceremony of installation, can rightfully claim to possess an influence which extends beyond the jurisdiction of the Lodge-room, and permeates the whole community. The brethren of Lawrence can fairly claim· to have called together one of the finest audiences that ever yet assembled on a Masonic occasion in Kansas."

Of course a grand ball and sumptuous banquet followed.

The Grand Secretary furnishes the correspondence report, noticing Canada for 1872.

M. W. Bro. Owen A. Bassett, was elected Grand Master; and the Grand Secretary was re-elected.

We have also received a very handsome pamphlet, containing the programme, &c., of the ceremonies at the dedication of the Masonic Temple at Leavenworth, on the 12th of February, 1874.

LOUISIANA.

A Special Communication was held at New Orleans, December 15th, 1873, to attend the funeral of Henry Rufus Swasey, P. G. M.

The sixty-second annual Communication was held at

New Orleans, February 9th, 1874. M. W. Bro. M. E. Girard, Grand Master; and R. W. Bro. J. C. Batchelor, Grand Secretary.

We copy the remarks of the Grand Master on Canada.

"The vexed question of Canada and Quebec, is still furnishing occasion for much comment, and bids fair to assume a very serious turn. The breach is widening and the harm is increasing—other parties have entered the lists, and several edicts of non-intercourse have been issued. All of this, instead of tending to appease the discord and restore harmony, must result in creating bitterness and increasing any animosity that might have existed. May we not hope that all concerned will reflect, that they can achieve more by conciliation and persuasion, than by any attempt at coercion? Will they not stop before the breach be made still wider, and all lend a helping hand to unite together again the broken links of a chain, that heretofore tied mystically all the Masons of America so closely, that they seemed in truth but one family, wherein no discord could enter, much less ever disturb the harmony, that prevailed so cordially among all.

"There is involved in this subject a question of Grand Lodge territorial jurisdiction, of serious concern to Canada, who believes that her rights heretofore fully recognized are now being trampled upon, and claims that her territorial jurisdiction, of which there could be, and was *at one time*, no question throughout its whole extent, is now wantonly and uselessly invaded: her pride is ruffled as she thinks her authority, of which she is jealous and tenacious, has been overturned by a newly born Grand Lodge, of Quebec, who in her turn thinks, she has the American doctrine of Masonic jurisdiction, being co-extensive only with recognized State lines, and the precedent of West Virginia and specially New Brunswick and Nova Scotia, together with the approbation and recognition of a very large majority of the American Grand Lodges to sustain her action, and she thinks she is right.

"There is no doubt that the result must eventually be in this case, as it was in that of West Virginia and others, in which all acquiesced as the only means of relief from the difficulty presented for solution. I believe the sooner this is done, also for the Grand Lodge of Quebec, the better it will be for all—that peace and harmony may again be restored to the American family.

"In connection with this notice of the estrangement of these Grand Bodies, I must call to your attention our action last year concerning the Grand Lodge of Canada, which grew out of our difficulty with the Grand Orient of France, whereby we have become estranged from the Grand Lodge of Canada, not irretrievably, I hope.

" Soon after our Grand Lodge had recognized as a thing accomplished, the existence of the Grand Lodge of Quebec, it so happened that the Grand Lodge of Canada, as they said: ' with a view of cementing the union between her and the Grand Orient of France,' effected an exchange of representatives. This appeared to us then, as if it were intended as an open and frank act of retaliation against us for our recognition of the Grand Lodge of Quebec, and consummated purposely to aid and abet the Grand Orient of France in their inimical and unjust course towards the Grand Lodge of Louisiana. We could not then, and under such appearances of the circumstances—laboring under the sting of what we thought was a wilful stab at our cherished doctrine of absolute Grand Lodge sovereignty, do less than break off and withdraw our representative from their Grand East. We think yet that the Grand Lodge of Canada, should not only not countenance in any way the Grand Orient of France in its arrogant and iniquitous conduct, but should go one step further and make them understand and feel their own opinion and condemnation of such conduct by refusing to lock hands with one who has set at defiance all the legal Masonic powers in America.

" However, the M. W. Bro. W. M. Wilson, Grand Master of Canada, in his Address alludes to this matter in terms of regret, and explains that the exchange of Representatives happened at an inopportune time, that drew attention to it so pointedly, and disclaims any intention of doing any injury or affront to the Grand Lodge of Louisiana; He says:

" ' It appears to me that the Grand Lodge of Louisiana has misapprehended our action in this matter. The Grand Lodge of Canada has for the past ten years been in friendly communication with the Grand Orient of France, and the formal exchange of representatives, although delayed, was made without the slightest reference to, or thought of, the difficulties which had sprung up between these Grand Bodies.

" ' With reference to the point at issue between the Grand Lodge of France and Louisiana, I must say that my sympathies are entirely with our sister Grand Lodge of Louisiana, but I fail to see that this Grand Lodge is called upon on that account to suspend friendly relations with a sister Grand Lodge,' and concludes by expressing 'the hope that at no distant day the two Grand Bodies will be again on terms of friendly intercourse and the reciprocal exchange of Masonic courtesies.' Their Board of General Purposes, through their President R. W. Bro. Thomas White, Jr. (who is the Representative of the Grand Orient of France), reviewing the Grand Master's Address, in their report approved by the Grand Lodge, say :

"'The Board has also to regret the withdrawal of their representative by the Grand Lodge of Louisiana, and agrees with the M. W. Grand Master, that it had arisen from a misapprehension of our action in relation to the Grand Orient of France. This Grand Lodge has never been influenced in its course by the opinions of other Grand Lodges on the difficulties which have arisen in the Province of Quebec, or by their recognition or non-recognition of our seceding brethren there.'

"It is therefore apparent that the act of the Grand Lodge of Canada was not done in malice or hostility against us, and we are glad indeed that they have said so ; we now hope sincerely this estrangement may be soon changed to a closer and firmer union and friendship than ever."

Also on their Lodge in the Island of St. Thomas.

" The charter to the Star in the East Lodge, was granted out of the usual way, without any previous dispensation, and by virtue of a resolution passed at your last grand communication, 'that a charter be granted to certain persons constituting the Star in the East Lodge, on the Island of St. Thomas, and that they return the charter they held from the Grand Lodge of Colon, to be retained in the archives of our Grand Lodge, until the Grand Lodge of Colon shall resume its public existence as a Grand Lodge.' The Star in the East, is now borne upon the register of the Grand Lodge of Louisiana, and I must say that the time set forth in your resolution, if construed strictly, when their original charter should be returned to them, will not come soon : when the charter was issued, the Grand Body issuing it had not a public existence, has never had and is not likely to have soon anything like a public existence. The document itself chartering them does not bear as signatures the names of the officers of the Grand Body who granted it.

"For this and other reasons, I feel bound to bring this subject to your notice and ask you to give it your serious attention.

"Your committee to whom the subject had been submitted, had been led to believe, as they reported, that the other lodges in the Island, 'Harmonic' Lodge, working under a charter from the Grand Lodge of England, and 'Les Cœurs Sinceres,' under the jurisdiction of the Supreme Council, 33°, A. and A. S. R. of France, were in friendly relations with the Star in the East. Since they have received a charter from us, and we have been communicating with them, our official information is quite different, and the other lodges there did not hold friendly relations, Masonically, with the Star in the East: so much so that their refusal to fraternize with them by visitation has been a subject of official correspondence which is on file, and on that score certainly, the committee and Grand Lodge have been led in error.

"This Lodge was chartered by the Grand Orient of Colon, in 1871. In 1872, they applied to the W. M. Grand Master Bruns, of South Carolina, for a *Dispensation* to enable them to continue their labors, alleging that the other Lodges on the Island would not recognize them, on the pretext that the Grand Lodge of Colon was not known to be in existence. Grand Master Bruns refused the dispensation, and his action was approved by the Grand Lodge. Their next step seems to be in 1873, and they knock at our doors, without informing us of their rejection by the Grand Lodge of South Carolina, and we immediately grant them a charter instead of a temporary dispensation; and with it they are in no better situation than they were before, for though holding a charter from the Grand Lodge of Louisiana, certainly known to exist as a Grand Lodge, they are still not recognized or allowed to visit by the other Lodges of St. Thomas. Their expectations, if such they had as they gave expression to, have not been realized.

"I must add to this portion of the history of this our Lodge in St. Thomas, that I have ample information that the W. Master of the Star in the East, is in full communion with the Masonic Powers of Colon from whom the Star in East received its charter in 1871, and who are still in existence, not as publicly as other Masonic Grand Bodies, but certainly as much so now as they have ever been. Indeed the Grand Orient of Colon is in full communication with other Masonic Bodies, and is actively engaged in the labors of Masonry, creating and organizing Masonic bodies throughout its jurisdiction, which it claims as extending over Cuba, St. Thomas, Porto Rico, St. John, St. Croix, and a portion of San Domingo. Doubtless if this Grand Body has vitality enough to organize new Lodges it should resume its authority over the Star in the East, and unless we wish to become trespassers in our turn, and play the part of the Grand Lodge of Hamburg and the Grand Orient of France, we can do nothing else but return to this Lodge their original charter, and recall that which we granted them last year.

• "But more important to us than this, is the question whether we may or should assume the control or protec· torate over any constituted Lodge of a foreign land and jurisdiction. It seems to me to be at least of very doubtful right or propriety, even with or without the express consent of the foreign Grand Body. Indeed in 1872, this Grand Lodge in a case parallel to this, the Tamaulipas Lodge, upon as urgent Masonic reasons as those suggested in behalf of the Star in the East, held that, 'we cannot take under our control Lodges which we did not create' and refused to do for Tamaulipas Lodge in 1872, what was done in 1873, for the Star in the East. This Grand Lodge thus appears as having received two reports inconsistent in their reasoning, and the Masonic law that should govern all cases of that character, and inconsistent in the definite action of this Grand Body. I believe we were right in 1872. What foreign Grand Body would have thought even of assuming the protection or control of any of the American Lodges during the bitter persecution of the Anti-Masonic partisan spirit of 1826. Were not some Grand Lodges apparently dissolved by the effect of the political frenzy of the powers of the day? Did the failure of the Grand Lodge to meet, dissolve the Lodges regularly created by them or annul the charters those Grand Lodges had granted? No, the Lodges remained regular, even though the Grand Lodge had ceased to meet: it might be 'dormant' for a time: but although obliged from overwhelming persecution to suspend its labors, it would not for that be dead or extinct, but over ready, the moment the storm of partizanship and persecution had blown over, as it did, resume its sway under the banners of universal benevolence.

"From 1862 to 1865 were not many lodges of Louisiana cut off from any communication with the Grand Lodge? Yet who of us thought of seeking the protection of any other Grand Lodge, by surrendering our charters and applying for dispensations. Who of us thought that we could need any such protection, or that it was necessary for us to prove and maintain our legal existence?

" Therefore, considering that the facts concerning the Star in the East Lodge were not truly known at the time the Grand Lodge acted upon their application, and that the Grand Orient of Colon is in full activity; that two inconsistent reports have been adopted on the subject of assuming control or protection over chartered and constituted Lodges in foreign lands. I now suggest that this matter of the Masonic law that should govern all such cases, involving the propriety and the legality of our action in granting a charter to the Star in the East, be specially enquired into and passed upon by the Grand Lodge; that we now maturely determine upon and establish, for our future guidance in such cases, *one* rule of action only."

This subject was disposed of by the adoption of the following report and resolutions :

"Your committee to whom was referred that portion of the M. W. Grand Master's Address relating to the Star in the East Lodge, in the Island of St. Thomas, cordially approving and endorsing the reasons set forth therein for our withdrawal from any quasi or inferential interference with the jurisdictional rights of the Supreme Council of Colon, and earnestly desirious of acting cautiously and justly on so delicate a subject, beg leave to submit the following resolutions :

" *Resolved*, That for the ample and sufficient reasons presented by the Grand Master, and it being shown that the Grand Orient of Colon is in sufficient activity, the charter to ' The Star in the East' Lodge, on the Island of St. Thomas, whereby she became one of the constituent Lodges of this jurisdiction, is hereby withdrawn, cancelled and anulled; and that the original charter now in the archives of this Grand Lodge be returned to her, whereby her fealty may be restored to the Supreme Council of Colon, to whom her Masonic obedience is properly and legitimately due.

" *Resolved*, That the M. W. Grand Master take prompt and immediate steps to carry this resolution into effect."

The session lasted five days, and a very large amount of local business was transacted.

From the report of the Masonic Board of Relief, on the terrible calamity at Shreveport, we extract as follows. Thirty-three brethren fell victims to the dread destroyer.

"On the 20th of August, 1873, an epidemic of yellow

fever broke out in this place more malignant in its features
and more fatal in its results, than ever known before, within
the zone to which this malady seems indigenous. On the
25th of August it was pronounced epidemic and on the 3rd
September the Howard Association was organized by the
election of L. R. Simmons, President. This association at
once put itself in connection with the New Orleans Howards,
and they—with the liberality characteristic of that well
known organization—requested us to make known our
wants that they might supply them. Means were at once
furnished and subsequently physicians · and nurses as required.

"The most experienced physicians of New Orleans and the
best medical talent was sent to our aid. Drs. Choppin, Bruns
and Davidson among others, and these gentlemen on their
return to New Orleans made a report of their labors, and
the result of their investigation, as to the cause of the
malady—a fearless, brief and pointed address—laying at
the proper door, the lamentable condition of the high-ways
and by-ways of the city under its years of maladministration
—a sad condition from which there appears to be no relief
under the existing government. Out of a population of
about ten thousand souls, six thousand fled from the scourge
during the latter days of August, and of the remaining four
thousand —in the latter days of September—fully one-half
were disabled by sickness, and before the epidemic ceased
in November the mortuary reports from the Howards, show
a mortality of seven hundred and fifty-nine.

" There was a black line drawn around us, by rigid
quarantine—the mails stopped and the only means of communicating with the outside world, was the electric tele-
graph. This was generously placed at our service and
messages of sympathy and relief came fo 'us from all
quarters of this generous nation—true to the instincts of
the Anglo-Saxon race. The Howards received most munificent donations—not only direct, but through our friends
in New Orleans; contributions were sent to the Mayor of
the city, to the Odd-Fellows, and the Hebrew Benevolent
Association, in orders, by wires, on the banks here, to pay.
From none were the donations for relief more rapid or more
generous than our own beloved, venerated and respected order
—the Fraternity of Ancient Free and Accepted Masons, up
to that time without an organized Board of Relief, to
represent the several branches of the great Masonic family
in this city. With no hope of getting—in such an hour of
death and darkness—a sufficient number of brethren to open
14

a Master's Lodge, R. W. Brother John G. McWilliams, Master of Caddo Lodge, No. 179, appointed R. W. Brother George A. Pike, a member of the board, which the necessities of the time required to be organized—to receive and disburse the charities bestowed upon us."

The committee on Masonic History reported progress, and were continued.

A handsome jewel was presented to R. W. Bro. James B. Scot, the former chairman of correspondence.

After considerable discussion, the following was adopted :

"*Resolved*, That any member in arrears of dues over twelve months, may by a majority vote of the Lodge at a stated communication, 1st. Be declared ineligible to hold office in the Lodge. 2nd. Be deprived of the right of speaking, or voting upon any subject before the Lodge, or both, at the option of the Lodge, and further, 3rd. Be directed in writing to pay the same within three months, or show satisfactory cause why he has not paid. After the expiration of which time, should he fail to satisfactorily respond, his membership may be declared forfeited, by a majority vote at a stated communication only; and such membership forfeited shall be considered as equivalent to suspension, *provided*, he may at any time, by paying all dues to the time of final action in his case by the Lodge, (in declaring his membership forfeited) be restored to membership by a majority vote."

The Grand Master was authorized to extend the hospitalities of the fraternity to the General Grand Encampment of Knights Templar, at its meeting in New Orleans, on the first of December next.

The following resolution was adopted on Hungary :

"*Resolved*, That in the absence of any definite and certain information as to the principles governing the Grand Orient of Hungary on the subject of the sovereign rights of Grand Lodges within their own jurisdiction, the request made by said Grand Orient for official recognition, and the interchange of Grand Representatives be *not concurred* in at present."

The report on correspondence, by Bro. Henry S. Jacobs, is exceedingly well written, and breathes a truly Masonic spirit. Our proceedings for 1873 are very kindly noticed, and our hopes of a speedy resumption of full fraternal relations, are cordially reciprocated. We copy his remarks on Brazil.

"The congratulations of the Masonic world that the dissensions prevailing amongst the fraternity in this country had entirely been healed by the amicable fusion of the two Grand Orients, seem to have been premature. Again have they broken out, and with undiminished virulence; and we have the sad spectacle anew presented to us of strife and division, threatening the general good and welfare of our institution and the progress of the noble teachings and purposes which we claim for it. The union of the two Grand Bodies, which took place a year ago, has been ruptured; and we have the two opponents once more seeking recognition, each as the legitimate Grand Orient of Brazil.

"We are disposed to keep aloof from both, and give Masonic recognition to neither. We have had enough trouble with 'Grand Orients;' and as a matter of wise precaution, added to the uncertainty which exists as to the legitimate claims of either,—despite the quasi endorsation of the *Lavradios*, by R. W. Albert Pike,—we most emphatically recommend the Grand Lodge of Louisiana to refuse recognizing either body, under the circumstances. No good can possibly arise to us, from interfering in these intestine quarrels, and we perceive much danger to ensue from being embroiled in such unseemly partisanship.

"The cause of the disturbed condition of the Masonic Order in Brazil, may be traced originally to political parties attempting to control the election of the Supreme Grand Master of Masonry in that country. The Viscount de Roi Branco, present Prime Minister of Brazil, was elected as such in preference to Saldanha Marinho, formerly Minister of State, a celebrated lawyer, and the head of the liberal party. A split ensued, and another Grand Orient was established, known as the ' Benedictinos,' on account of the lodge being located on a street of that name, while the other Grand Orient is known as the 'Lavradio,' likewise on account of the name of the street on which it is located. The different Lodges of the country then divided their allegiance, some adhering to the Lavradio, while others acknowledged the Benedictinos; and this state of affairs will continue, apparently, for some time, as political feeling in that country runs high.

"From all accounts, it appears that in the Brazils there is a facility in admitting persons to the Masonic Order without proper regard to their worthiness; thus, in some country localities, members of one Lodge are not admitted into some other Lodge, on account of their being well known as disreputable men. As a consequence, Masonry is no longer respected there as it used to be.

" As to recognizing one or the other of the two Grand Orients, as the one most deserving of respect, it is of course a farce, as their publications will show that each one has committed, and continues to commit, all manner of Masonic irregularities. The Catholic clergy of Brazil are very much opposed to the Masonic Order—to such an extent, in fact, as to actually require government interference to obtain burial for Masonic dead in consecrated ground."

The late date at which these proceedings are received, being just on the eve of going to press, forbids an extended notice, and will also account for the absence of remarks.

M. W. Bro. M. E. Girard, was re-elected Grand Master; and R. W. Bro. J. C. Batchelor, was re-elected Grand Secretary.

MASSACHUSETTS.

Quarterly Communication held at Boston, June 11th, 1873.

A large amount of local business was transacted.

A special Communication was held at Haverhill, June 24th, 1873, for the purpose of laying the corner stone of a new Masonic Temple.

An interesting feature of the proceedings, was the presence of seven Brethren, aged from 72 to 82, who had signed the famous "Declaration," issued December 31st, 1831.

At the quarterly Communication held Sept. 10th, 1873; the committee to whom was referred a Communication from the Grand Lodge of Hungary, reported that "the Grand Master and the Grand Secretary be requested to exchange acknowledgements of the recognition as a Masonic authority, and of our desire for fraternal relations, also to inform them, that it is contrary to our usages, to exchange permanent diplomatic representatives," and the report was adopted.

The 140th annual Communication was held at Boston, December 10th, 1873. M. W. Bro. Sereno Dwyght Nickerson, Grand Master, and R. W. Bro. C. H. Titus, Grand Secretary.

The Grand Master mentions the death of their Senior Past Grand Master, Bro. G. M. Randall, Bishop of Colorado.

He reports most of the Lodges in a prosperous condition, and a satisfactory increase of zeal and earnestness in the study of the ritual, and in the discharge of Lodge duties.

We quote the following from the very excellent address of Bro. Nickerson:

"I have endeavored to check as far as lay in my power the too prevailing inclination for public Masonic ceremonies and displays, and for publishing to the world reports of Masonic elections and proceedings. I fear that in too many instances such parades and publications are prompted principally by a desire on the part of the Brethren who are made conspicuous, to glorify themselves before the public, and thus contribute to their own social, political or pecuniary advancement. I believe it to be for the interest of the Institution to avoid publicity as far as possible. Its rapid growth and great popularity since the revival have led to the formation of an innumerable host of secret societies, many of which have copied our regalia, our form of government, our titles, and even mimicked our ritual and ceremonies. The latest of these organizations, formed ostensibly for the protection of farmers against railroad imposition, has gone so far as to adopt and use a burial-service, which is described as 'impressive, though long, including selections from Scripture, addresses, scattering of flowers on the grave, and closing with the depositing of a handful of earth by the *Master*, with the formula, 'In the name of the Grange, I now pronounce these words: *Brother*, farewell!'"

"It is certainly highly unbecoming and improper for any Mason to encourage or promote the adoption by any other organization of the peculiarities of Masonry. They should be considered sacred.

"The effect of these imitations is to lead the uninitiated to regard these associations as on an equality with our Institution, perhaps conceding the latter to be a little older and more respectable. Some of these organizations undoubtedly have worthy objects in view, but they follow Masonry at a long interval. They are modern, local and short-lived, while Freemasonry is ancient, universal and immortal.

"In this connection I cannot refrain from condemning in the strongest terms the transmitting of Masonic notices upon postal cards and in unsealed envelopes; the advertising of Lodge meetings in the public prints, and especially of the work to be done at such meetings. Such practices are totally at variance with the time-honored usages and customs of the Fraternity, and can only tend to that familiarity which breeds contempt.

"Nothing will more surely maintain the dignity and high importance of Masonry than a return to the good old practices of the fathers, to guard with jealous care the work of the Lodge and everything connected with it; to keep and conceal it from the profane, absolutely; and to communicate it only to those of the Craft entitled to know it, and to them only under proper circumstances, and with the most careful restrictions; to avoid appearing in public as Masons except upon strictly Masonic occasions, and those of the highest importance, sanctioned by long usage; never to write or print Masonic intelligence for the gratification of the curiosity of the profane, or the vanity of the initiated. We have wandered far from this high standard, and the return may be difficult; but I am convinced that the closer we confine Masonic affairs to Masonic breasts, the better it will be for the Fraternity and its reputation.

"In June last, with the approval of the Board of Directors, I purchased the Masonic Library of Bro. Leon Hyneman, which he had been collecting for the past twenty years. It was particularly valuable to us, as it contained upwards of twelve hundred numbers of the Proceedings of the Grand Bodies which we lacked, many of which could not be obtained from any other source at any price. It also comprised full sets of many Masonic periodicals, some of which are now very rare; and a large collection of miscellaneous Masonic works. Included in this purchase was a very large number of duplicate Proceedings of Grand Bodies which can be readily sold when not required for exchange.

"The Library of this Grand Lodge now comprises probably the fullest collection of the Proceedings in existence. Of many States we have complete series of Proceedings of all the Grand Bodies, and of many others the series is complete for a part of the Bodies. Our list of Masonic periodicals is is very full, and they are exceedingly valuable. During the past year the use of the Library has considerably increased, and is now constantly consulted by Brethren of other jurisdiction, as well as our own."

He recommended that the rank of Honorary Past Grand Master, should be conferred on R. W. Bro. Charles W. Moore, who was then lying on his death bed, and in doing so, he mentions as a *quasi* precedent, that in 1845, Dr. Oliver and Dr. Crucefix, both of England, were elected Honorary members of the Grand Lodge of Massachusetts, the former with the rank of Past Deputy Grand Master, and the latter with that of Past Senior Grand Warden.

The Grand Lodge unanimously adopted the following preamble and resolution, thus rendering a graceful and well merited tribute, to the life long services and zealous devotion, of Bro Moore to the Fraternity at large :

" WHEREAS, R. W. Bro. Charles W. Moore, for more than forty years, without interruption, has been a member of our Grand Lodge; its staunchest friend during the days of adversity and peril ; its advocate and councellor in prosperity ; and whereas, our Brother has devoted his life to the interests of Freemasonry in all its branches, and especially to those of this Grand Lodge,—therefore,

" *Resolved*, That the Grand Lodge of Massachusetts do now promote our R. W. Brother, Charles Whitlock Moore, to the rank of Honorary Past Grand Master, and that hereafter he be recognized and respected accordingly."

We also copy the following, showing how this action was received by Bro. Moore. The scene must have been deeply affecting :

" REPORT OF DR. LEWIS FROM BRO. MOORE.

" IN GRAND LODGE, December 10th, 1873.

" The committee appointed to communicate to R. W. Bro. Charles W. Moore, the action of the Grand Lodge in unahimously electing him to the rank and privileges of Honorary Past Grand Master, has attended to the duty assigned him and respectfully reports :—

" The announcement of the action of the Grand Lodge, for the moment, re-animated his dying features and lighted up his fading eyes. With grateful emotion he expressed his benediction to his Brethren, and added that this tribute was worth living for and worth dying for. Ho expressed his full consciousness of this last bestowment of the appreciation of his labors, and of the solace thus administered in the last moments of life.

"It smoothed his pillow of death, and sweetened the bitter cup of that libation of which we must all sooner or later partake.

WINSLOW LEWIS."

Bro. Moore died a few days after the meeting of Grand Lodge, and the whole Craft will mourn his loss. We make no apology, for inserting the following address of the Grand Master, after his death :—

"In February, 1822, he applied for initiation in Massachusetts Lodge, then, as now, standing third in the list of Boston Lodges. He was accepted, and would have been received on the evening of his coming of age, but for business engagements which called him to the State of Maine. With the consent of Massachusetts Lodge he was admitted in Kennebec Lodge, of Hallowell, in May following, and was raised to the sublime degree of Master Mason on the evening of the 12th of June. He returned to Boston in July, and on the 10th of October was admitted to membership in St. Andrew's Lodge.

"In 1825," says Bro. Moore, 'I established what was the first Masonic newspaper, not only in Boston, but in the world, the Masonic Mirror,'—in which, to the best of my ability, I fought the battle of Masonry against Anti-Masonry from that year up to 1834, and sustained it subsequently till 1841, in the Masonic Department of another paper. In November of the latter year I started the Freemason's Magazine,' as an *exclusively* Masonic publication, and the only one then in the world based on the principle.' It was continued without interruption until his death.

"In the year of his admission to St. Andrew's Lodge, 1822, Brother David Parker was its Worshipful Master. 'On the 12th of November of that year,' says Bro. Moore, 'at the election of officers, Brother Parker, in making up his appointments, did me the honor to invest me with the jewel of one of the subordinate officers of the Lodge, I having then been a Mason but six months. I look back with grateful pride upon that appointment as the first step of a long career of official duties; for, from that time to the present, a long half century of Masonic life, I have no recollection of ever having been free from official duties and responsibilities .

in some one or more of the various divisions or branches of our Institution."

"He was elected Master of St. Andrew's Lodge by a unanimous ballot in November, 1832, and re-elected Nov., 1833, but having, in December following, been elected Recording Grand Secretary of the Grand Lodge, he was under the necessity of resigning the office of Master—the two offices being incompatible. He was, however, the same evening, elected Secretary of St. Andrew's Lodge, which place he held for sixteen years, when he resigned.

"In 1826, that remarkable and most groundless persecution, known as the 'Anti-Mason Excitement,' broke out in the western part of the State of New York, and speedily spread itself over all the neighboring States. In 1830 and 1831 it raged with unmitigated violence and virulence in Massachusetts. Here, as elsewhere, it was carried into all the relations of social life ; the ties of kinship and of friendship were rudely severed; the springs of sympathy were dried up ; confidence between man and man was destroyed ; the dark demom of persecution ran riot throughout the length and breadth of the land ; members of the Masonic Institution were broken up in their business, denied the lawful exercise of the civil franchise, driven with ignominy from all public offices, from the jury-box and from the churches ; subjected to insult, injury and contumely, in their daily walks, hunted down as felons, and only saved at times from personal violence, through the cowardice of their wicked persecutors. It was at this time, and when mercilessly beset and assailed by their infuriate foes, that the Grand Lodge, through the expiration of its lease, was required to vacate the rooms it had occupied for some years previously in one of the public buildings of the city. It determined, therefore, to erect a Masonic edifice of its own. For this purpose it purchased the land on which the old Masonic Temple, on the corner of Temple Place, now stands, and immediately commenced the building. By its Act of Incorporation, granted in 1816, the Grand Lodge was authorized to hold real estate not exceeding the value of twenty thousand dollars, and personal estate not exceeding the value of sixty thousand dollars.

"Anticipating no difficulty in obtaining a modification of the charter reversing the proportions named, the Grand Lodge went on with the building, and in March, 1831, petitioned the Legislature accordingly. 'The petition was immediately attacked in violent and abusive language by

15

the Anti-Masonic members of the House, but was finally
referred to the Committee on the Judiciary. The committee
made their report, at the end of the session, in favor, as was
expected, of the petition of the Grand Lodge. After a
stormy debate, the report was rejected by a vote of one
hundred and twenty-eight in the affirmative, to one hundred
and thirty-three in the negative. A motion to reconsider
was lost on the following day, and the Grand Lodge was left
without its remedy. It had undeniably exceeded its corporate
powers, and had thereby endangered its property.

"Remonstrances and petitions were prepared in great
numbers, to be presented to the Legislature in case the Grand
Lodge renewed its petition at the session of 1832, as was
expected. But in this our enemies were disappointed; no
action was taken.

"The year 1833 was one of great anxiety to the Grand
Lodge. It had gone on with and completed its new Temple;
the Legislature was to re-assemble in January; the Grand
Lodge had exceeded its corporate powers, and its property
was still in danger. The inquisitorial committee, so pertina-
ciously asked for by its enemies, would then probably be
appointed. Before that committee, the leading Masons of
the State would, undoubtedly, be summoned: an oath would
be proposed which they would not take; questions be put to
them which they could not and would not answer. The
only alternative was imprisonment!

"With few exceptions, the leading Masons in the city
were prepared for this; others were not. All naturally
desired to avoid the issue, if it could be done without
dishonor. How was this to be accomplished?

"Councils and extra meetings of the Grand Lodge were
held, various propositions were submitted, debated, and
rejected. On the 20th of December (eleven days before the
assembling of the Legislature), nothing had been decided
upon. The committee, appointed at a previous meeting,
reported that they had not been able to agree upon any
course which they could recommend as free from objection,
and they were discharged.

"Thereupon Brother Moore moved 'that a committee be
appointed to consider the expediency of surrendering the
Act of Incorporation of the Grand Lodge, and reported the
next meeting.'

"The members of the Grand Lodge were not disposed to
surrender anything. Their temper had been sorely tried,
and was now decidedly above fever heat.

"The resolution was adopted, and the following named Brethren were appointed as the committee: R. W. Brothers Francis J. Oliver, Augustus Peabody, Joseph Baker, John Soley, and Charles W. Moore; all being among the ablest, and the first four among the oldest members of the Grand Lodge.

"On the 27th of December the committee reported recommending the surrender of the Charter, and the presentation to the Legislature of a Memorial which Brother Moore had prepared. Both the recommendation and the Memorial were adopted by a unanimous vote of the Grand Lodge, without amendment.

"The Memorial was presented to the Legislature by the Hon. Stephen White, of Boston, on the first day of the session. 'The surrender was accepted. The authority of the Legislature over the Grand Lodge was at and end; the property of the latter was secure, and the Fraternity of the whole Commonwealth could now sit down under 'its own vine and fig-tree,' regardless alike of Legislative interference and of Anti-Masonic malice and impertinence.

"In the meantime the Masonic Temple had been conveyed to Brother Robert G. Shaw, an honorable and honored merchant of Boston, who, after the storm had passed, transferred it to Trustees for the benefit of the Grand Lodge.

"It has been well said that 'the Declaration' of 1831, the 'Memorial' of 1833,—both written by the same hand,—and the triumphant acquittal on a charge of libel, in the same year, of the author of these celebrated documents, were the three blows which killed Anti-Masonry in Massachusetts, and redeemed the Masonic Institution from seven years of obloquy and unparalleled opposition."

"From the History of Columbian Lodge, by R. W. Brother John T. Heard, we gather the principal facts of Bro. Moore's Masonic life, as they were obtained from his own lips. In 1825, he was made a Royal Arch Mason in St. Andrew's Chapter, and having filled most of the offices in that Body, he was, in 1840, chosen its High Priest. He was subsequently elected Grand High Priest of the Grand Chapter, in which he had previously sustained nearly all of the subordinate offices, including that of Grand Lecturer. He was made a Knight Templar in Boston Encampment in 1830, and was its Grand Commander in 1837. He was afterwards Grand Commander of the DeMolay Encampment, of Boston. In 1841 he served as Grand Master of the Grand Encampment of Massachusetts and Rhode Island. In 1832 he received the

Royal and Select Masters' degrees in Boston Council, over which he presided for ten or twelve years. The Thirty-third Degree of the Scottish Rite was conferred upon him Nov. 13th, 1844, and he afterwards served as the Grand Secretary General of the Supreme Council for the Northern Jurisdiction of the U. S. A. He held various offices in the General Grand Encampment of the United States, and was, for a time, its third officer. He was Secretary of the Board of Trustees of the Grand Charity Fund for sixteen years, and afterwards of the Board of Trustees of the Masonic Temple. 'In short,' says Bro. Heard, 'he has filled nearly every office in a Lodge, Chapter and Encampment, holding each several years. He has rarely failed to occupy less than three or four, and frequently five or six official stations at the same time."

The Grand Master and Grand Secretary were re-elected.

In the bulky volume we are reading we find a large appendix, containing biographical sketches of the Chaplains of the Grand Lodge of Massachusetts, appointed since 1796. They are exceedingly interesting, and are embellished with numerous portraits.

A quarterly Communication was held at Boston, March 11th, 1874.

A petition for formal healing, was presented by an individual who had been twice rejected, by the Lodge in Massachusetts, in whose jurisdiction he resided, and who, afterwards, while on a visit to Scotland, received the degrees there. His petition was not granted, and from the report of the committee on the petition, we learn something of the rules laid down, to be observed in such cases. They are:

" For, indeed, no Lodge, by solemn vote, can be presumed to desire the formal healing of a person which it has rejected in the exercise of its loyal Masonic duty, unless he brings himself within the rule and practice of the Grand Lodge in such cases. That rule and practice, so often laid down in similar applications, is this: the petitioner must show that his irregular receptions of the degrees proceeded from a pardonable ignorance of our regulations, and, of course, with no intent to violate, them; that it was in good faith, and that he is at least, *prima facie*, worthy of a lawful connection with the Fraternity; or, in other words, that his error was one of *form* alone. If either of these elements be wanting,

the petitioner rightfully fails in his application for healing.
In the present case, from what has been already observed,
the good faith of the petitioner in receiving the degrees in
the Scotch Lodge, does not, in the judgment of your
committee, sufficiently appear to warrant the Grand Lodge
in the granting of his petition. There has, furthermore,
been filed in this case a document, upon the inspection of
which, at least, very grave doubts arise as to the moral
fitness of the petitioner to become legitimately connected
with the Fraternity. The suggestions of this document, had
they been made to Ionic Lodge, might have caused its members to hesitate in the adoption of the vote before spoken of.
Your committee, considering how accessible the printed
Proceedings of the Grand Lodge often are to the eyes of the
profane, do not think it wise to place upon record many
statements affecting personal character, that are presented.
in such cases. It is enough that all documents on file, are
open to the inspection of the Brethren who desire to examine
them. Upon the whole case, your committee are constrained
to recommend that the prayer of the petitioner be denied."

The Grand Master, announced with great pleasure, the
settlement of the Quebec difficulty.

MICHIGAN.

A special Communication was held October 2nd, 1873, for
the purpose of laying the corner stone of the new State
Capitol at Lansing. The ceremonies were peculiarly imposing and appropriate. We observe that our M. W. Grand
Master, W. M. Wilson, was present as a visitor, and was
assigned a distinguished position in the procession. We
copy the conclusion of the Grand Master's eloquent address.

" On the rugged coast of Scotland there runs out from the
Grampian Hills a rocky headland, known to all Scots as
Craig Ellachie. The turf cottages of clan Grant are in
sight of its hoary head, and its earnest but dependent
peasantry have for their war-cry —'Stand fast, Craig
Ellachie.' The wild warriors of the hills, serving in the
armies of England, are said, by the eloquent March, to have
carried that cry around the world; and whenever it runs
along their line, whether making the terrible charge or
resisting the more fierce attack, the brave Highlanders
assume to themselves the steadfastness of the rock which
looks down upon their distant homes.. The rememberance

of that rugged and storm-beaten craig nerves the heart of
the Scottish soldier whether shivering in the icy winds of
the north or panting in the heat of the tropics. Wherever
the hour of peril finds him, and his thoughts wander away
to the home of his childhood, the cry comes back to him
from that hoary rock, 'Stand fast.'

"And so, from the sturdy defenders of the truth, in all
time, there comes to us, in all seasons, the clarion cry,
'stand fast.' The example of their constancy rises up,
amid all the conflicts of the past, as a rocky headland that
faces the storm or that carries a beacon on the shore of a
treacherous sea. Let us assume the strength of their faith
and of their courage; let us take up the cry that comes
down to us from the ages; let us give it new life and new
power by our fidelity to truth, to liberty and to equal rights;
and in all times of danger, and to all who serve the State,
let our watchword be—' Stand fast.'

"The Romans possessed a shield, said to have descended
from Heaven, and so long as it remained at the Capitol, the
sceptre of empire could not depart from the nation.

" We, too, have a shield, whose protection spreads over
every vulnerable part of the State. But its Divine origin is
no fable; and so long as it remains among us, our prosperity
and happiness will be maintained inviolate. It is *The
People's Love of Liberty!* God grant that this love may
warm the heart of every citizen, may always protect the
citadel of our political rights and nerve the hand that casts
the ballot:

" The mighty weapon, firmer set
And better than the bayonet—
A weapon, that comes down as still,
As snow-flakes fall upon the sod,
But executes a freeman's will
As lightning does the will of God."

The thirtieth annual Communication was held at Detroit,
on the 27th day of January, 1874. M. W. Bro. Hugh
McCurdy, Grand Master; and R. W. Bro. Foster Pratt,
Grand Secretary.

The Grand Master records the death of P. G. M. Francis
Darron. He issued ten dispensations for new Lodges. Two
Lodges of instruction were held during the year, one at
Kalamazoo, and the other at Grand Rapids, both well
attended. The Grand Master officially visited a number of
Lodges, among them five on Lake Superior.

He decided, " that a Lodge, grand or subordinate, has no Masonic right to collect dues from non-affiliated Masons residing within its jurisdiction ; and that a candidate who cannot *both read and write is not qualified to be a Mason.*

We also copy the following important decisions :—

" *Question.*—Does Masonry require a candidate to avow a belief in the Divine authenticity of the Holy Scriptures?

" *Answer.*—No. Symbolic Masonry acknowledges God' and demands of its votaries a declaration of belief in the *existence* of God—Jehovah—a supreme being. This is demanded because we seek Masonic association only with those whose moral natures and conduct are restrained, and whose Masonic obligations are made binding by such belief.

" But Masonry is not religion, nor is it a sect,'neither does it enforce any theological *interpretation* upon a Mason's belief. Its demands in this respect are fully satisfied when the existence of God is acknowledged as *a fact.* It, in like spirit, accepts the earth, the sun, the moon, the stars and man himself as *facts*, and does not require any interpretation of the facts. The Indian who believes in the 'Great Spirit,' and the Jew who reverently adores the 'Great Jehovah '—the Trinitarian and Unitarian—the Calvinist and Armenian — the Catholic and the Protestant — the Mohammedan and the Hindoo can all harmoniously kneel at Masonic altars and recognize their mutual fraternal relations. This is so, because each knows that every other brother, who kneels there has avowed his belief in the existence of a Supreme Being, and, furthermore, because each one knows that his own *interpretation* of his own belief will not be questioned or challenged, neither will his freedom of conscience be restricted or controlled by Masons or Masonry.

" This is one of the grand secrets of that wonderful vitality which Masonry has always shown, from its origin in a remote antiquity down through all the variations and devisions of religious belief, until the present day; when we see, within its mystic fold, the representatives of nearly every race and nation, and the disciples of nearly every faith in the known world. And it is because Masonry permits us thus to meet at her altars as *men*—as the representatives of a common humanity—and as brothers who trace their origin to an Universal Father, that it is the only human institution which presents the sublime spectacle of a really universal brotherhood.

" While our landmarks admit no Atheist to our ranks, they do not authorize us to demand of a candidate or a brother any declaration of his specific belief concerning the origin of the Holy Scriptures, the manner of their communication to man, or the precise signification of their contents. We, as Masons, do not undertake to decide questions on which theologians themselves do not agree. The Bible, the square and the compasses are recognized lights in Masonry; and we have no more right to demand that the Mason or the candidate shall declare what he believes to be the origin or the nature of the Bible than we have to require him to declare what he believes to be the origin or the nature of the metal in the square. The former we leave to the theologian and every man's conscience, and the latter to the chemist and to every man's investigation. The uses we make of these Masonic lights *do not require* that these questions be mooted or decided by us.

"Inasmuch, therefore, as our landmarks do not demand of the candidate any declaration *of faith or of religious belief,* except that of the existence of a God—a Supreme Being— the Great Ruler of the Universe:

" It is ordered that the Lodges of this Grand Jurisdiction can neither *add to nor take from* the requirements in this respect, which were established by our ancient brethren.

" *Question.*—A brother from another Grand Jurisdiction has petitioned my Lodge for membership, and files with his petition a dimit from his Lodge *only;* is that sufficient evidence?

" *Answer.*—No. A constituent Lodge of this Grand Jurisdiction cannot be presumed to know, except on proper evidence, that a Lodge in another Grand Jurisdiction is working under a regular and unforfeited charter. A certificate of dimit, purporting to emanate from some foreign Lodge, is not of itself sufficient evidence of the regularity and good standing of the Lodge issuing it. But, if such certificate of dimit have attached thereto the certificate of the Grand Secretary under the seal of said foreign Grand Jurisdiction, that the said dimiting Lodge is regular and in good standing, the evidence required by our regulations is complete.

" *Question.*—In a Masonic trial is it competent to receive evidence to impeach the general reputation of a brother in good standing?

" *Answer.*—No. The general reputation of a brother in *good standing* cannot be impeached, and every brother must bo doomed and considered to bo in good standing until convicted of a *Masonic offence*.

"*Question.*—At our last regular, previous to taking a vote, a number of the brothers requested that it bo taken by calling the ayes and noes. I have deferred taking tho vote until I know that such a vote is proper.

"*Answer.*—A vote cannot be taken in a Masonic Lodge by calling the ayes and noes. The ancient methods of voting aro sufficient for all purposes, and innovations should not bo permitted.

"*Question.*—Can a brother bo tried for an offence committed before ho was made a Mason ?

"*Answer.*—It is generally conceded that ho cannot; but I hold that every brother may bo dealt with Masonically, for an offence involving moral turpitude committed by him previous to being made a Mason; provided, the Lodge accepting tho candidate had no notice at tho time of such acceptance that ho was guilty of tho offence charged ; and, provided further, that charges bo preferred against the brother within one year from tho time tho Lodge received such notice.

"*Question.*—Is it proper to prefer charges against a brother who is suspended?

"*Answer.*—Yes. A brother under suspension for one offence may bo proceeded against for the commission of any other offence or unmasonic conduct. A sentence of suspension is not a bar to trial on an offence for which ho has not been already tried and suspended."

Ho has the following on non-affiliates :

" That wo have in this State a large number of unaffiliated Masons is a fact for which I think our affiliation fee is, to a great extent responsible. My objection is not against the amount of tho tax but against any tax. A brother removing from a sister jurisdiction into this should be at liberty to join us without paying any fee. Ho should bo regarded, as ho is, a member of our family, and bo made to feel that it is his right to join us in our work, if wo need workmen, without paying a fee for a mere privilege. I therefore recommend that all fees for affiliation bo abolished."

A new " Penal Code " was considered and adopted. It gives tho method of procedure in trials with great particularity.

16

All fees to Grand Lodge for affiliation were abolished.

It was decided that a History of Masonry in Michigan should be prepared.

On the question of colored Masons, claiming recognition, we find that their requests were laid on the table, and the following action had :

"THE BALLOT BOX—THE DOOR TO MASONRY.

"M. W. Bro. Henry Chamberlain presented the following preamble and resolutions, and moved their adoption :

"WHEREAS, Petitions or requests have been presented to this Grand Lodge, from persons who represent themselves to be Freemasons, and members of Lodges claiming to hold charters under a Grand Lodge of Ancient Free and Accepted Masons of the York Rite—colored—of the State of Michigan ; and,

"WHEREAS, This Grand Lodge has taken no action upon said petitions or requests, except to respectfully receive them, therefore,

"*Resolved*, That this Grand Lodge, having for over thirty years exercised an exclusive and lawful jurisdiction of the several degrees of Ancient Craft Masonry within and throughout this State, all so-called Lodges existing or pretending to exist within this State, not acknowledging allegiance to this Grand Lodge, and not working under its Charter or Dispensation, are *clandestine*, no matter from what source they may have derived their pretended authority, and cannot be, in any manner Masonically recognized by this Grand Lodge.

"*Resolved*, That this Grand Lodge does not dictate, and has not, at any time, undertaken to dictate to its constituent Lodges, what shall be the color of their members, or of their Masonic material.

"*Resolved*, That all persons having the qualifications required by our ancient regulations, who desire to be made Masons, are referred to the constituent Lodges of this Grand Jurisdiction, with the assurance, that all who have such qualifications, and can pass the scrutiny of the ballot, will be received without question.

"Adopted by an unanimous vote."

Bro. Robert H. Morrison, of Sturgis, was received and

welcomed as the Representative of the Grand Lodge of Canada.

Grand Secretary Foster Pratt has an able report on correspondence. He takes strong ground against Vermont and Illinois on their action on the Quebec question. Canada for 1872 and 1873 is noticed.

M. W. Bro. W. L. Webber, was elected Grand Master, and the Grand Secretary, was re-elected.

MINNESOTA.

Twentieth annual Communication held at St. Paul, January 14th, 1873. M. W. Bro. Grove B. Cooley, Grand Master; and R. W. Bro. Wm. S. Combs, Grand Secretary.

The Grand Master issued dispensations for nine new Lodges, and made a number of official visitations.

The following extract shows how an energetic chairman rises superior to all difficulties, and proves himself equal to any emergency:

"By direction of the Most Worshipful Grand Master, I called a meeting of the committee at the office of the Grand Secretary, December 30th, 1872, at two o'clock p.m. At the hour appointed I 'assembled' in due form, and no other member of the committee being present, I proceeded to revise the Constitution, and my labors progressed with the highest degree of harmony and unanimity, until about four o'clock, when another member of the committee appeared, who, not holding the same general views on the principal points at issue, retarded rather than advanced the work of the committee. The committee, therefore, adjourned *sine die*, and the following are the views of the chairman only, he not having had, subsequently, an opportunity to confer with other members of the committee."

The next extract shows that the Grand Treasurer performs his onerous duties with fidelity. He certainly should have an assistant.

"To THE M. W. GRAND LODGE OF MINNESOTA:

"The undersigned respectfully reports that he has

neither received nor paid out any moneys belonging to this Grand Lodge since the last session thereof.

" He still has on hand the same four dollars and twenty-two cents, as stated in last annual report. See printed proceedings of 1872, page 29.

" All of which is respectfully submitted.

GEO. L. OTIS,
Grand Treasurer."

The Grand Lodge recognized the new Grand Lodges of British Columbia and Utah ; but from the meagre information at hand, they decided to take no action regarding the Grand Orient of Brazil. They declined fraternal intercourse with Quebec, until that Grand Lodge should be recognized by the Grand Lodge of Canada.

Canada for 1871 is kindly noticed in the report on correspondence, which is by Bro. A. T. C. Pierson, and is written in his usual excellent manner.

M. W. Bro. Chas. Griswold, was elected Grand Master ; Bro. Combs declined re-election, and R. W. Bro. E. D. B. Porter, was elected Grand Secretary.

MISSOURI.

Fifty-third annual Communication held at St. Louis, October 14th, 1873. M. W. Bro. Samuel H. Owens, Grand Master; and R. W. Bro. Geo. Frank Gouley, Grand Secretary.

The address of the Grand Master is an extensive and well-written document. There are nearly 500 Lodges, and 30,000 Masons in his jurisdiction, and he has found it no easy matter to fill the office. He records a large number of decisions, and other official acts. We extract the following on Dispensations refused :—

"I have during the year refused many petitions for dispensations. Some of them so ridiculous in their nature that I will not present them to the Grand Lodge. From the many I have selected the following to report:

"The Senior Warden of Medoc Lodge, No. 335, asked for dispensation to hold election for officers. The reasons given were that the Junior Warden was dead, and the Master resided some fifteen miles away. The Senior Warden was all right, and could govern the Lodge as well as though he were Master. I therefore declined to issue same.

"Potter Lodge elected a Master and Senior Warden who refused to be installed, and asked for a dispensation to hold another election. Understanding that the Lodge was doing better than it had been doing for a long time under its present officers, I declined to grant the same, as they held over under the law until their successors were elected and installed.

"The Worshipful Master of Ituria Lodge, No. 406, petitioned for dispensation to confer the degrees on a Dr.———, in less time than the law allows. Benson, the Dr., was going to visit the Vienna Exposition in Europe—was a 'good man' —had lived in the jurisdiction of the Lodge twelve years. I declined to do so, believing I had no such authority, and would not have exercised it in such a case if I had.

"Five other petitions came in soon after the above, all asking me to allow the candidates to receive the degrees in less time than the law allowed. In order to put a stop to such petitions among Masons who would read, I published my views in the *Freemason* on that subject, as follows:

"WANTS 'TO GO THROUGH QUICK.

"To save the Craft the trouble of making any more applications to me for a dispensation to allow a candidate to take the degrees in less time than is prescribed in the By-Laws, and to relieve me of that much correspondence, I wish to say that, according to my views, the Grand Master of Masons in Missouri has no right or power to issue such dispensations. The Grand Lodge, at its session in 1850, announced its opinion on that subject, by a resolution, which will be found on page 14, of our book of Constitutions, note 9 g. But even if the Grand Master possessed this power, I cannot conceive a case wherein I would exercise it.

"We have, within this Grand Jurisdiction, near five hundred Lodges (more than we ought to have), and these so distributed that nearly every man resides almost within the 'sound of the gavel.' He never thinks of becoming a Mason until his business or pleasure calls him away from home, when suddenly he thinks it would be good to be a Mason. He has no time to wait the required time, and some enthusiastic member of the Lodge, who is a particular friend of the would-be Mason, asks the Grand Master for a dispensation. The petition for the dispensation never fails to inform the

Grand Master of the fact that the candidate is ' a good man
—the very best material we can get,' &c. Now all this may
be true, and doubtless is true, but he is no better than any
other men in the Lodge, who have become Masons for the
purpose of being ' serviceable to their fellow man,' and not
that it would be a letter of recommendation to them in
foreign or strange communities. One party stated that the
candidate wished to visit the Vienna Exposition, and had
not time to wait. He also was a *good man*, and had resided
twelve years in the jurisdiction of their Lodge. I thought he
had been there long enough to have taken the degrees,
without any dispensation.

" Notwithstanding the fact of the existence of the resolution of the Grand Lodge, above referred to, I have had six
petitions for such dispensations, all of which have, of course,
been refused."

The Grand Lodge declined to recommend a Masonic
Mutual Benevolent Society.

Pages are dedicated to the memory of John F. Ryland,
Past Grand Master ; W. D. Muir, Past Grand Master ; and
M. M. Tucker, Grand Lecturer.

We find, as usual, an elaborate report on correspondence
by Bro. Gouley. We take the following from his notice of
Canada for 1873.

" The annual Address was a lengthy and most complete
report of official transactions, and proves the Grand Master
to be one of those officers who appreciate their duties and
fulfil them. When the Grand Lodge of Vermont injudi-
ciously (and as we think, illegally) severed communication
with the Grand Lodge of Canada, unless she should recognize
Quebec, Brother Wilson, with a commendable regard for the
dignity of his own Grand Lodge, at once retaliated with a
proper spirit, and so did Brother T. Douglas Harington, the
Grand Representative of Vermont, and one of the most
distinguished Masons of our country, and one who has done
more for Quebec Grand Lodge than any other member of
the Grand Lodge of Canada. Vermont went just one step
too far and put her foot in it, and she cannot pull it out too
soon, even if she loses a shoe by it—better lose her slipper
than her honor.

" The Grand Master paid a deserved tribute to the
memory of the Earl of Zetland, who was for over a quarter

of a century the worthy distinguished Grand Master of England. He also refers to the issuing of a warrant to 'The Royal Solomon Mother Lodge,' at Jerusalem. We regret that at the organization of that Lodge only *four* chartered members were present, hence the work they did was illegal under the law of the Grand Lodge of Canada. We hope that this defect may be remedied by the Grand Lodge of Canada, as we would like to see such Lodge maintained.

" The Grand Lodge took no active part in the Quebec case, having undoubtedly decided to rest the case where it was, and to leave the consequences where they properly belong, viz : with the arbitration of right and justice."

In his review of Texas, we find the following comments on the question of a candidate who does not believe in the Divine authenticity of the Scriptures, and denies that such belief is a pre-requisite to initiation. They have our approval :—

" This decision is certainly most extraordinary, from the fact that there is no 'Ancient Regulation' or 'old charge,' or anything else in the grand universal principles of our institution which calls for any such declaration of belief. If it were so, then no Hebrew could become a Mason without perjury.

" The committee were evidently in a quagmire, for they seem to have floundered through the case like a lot of sturgeons in a net; they just fairly broke through the thing, having found themselves caught among the inconsistent precedents of former decisions. To tell the whole long and short of this story, we simply say that all such regulations or restrictions in the institution of Freemasonry, are nothing less than double-barrelled nonsense. If a profane from Constantinople wanted to be initiated, we should honestly and truly present him the Koran, for the simple reason that that was the book they accepted as the 'Great Light,' although we might not believe a word in its 'divine inspiration.' If we were in Portugal we would present the Douay Bible because they accept nothing less, and we would not set up our prejudices against their knowledge. If we were a Jew we would present the Old Bible, although we might believe in nothing but the New Testament. In other words, we would obligate ourselves in all truth, honor and fidelity towards our brethren, upon any pledge they might designate, and feel as much bound to live and die by that obligation, as though we had selected the book ourselves. But as to compelling a candidate to declare a certain belief in any particular religion, it is wholly inconsistent with the fundamental principles of Freemasonry, and subversive of its very existence as a cosmopolitan institution, and without this character it is nothing. We sincerely hope that the Grand Lodge of Texas, in order to be in harmony with the rest of the world, will at once repeal the work alluded to on page 280, vol. 2, Ruthven's Reprint. Such a requirement *is an innovation*, and is not tolerated by any other Grand Lodge in the world."

M. W. Bro. Rufus E. Anderson was elected Grand Master; and the Grand Secretary was re-elected.

MONTANA.

Ninth annual Communication held at Helena, October 6th, 1873. M. W. Bro. J. R. Boyce, sen., Grand Master; and R. W. Bro. Cornelius Hedges, Grand Secretary. All the sixteen chartered Lodges were represented.

The Grand Master decided that charges could not be disposed of by indefinite postponement. He suspended one Worshipful Master for being frequently intoxicated, " to scandal of our fraternity." He set aside the decision of a Lodge, and ordered a new trial, in a case where a Senior Warden was charged with gambling, and confessed the charge to be true, yet the Lodge found him not guilty. In all of which proceedings the Grand Master has our hearty commendation. We copy some of his valuable remarks:—

" In my addresses to them I have tried to urge upon the Lodges the necessity of practical Masonry, especially calling their attention to the standing resolution of the Grand Lodge passed in 1870, denouncing as high treason against the most vital tenets of Masonry, the crimes of gambling, drunkenness, licentiousness, and profanity, realizing that the time has now come in our history when we must assume our true position and place ourselves right before society, relative to these sinners. They are too flagrant a violation of our teachings, and too commonly practiced to be longer passed lightly over; the mantle of charity will no longer cover them, and the hour for action has come; we may no longer shun the responsibility of respecting the opinions of society; the

Grand Lodge has placed her seal of condemnation on these practices, and our sister Grand Lodges have approved, yet these wholesome regulations have remained on our statutes a dead letter, unpracticed and unenforced. Brethren, otherwise good and true, have well-nigh ruined themselves; our Lodges have been mute; a mawkish charity has held them back from enforcing our laws, and our beloved Order has lost, in a great measure, her prestige as the harbinger of morality. Good Masons stand appalled at the fearful violation of Masonic law, and society condemns the flagrant violation of what all know to be Masonic duty. These departures from duty must cease, or we lose our heritage. Brethren, we have good material; men, as true as steel; men, who would ornament any society on earth, if we will only break off the rough corners, and fit them for the builder's use. But we have rested in the glory of our beautiful ritual, admired its grandeur, and the drapery in which it is clothed, and forgotten that without exemplification in every-day life it is only a relic of the misty past. Masonry is either something to be practiced, or its teachings are valueless. It teaches sublime truths; it arrays itself in gorgeous drapery; it points grandly to the beautiful, the good, and the pure; it elevates the evergreen of immortality; it tells of high duties and glorious hopes; it lifts the veil of the future and points to immortality and a glorious resurrection and eternal life; yet how far below these grand visions and duties do we practice. Brethren, can we hope longer to maintain our heritage and enjoy our birthrights, unless we live Masonry as well as teach it?"

The Grand Lodge dedicated the Temple in which they were convened, with appropriate ceremonies. The building cost about $25,000.

It was decided, that an appeal can be made from the decision of a Lodge to the Grand Lodge, but not to the Grand Master.

The brethren were entertained, and their spare time occupied, in a very meritorious way, by the reading of the report on foreign correspondence, which is well written by the Grand Secretary, and in which Canada for 1872 receives kindly mention.

M. W. Bro. Solomon Starr, was elected Grand Master; and R. W. Bro. C. Hedges, was re-elected Grand Secretary.
17

NEBRASKA.

Sixteenth annual Communication held at Nebraska City, June 17th, 1873. M. W. Bro. W. E. Hill, Grand Master, and R. W. Bro. W. R. Bowen, Grand Secretary.

The Grand Master issued dispensations for eight new Lodges. He discouraged the formation of several others, where suitable rooms could not be procured. He reports that the rule requiring a fee of ten dollars, for special dispensations, seems to have materially lessened the emergent cases, "that is the most of cases are not emergent, when they cost ten dollars." He recommends the continuance of schools of instruction, and issued an edict against a "grand gift concert."

It was decided, that the principle standing Committees should meet two days in advance of Grand Lodge.

It was proposed to compel not-affiliates to join some Lodge, but the Grand Lodge adopted the following report in opposition thereto :—

"That while we deprecate the growing tendency to nonaffiliation, yet your Committee are of the opinion that 'a compulsory method of keeping Masons within the Lodge, after they have once been made, is repugnant to the voluntary character of the institution.

"Your Committee are of the opinion that it is unwise on the part of any Lodge to refuse application for a dimit on the part of a member in good standing, made in legal form and in good faith.

"Your Committee believe that although dimission made with the intention of a total disseverance from the Fraternity, is a violation of a Masonic duty, yet there is no power in a Lodge to refuse to act upon an application for a dimit when legally demanded."

The following report was also adopted. The petitioners claimed to be "A. F. Y. M.," working under a Warrant granted by the "M. W. King Solomon, Grand Lodge of Kansas :—

"Your Committee on charters and dispensations, to whom was referred the application of certain persons claiming to

be the officers of W. D. Mathews Lodge No. 8 of the jurisdiction of the State of Kansas, (said Lodge being located at
Omaha, Nebraska,) praying that a warrant be granted to
said Lodge by this Grand Lodge; and upon which the said
Lodge will sever its connection with the jurisdiction of the
State of Kansas,—have carefully considered the same, and
find no evidence of any kind whatever that any such Lodge
exists, or that any of the persons signing said application
are Master Masons: and we therefore recommend that said
application be not granted."

We also copy the following resolutions which were adopted:

"*Resolved*, 1st, That the trafficing in lottery tickets, and
all schemes, enterprises, and games of chance, are corrupting
and demoralizing in their tendencies,—and as such are
offences against the fundamental principles of Masonry;
and all persons guilty of such practices shall be subject to
the same penalties as the liquordealer, the habitual drunkard,
the profane swearer, or professional gambler.

"*Resolved*, 2nd, That subordinate Lodges are hereby
required to take cognizance of violations of the foregoing
resolutions; and to bring to trial, conviction and punishment, all Masons within their respective jurisdictions who
shall wilfully violate the same.

"*Resolved*, 3rd, That any subordinate Lodge which shall
fail to punish a flagrant violation of the forgoing resolutions
shall be liable to forfeiture of its charter; and the Grand
Master is authorized, in the exercise of a wise discretion, to
suspend the charter of any subordinate Lodge which shall
fail to enforce a due regard for these resolutions, or which
shall in any manner countenance any lottery, gift enterprise
or scheme of chance."

A report on correspondence is by Bros. E. E. Livingstone,
and J. M. Wise, from their notice of Canada for 1872, we
extract the following:—

"The report of the Committee on foreign correspondence
is from Bro. E. Mitchell, and reviews in a courteous and
fraternal spirit, the proceedings of thirty-three Grand Bodies.
Nebraska for 1871 received a kindly review. We observe
that Canada italicises the one dollar per annum salary many
of our officers receive: and inasmuch as many other Grand
Bodies have seen fit to do likewise, we rise to explain: that
under our laws unless an officer receives a stipulated amount
of salary, he cannot be compelled to reimburse any lost or

misappropriated funds, and hence, without being as munificent and GRAND as some of our older and wealthier sister Grand Lodges in the salary business—we simply protect our funds under the law from any back salary grabbing, by fixing a definite remuneration, which enables us to collect, you know, in case of accidents."

Under the head of Mississippi we find our own views as stated in former reports, ably upheld and concisely expressed:—

"That where a subordinate Lodge suspends or expels a member, and the case is brought before the Grand Lodge on appeal, and the latter reverses, or sets aside the judgment of the former, that act places the brother who had been suspended or expelled, exactly in the relation to the subordinate Lodge, which he held before charges were preferred against him.

"That when a subordinate Lodge passes sentence of suspension or expulsion, upon charges properly brought, and the case goes before the Grand Lodge on appeal, and that body reviews the proceedings in the case, and orders the subordinate Lodge to re-try the case, the brother stands in his relation to the Lodge, as one 'under charges.'

"That when a like cases goes before the Grand Lodge on appeal, and that body affirms the decision of the subordinate Lodge, the Grand Lodge possesses the power to, and may restore the suspended or expelled person to the rights and privileges of a non-affiliated Mason. Only this, and nothing more."

M. W. Bro. Martin Dunham, was elected Grand Master, and the Grand Secretary, was re-elected.

NEVADA.

Ninth annual Communication held at Virginia, November 18th, 1874. M. W. Bro. W. A. M. VanBokkelen, Grand Master; and W. Bro. M. J. Henley, Grand Secretary, pro tem.

The following paragraphs from the address of the Grand Master, will be found interesting :—   '

"We often, I am sorry to say, too often, hear the remark: 'Masonry is my religion: Masonry is all the religion I need.' Believing this idea, as it is often urged by some of

our older brethren as an excuse for the neglect of their
religious duties, to be not only a pernicious doctrine, but
one which if allowed to gain full sway is bound to sap the
very foundation of our Fraternity: I cannot allow the
present occasion to pass without raising my voice against it.
Religion is defined as 'The recognition of God as an object
of worship, love, and obedience; a system of faith and
worship.' As used by the brethren when claiming Masonry
to be a sufficient religion for them, it means that Masonry
contains every thing essential to their salvation, or their
gaining admission into the eternal presence of God. From
this proposition I most emphatically dissent. Masonry
merely seeks to throw around its charmed circle the sanction of the great truth, that God is the Universal Father to
whom we all owe filial obedience. It is a beautiful system
of morals, but does not inculcate the practice of those morals
for any higher reason than our duty to society. Its object
is not to save fallen man, and it does not *profess* to save him.

"Non-affiliation is a growing and ever-increasing evil
under the present social condition and popularity of our
Fraternity, which induces many to unadvisedly seek dimission within our doors, and entirely too many to receive the
degrees with a view solely to their personal aggrandizement.

"There should be some means devised by which non-
affiliates may be prevented from visiting our Lodges, and
joining in our private and public ceremonies. If we endorse
them to the world as good Masons, by allowing them to join
in our public ceremonies, the world has a right to expect
that we will in the hour of trouble minister to their wants,
and allow them to draw from a treasury to which, in the
hour of their ability, they have persistently refused to
contribute. The only feasible plan for accomplishing this
end, which has been suggested to me, is to require that the
Master of the Lodge shall upon every festal or public
occasion, and as much oftener as may be deemed expedient,
either in the opening ceremonies, or subsequent thereto,
demand of each brother present who is not a member of
that Lodge, an answer to the following or similar questions
which have been adopted by Elko Lodge, No. 15:

"*Question.* Are you a member in good standing of any
regular Lodge of Master Masons, or have you dimitted
therefrom? (To know that you are a member in good
standing, you must know that you are clear of the books
according to the Constitution of the Grand Lodge and the
by-laws of the Lodge of which you are a member.)

"*Question.* What is the name, number, and location of the Lodge of which you are a member, or from which you dimitted?

"*Question.* What is the date of your dimit?

"*Question.* How long have you resided in the jurisdiction of this Lodge?

"*Question.* Have you applied to any Lodge for membership since holding the dimit which you now have? If so, when and where did you make your last application?

"And also cause the Tyler to propose the same questions to all who may apply for admission after the examination in the Lodge. And then, if necessary, to enforce Section 111 in its letter and spirit.

"The correspondence had during the year with the Grand Lodge of Canada has terminated most happily, and amicable relations have been restored between the two Grand Bodies. The offensive letters having been withdrawn, our resolution of September 19th, 1872, was by its own terms repealed, and I so directed the Grand Secretary to instruct the Craft. The Board of General Purposes investigated the matter of the initiation of Bro. Craig, and concluded that it was the result of an error, and not an intentional violation of jurisdictional rights: in which conclusion I concurred. I would now suggest and recommend the propriety of declaring by resolution that no offence was intended by the rather too strong language in our resolution of September, 1871."

Resolutions were introduced, to have a general congress, or convocation of Freemasons at the Centennial, in Philadelphia, in 1876, but they were not adopted.

In one case, a sentence of suspension by a Lodge, was changed to expulsion; and in another, a reprimand was increased to suspension—both cases on the ground that the Lodges were too lenient. In neither case does there appear to have been any appeal from the decision of the Lodge, and we are at a loss to see what business the Grand Lodge, or committee on grievances, had with the cases; or how they could assume to revise the action of the Lodge, without any appeal.

We copy the following, with reference to our former correspondence :—

"M. W. John C. Currie, from the special committee, reported as follows, upon that part of the Grand Master's address relating to the Grand Lodge of Canada :—

"To the M. W. Grand Lodge of F. & A. M. of Nevada:

"Your special committee, to whom was referred the matter of difference between this Grand Lodge and the M. W. Grand Lodge of Canada, beg leave to report the following resolution:

"*Resolved*, That it is the sense of this Grand Lodge, in explanation of the resolution passed by it at its annual Grand Communication, held in September, 1871, as to the petition of James R. Craig, for membership, that nothing offensive was intended by the language used in that resolution, although the said language was forcible, and intended to be emphatic.

All of which is respectfully submitted.

J. C. CURRIE,
A. NICHOLLS, } *Committee.*
DAVID E. BAILEY,

"Which report was received and the accompanying resolution adopted."

The report on foreign correspondence covers 179 pages, and is an elaborate and exhaustive review of 47 Grand Lodges, including all in North America, The author is Bro. R. H. Taylor, and he proves himself to be an able writer, and well qualified for a "reporter." He has taken the trouble to compile a digest of the decisions found in the different proceedings, and has arranged it in alphabetical order, making it very useful for reference.

Canada for 1873 is fully noticed, and your committee are touched up very nicely in this way:—

"Speaking of the laying of the corner stone of a church, by the Grand Master of the District of Columbia on a Sunday, he says:—

"'We think that the laying of a corner stone, albeit of a church, is *work*, and secular work as well, and that it should not be done on the Sabbath day.'

"Corner stones ought not to be laid at all! Because we shall be sure to invade somebody's Sabbath. Masonry is universal, is confined to no nation, sect or creed. Sunday is claimed by the Christians, Monday by the Greeks, Tuesday by the Persians, Wednesday by the Assyrians, Thursday by the Egyptians, Friday by the Turks, Saturday by the Jews,

Therefore on none of these days let us lay corner stones, for they are all days of 'rest,' in which we should do no ' work.' "

We are still, however, of the opinion that Masonry inculcates obedience to the laws of the land in which we live.

He has the following paragraph on our remarks on Louisiana :—

" The reasoning of the last sentence above quoted seems to us to be ill-founded.   We admit, that in personal relations, the fact that A and B are unfriendly to each other may furnish no reason why C should not be upon amicable terms with A and B.   But the matter of Grand Lodge comity, and the invasion of Grand Lodge sovereignty, stand upon a different footing.   A wound in that direction, strike where it may, affects the whole body.   And have you not heard this saying ?—'Inasmuch as ye have done it unto one of the least of these, my Brethren, ye have done it unto me.' "

Our Grand Lodge sovereignty was invaded, and both Louisiana and Nevada uphold the invaders.   We do not uphold France in her invasion of Louisiana, and Bro. Taylor's quotation is entirely inapplicable to us, but comes home directly to Nevada.   The wound given us affected all Grand Lodges, and should have been resented by all, and it comes with an ill grace from any recognizer of Quebec, to reproach us with any action on that score.   Our record is clear, and we have always upheld Grand Lodge sovereignty. Not so, Nevada.

M. W. Bro. Horatio S. Mason, was elected Grand Master; and R. W. Bro. S. W. Chubbuck, Grand Secretary.

NEW BRUNSWICK.

Sixth annual Communication held at St. John, Sept. 24th, 1873.   M. W. Bro. John V. Ellis, Grand Master, and R. W. Bro. F. Bunting, Grand Secretary.

The Grand Master in his address, refers, to the death of the Earl of Zetland, and to an interchange of representatives with Scotland, New Jersey, and Michigan. We report the following:—

"A communication has been received from Worshipful Brother D. E. Seymour, our Representative at the Grand Lodge of Maine, informing us that the Alley Lodge at Upper Mills had been making Masons of persons whose residence is within the jurisdiction of the Grand Lodge of Maine. The Grand Secretary has brought the matter under the notice of Alley Lodge, asking for information, and has assured the Grand Master of Maine that no such invasion of the territory occupied by his Grand Lodge will be permitted by the Masonic authorities in the Province of New Brunswick. The correspondence is not yet closed; but there is nothing in the matter to call for immediate action on the part of Grand Lodge. It is but just to state that the position of Alley Lodge is very peculiar. The community in which it is located may fairly be stated to exist on both sides of the boundary line, which is here but a narrow stream; and a man at one time of the year may reside on one side of the line, whilst at another time he may reside on the other. On a recent visit to the Lodge I found to my surprise that the Worshipful Master and many of the officers were residents in the United States. The greeting that I received from them was most cordial, and the fact that we hailed from different nationalties seemed to intensify our fraternal regards for each other. I exhorted the Worshipful Master to be exceedingly careful in respect of the candidates whose application he received.

"An application was made to the Grand Secretary on behalf of certain gentlemen claiming to be Masons, and working on the line of the Intercolonial Railway, in the Province of Quebec, for Masonic instruction. They thought that as they were over 200 miles away from the nearest Lodge in the jurisdiction within which they lived, and that as Restigouche Lodge, No. 25, was only seventy miles distant, some opportunity might be given to secure for them the instruction through that Lodge which they desired. While fully appreciating their zeal for Masonic knowledge, I felt that as they lived within another jurisdiction, no official steps could be taken to meet their wishes. The Grand Secretary so informed them.   *   *   *

"An application was made to me personally, by a brother hailing from a sister jurisdiction, to issue a circular as Grand Master, to all the Lodges in the Province, asking them to subscribe, through the office of the Grand Secretary, to a

18

book of which he was the author. The brother was suffering
from a severe infirmity, which prevented him from making
a personal canvass through the country, and he came armed
with printed letters and circulars, such as he desired to have
issued here, from the Grand Master and other Brethren high
in position in the jurisdiction in which he had resided.   I
sympathized deeply with his misfortune, and felt keenly my
regret that a sense of duty compelled me to refuse his
request. Our Constitution prohibits private Lodges from
issuing certificates to enable brethren to proceed from place
to place seeking aid. I not only felt that in a case of this
kind, the Grand Master ought not to do what was pre-
eminently contrary to the system here established among
our subordinate Lodges; but that if the Grand Master proceeded to endorse the works of one brother, he would have
to do it for another, and that it would be hard to draw the
dividing line; one day it might be books, another day it
might be some other article of commerce. If I asked the
Lodges to help an infirm brother to sell what might be an
inferior book, could I refuse an able-bodied brother my
countenance and official signature when he desired to sell
Masonic books?   I must confess that the fact that, brethren
holding sway in jurisdictions whose subordinates are numbered by hundreds, had issued such circulars, and lent the
names of their Grand Lodges to such a system of canvassing,
made me somewhat doubtful as to whether I was right in
refusing the demand.   But my views of the principles
involved overcame my fears and I declined the request."

From the report of the Board of General Purposes, we
make the sub-joined extract :—

"As to the, third charge, W. Bro. Logan, having, by
'instituting a strong personal canvass for himself,' gone
counter to that portion of the ancient charges wherein it is
laid down that 'all preferment among Masons is grounded
upon real worth and personal merit,' and that ' any canvassing made or used by any brother of a Lodge, urging his own
claims on the office of Worshipful Master, is highly improper
and unmasonic, and subversive of the salutary rule that a
Master should be chosen by the unsolicited and free choice
of the members, grounded alone on merit," it was necessary
to censure the proceeding, and the R. W. Deputy Grand
Master was directed to pronounce such censure prior to the
installation of W. Bro. Logan as W. Master."

The question of the recognition of the Grand Lodge of
Quebec was deferred until the next annual Communication.

The Grand Master and Grand Secretary were both re-elected.

NEW HAMPSHIRE.

The annual Communication was held at Concord, May 21st, 1873. M. W. Bro. Nathaniel W. Cumner, Grand Master; and R. W. Bro. Abel Hutchins, Grand Secretary.

The Grand Master's address was brief, and to the point.

Reports were presented by five District Deputy Grand Masters, giving full particulars of the condition of the Lodges.

One Lodge protested against a former report of a District Deputy Grand Master, as follows :—

"PROTEST OF RISING STAR LODGE.

" To THE M. W. GRAND LODGE OF NEW HAMPSHIRE :—

" Respectfully represent the officers and brethren of Rising Star Lodge, No. 47, at New Market.

· " That by the report of the District Deputy Grand Master of Masonic District, No. 1, for the year 1872, they feel that great injustice was done to them as men, as Masons, to their Lodge, and to the cause of Masonry, by the misrepresentations and insinuations therein set forth ; and they feel it a duty they owe to themselves and to the Institution, to earnestly *protest* against the same.

" The report commences by saying : ' Though harboring the best of fraternal feelings toward the brethren of Rising Star, yet we feel bound by our Masonic honor to say that this visitation was eminently unsatisfactory, and this feeling was shared in common with the R. W. District Grand Lecturer of this District, who was present.,

" Whether this report is the emanation of the ' best of fraternal feelings,' and the effect of the binding force of ' Masonic honor,' we will not assume the province of determining, but leave the question to be decided by the M. W. Grand Lodge. Let them judge from the tone and spirit of said report ; we are content to rest this point of our case there.

" If the visit was so ' eminently unsatisfactory,' it would seem that Masonic duty would require that the reasons for that dissatisfaction should have been then and there made known, which was not done. Nor did the R. W. District Grand Lecturer, who, the report states, shared in this feeling, express any dissatisfaction at the time, nor since, to our knowledge.

"In conferring the degree (Fellow Craft) there may possibly have been some verbal variance from the Work of the Grand Lodge. The same *may* have been true of the Lecture ; but in neither was there anything essential, or of consequence enough to be noticed by any others present, some of whom at least, we venture to say, are as well informed in the Work and Lectures, and as quick to detect errors, as this R. W. District Deputy Grand Master. And if this had been as represented in this report, Masonic duty would seem to dictate that attention should have been then and there called to the errors, more especially as the District Grand Lecturer was there present for the express purpose of correcting errors of this kind, which was not done. Masonic duty, to say nothing of Masonic charity, would point this out as a more proper and just course than to sit by in silence, letting such errors pass unnoticed, for the purpose of making them the occasion of unkind animadversions in this report.

"That we do and have occupied a hall that is also occupied by other ·organization, is true. This is not a matter of choice on our part, but of necessity. It was the only hall in the place that we could procure, and we were left to the alternative of occupying this or not meeting at all.

"The report goes on to say : 'The hall is situated within six or ten feet of an occupied dwelling house, the windows of which being opposite and on a level, Masons can draw their own inference from such contiguity.'

"The dwelling house referred to is more than twenty feet from that part of the building in which our communications are held. The hall is in the third story, while said house is but two stories high, so that in fact the bottom of the hall windows is as high or higher than the eaves of said house. Besides, only one window of our hall can be said to be opposite said house, in any sense : for that part of the building containing our hall, extends back and beyond said house, and the other windows are in that part so extending beyond said dwelling ; and we may add all of said windows are darkened by close and suitable curtains.

"Again, the report says : 'Nor is the entrance to the hall through Solomon's Porch.' We confess our ignorance of what is meant by this assertion. It has never been the fortune of any of us to visit a Lodge where the entrance was through 'Solomon's Porch.' We think that the most any aspire to is a symbolical representation, explained by allegorical allusions. Whether intended for a covert insinuation under which an insiduous blow might be given to gratify some private pique, or for some other purpose, we are in ignorance.

"This report makes not the slightest or most distant allusion to the manner in which our records are kept, or to the condition of our finances; an omission, it seems to us, of a very important matter, and one to which much prominence is given in the reports of our sister Lodges in the same District. It appears to us that there was a preconcerted design to maintain silence in reference to any matter upon which censure could be bestowed. This seems the more apparent from the fact that the author of the report finds kindly excuses for other Lodges, for shortcomings similar to those for which he can find only censure and unkind criticism for us.

"While we cordially extend to our brother that mantle of Masonic charity for which he asks, and which we, as well as himself, feel that he needs, we most sincerely think that great injustice has been done us by his report, and we respectfully ask that this, our earnest *protest* against said report, may be placed upon the files of the M. W. Grand Lodge, and that the same may be printed in their next annual journal of proceedings.

"ALVIN W. KELSEY,   "CHARLES E. TASKER,
    "*Secretary*.   "*W. Master.*"

A capital report on correspondence was presented by Bro. John J. Bell, covering two years operations. Canada for 1871 and 1872 receives a favourable notice.

M. W. Bro. N. W. Cumner, was re-elected Grand Master; and R. W. Bro. John A. Harris, was elected Grand Secretary.

NEW JERSEY.

Eighty-seventh annual Communication held at Trenton, January 21st, 1874. M. W. Bro. William E. Pine, Grand Master; and R. W. Bro. Joseph H. Hough, Grand Secretary.

The Grand Master suspended a Worshipful Master who had passed a candidate without previous examination as to his proficiency in the first degree.

From his decisions we take the following:—

" Members of Lodges who are more than twelve months in arrears for dues, upon whom written demand for payment has been made by the Secretary, by notice mailed to their last known place of residence, may be suspended, in accordance with the requirements of the 17th General Regulation, notwithstanding the notice be returned to the Secretary as an undelivered letter.

" It is not necessary that an applicant for visitation should satisfy the examining committee by documentary evidence, of his good standing as a Mason.

" A brother making application to visit a Lodge (if not avouched for) is, by courtesy, entitled to an examination; and a motion tending to debar him of this privilege should not be entertained by the W. M.

"A Lodge authorized by the Grand Lodge to work in the German language, has also the right to confer the degrees in the English language, in case the candidate is not sufficiently conversant with the German language to fully comprehend the ceremonies of initiation."

He is still of the opinion that the services of the Grand Lecturer can safely be dispensed with.

Under a former resolution, the Lodges were requested to assist in creating a Masonic Hall and Widows' and Orphans' Fund. Only $383 53 were received in answer to his request, and the Grand Master recommends that the several amounts be returned to the contributors, " there being no probability that the amount will ever aggregate to a sum sufficient to realize the object for which the fund was originally intended."

He endorsed the appeal for aid of the Mount Vernon Ladies' Association.

A revised Constitution and By-Laws was adopted.

The recommendations of the Grand Master noticed above, were all adopted by the Grand Lodge, and the sum of $500 was voted to the Mount Vernon Ladies' Association.

The report on correspondence is by Bro. Marshall B. Smith. He reviews Canada for 1872 and has the following comments on the report of the Board on the circular from Louisiana :—

"Now we do not believe that there is, in the abstract, any American *doctrine* of Masonry; and yet, that European Grand Lodges do not, as a general thing, endorse the American *view* of Grand Lodge Sovereignty, is evident not only from the aggressions upon our territory, but also from the letter which a very distinguished foreign brother, Bro. J. G. Findel, addressed two years ago to the Grand Master of Massachusetts. Bro. Findel writes : " We don't acknowledge the principle that only *one* Grand Lodge can exist in a State ; we deem it unmasonic." We of New Jersey have thus far viewed the Quebec question from this ' American ' stand point, and it appears to us that our brethren of Canada, in view of their present difficulties, will find adherence to this 'doctrine ' the safe side, and, in the light of Masonic Jurisprudence, the strong side."

We have not the Louisiana circular at hand in order to quote its exact language, but it is sufficient for our present purpose to state that it set forth in unmistakable terms that unless we, in conjunction with other Grand Bodies, gave in our adherence to the "*American*" *doctrine* in connection with the sovereignty of Grand Lodges within their territorial limits, non-intercourse of friendly relations would be declared against us. We were, up to the time of receiving the circular, unaware of the existence of any *American* as distinguished from *Masonic* doctrine, which could be made at all binding on the whole order, hence the rejoinder given thereto by our Grand Lodge.

Bro. Smith has somewhat spoilt his open confession of having no belief in any "*American doctrine*" of Masonry, by bringing to the foreground a writer of some renown who has given utterance to the fact that he does "not acknowledge the principle that only *one* Grand Lodge can exist in a State ; he deems it unmasonic," but notwithstanding Bro. Findel's views as communicated " to the Grand Master of Massachusetts some two years ago," a dispassionate examination of the position assumed by the Grand Lodge of Canada on this subject must lead every candid mind to admit its correctness.

Sectionalism can have no place in the fundamental laws of Freemasonry. The Order is cosmopolitan and its usages and general laws must of necessity be universally recognized to be of any advantage or binding upon the whole institution.

There has been no stronger upholder of the generally accepted *Masonic* law of the sovereignty of Grand Lodges within their territorial jurisdiction than has the Grand Lodge of Canada, and had a number of the Grand Lodges, who have of late been so wonderously captivated with the enforcement of the *American* doctrine against foreign aggression, when an opportunity was presented to them, supported and carried out the true *Masonic* doctrine, this Grand Lodge would not now have to complain of the successful invasion of her jurisdiction, the fundamental principles of Masonic government would have been sustained and the Grand Lodge of Quebec could only have been established upon well recognized constitutional law.

M. W. Bro. Wm. A. Pembrook, was elected Grand Master; and R. W. Bro. Joseph H. Hough, was re-elected Grand Secretary.

NEW YORK.

The annual Communication was held at New York, June 3rd, 1873. M. W. Bro. Christopher G. Fox, Grand Master; and R. W. Bro. James M. Austin, Grand Secretary.

(Might we suggest to Bro. Austin that his Proceedings would be vastly improved by the absence of the abominable wood-cut which defaces the first page.)

The Grand Master's address is eminently practical and contains a large amount of matter in a small compass. During the year dispensations were issued for seventeen new Lodges and five other applications were refused. He mentions a number of public ceremonies and recommends the compilation of a code of laws. A fair for the benefit of the Hall and Asylum Fund was held in New York and continued for four weeks. It resulted in adding to the fund the handsome sum of nearly $40,000.

A large amount of local business was transacted, and the

condition of the craft is described as harmonious and prosperous.

The report on correspondence by Bros. James Gibson Charles Sackrenter, and James E. Morrison, is elaborate and extensive. Our proceedings for 1872 are kindly noticed. We copy the following valuable article on the

" LAWS ENABLING LODGES TO TAKE AND HOLD PROPERTY.

" There is much said in the various transactions, against the acceptance by Lodges of acts of incorporation by State Legislation. We concur in the suggestions, that none such should be accepted by any Lodge of F. and A. M., and if obtained and accepted, the authority of the Grand Lodge should be exercised to prevent any use of it by the subordinate Lodge. But when our jurisdiction is attached, as approving or accepting such acts, we beg leave to say that there is no ground whatever for the allegation, except in two or three instances, exceptional in their character, and occurring many years since, and which have none of them ever been approved by the Grand Lodge.

" The history of the action, judicial and legislative in this State, on this subject, is this. In the year 1857, the Court of Appeals of this State, and the highest Court in it, heard and determined the case of Austin against Searing (16 *New York, Reports* 112), which was an action brought against the former treasurer of a Lodge of the I. O. of O. F., and others, to compel payment and restoration of the property and funds of the Lodge in his and their hands, at the time of their expulsion, to the members in good standing of the Lodge on its charter being restored by the Grand body of that Order. The case involved the rights of all voluntary, unincorporated associations to hold property and enforce any right in the courts, in other words to determine whether such Bodies had any *status* in the courts for the protection of their property. The questions thus raised were vital to the welfare of the Fraternity of Masons as to the I. O. of O. F.

" The Court of Appeals determined the case in favor of the defendants, deciding substantially that such Lodges being composed of unincorporated associations, the members were individually tenants, in common, of all the property, and each individual member, getting any part of it, could hold possession as long as he pleased if he did not sell or destroy it, and that the body itself, or association, as such,

19

had no rights which the courts would protect. Our Lodges for many years after suffered under the evils flowing from that decision—wicked men getting possession of their property, as treasurers, trustees, or otherwise, and converting it to their own use with impunity, and Lodge funds were in constant danger from this source.

"To remedy these evils, the Legislature of the State was invoked, and in 1867, an act was passed, not *incorporating* Lodges, but merely *enabling* them to take and hold property. This act will be found in the Laws of New York for the year 1866, and is chapter 317 of the Acts of the Legislature for that year, and is also in the Appendix to the Transactions of the Grand Lodge of New York for 1869, at p. 303. It is entitled : 'An Act to enable Lodges and Chapters of Free and Accepted Masons to take, hold and convey real and personal estate.' The first section of this act provides that ' whenever any Lodge of Free and Accepted Masons, which is or may hereafter be duly chartered by, and installed according to the general rules and regulations of the Grand Lodge of Free and Accepted Masons of the State of New York, shall be desirous of having the benefit of this act, it shall and may be lawful for such Lodge, at any regular communication thereof, held in accordance with the Constitution and general regulations of the Grand Lodge aforesaid, and in conformity to its own by-laws, to elect three trustees for such Lodge for the purpose aforesaid.' . The first three elective officers of the Lodge are required to make a certificate of such election, and after its execution it is acknowledged, and is to be filed with the Secretary of State. And ' such trustees and their successors shall thereupon be and become entitled to all the benefits, rights and privileges granted by this act, to and for the use and behoof of said Lodge.'

" The second section provides for dividing the terms of the three trustees so that one shall be elected each year, and for filling vacancies. The third section enacts that a trustee being expelled, etc., his office as trustee hereby becomes vacant. By the fourth section the trustees are authorized to take property, real or personal, by gift, grant or devise, and, whether given directly to the Lodge, or in trust for it, and thus, by statute, technically ' executes the use,' and vests the legal and equitable title in the trustees. The fifth section requires the trustees to ' at all times obey and abide by the directions of such Lodge, duly passed at any regular or stated Communication thereof, according to, and not contravening the Constitution and Laws of this State, or of

the Grand body to which it shall be subordinate, or of the
Lodge aforesaid ;' and provides that if the Lodge shall be
expelled, or its warrant forfeited, its property, after payment
of debts, shall be paid over to the trustees of the Masonic
Hall and Asylum, to remain for three years; and if not,
within that time, reclaimed according to the Constitution and
General Regulations of the Grand Lodge, the same is to be
applied to the benevolent purposes of said Hall and Asylum.
The Legislature also, by another section declares the act a
public one, and ' to be benignly construed in all courts and
places to effectuate the object thereof.'

"This act, it seems to us, avoids the objection which exists
to incorporating the Lodge, and at the same time accom-
plishes the object, by enabling them to take and hold
property, and protect and enforce their rights over the
same.

" The objections to an incorporation of the Lodge, seem to
us insuperable. They arise out of the rules of law, applied
by the courts, to all corporate bodies. Thus whenever a
corporation is created, the organization becomes the creature
of law, and is subject to the visitation of the courts for a
variety of purposes. Thus the validity of a Masonic election
for Master, would be examinable in the courts, in such case,
with the right to put the one adjudged to have been legally
elected, in the Oriental Chair. The expulsion, or suspension
of a member would also be the subject of an examination in
a court of law, and if it was determined that the same had
been unjust, or irregular, the court might order his restoration. The validity of a by-law of a corporation is also
examinable in the courts, and even the question of its
reasonableness; and if deemed unreasonable, it will be set
aside ; and one expelled for its violation, will be ordered to
be restored. This last was held by the Supreme Court of
Pennsylvania, as to a by-law forbidding one member from
vilifying another, on pain of expulsion; the court holding
that the penalty of expulsion was too severe, the restoration
of the offender was ordered.

"There are other evils arising from an incorporation,
which, for obvious reasons, can only be alluded to without
specification. Thus attempts to enforce Masonic duties and
obligations, would necessarily be futile, because our Lodges
would never submit to their being examined, and their
reasonableness or propriety, made the subject of judicial
examination and determination.

"We have endeavoured to show, as far as we felt it

permissible, the propriety and indeed danger of *incorporating Lodges*, because we know that many Lodges have become so unthinkingly, or not being aware of the consequences. We would suggest that the Grand Lodge prevent it in future, and cause such as have, to surrender, or cease to act under the charter.

"The act we have stated, and explained, under which the Lodges in this State, have become, through trustees of their own chosing, enabled to take and dispose of real and personal estate, is not, as we think, subject to these objections, and is safe to use for the purposes specified in it. The act was prepared on the basis of the law of New York, allowing religious societies to become incorporated. By this act trustees are authorized to be elected, who take and hold the property of the Church, subject to the direction and control of the congregation, but the Church is not incorporated. The latter can therefore expel from the Church, repel from the communion, or pass sentence of final excommunication, without such action becoming the subject of judicial examination in the courts. If the Church which controls the spiritual concerns, whether minister and session, parson, priest, or rector were the corporation, their decisions in matters of spiritual discipline, especially on an excommunication, would be examinable in the courts, and thus their action against sinners would be controlled by a court too often, we fear, composed of infidels and unbelievers, and sometimes of wicked and corrupt men. No doubt these reasons induced the action by which the trustees of the temporal organization only are incorporated, leaving the congregation, or the organization controlling spiritual affairs, like the Lodges under our act, only connected with it by the authority to elect and control the trustees.

"We have deemed it necessary to be thus full in the statement of this subject, because, not only of its importance to the Craft, but that our jurisdiction has been for some time past, thought by some to have been unfaithful to its duty in allowing the proceedings we have stated to be taken under the act."

M. W. Bro. Christopher G. Fox, was re-elected Grand Master; and R. W. Bro. James M. Austin, was re-elected Grand Secretary.

NORTH CAROLINA.

Eighty-seventh annual Communication held at Raleigh, December 1st., 1873. M. W. Bro. John Nichols, Grand Master; and R. W. Bro. Donald W. Bain, Grand Secretary.

From the lengthy address of the Grand Master, we extract the following.—

"The meeting here to-night carries me back in thought to the re-organization of this Grand Lodge in the town of Tarboro, eighty-six years ago. The State and nation had just emerged from a terrible civil war with the mother country. Our people were impoverished, our laws in confusion, and our currency worthless.

"During that war many of the brethren who had constituted the membership of the Masonic Lodges in North Carolina had fallen in defence of their country. A number of subordinate Lodges had ceased to work, and our Grand Lodge itself had been despoiled, and its records destroyed by the British army, in the town of Edenton. At the date of the meeting at Tarboro, this State had not adopted the Federal Constitution, nor had Gen. Washington taken upon himself the oath of office as the President of the new nation. It was thus at a time previous to the organization and establishment of both the nation and the State, that the Masons of North Carolina met for the purpose of re-organizing their Grand Lodge. The character of the persons composing that convention, as well as of those who controlled the Grand Lodge for many years after its re-establishment, should be a source of pride to every Mason in the State. A reference to the proceedings of this Grand Lodge will show that the men who were foremost as commanders in the armies, and who, after peace was declared, shaped and controlled the destinies of this State, were men high in the Masonic councils. As long as our State has a history will the names and services of Samuel Johnston, Richard Caswell, William R. Davie, Wm. Polk, John Louis Taylor, Montfort Stokes, John Hall and others, be remembered; and these are the men who have shared the honors of this Grand Lodge, and illustrated in their lives the principles of Freemasonry in our midst.

"The records of our Grand Lodge from its organization in December, 1787, to the present time, are carefully preserved in the office of the Grand Secretary. They embrace much curious and valuable information in regard to the establishment and progress of the Order in the State, and in my opinion something should be done toward preserving them from decay and from destruction by fire.

"As the early history of Masonry in this State has received considerable attention during the year now drawing to a close, I deem it not inappropriate to recommend that a committee be appointed at this session of the Grand Lodge to collect such materials bearing on this subject as may be had, and submit them at our next, or some succeeding annual communication, with a view to publication."

He also recommends the preparation of a digest of the decisions of the Grand Masters, and says that their present plan of publishing the names of suspended and expelled Masons, by sending notices thereof to all the Lodges, is highly objectionable. He refused several applications to legalize the election of brethren, as Worshipful Master, who had not served as Wardens.

We copy an important decision with the Grand Master's reasons therefor:—

"*Have Lodges U. D. Territorial Jurisdiction?* A case involving this question was submitted for my decision during the year. I decided it in the negative, for the following reasons : The Grand Lodge holds and exercises jurisdiction over the entire State, and I gave it as my opinion that it alone could sub-divide that territory. Dispensations for new Lodges are obtained as. follows : Seven or more Master Masons wish to form a new Lodge. They make the fact known to the nearest chartered Lodge, and ask that Lodge to recommend them to the Grand Master as persons suitable and in every way qualified to rule and govern a new Lodge. The chartered Lodge gives the recommendation, and on that the Grand Master issues to them a warrant, authorizing them to INITIATE, PASS and RAISE, but such a Lodge possesses no powers except those specially delegated by the Grand Master. A Lodge U. D. cannot try or discipline the Masons composing it, nor those living nearer it than to another Lodge. It cannot form By-laws, and cannot affiliate Masons —these prerogatives belonging only to chartered Lodges.

"It is required that each Lodge U. D. shall send up a specimen of its skill to the Grand Lodge, and if its work is approved, a charter is granted by that body, and it *then* takes its position as a Lodge with powers and privileges equal to those of any other Lodge in the jurisdiction.

"The question recurs : If a Lodge U. D. does not possess territorial jurisdiction, where is it to obtain material with which to work? It is answered : The recommendation of the nearest chartered Lodge on which the warrant is issued, is a permit authorizing the Lodge U. D. to enter its quarry, and appropriate to its own use, and work up such material as it there finds unappropriated. (In some jurisdictions no dispensations to form new Lodges can be issued without the recommendation of *all* the Lodges whose jurisdiction shall be affected by such dispensation. I am not sure but this is the correct view, yet it is not the law in this State.) The Lodge U. D. cannot use any material already received or rejected by the chartered Lodges, and being in a sense *a tenant by courtesy*, it cannot object if the chartered Lodges continue their work in the same quarry; for they have prior rights, and may still use any material not rejected or received by the Lodge U. D.

"The Grand Master is the supreme head of the *Masnos* in the State; but, in my opinion, he has no power to add to or reduce the territorial jurisdiction of the Grand Lodge, or of any subordinate Lodge, and cannot, therefore, by a dispensation, divide the territory of a chartered Lodge by giving a part of such territory to a Lodge U. D. The Grand Lodge alone possesses and has the right to exercise exclusive jurisdiction within its territory, and it alone may sub-divide that territory."

St. John's College receives full notice and it appears they have now got their "elephant" into good working order, and in a fair way to prove a perfect success. The Grand Master says :—

"*St. John's College!* Be not alarmed, I am not going to repeat the 'old, old story,' which has been so often heard in this hall, the very mention of which seemed to bring with it some evil omen to the minds of the brethren, which all sought to escape. I do not now propose to review the history of that Institution, nor is it necessary to do so. If there are any unpleasant memories associated with its past history, let them be forgotten, and let us look forward with the fond hope that the bright anticipations of the projectors of that noble enterprise may be more than realized in the glorious cause which now unites the hearts of every true friend of the Orphan Asylum.

"By reference to the printed proceedings of 1872, page 223, it will be seen that four short resolutions, embracing in

all eleven lines of printed matter, settled (let us hope for
ever) a question which has perplexed this Grand Lodge for
the last dozen years or more.

"At the time the Grand Lodge took this action few had
faith in the project. But with a will and an energy equaled
only by the goodness of his heart, the brother selected
to make the experiment entered at once · upon the
discharge of his duties. Like a mariner without compass,
knowing not in what direction he was drifting, but with a
steadfast faith in the noble cause in which he had embarked,
he relied upon the free-will offerings of an enlightened and
sympathizing public, and the blessings of God. His labors
have been blessed beyond the expectations of the most
sanguine friends of the enterprise."

The Grand Lodge adopted certain rules and regulations,
as a basis of organization for the Asylum, and Bro. J. H.
Mills was re-elected Superintendent.

Bro. Robert Bingham proffered to educate all orphans,
sons of Masons, free, at his school at Mebaneville, and
thanks were voted for his generous offer.

The committee on jurisprudence, among other items,
reported that

"In reference to the resolution of inquiry of Bro. C. C.
Clark as to what is the proper mourning for Masons, we
report that, upon burial occasions, Masons should appear
clothed in black as nearly as practicable, with white gloves
and aprons, officers with their jewels, and all with black
crape upon the left arm above the elbow.

"According to the ancient usages, Master Masons have the
right, in their discretion, to wear in addition thereto, a
piece of blue ribbon overlaid with a narrow black ribbon,
upon the lappel of the coat; but, this is left to individual
choice, and is no part of the prescribed uniform."

And the report was adopted.

There is no report on foreign correspondence.

The Grand Master and Grand Secretary were re-elected.

NOVA SCOTIA.

The eighth annual Communication was held at Halifax, June 4th, 1873, M. W. Bro. the Hon. Alex. Keith, Grand Master; and R. W. Bro. Benjamin Curren, Grand Secretary.

The Grand Master reports the satisfactory and healthy progress of the Order during the past year. He does not approve of dual membership; and refused a number of applications to shorten the time between the degrees. He issued dispensations for two new Lodges.

The Grand Lodge attended, in a body, the funeral of the late Governor of Nova Scotia, the Hon. Joseph Howe.

The trustees of the Masonic Hall in Halifax dispute the right of the Grand Lodge to the eight shares of the Hall property, held by the former district Grand Lodge of Nova Scotia, and a special committee was appointed to take steps to settle the question.

It was resolved that Lodges may return as "missing," any member whose residence or address is not known for three successive years, and that Lodges be exempted from dues for such members while so "missing."

A resolution was also adopted to pay the expenses of the District Deputy Grand Masters.

Bro. George T. Smithers is the author of a capital report on correspondence.

The Grand Master* and Grand Secretary were both re-elected.

* Since dead.

OHIO.

Sixty-fourth annual Communication held at Columbus, Oct. 21st, 1873. M. W. Bro. Asa H. Battin, Grand Master, and R. W. Bro. John D. Caldwell, Grand Secretary.

The Grand Master reports that the condition of the Fraternity, in the subordinate Lodges, is entirely satisfactory. He issued dispensations for ten new Lodges. He decided one question as follows:

20

·" When a Lodge, duly chartered and constituted, located in an incorporated village, and such village afterwards, by action of the proper civil authorities, becomes annexed to and constitutes a part of a city, such annexation does not in any manner effect the territorial jurisdiction of the Lodge.

"I admit that considerable may be said upon both sides of this question ; but it seems to me that, when the territorial jurisdiction of a Lodge is fixed and defined by the action of this Grand Body, nothing but its action can in any manner alter or change it. I submit the decision to you for careful consideration, and believe that further legislation, defining the jurisdiction of Lodges in such cases, ought to be had by this Grand Lodge. The question will undoubtedly arise, at no distant day, in other portions of the State, and the effect upon Lodges of similar annexations of contiguous territory to cities ought not to be left for a moment in doubt."

The following report of the committee on grievance, on the duty of Lodges to re-imburse necessary funeral expenses of members dying abroad, was adopted by Grand Lodge.

" Your committee, to whom was referred the complaint of Cheyenne Lodge No. 16, of Wyoming Territory, against Belmont Lodge, No. 16, of Ohio, for neglecting to refund .moneys claimed to have been expended by said foreign Lodge for funeral expenses in the Masonic burial of a brother, said to have been a member of said Ohio Lodge, and who died in the jurisdiction of said foreign Lodge, have had the same under consideration, and, upon careful examina-tion and consideration, find no evidence that *in fact* said Ohio Lodge has ever received information of such expenditure or the decease of said brother. Nor is there any evidence before this committee that the person buried was a Mason, or, if so, that he was a member in good standing of said Ohio Lodge, and so entitled to claim Masonic charity and burial. Your committee are further of opinion that this Grand Lodge has no jurisdiction to *compel* a subordinate Lodge to refund money voluntarily laid out by a foreign Lodge in Masonic charity to a member of the former ; but we emphatically say, and so ·state as the sense of this Grand Lodge, that Masonic charity and duty require that Lodges should extend to all their worthy destitute members, whether within or without their territorial jurisdiction, all needed help ; and that when and wherever such members may die,equally with their more fortunate brethren, they, in their last moments, have a right to Masonic care and sympathy, and, after death, to Masonic burial ; and that, if these charitable and friendly offices are kindly extended to members of Lodges within this jurisdiction by foreign Lodges, it become the duty of the former, so far as they may be able, to reimburse the latter for their expenditure in so doing."

The report on correspondence is by Bro. John L. Stettinius, and notices Canada for 1872.

Memorial pages and obituaries are dedicated to Bros. Wm. B. Thrall and Wm. Fielding, Past Grand Masters.

The Grand Master and Grand Secretary were both re-elected.

OREGON.

Twenty-third annual Communication held at Portland, June 9th, 1873. M. W. Bro. T. Mc.F. Patton, Grand Master, and R. W. Bro. R. P. Earhart, Grand Secretary.

The Grand Master granted dispensations to four new Lodges. He refers to the rapid increase of the Educational Fund, and recommends that it should be permanently invested. It now amounts to nearly $14,000. He appears to have performed the duties of his office, faithfully, having personally visited thirty-two, out of the forty-four Lodges. In doing this he was required to travel 2,873 miles, 560 of which was by stage.

A handsome jewel was presented to R. W. Bro. J. E. Hurford, Past Grand Secretary.

It was resolved to establish a Grand Lodge Library.

The committee on records of subordinate Lodges, found one Lodge, whose records show that the second section of the Masters degree, was conferred while at refreshments, and others who use the phrases " More Honorable," when speaking of the F. C. degree

The Grand Lodge of Quebec was recognized.

Bro. S. F. Chadwick, is the author of the report on correspondence, Canada for 1872 is noticed.

All the Grand officers were re-elected.

' RHODE ISLAND.

The semi-annual Communication was held at Providence, November 18th, 1872.

The committee appointed for that purpose, reported that they had destroyed all work written by the authority of the Grand Lodge.

M. W. Bro. Thomas A. Doyle, P. G. M., was presented ' with an elegant jewel of solid gold, an apron, and a hand-somely engrossed vote of thanks, for his services as Grand Master during the past seven years.

The eighty-third annual Communication was held at Providence, May 17th, 1873. M. W. Bro. Lloyd Morton, Grand Master: and R. W. Bro. Edwin Baker, Grand Secretary.

We take the following paragraph from the report of the committee on the report of the Grand Secretary:—

" Your Grand Secretary recommends to your consideration the subject of authorizing the establishment of Chapters of the Order of the Star in the East of so-called Androgynous Masonry. Such a thing, of course is not Masonry in any sense, and over anything else, this Grand Lodge has never in the past sought to have authority or extend its patronage, and in our opinion should not in the future.

" It is an affair of no moment to this Grand Lodge under what organization outside of Masonry, the Brethren may choose to meet socially or otherwise."

The Grand Master made the following decisions:—

" *Question.*—Can a Mason voluntarily withdraw from the Order of Freemasonry ?

" *Answer.*—It is not within the power of any Mason, or any body of Masons, to voluntarily withdraw from the Order of Freemasonry.

" *Question.*—Can a person who has a deformity of the feet, commonly called "club feet," receive the degrees of Free-masonry ?

" *Answer.*—No man, who is unable to perform every part of the work in the three degrees of symbolic Masonry, without artifical aid, is eligible to receive those degrees.

"A Lodge of Masons contributing to the relief of a distressed sojourning Mason, has no right to demand reimbursement from the Lodge of which such distressed sojourning Mason is a member.

"No Lodge has the right to contribute to the relief of any of its distressed members, while such members are sojourning within the jurisdiction of another Lodge, unless the consent of such Lodge is first obtained.

"In addition to the above, I have made several decisions which were of local importance only, and of temporary significance; most of them also have been provided for in our revised Constitution."

He also recommends as follows:—

"Again we are, as far as my knowledge extends, the only Grand Lodge in the United States of America which does not sanction assessments upon its members on the part of subordinate Lodges.

"It seems to me the time has now arrived to sanction such a course, in order that subordinate Lodges in this jurisdiction may be enabled to exercise that charity which is one of the fundamental principles of our Order.

"Therefore I do earnestly recommend to your serious consideration the propriety of ordering each subordinate Lodge in this jurisdiction to assess an annual tax upon each of its members, the tax not to exceed five dollars per annum, with penalty annexed for non-payment of the same."

Reports were also presented by several District Deputy Grand Masters, showing the Lodges generally in a prosperous condition.

M. W. Bro. Nicholas Van Slyck, was elected Grand Master; and R. W. Bro. Edwin Baker, was re-elected Grand Secretary.

SOUTH CAROLINA.

The annual Communication was held at Charleston, Dec. 9th, 1873. R. W. Bro. J. B. Kershaw, Deputy Grand Master, presiding, and R. W. Bro. B. Rush Campbell, Grand Secretary.

A brief address was read from the Grand Master, M. W. Bro. R. S. Bruns, who was then lying seriously ill. He reports a most gratifying improvement in the condition of the Lodges, and bids the brethren an affectionate farewell. A resolution of sympathy was then immediately passed by Grand Lodge.

A Masonic Board of Relief, similar to those in our cities, has been organized in Charleston, and is now stated to be a most admirable institution, supplying a want long felt in that jurisdiction.

The Grand Lodge committee on charity, thus explains its scheme of operation:

" There are some fourteen city Lodges, each separate and distinct from each other, each having its committee on charity. Experience has shown that many, even worthy applicants for relief, being Masons from abroad, and widows and orphans of Masons not connected with Charleston Lodges, would apply to the various Lodges in the city, and frequently receive an undue share of Masonic charity by reason of the Lodges acting independently and without concert or information as to each other's actions. For the same cause, it not unfrequently happened, that worthy brothers from abroad, finding themselves in distress, would be unable to apply to fourteen different committees on charity, and thus fail to receive a proper amount of assistance. Again, there being no central body to correspond with other Boards of Relief or kindred Masonic Bodies, and thus obtain information, and keep a record of persons assisted, our Lodges were subject to the impositions of cheats and cowans.

"The Masonic Board of Relief was therefore organized to supply this want, and is composed of three representatives from each Lodge, contributing to it. Your committee on charity were also admitted to seats on the Board.

"The Board does not interfere with the charities of the Lodges to their own members, but simply relieves them from all outside applications, by first dispensing charity to those who were worthy to receive it, provided they were not connected with a city Lodge, and by means of rigid examinations, correspondence with kindred organizations in other States, careful and circumstantial records of applicants, and, in short, by every means in its power, detects and exposes unworthy applicants.

" Since the organization of the Board, your committee have dispensed your charity through that channel, and feel that the same has been more properly and understandingly bestowed than ever before."

The committee on jurisprudence, presented a very sound and valuable report, from which we extract as follows:

" The report of the R. W. D.D.G.M. eighth District submits the following, upon which the judgment of this M. W. Grand Lodge is asked : ' What is the status of a Mason who was a member of two Lodges, and has been erased from the roll of one Lodge for non-payment of dues ? Is he a member in good standing in the Craft ?' To this enquiry, the current of Masonic decisions seems to reply, that erasure from the rolls of a Lodge for non-payment of dues deprives the brother of membership in that particular Lodge, but does not effect his general relation to the Craft. The question has been much discussed, and is not free from embarrass-ment, but such is the general current of decisions, and the provisions of the Constitution of the Grand Lodge, and the committee report in conformity thereto.

" The report of the R. W. D. D. G. M. fifth District also pre-sents two questions of Masonic law ruled by him. First. That a Junior Warden, who, by request, prefers charges, is to be viewed in the light of an accuser, and ought to retire, as such, when the trial is concluded. At the Communication of 1870 this was decided, and the committee concur in the ruling of the R. W. D. D. G. M. Second. That a brother under charges had the right of voting on an application for membership, since he should be regarded as innocent until convicted. In the correctness of this ruling, also, the Committee fully concur.

" The report of the R. W. D. D. G. M. fourth District submits two points of law which he has decided, and upon which he desires the opinion of the M. W. Grand Lodge. Time will not permit the committee to discuss the law, or assign reasons for their opinion ; they are obliged, therefore, merely to state the points. The first is as follows : A profane was balloted for and elected, and at the next com-munication, a member, who had not been present when the ballot was taken, appeared and informed the Worshipful Master, that he objected. The committee are of opinion that a member who was absent at the ballot, cannot, by a mere objection, prevent one who has been elected from being initiated. If there is objection, the member should state those objections, and upon them the Lodge can decide. Had the objecting member been present at the ballot, the right belonging to him could have been exercised; but, by his absence, he forfeited his naked right, and to set aside the order of the Lodge, should assign a reason, the validity of which the Lodge could pass upon. The committee append a resolution, the adoption of which is recommended.

" *Resolved,* That when a candidate has received a favorable ballot, the naked objection of a member not present at the ballot will not prevent the Degree balloted for being conferred. The objector is required to assign a reason for his objection, or prefer charges, as the case requires, and upon the validity of which the Lodge shall pass."

The following resolution was proposed and adopted:—

" WHEREAS, This hall was built by Masons for their benefit, and as the subordinate Lodges in Charleston have made complaint to this Grand Body that their work has been interrupted by music and dancing in this hall, therefore be it

" *Resolved,* That this hall shall not be rented for that purpose, or any other that would conflict with the work of subordinate Lodges, unless the hall committee remedy the evil complained of."

The Grand Secretary gives a very good report on correspondence, in which our proceedings for 1872 are reviewed.

M. W. Bro. Joseph B. Kershaw, was elected Grand Master; and R. W. Bro. B. Rush Campbell, was re-elected Grand Secretary.

TEXAS.

Thirty-seventh.annual Communication held at Houston, June 4th, 1873. M. W. Bro. Wm. Bramlette, Grand Master; and R. W. Bro. Geo. H. Bringhurst, Grand Secretary.

The address of the Grand Master shows a large amount of work. He strongly denounces the liquor traffic, and believes that the retailing of spirituous liquors is not a legitimate business for a Mason.

The Grand Lodge dedicated a new Masonic Temple, with imposing ceremonies.

From the address of the Grand Orator on that occasion, we extract the following :—

" We realize and accept the fact, that man everywhere, in all conditions and circumstances—from the time that he is hushed to sleep on his mother's bosom, by his mother's lullaby, to the time when some kind brother wipes the death damp from his brow—needs *help*. And we purpose to help him; help him in every way; relieve his necessities, comfort his distresses, sympathize with his misfortunes, encourage him in the right, and prevent him in the wrong. These are our principles. To aid in their practice and development, this Order was organized; this house has been built. Can any say them nay? Do they not commend . themselves to your favor? Do you not already approve them; and are you not ready to say, that wise and good men everywhere, must bid 'God speed' to an institution resting on so solid a foundation?

"In this epitome, I have disclosed to you all the concealed workings, all the secret purposes of Freemasonry. You now understand why and how it has lived so long—how it has survived the rise and fall of empires—the storms and shocks of revolutions, and why to-day, its grand proportions are nowhere marked by 'decay's effacing fingers.' This is why Freemasonry has now, more than a general—almost an universal existence. It is, *because* it unfurls the banner of Brotherly Love, Relief and Truth, in every Nation and State, of both continents, and on the 'far off Isles of the sea,' that it has millions of faithful followers, who are learning and teaching lessons of Fraternity, Benevolence and Charity."

*   *   *   *   *   *   *

" Whatever may be said of Masonry in the past, or what-ever may be its future fate, *we know*, that in Texas, it has put out the fires of discord, dried up the tears of distress, given food and clothing to the hungry and destitute, encouraged the orphan, cleared up the gloom from the pathway of struggling merit, and kept back the maddening torrent of passion which would precipitate man in deadly conflict with his fellow man.

" With such a record of the past, with so much prosperity in the present, our hearts should be filled with gratitude to our merciful and Supreme Grand Master for his mercies and blessings, and we should be incited to more diligence and greater exertions for the future."

The following is the concluding part of the report of the committee on jurisprudence, which was adopted by Grand Lodge.

" That report shows that this Grand Lodge has no official knowledge of, or communication with, any Masonic body

21

known as the Grand Orient of Mexico, under whose jurisdic‐ tion Tamaulipas Lodge is said to have its existence. As we do not know the supposed Masonic Mother to be legitimately constituted, neither can we know or recognize her children to be so; although the letter asserts that, the Grand Orient of Mexico is 'recognized as a legal body by the Supreme Council of 33° of Charleston, S. C.'

"To that assertion, we respectfully ask, what sort of a Masonic body is the Supreme Council of 33 ?° What Grand Lodge of A. F. & A. M. recognized by us, vouches for that Supreme Council, as a legitimate head or authority in A. F. & A. Masonry ? We know of none such, and are not in Masonic communication, as a Grand Lodge, with such a Council, any more than with the Grand Orient of Mexico. Neither of them are Masonic Grand Bodies recognized by our Order of Masons, and it follows that the brethren of Rio Grande Lodge are mistaken in supposing that the members of Tamau‐ lipas Lodge of Matamoras, are 'their brothers,' or entitled to the exchange of those 'civilities and courtesies due from one Masonic body to another.'

"We beg further to submit that this tendency, now so apparent, for fraternization with other charitable · or mystic institutions, needs to be checked, rather than encouraged. It may lead to awkward complications, if not to serious injury to our time-honored Order and its principles. There is ample room for the good designed to mankind by each and all, in their several spheres ; and friendly relations may continue to exist among all, without too much intimacy, and certainly without placing all on our level. The path of peace and safety is for each fold to feed in its own pasture. All of which is perfectly consistent with the individual liberty of every Mason."

A resolution was adopted, that hereafter no dispensation or charter shall be issued in the name of any living man.

We are much pleased with the report on correspondence by Bro. E. H. Cushing. He reviews a large number of proceedings, including ours for 1872.

M. W. Bro. James F. Miller, was elected Grand Master, and the Grand Secretary was re-elected.

We were very much gratified to make the acquaintance of Bro. Miller, on his visit to Canada, last summer. We hope that he enjoyed his northern trip, and that he may be induced to give us a longer visit next time.

UTAH.

Second annual Communication held at Salt Lake City, November 11th, 1873. M. W. Bro. R. H. Robertson, Grand Master; and R. W. Bro. Christopher Diehl, Grand Secretary.

The Grand Master delivered an excellent address. He congratulates Grand Lodge on the prevalence of peace and harmony; and says :—

" Notwithstanding the political, religious and financial conflict of ideas that has disturbed and agitated our community, and which, in some particulars, is peculiar to Utah, Masonry has pursued the even tenor of her ways, participating not in strife, but always teaching those great moral principles that lie at the very foundation of our Institution, and which tend, at all times and in all nations, to promote brotherly love and fraternal fellowship; and which teaches man to clothe and shelter the destitute and helpless, feed the hungry and provide for the needy, and always promote ' peace upon earth and hushes the war-cry of hatred.'

"While we look upon our history with pleasure rather than regret, let us learn wisdom from the past, and apply it for the more faithful discharge of our duties in the future, and as we go forth to perpetuate the work so nobly commenced, never forget the lessons of morality and fraternity so carefully inculcated about our altar."

He condemns "Gift Concerts," thus :—

" I have before me a circular entitled " Grand Gift Concert! 10,000 prizes ! $250,000 in currency to be given away !" for the benefit of the Masonic Relief Association of Norfolk, Virginia. It is said that the proceeds of this enterprise will be used for the purpose of procuring funds necessary for the completion of the Masonic Temple at that place. ''Tis true, pity 'tis, 'tis true,' In the language of the Grand Lodge of Nebraska, ' We view with abhorance any attempt on the part of Lodges or members of Lodges to give the aid of Masonry, in an organized or unorganized form, to any lottery or gift enterprise whatever.'

"It is a ' modern innovation ' upon our Order, and subversive of the great principles we seek to inculcate. Let

Masons everywhere frown upon any attempt to soil its fair
name.   Our Order is too old to 'take chances.'   I regret that
our brothers of Norfolk resorted to such a scheme.   I fear
they 'give away' too much 'currency.'"

He recommends that each Lodge should secure a suitable
piece of land on which to build, also that the Grand Lodge
should be incorporated; and concludes as follows: —

'   "But let judgment and not prejudice control your action
in this regard.   We want 'good men and true.'   Our position
is peculiar and our surroundings anomalous.   We must
grapple with the situation as we find it, and 'let justice be
done, though the heavens fall!'

"Some of our sister Grand Lodges seem at a loss to understand us.   One smiles at our diminutive proportions, while
another wonders why the head of the church is not at the
head of the Masonic Fraternity in Utah.   To such we say,
in our Lodge room we know no creed either in politics or
religion.   The universality of Masonry is such that we
cannot, even if we so desired.   And yet we distinguish here,
as Masons do elsewhere, between law-abiding and law-defying
citizens; and we shut our Lodge doors against those persons
who have—and I believe would again—prostitute Masonry
for the building up of priestly rule and power.   Neither do
we want, nor do we intend, to have the history of Masonry
in Nauvoo repeated in Utah.   We must allow no discordant
element to enter our Lodges.   It would disturb the peace
and harmony that prevails among the Craft.   ·

" Brothers, let us, with zeal and fidelity, continue this good
work, turning neither to the right nor the left, and I assure
you that 'that Order of Brotherhood which teaches man to
do justly, love mercy, and walk humbly before his 'God,' will
live and continue to increase in power.   Its quiet and loving
influence will penetrate the remotest parts of our Territory,
and be felt in every hamlet of our beautiful valleys: and it
will do much to correct the wrongs now existing, and to
redeem our fair Territory from the curse of polygamy and
its concomitant evils."

The Grand Secretary has been very industrious in securing
the foundation of a Grand Lodge library, and has made a
very good commencement.

He is also the author of the report on correspondence, of
which the beginning only is printed.   ·

M. W. Bro. Louis Cohn, was elected Grand Master, and the Grand Secretary was re-elected.

VERMONT.

The annual communication was held at Burlington, June 11th, 1873. M. W. Bro. Park Davis, Grand Master, and R. W. Bro. Henry Clark, Grand Secretary.

They have now 100 Lodges in the State, and the Grand Master thinks that is as high a number as it is desirable at present to attain. We copy one of his decisions, which we think questionable.

"In balloting for the officers of a Lodge a vote for a person not a Mason should be excluded in the count. The whole number of votes being twenty-eight, including one such vote, the latter could not be counted; and a member of the Lodge who was eligible to the office of Master, receiving fourteen proper votes upon such ballot has a majority of the lawful votes, and should be declared elected,"

We think the vote excluded by the above decision, was a legal vote, and the candidate who received fourteen votes, had not a majority of the legal votes cast. An illegal vote is one cast by a brother who is not entitled to vote, and the vote excluded was just as much *against* the candidate as the other thirteen. We should have ordered a new ballot, until one had a majority of the legal votes cast.

The following resolution created quite a discussion :—

" Bro. A. A. Hall presented the following resolution :—

" *Resolved*, That while this Grand Lodge fully recognizes the doctrine laid down in the ancient Constitutions ' that it is the duty of every Mason to belong to some regular Lodge,' yet as our Institution is a voluntary one, it is the undoubted right of any member of a Lodge, in good standing to request a dimit, without giving any reason therefor, and when such a request is made it is the duty of the Lodge to grant it.

" *Resolved*, That unaffiliated Masons shall be deprived of all Lodge rights and benefits, and shall not be allowed to visit except with a view of petitioning the Lodge for membership.

After some speaking, Grand Master Davis "said that he held that when a question of right or expediency came into consideration we should do what is *right*. He advocated the adoption of the resolutions in a strong and earnest argument, on the ground that they were right in principle, but that a large number of States had taken the position he advocated —some eighteen or more States—that it was the inalienable right of a brother to receive a dimit—and the duty of a Lodge to grant it without requiring a reason for petitioning therefor, if the brother was in good standing in his Lodge.

"Bro. George F. Skiff briefly opposed the adoption of the resolution.

"The Grand Master again addressed the Grand Lodge, and moved an amendment to the first resolution by inserting the words 'that a reason satisfactory to the Lodge be given.'

"Bro. William Hidden thought the matter better be left where it has been for years past, and moved to dismiss the resolution; which was disagreed to. Thereupon the amendment offered by Grand Master Davis was agreed to; the question being shall the resolutions as amended be adopted. It was decided in the affirmative by a yea and nay vote— yeas 192, nays 39."

We think the first resolution, as introduced, should have been passed without the amendment.

It was decided, that a dimitted Mason has not lost the right to prefer charges, but that such charges should be duly considered in all cases, and

"If, on investigation, they are decided to be well founded, should be prosecuted to a trial. The dimit does not release a brother from his obligation to watch the portals of the Lodge to see that 'the honor, glory and reputation of the Institution may be firmly established, and the world at large convinced of its good effects.'"

Bro. Henry Clarke from the special committee on the invitation of the Committee of Arrangements for the Inauguration of the Ethan Allen Statue in the city of Burlington, July 4th, 1873, reported that it was the opinion of the committee.

"That the invitation should be courteously declined for the reason, that it was not in accordance with ancient custom for the Grand Lodge or its subordinates to join in public processions of that character, unless to perform some part of the service."

The report was adopted, and the Grand Secretary instructed to acknowledge the courtesy of the invitation, presenting the thanks of the Grand Lodge therefor and decline participation in the services, because of the ancient usage and customs.

In the report of the D. D. G. M. for the twelfth district, we find this paragraph :—

" Washburn Lodge—It always gives me pleasure to visit this Lodge either officially or otherwise. The circumstance of this Lodge being located at Danville, the very hot-bed of Morgan anti-Masonry, may have had something to do with creating this Lodge in perfect harmony, be that as it may, there is no Lodge in this jurisdiction where the brothers love each other and the Institution so well. The Lodge has done but little work in making Masons the past year, but what has been done is well done. The first installed Master still presides, a fact that I think all Lodges should imitate. Get a good Master then keep him."

The appendix contains the "Settlement of the difficulties between Canada and Quebec," and the following is Edict of the Grand Master :—

"GRAND LODGE OF VERMONT.

GRAND MASTER'S OFFICE.

" To all whom it may concern :

" WHEREAS, the Grand Lodge of Vermont at its annual Communication, A. L. 5871, extended to the Grand Lodge of Quebec, full and fraternal recognition: and

" WHEREAS, on the 9th day of December, A. L. 5872, pursuant to a resolution of said Grand Lodge, adopted at its annual Communication, on A. L. 5872,—it having been made to appear that the Grand Lodge of Canada then asserted jurisdiction over certain Lodges, existing within the territorial limits of the Grand Lodge of Quebec, and in other respects had violated and then continued to violate the jurisdiction of the last named Lodge, and wholly to disregard its Masonic Sovereignty over the Province of Quebec—the Grand Master then issued his edict of non-communication, forbidding all Masonic intercourse on the part of the Masons of Vermont with the members of the Grand Lodge of Canada, and its subordinate Lodges; and

" WHEREAS, it has been made to appear that, at a meeting of the joint committee appointed by the Grand Master of the Grand Lodges of Canada and Quebec respectively, with full power to settle all questions of controversy between them, holden at Montreal, on the 17th day of February, A. L. 5874, all matters of Masonic differences existing between said Grand Lodges were fully and amicably adjusted, and by the terms of said adjustment the Grand Lodge of Canada has withdrawn all claim to Masonic jurisdiction within the Province of Quebec, and has ceased to assert the same therein.

" THEREFORE, by virtue of the authority vested in me, as Grand Master of Masons in the State of Vermont, I do hereby *Revoke* and *Abrogate* said edict of non-communication, and

" THEREFORE, from and after this date, on the part of the Grand Lodge of Vermont, grant to brethren holding allegiance thereto, liberty to hold Masonic intercourse, with the members of the Grand Lodge of Canada, and the Masons under its jurisdiction in as full and fraternal a manner as though said edict had not been issued.

"Done at St. Albans, State of Vermont, this 28th day of February, A. L. 5874, A. D. 1874.

"PARK DAVIS,
     " *Grand Master.*

{ SEAL. }

"HENRY CLARKE,
     "Grand Secretary."

The Grand Master and Grand Secretary were re-elected.

VIRGINIA.

The annual Communication was held at Richmond, Dec. 8th, 1873. M. W. Bro. R. E. Withers, Grand Master, and R. W. Bro. John Dove, Grand Secretary.

From the address of the Grand Master, we make the following extracts:—

" During the last year, on application of the Masonic Relief Association of Norfolk, I granted permission to that organization to address a circular to each of the subordinate Lodges in this jurisdiction, asking assistance for the completion of a Masonic Temple, by the purchase of tickets to a Gift Concert. My action in this matter was not taken without great hesitation, and strong doubts of its propriety. Believing the tendency of such enterprises,at least,of doubtful character, nothing but the entire confidence I felt in the brethren who proposed to conduct it, and a conviction that it afforded the only prospect of relief from a most embarassing complication, threatening ruinous pecuniary loss to the Fraternity of that city, induced me to give it my sanction; and though precedent furnished by this Grand Lodge can be cited to sustain my action, yet I feel constrained to indicate my desire that this additional precedent may not hereafter be pleaded to justify a resort, on ordinary occasions, to this method of raising funds.

"In August last, I was the recipient of a communication from Most Worshipful Charles F. Stansbury, Grand Master of Masons in the District of Columbia, enquiring as to the 'relative positions and authority of the Masonic Fraternity and the Order of Odd Fellows, at funerals, where the deceased had been a member of both organizations.' In response, I forwarded him a copy of the resolution adopted by this Grand Lodge, 'repealing the law prohibiting persons other than Masons from acting as pall-bearers at Masonic funerals.' constituting the only regulation on the subject. In this connection I will say, that having been called on by the Worshipful Master of Lodge No. 120, to sustain his decision prohibiting the passage of a procession of other organizations through his Lodge, when convened to bury a Brother, also a member of another Order, I did not hesitate to confirm his action. I cannot avoid giving expression to my regret that this Grand Body has opened the door to these embarrassing questions of precedence, &c., by departing from what I am constrained to regard as true Masonic law, in admitting non-affiliates or profanes, within the precincts of a titled Lodge, duly opened, whether as pall-bearers or otherwise. The exclusiveness of our Order being thus invaded, it becomes exceedingly difficult, if not impossible, to draw the line which shall fix the relative rank,dignity and ceremonial, of different organizations on a satisfactory basis.

"I have declined to issue dispensations in several cases authorizing Lodges to confer all the Degrees at one meeting. or to consider petitions for initiation within less that one month after presentation. My conviction, after long observation, is that the interests of the Order are rarely subserved

24

by the initiation of parties who desire the Degrees only
when about to travel, and who have previously neglected
every opportunity of uniting themselves with the Order."

That "Gift Concert," for Masonic purposes, has been
almost universally condemned. We would hardly have
believed that any Grand Master would have sanctioned so
questionable a method of raising funds. It is nothing more
or less than gambling, and is totally at variance with all
our teachings of morality. We should practice what we
profess, and those Gift Concerts should not be tolerated in
connection with Masonry, nor in any other connection for
that matter.

The Virginians claim to have been the first to establish
Masonry in America. The Grand Secretary says:—

" Another important addition presented itself, involving
a somewhat disputed point, to whom was the honor due of
first establishing Masonry in America. This I have proved
from authentic records, was accomplished by Virginia, and
which required much labor, and time, as it necessarily
involved a history of Masonry in Virginia from 1733 to
1777, a space of 44 years before this or any other Grand
Lodge was formed according to law."

One D. D. G. M. says:—

" After an experience of over twenty years, he feels
satisfied that inefficiency of the officers, the rapid rotation of
Worshipful Masters, is a most fertile cause of the loss of
Masonic interest among the members, and of the consequent
downfall of the Lodge."

Canada for 1872 and 1873 receives notice, in the report on
correspondence, by Bro. B. R. Welford, Jr.

M. W. Bro. W. H. Lambert, was elected Grand Master,
and R. W. Bro. John Dove, was re-elected Grand Secretary.

We have also to acknowledge the receipt of "a final appeal
of the M. W. Grand Lodge of Virginia, to the Grand Lodge
of Hamburgh, and the Grand Orient of France, to reconsider
and withdraw their unmasonic action in invading other
Grand Masonic Jurisdictions;" under date of April 1st, 1874.

WASHINGTON.

Sixteenth annual Communication held at Olympia, Sept. 3rd, 1873. M. W. Bro. Granville O. Haller, Grand Master, and R. W. Bro. Thomas Milburne Reed, Grand Secretary.

In his annual address, the Grand Master recommends the appointment of District Deputies, and the adoption of the system of dropping for the non-payment of dues. He reports that he had revoked the charter of Alaska Lodge, and concludes as follows :— ·

" The good Mason is ever studying the hidden' meanings of our symbols—perfecting himself in speculative Masonry —and practicing the precepts of our Order. He is the brother 'who can best work and best agree.' He is no sluggard, but is ever passing from the W. to the E. in search of Light; by careful study and industry purifying his intellect and rising higher and higher in the scale of humanity. He, when reviled, reviles not, for a soft word turneth away wrath. He can listen, without being offended, to the criticisms of his enemies and of the envious, as they are more likely to expose the weak points in his nature and conduct than the criticisms of friendship, and thereby enable him to become a more perfect ashlar. He will, by little acts of kindness and of charity, make himself dear to his brethren and perhaps to the people at large, so that when he enters upon the Level of Time in that undiscovered country from whose bourne no traveller returns, he will be missed —the void will be felt,—and we may be proud of our departed brother.

" The higher teachings of Masonry, say truly,—'Those things that can survive us—our works—our words—our immortal thoughts—our influences—and the effects of good deeds—are more to the world that survives us, *than we our- selves are.*"

" But even more might be positively affirmed of a good Mason, and, then there is a negative point of view, which should not be overlooked, but I have| already trespassed largely on your time and patience, and must be brief. The true Mason *will not* let the left hand know what the right hand bestows in charity, while he may reprehend and admonish his erring brother, he *will not* expose the faulty brother unnecessarily ; in short, he will do unto others as he would that they should do unto him.   Let us always keep in mind Pope's universal prayer :—

"Teach me to feel another's woe,
To hide the faults I see ;
That mercy I to others show,
That mercy show to me."

A charter was granted to one new Lodge.

By the adoption of the report of the committee on juris-prudence, the recognition of the Grand Lodge of Quebec was withheld.   The committee say that political bodies in their partitions or divisions of territory cannot disintegrate Grand Lodges, nor abridge the jurisdiction of any Grand Lodge.

The committee on correspondence do their best to be brief. They present a very readable report, and amongst others review our proceedings of 1872.   The report is signed by Bro. T. M. Reed, Grand Secretary.

M. W. Bro. David C. H. Rothschild, was elected Grand Master; the Grand Secretary was re-elected.

WEST VIRGINIA.

The eighth annual Communication was held at Wheeling, Nov. 12th, 1872.   M. W. Bro. Thos. H. Logan, Grand Master, and R. W. Bro. O. S. Long, Grand Secretary.

The address of the Grand Master is brief and practical. He issued five dispensations for new Lodges, and reports the Craft generally in a prosperous condition.   We quote two of his decisions :—

"A brother under suspension for non-payment of dues can be tried under charges of unmasonic conduct.   He cannot appear in the Lodge during his trial, except by his attorney, who must of course be a Master Mason.   He can, however, appear before a committee.

" A brother who had lost his right leg (after he was made a Master Mason), was elected Master of his Lodge.   The question of his eligibility having been referred to me, was decided in the negative."

On the latter of these questions, the committee on jurispru-dence differed from the Grand Master; they say :—

"Your committee think the decision was correct in the particular instance, but are of opinion that the loss of a leg by a Master Mason does not necessarily render him ineligible to the office of Master, as it certainly would not, in their opinion, if the loss had been so supplied by mechanical aids as to enable him to conform in all respects to our Ritual."

However, the Grand Lodge sustained the doctrine, as announced by the Grand Master.

The Grand Master and Grand Secretary were both re-elected.

WISCONSIN.

Twenty ninth annual Communication held at Milwaukee. June 10th, 1873. M. W. Bro. Henry L. Palmer, Grand Master, and R. W. Bro. Wm. T. Palmer, Grand Secretary.

The Grand Master issued five dispensations for new Lodges. He does not approve of shortening the time for degrees. We quote a part of his remarks on this subject:—

"In my judgment, the provisions of the Constitution of the Grand Lodge which require that a petitioner for the degrees in Masonry should be a resident within this State, and within the jurisdiction of the Lodge to which he presents his petition, for a period of time sufficient to enable the members to learn something of his character, qualifications and fitness for initiation, as well as those other provisions of the Constitution designed to prevent the too hasty advancement of initiates, are eminently wise, and ought not to be lightly dispensed with. It is often an unpleasant duty for a Grand Master to decline requests of this character, when by complying with them he could oblige some of his brethren. But a due regard to the obligation resting upon him very often compels him to deny requests which those by whom they are made hastily think he ought to grant."

A committee was appointed to locate schools of instruction, and their report, which was adopted, named eighteen places at which these schools were to be held.

Bro. George E. Hoskinson is the author of the report on correspondence, which is one of the best we have seen. His views, as expressed in the subjoined extracts, are correct in the main, and worthy of note.

"There are 'two rights' which pertain to every member

of a subordinate Lodge. The right of standing at the door
of Masonry, and, by simply objecting, to prevent the intro-
duction of unwelcome material into his Lodge, whether the
same be on an application for initiation, passing, raising,
affiliatioñ or visiting; and the right to withdraw from his
Lodge at any time upon payment of all arrearages of dues,
without question, let or hindrance. Once a candidate has
been started by a Lodge on his Masonic career he becomes
invested with Masonic rights, and these may not be set aside
by a frivolous objection. But at the starting point the ' I
object ' is sufficient.

" We hold these propositions to be self-evident, inasmuch
as Lodges are merely adjuncts of Masonry, not necessary to
its preservation, and therefore incompetent by reason of
their inferiority to annul or impair by a local regulation,
rights and powers conferred by a sovereign authority upon
every brother when raised to the sublime degree of Master
Mason.

" We trust the time is coming when such cast iron regulations are the things of the past. It is an open question,
indeed, whether ' once a Mason, always a Mason,' until
disqualified for that title by the commission of crime,
whereof he has been duly convicted, be not good Masonic
law. We believe it is, and that suspensions and exclusions
from all Masonic rights, if from any cause, a brother fails to
respond to a pecuniary assessment made upon him, practically operating as an expulsion from Masonry, are violations
of the fundamental principle of Masonic charity. Charity
begins at home, nor do we regard Masonry as an insurance
institution, where if the premium be not paid at the tick of
the clock, the policy is forfeited. Far from it. Some lighter
punishment should follow the non-payment of assessments.
Our system of ' exclusion ' comes pretty near the mark, but
we cannot say we advise or recommend its adoption elsewhere; perhaps the Connecticut system of striking from the
' rolls ' is better. We would have a system of registration,
and an exclusion from participation in the business of the
subordinate Lodge, while the non-paying member was
' registered,' but he should be regarded as a Mason, whom
we have vowed to recognize, to support, to protect. He
may be unworthy, so often our natural brothers are
unworthy, but all the same we recognize the justness of
their claim to our fraternal regard. Subordinate Lodges
are a modern invention, perhaps not exceeding a hundred
and fifty years in age, and the regulations which have grown
up with them partake very frequently, more of the selfish
commercial cast of the age, than the benign character of

Ancient Masonry. Brethren, let us make the entrance to Masonry as difficult as we may, but once we take a brother to our hearts let us hold him fast 'by hooks of steel,' and not ignominiously kick him out of our temple because he owes $2 00 for last year's dues."

In his notice of Canada for 1872, we find the following:—

"A resolution that 'all business in private Lodges in connection with this Grand Lodge be conducted in the third degree,' was ruled out of order by the Grand Master 'inasmuch as the notice did not state that it was an amendment to the Constitution.' According to our ideas the resolution was superfluous as no general business can be transacted in any other than a Master Mason's Lodge."

In this latter sentence, Bro. Hoskinson displays a lamentable ignorance of the practice of the oldest and most influential Grand Lodges. In our Lodges the general business is always transacted in the Entered Apprentice degree. In this, we follow our Mother Grand Lodge of England, and all the European Grand Lodges. The Grand Lodges of the United States have departed in this respect from Ancient Custom, and for no good reason, that we can see.

In his review of Georgia, he again reverts to suspensions for non-payment of dues.

"We hold that there is a vast difference and a wide distinction between a suspension for non-payment of dues and other Masonic offences. We believe there is nothing criminal or unmasonic in owing a few dollars, and we fail to see how a debt to a Lodge is of any more importance than a debt to a brother Mason. Yet we despise as heartily as Bro. Blackshear those mean, shiftless, worthless deadbeats, who occasionally sneak into a Lodge, and while enjoying all the benefits of the organization refuse to aid in its support; nevertheless, they are Masons and have rights. We believe the best way for the Lodge is to dimit such members on its own motion. If they fail to pay their dues after they have run a year, and after being thrice demanded, dimit them, balance their account, send them a receipted bill, and carry it over to the debtor side of the Charity Fund. There will be less timber, but what there is will be sound."

M. W. Bro. R. DeLos Pulford, was elected Grand Master; and R. W. Bro. George E. Hoskinson, was elected Grand Secretary.

CONCLUSION.

We have thus far endeavored to give as clear an account as possible of the most important and interesting matters that are taking place in the Masonic World around us. We find many things to praise, few to condemn. The Craft, in general, is highly prosperous, and in every one of the volumes we have been perusing, we find ample evidence of the beneficent effects of our Institution. We find the widow and orphan relieved and protected; we find the distressed brother assisted and sent on his way rejoicing; and we find the great calamities of epidemic sickness and death, or other extensive misfortunes, only serving to bring out more strongly into relief the great Bond that unites the Brotherhood.

We also see, no less strongly exemplified, the cardinal tenets of our fraternity—Temperance, Fortitude, Prudence and Justice. We see a noble army of workers, actively engaged in promulgating those great principles, both by precept and example; and wherever their standard is raised and supported, we find the general morality of the people increased, and society adopting a more virtuous tone.

Let us, then, each take heed to himself. Let each brother feel that he is looked to as an example, both by his younger brethren and the outside world, and let him so act as becomes a *Mason*, as one of those who are earnestly striving for the general welfare of their fellow creatures.

***

We have, so far, avoided statistics, but they are not less interesting and useful on that account. However, we have preferred giving them in a tabulated form, and as we are always anxious to save ourselves as much trouble as possible, and at the same time to give our brethren the best that can be had, we have decided to appropriate the labors of Bro. William H. Hill, the chairman of correspondence of California. We tender him our acknowledgements, for his valuable statistical table, which we append hereto, together with his remarks thereon. As he says, it will well repay a careful examination, and it gives about the best view that can be obtained of the remarkable spread of the Craft in the States and Canada.

Grand Lodges.	No. of Lodges.	Initiated.	Members.	Net Increase.	Net Decrease.
Alabama,	390.	755	10,643	—	78
Arkansas,	309	960	10 179	348	—
British Columbia,	9	17	301	6	—
California,	190	706	10,078	169	—
Canada,	281	1802	12,168	1668	—
Colorado,	19	95	1,079	86	—
Connecticut,	109	821	14,845	—	251
Delaware,	21	134	1,046	18	—
District of Columbia,	19	—	2,443	23	—
Florida,	65	162	2,100	374	—
*Georgia,	268	—	13,921	—	—
Idaho,	8	38	272	—	10
Illinois,	677	2887	36'775	272	—
Indiana,	467	2231	26,216	1892	—
*Iowa	327	1284	15,134	593	—
Kansas,	130	530	5,078	2653	—
Kentucky,	453	1664	20,649	487	—
Louisiana,	155	459	7,178	—	399
Maine,	165	1015	17,224	653	—
Maryland,	83	183	5,410	58	—
Massachusetts,	202	1830	23,217	1711	—
Michigan,	304	1745	24.622	626	—
Minnesota,	93	453	4,945	—	273
Mississippi,	308	1034	11,528	40	—
Missouri,	445	1691	23,118	2439	—
Montana,	18	37	643	93	—
Nebraska,	38	220	1,706	127	—
Nevada,	17	88	1,180	152	—
New Brunswick,	28	206	1,926	175	—
New Hampshire,	71	413	7,487	371	—
New Jersey,	134	—	10,569	662	—
New York,	683	5300	79,849	903	—
North Carolina,	229	457	11,216	66	—
Nova Scotia,	59	417	2,478	212	—
Ohio,	423	2041	29,267	5180	—
Oregon,	44	188	1,757	169	—
Pennsylvania,	344	2577	34,772	1544	—
Quebec,	38	219	1,606	110	—
Rhode Island,	25	193	3,915	526	—
South Carolina	157	198	6,600	124	—
Tennessee,	354	1326	19,538	137	—
Texas,	327	1465	16,610	2113	—
Utah,	4	37	165	41	—
Vermont,	95	592	8,099	—	—
Virginia,	238	—	8,468	88	—
Washington,	16	61	550	54	—
West Virginia,	58	314	2,664	256	—
Wisconsin,	170	632	9,386	—	—
Totals,	9,067	39,487	590,721	27,219	1,011

*Statistics of previous year.

"These statistics are suggestive, and will repay their careful study. The total, it will be seen, far exceeds that of last year, and the remarkable increase in some jurisdictions may be *apparent* only, arising from a more careful revision of previous statistics. We particularly refer to Kansas, Missouri, Ohio, and Texas. If the figures in our column of 'Net Increase,' do indeed indicate the actual growth of the year, then our brethren of these jurisdictions are to be congratulated upon their remarkable prosperity, provided the material worked up be good and sound.

"It will be seen that in the United States and British Provinces there are 9067 Lodges, with a aggregate membership of 590,721. The initiations during the year (omitting the District of Columbia, Georgia, New Jersey, and Virginia, from which no returns of initiations were given), amount to the very respectable number of 39,487. And after deducting the suspensions, removals, and deaths, the net increase over 1872 appears to be 26,208. We do not believe that if Bros. FINNEY, BLANCHARD, PIUS IX & COMPANY could gather their malignant ' Antis ' into Lodges, they would equal in number this net increase of our Fraternity. So may it ever be, so long as we only take in ' good men and true.'"

In conclusion, we tender to our *confreres* of the quill abroad, our hearty thanks for the many flattering notices of our last effort. These reports are becoming more valuable, year by year, and it is our desire, as it is, doubtless, that of all the reporters, to make these annual reviews permanently interesting, and worthy of preservation in any collection of Masonic literature.

All which is fraternally submitted.

HENRY ROBERTSON,
Chairman Com. on Foreign Correspondence.

Collingwood, Ont., June 1st, 1874.

\

www.ingramcontent.com/pod-product-compliance
Lightning Source LLC
Chambersburg PA
CBHW030622030726
47497CB00006B/1606